PLAYER MANAGER 3

PLAYER MANAGER 3

TED STEEL

Podium

THE STORY SO FAR

SEASON 2022/23 - THE THIRD HALF

Max Best has been cursed with the abilities of a top football manager. Thanks to the curse-giver's sloppiness, there was an unexpected side effect: he is also a fantastic player. As he was about to apply for the player-manager role at bottom-of-the-table Telford, he was offered the position of director of football at Chester Football Club—but first he must convince its fans he's the right man for the job.

PLAYER MANAGER 3

What is a club in any case?

Not the buildings or the directors or the people who are paid to represent it. It's not the television contracts, get-out clauses, marketing departments or executive boxes.

It's the noise, the passion, the feeling of belonging, the pride in your city.

It's a small boy clambering up stadium steps for the very first time, gripping his father's hand, gawping at that hallowed stretch of turf beneath him and, without being able to do a thing about it, falling in love.

—*Sir Bobby Robson,* Newcastle: My Kind of Toon

CRACKERS

Monday, December 26, 2022.

The day after Christmas is Boxing Day. It's called Boxing Day because there's no boxing but there's loads of football.

Football?

While the sensible German leagues have a lovely old winter break and those footballers spend Christmas wrapped up warm and snug with their loved ones, the British play—get this—*even more* football! Christmas Eve! Boxing Day! New Year's Eve! New Year's Day! Did you enjoy your day off? Great! Get back on the pitch; we're playing Stoke at 8. Wait, that's on Wednesday. Today it's Oxford at 3. What do you mean you're tired and you want to see your kids? Shut your gob and get warmed up!

Eight days ago, after the immortal World Cup final between France and Argentina, the managing director of Chester Football Club, Mike Dean, offered me a job. A job that didn't exist yet and showed no signs of existing. It was my opinion as a professional ghoster that he was dragging his heels. Did he have cold feet? Or was he simply waiting until the January transfer window opened?

MD was strangely sensitive to the outside world's opinion of him. Chester signing a twenty-two-year-old director of football (me) would have been the only topic of conversation in the boardrooms of England's sixth tier. An obvious source of mockery. *What are they smoking over there at the Deva Stadium?* On the other hand, Chester signing the league's best player (also me) by giving him a meaningless job title— yeah, MD would have pulled off quite the coup.

Whatever the root cause was, the delay in finding a path forward had been doing my head in. I decided to give MD what professional football players call "a kick up the arse." Chester's next league game could not have been more perfect for my purposes.

Me: Are you going to the Boxing Day match?

MD: Yes.

Me: See you there! *Winky face emoji.*

"Oh!" said Emma, my blonde bombshell girlfriend, who had forgiven me for a minor Christmas meal falling-out with her father.

"What?"

"This stadium. It's really nice!"

"Yeah," I agreed, peering out of the passenger window. The New Bucks Head was the home of AFC Telford United, yet another phoenix club, risen from the ashes of its former ownership. "That *is* nice. Looks like a real stadium."

"Maybe you *should* have taken this job."

"It's still available," I mused. Telford were bottom of the league by a considerable distance. Everyone thought they were finished, but I knew I could save them. There was only one fly in the ointment—I wanted to save Chester; I had friends there.

Emma wound down her window and spoke to a man in a luminous orange coat. A blast of cold air hit me like a forearm smash. "Max Best plus one," she said.

He looked down at a clipboard. "Ah yes," he said. "The guest of honour. Go right to the front. Roll up to the Chester team bus there, then go a little farther. The spot says *Home Manager.* Can't miss it." He lowered himself so he could get a better look at us. No, not at us. At *me.* Imagine wanting to look at *me* when Emma was *right there.* I couldn't read his expression. He stood straight and gestured for us to drive on.

"The manager's spot," said Emma, with a wry smile. "What did you tell them?"

I tried to hide a smirk. "Just said I was coming. No reason they'd roll out the red carpet for little old me."

"Yeah?" She turned into our spot. "Just to be clear today, Max Best, if you tell another person I was on *Geordie Shore* I'll do something that one of us will regret."

"Huh?" I said. "I only said that once. With Mike Dean. Ha! Reminds me. I got a text from him last week asking which season you were in. I think he's watching it from the start, just in case he can catch you in a tight dress."

"I don't mean Mike. I mean your mum." We got out of the car and looked left and right. I pointed to a series of big glass doors that looked like a main reception. Emma headed that way. "I see you forgot already. You were trying to change the topic from that phone game that your mum and Anna were playing. What was it called?"

"*Soccer Supremo*," I said, shuddering at the memory. I'd recently asked my mother's friend Anna for help understanding my curse. That involved making her explore my old copy of *Champion Manager*—the game *Soccer Supremo* had ripped off. After I left she had spent ten pounds—exorbitant—buying the latest mobile version. She was utterly addicted; managing Blackpool Football Club had taken over her life. Anna knew better than to ask me about the game because even looking at a static image made me feel sick, but mum had asked me what the latest killer formations were and who were the cheapest wonderkids. I'd tried to deflect in small ways before going nuclear by mentioning mum's passion: reality TV.

Emma nodded. "*Soccer Supremo*, right. Your mum was asking how many seasons it took before the game would start producing 'regens,' and that's when you said I was on *Geordie Shore*. That distracted her until I said you were joking."

"Remind me to teach you the 'Yes, and . . .' rule."

"Then you said I was on *Love Island* and she said 'pah' because she would have remembered. *Then* you asked her to tell Anna what happened in the *Love Island* 'movie night' scandal and your mum went on a big rant and the game was forgotten. Why would you rather talk about reality TV than football?"

"I want to *be* a soccer supremo," I said. "Not *pretend*. And I don't want to talk about football twenty-four seven. All right. On the other side of this door is a little place I like to call *The Future*. Have you been practising your WAG face like I told you?" WAG means Wives and Girlfriends. It's tabloid newspaper shorthand for talking about the partners of football stars.

She laughed. "You don't get to tell me what I do with my face. What's WAG face anyway?"

"I'll show you." I took her arm, turned her towards me, and asked her to close her eyes. I imagined I was married to Jack Grealish. What face would I have? "Okay, open."

She was still wiping the tears away when we were met by Telford's most senior hospitality volunteer. She would have smiled at us anyway, but seeing the huge grins on our faces brought one to hers.

She introduced herself, apologised for how cold it was, then got down to business. "Right, then. You said you'd like to wander around. By all means, have a gander. We're proud of this old place, so we are. Let me get you your tickets. Just in case anyone stops you when you move from section to section. Oh. Now, *that's* odd."

"What is?"

"I've got *two* envelopes for you. Let me check this." She pulled the first one open and nodded. "Yes, these are from us. That's our VIP section. Good view. So what's this one?" She opened the second envelope. "Oh! These are from Chester FC. Why would they do that? I'm sorry. It's none of my business."

"That's all right."

She offered both envelopes. "So, which do you want?"

I smiled at her. "I'll take both. If I don't like the company in one place, I'll try the other." She gave me a wobbly smile like I was making a joke she didn't understand. I gently gripped the envelopes between my thumbs and index fingers until she let go. "Lovely stuff," I said. "Thank you very much."

She scratched the back of her head. "I thought you were a player."

"Can you keep a secret?" I said.

"No," she said.

"Perfect. Chester might be offering me a job. The board that represents the fans have to meet and approve it. But if they don't hurry up, I'll apply for the Telford position."

"You don't mean manager?"

"Player-manager." I smiled.

"You're very young," she said, full of doubt.

"I might have the body of a twenty-two-year-old, and the emotional maturity of a . . ." I turned to Emma. "What did we agree?"

"Sixteen."

"Sixteen-year-old. But I've got the . . . Huh. I don't know how to finish that sentence."

"Parking space."

"Yes! I've got the parking space of a fifty-year-old football manager. And all my own hair. If anything, I'm overqualified."

The hospitality lady gave me the warmest smile she could generate. "Enjoy the match, Mr. and Mrs. Best."

"That's an encounter she'll never forget," Emma said.

"That's what I do best."

"Which seats first? Telford or Chester?"

"Telford."

"Oh! Plot twist."

A steward told me where to go. I went at one mile an hour up the stairs, taking in the stadium. From inside it was even more impressive. It was a real football stadium, four-sided, well thought out. Great disabled access. It had been built with care and with the fan experience in mind. I wanted it. I wanted it a lot.

Another reason to walk slowly was to try to catch sight of Mike Dean. I spotted him gladhanding some bigwigs. Presumably his Telford equivalents.

I paused.

"What vibe do you want?" said Emma. She enjoyed my little games. Most of her life involved being a lawyer, looking through fine print, cross-referencing documents. Utter tedium. Sometimes she threw herself into my role plays with an enthusiasm I found disquieting. When I'd pretended she was my deranged stalker she was all too believable.

"Hmm," I said. "How about . . . one of us offers blistering football analysis while the other looks like sex on legs and gets some old white men thinking of long, debauched nights in tawdry hotels?"

She nodded. "Football analysis. Got it." She rubbed her nostrils while sniffing, and said in a pastiche of Chester's awful manager, Ian Evans: "Four-four-two, get up their arse, keep it tight first fifteen." I bit my lip. The football dinosaur persona slipped off her face and she flushed. "What?"

I jerked my head towards the gathering. "You're fantastic. Let's go before icicles start forming on me."

"Mike!" I said, barging into the group. "Nice to see you. I thought you were on holiday. You didn't reply to my last eighteen or nineteen phone calls."

He rolled his eyes slightly and introduced me to the Telford lot. "Everyone, this is Max Best. Darlington's mystery winger. Nine goals in five starts. Max. Glad you got my tickets."

"What? No, MD. I'm here by invitation of Telford. They haven't said it out loud, but I think they'd like me to apply for the manager's job. They must have heard about me heroically beating Man City's under-sixteens with a team of much older, more experienced players."

There were some awkward smiles from everyone except MD. He said, "Can I speak to you privately for a moment?"

"You're always asking to speak to me privately! Weird habit. You know I long to save a club from relegation. Isn't it funny that two relegation-threatened clubs should be playing each other just as I'm scratching around for an opportunity? So convenient! But while I always liked the abstract *idea* of saving Telford, now that I'm here I find myself enchanted. Look at it! Guys, I love your stadium. I love the area. I love my parking space." To MD I added, "They gave me the manager's spot." Then to the dudes, "It's good you haven't chosen one yet. The chosen one, AKA the frozen one, may be closer than you think."

"Well, it's Christmas. Hard time to arrange meetings and such," said one Telford dude. "And with all the postponements recently, we haven't really missed out on having a manager, if you see what I mean."

I nodded rapidly. "Yep yep yep. Thing is, if I'm running a football club, I'm going to use the January transfer window to find new players, aren't I? Beef up the squad. It's no good me getting a job mid-January, is it Mike? Need it *now*, don't I? To hit the ground running. Get stuck in," I said, giving him a gentle little punch to the belly.

He inhaled and put his hand to his forehead. "I'm going as fast as I can, Max. It would help *enormously* if you sat in the seat I organised."

"Enormously?" I said, whipping out the Chester tickets.

"Enormously."

"Then I shall so do."

I took a step away, and one back again. I lowered my voice in the pretence that MD wouldn't be able to hear me. "But just in case, do you guys have an application form or something like that?"

The main Telford dude seemed confused. "For the manager position? Are you serious?" Three faces showed that I was: mine, Emma's, and MD's. The man continued. "There isn't a form as such. We'll take applications and conduct interviews. It's clear you're a special player, but do you have any qualifications? Experience? It's a tough job."

I waved his worries away. "If I came for an interview you would literally be spellbound. Don't worry about that. As for qualifications, how about this?" I half-turned and pointed to spots on the pitch that would soon be filled with players. "If I know your caretaker manager, and I think I do, he'll send out a solid four-four-two. Solid being a polite way of saying ultra-defensive." I proceeded to name the starting lineup, who would take the corners, the left and right set pieces, penalties, and captain. The tactics screen told me all this. It also showed me that one player's stamina was written in red. "Huh. That second striker looks injured to me. Either he's been rushed back from injury or he's done it in the warmup and not told anyone. Naughty boy! I'd soon stamp that out. That's team spirit cancer, that sort of thing. But you're probably more interested in what Chester will get up to." I did the same thing with the away team, but slowed down near the end to look at individual instructions. "Aff, that's what they call the Irish guy playing left-mid, is Chester's most dangerous player. So Ian Evans has instructed him . . . hold on, let me double-check this . . . has told him *not to attack*. What the fuck? Mike! We need three points today! Telford are bottom of the fucking league! If Evans plays for a draw today I'm going to spontaneously combust."

He was giving me a strange look. "Ian Evans is a very experienced manager. I'm sure he has a plan he thinks will win us the match."

I found myself trying to loosen my jaw. "Riiight."

We went to the Chester seats. I was fuming—not enough to warm me up—and through a shimmer of frustration I realised Emma was chanting something. "What?"

"Burn the witch! Burn the witch!"

It calmed me all the way down. I gave her a lopsided smile. "You know I'm good at this here football malarkey. Why's it so weird I'd know the teams?"

"Not so long ago, you told me you didn't know anything about Telford. A week ago you didn't know what colours they played in. Now you know their tactical plans down to the subatomic level."

"I studied. I've got a brain the size of a planet. Not to be rude but until recently I was managing elite players in the sport's biggest tournament. This match is remedial."

"Sure, sure. Oh, Max, just out of interest. *When* did you study? Because we've spent almost every waking minute together for a week. And when you've had spare energy, I've found ways for you to use it."

I grinned at the memories. "Remember when you thought I was playing *Merge Mountain* on my phone? I was actually researching that." I jabbed my thumb backwards. "Now," I said, pointing forwards, "MD wants us to sit in those two seats there. Obviously one of the people on either side is on the board."

At some point in the last week, Emma had begun mocking me by intoning "the board" in a deep, menacing voice whenever I mentioned it. She did so now. "The board."

"Use your womanly intuition to guess which one is the board guy."

"The board," she said. Then she shook her head. "If I had any womanly intuition—whatever the fuck that is—I wouldn't have invited you to meet my dad, would I?"

I looked up at the terrace's roof. "I thought we'd agreed not to bicker."

"We half-agreed. You said yes; I said no." She tilted her head. "Got to be the blind guy, right?"

"Right."

We shuffled along the row and I sat next to the dude with the cane. Emma sat to the right of me. The match kicked off.

"Hey, Emma," I said, a bit louder than normal. "I've got some tactical insights into this contest. Would you like to hear them?"

"Oh, yes please my boyfriend, Max Best," she said. She pulled her phone out and got stuck into WhatsApp while I repeated the spiel I'd given to the bigwigs. She tuned out so completely that when I was done I had to give her a little bump on the shoulder. "Er . . . gosh. That was fascinating. So it's true what they say?"

"What do they say?"

"You're not just a pretty face." She leaned in for a kiss and got one.

The blind guy to my left tapped his cane on the concrete floor three times. "What a performance! Seems like you're onto us," he said. He had a wide, round face with short, wispy hair. His eyes were closed and he held his face close to a smile. He pushed a hand out. "I'm Crackers." I shook it. Crackers is *English* English for crazy.

"Max Best. Next to me's my girlfriend, Emma. She's very attractive. Do you want to palpate her face?"

Emma punched me. Crackers laughed. "I don't generally go round fondling strangers. I'm blind, not psychotic. Hollywood has a lot to answer for."

"Crackers, listen," I started.

"I'm all ears," he said, which I guess was a disability joke.

"Is this Mike's plan? To get this job, I have to meet the board one by one in a variety of increasingly intense situations? First, a random encounter with a blind man. Will Max be kind and considerate, not knowing that the man holds his future in his hands? The next one, I'm trapped in an escape room with a librarian from South Chester. The seventh, Bulldog and I are pushed into a cage and only one can leave."

"Bulldog?"

Oops. Forgot to code switch. "Didn't I hear one of the board was called Mr Bulldock?"

He shook his head. "No. Why does your missus keep mumbling 'the board' like that?"

"Because she has the emotional intelligence of a sixteen-year-old," I said. "Is that the plan, though? This delay is murderous. If I get the job, I want to get going. Get started. January is key to the whole thing! And if it's not going to happen, I'd appreciate being told as fast as poss. The delay is literally costing me money. I'm close to broke. It's not fair to keep me hanging."

"I can't say I know Mike's plan, or that there's a plan as such. It's a strange thing he's proposing. We can't rush into it."

"That's fair," I said. "But there's not rushing and there's going at the speed of a glacier."

"Glaciers are fast these days," said Emma. "Global warming."

"Thanks, babes. What I'm saying, Crackers, is let's get you dudes in a room and I'll wow you all and get it over with."

"Max, it's Christmas. And New Year's. You can't get everyone in one place so easily. And for something major like this, you'll need to meet us face to face. We represent different types of fans. We've got different specialties and interests. What's essential to me is tedious to someone else. You can't do it all in one go. And we're representatives for the wider fan base. If we give you this position and it goes tits up, we have to explain to CFU that we went through a proper process. You get that, right?" CFU was City Fans United, the association that owned Chester.

"Of course there should be a process," I said. "For normal jobs for normal people. You should think of me as a celestial being, though. People often describe me as a floating megabrain. I know everything about football except how to lose. I'm a million-pound player offering my services at minimum wage."

"That's even more reason to slow down," said Crackers, which seemed wise at the time but later sounded deeply stupid.

"All right, fine. Let's do the interview."

"Interview?"

"You want to check me out, right? Okay. I'm here."

He chuckled. "This is a simple meet and greet."

I shook my head. I wasn't into this. Would I do it if there was no alternative? Maybe. But I had three *amazing* alternatives. Become the player-manager of Telford and achieve all my goals. Win the league with Darlington. Or sack the whole thing and make sick amounts of money playing for a big team and *then* do the minimum wage "save the soul of football" thing. "What's your area of interest?"

"Three main ones. Disabled access, of course. The atmosphere in the ground. And taking pride in the team. Chester are a pretty big deal in these parts, and I like that. I like feeling like someone. You probably don't understand what I'm talking about."

"I'm a Manchester United fan. So yeah, I do. But there's a big problem."

"What's that?"

"You like being a big fish in a small pond. Where I'll take Chester, you'll never be able to think that. We're going to the biggest pond of all. What's the smallest kind of fish?"

"Minnows are famously small."

"All they do is swim around and get eaten, right? That's their whole deal. That's like . . . Norwich City. Wigan. I don't know. We're not going to be them."

"Failed analogies aside, what are you trying to say?"

"I'm going to turn Chester into some kind of piranha. Yeah, small. But a menace." I imagined meeting a rival director of football one day in the future. "Yeah, you can feel smug that you're bigger. But we've got fucking teeth, mate, and while you were polishing your 1995 Anglo-Italian cup trophy, we've just chewed your legs off."

Crackers seemed to enjoy this line of thinking. "How would you take us to this bigger pond? And I suppose it's only fair to ask . . . what fish are you competing with . . . that has legs?"

I shook my head. As much as I liked Crackers, there was no way I was going to have this conversation seven times. That was absurd. "Crackers, you come to support the team and feel the atmosphere first-hand and all that. It must be spine-tingling sometimes. But you don't normally sit there and not watch the action, right? If I wasn't here, you'd be listening to the radio?"

"That's right. *Seals Live*." Chester were nicknamed the Seals, after their old stadium.

"Ah! I've seen the links on the website. It's the same tech as *Darlo Fans Radio*. Big fan of that. Emma found out how to listen to the old episodes and since then I've been listening on a loop."

"To the bits about himself," she said.

"Well, yeah," I said. "What else? The bits that aren't about me? Dull as dishwater. Why would I care about those? This *Seals Live* show, it's good, is it?"

"Oh, yes. Boggy does a great job. Very enthusiastic. Normally, anyway. We haven't had much to cheer recently."

"Tell you what," I said. "I'm off to the toilet but you listen to a few minutes and see if I was right about the tactics and that injured player. See if . . . Boggy? . . . notices. I'm keen to get a sense of the guy."

Crackers didn't know what to make of that. "Why?"

"Oh, no reason," I lied, chuckling.

Emma leaned across me. "He's plotting some mischief. But don't worry. He means well."

I eased past Crackers into the aisle and sent Emma a text.

She read it and shook her head at me. When I simply smirked at her, she replied by text that my idea was *not* a good idea.

I mimed putting earphones in. She shrugged. *Why?*

I mimed kissing my bicep and sent her a link. Then I snuck off.

Dramatic Extremely Fake Point of View Change!

Crackers, or Cracky to his closest friends, was starting to wonder where Max Best had gone. Not to the toilet—that had been an obvious lie. The man wanted this job, didn't he? Surely he could spend at least one half of one match trying to schmooze a board member. Maybe Cracky's first thought had been right—the man was much too young. What could a twenty-two-year-old possibly know about anything?

And yet it had been uncanny how accurately Best had predicted what would happen. Not the lineups—there were hundreds of ways he could have known those. But the names of the set piece takers and which side they'd take them from. The fact that Aff wouldn't bomb forward to get crosses in. And most implausibly, the fact that the Telford striker had been subbed off after only five minutes. Such things were hard to explain.

Crackers turned the volume of his earphones up and found that the early stages of the match had sapped Boggy's passion.

"A very drab affair so far," said the *Seals Live* commentator. "A game of little quality and few chances. It does seem that both teams have set up hoping for a draw. I must say it's thin gruel for a bumper Boxing Day crowd here in Bucks Head. Er . . . excuse me? Hello? No, that's not plugged in. No! Don't touch that! We're live! We're on air! But who *are* you?" A tiny pause. "Oh." There followed a lot of clicking and crackling. "Um. Why don't you introduce yourself?"

"Hi, everyone! I'm superstar football player Max Best. I'm gate-crashing your broadcast to announce my application for the position of Chester's director of football."

Crackers gasped.

To his right, the girlfriend groaned. "Fucking hell, babes," she muttered. Crackers felt her twist in her seat to look at him. There was a smile in her voice. "So . . . now you've met Max, then."

SEALS LIVE

Boggy was in his forties, average height, slim, tidy beard, glasses. My sense of him was that he'd had some media training in his youth, or had studied journalism, but it hadn't quite worked out for him as a career. So volunteering to narrate the Chester matches kept the old flame alive and gave him some status in the fanbase. I listened to him for a few minutes before I invaded his space. He was biased in the sense that he wanted Chester to win, but not to the extent that he'd refuse to believe the evidence of his own eyes, like many fans did. He'd call out Chester's bad fouls and mistakes and he very clearly longed to see some good football.

His home for this occasion was at the back of the small media area in the main stand. Those seats had very slightly more space than average, and the incredible luxury of working plug sockets. Boggy was squashed up behind a big laptop that had dozens of tabs open and many things sticking out of holes, including two USB microphones that we held to our mouths. At some point he'd dropped a pen, but bending to get it would have risked part of his setup popping out.

My being there was incredibly stressful for him, but also exciting. A lot more exciting than the match, that was for sure. Boggy was wise enough to hear me out. This was radio gold. A big ON AIR icon on his laptop showed me that the listeners could hear us. "Mr. Best, I'm confused. Chester doesn't have a director of football."

"Call me Max, Boggy. You're right, but I hope to—"

He cut across me to describe what was happening on the pitch. "Aff passes back inside. Topps powers forward! He's got options left and right." Slight pause. "He doesn't like either. He turns and plays it to Carlile in the right-back slot. Er . . . this is great possession for Chester."

I laughed down the mic—a much more charming and rounded laugh than normal. Of the listeners, only Emma would know it was fake. "Boggy, be serious. They're playing for a *draw*. Almost nothing's going to happen in this half. Let's have a chat."

"I've got to describe the match for the people listening at home."

"Of course you don't. It's just throw-ins. Tell you what, if anything interesting happens I'll point it out. I promise. Now, you're right. There isn't a director of football position. There are discussions about creating one so that I can come to Chester and use my talents."

"Your talents as a player? You want to be player-DoFfer? It doesn't roll off the tongue."

"Neither does ice-cream but it's still delicious. How about I describe what I see myself doing? Give you the five-minute pitch. Oh, and I see there are eight hundred people listening online. Listeners, go ahead and leave your questions in the chat and I'll answer the best ones later."

"But Max," said Boggy. "Why turn up unannounced like this? We could have arranged it. Promoted it. I'm sure people would be really interested."

"Yes, I agree. That would have been better. To be honest, I'm only here to cut through some red tape. The fan representative board, seven people, want to meet me and hear my ideas. One at a time. That's seven meetings, Boggy. Now, I'm *willing* to have seven meetings, if only to prove how determined I am to do this job. But I don't want to have to say the same thing over and over again. I hate saying the same thing over and over again. Boggy. Do you know what I hate?"

He smiled. "Saying the same thing over and over again."

"Right. So, live on your show, I'll tell everyone what I'm about. And then I'll meet the board and we can skip to the bits they don't like or address their particular interests."

"They might not like you blurting it out like this."

"Why? Is it a secret? This isn't just about respecting the board and their right to set up the process however they want. I'm in the process, too, and thanks to the process, I'm in limbo."

"Limbo? Is that why you're not playing for Darlington right now?"

"Yes. I told my manager, David Cutter, that I wanted to interview for a position elsewhere and he said he only wanted to pick players who were committed to Darlington. Fair enough, some of you might think, although it goes without saying I would be absolutely crushing Scarborough right now. They're a good team but they concede a lot of goals. I'm paid by the match, and most of my income is from goal bonuses. Being here has cost me a luxury sofa." I did that laugh again. "Manchester luxury, not London luxury."

"One of those where you lean back and . . . ?" He mimed kicking his legs, which I'm not sure was great radio.

"Yeah. But you know what? Thinking about putting my feet up has given me an idea. Why don't I do co-comms with you for the rest of the half? Then I'll go buy a burger and a space heater, and at the start of the second half I'll lay out my pitch. So everyone at home, call your friends, text them, post this link to all your socials. Let's get thousands of Chester fans listening in. In the meantime, you can get to know me as a player. Go to your favourite video app and type 'Max Best Player of the Season' or 'Max Best scores from a corner' or 'Max Best scores four goals in forty-five minutes so he can spend the second half watching the World Cup.'"

"No, really? I watched that game! It was almost the only football in the country that day. I thought you'd picked up a knock."

"Boggy, it was bloody freezing. Four goals, pay the mortgage, three points, top of the league, job done, hot shower, let someone else freeze his er . . . knees off in the second half. Can I swear?"

"No, thanks."

"All right. Boggy? We've got a plan. Still nil–nil here with no shots. Let's talk about Chester's rest defence."

"Rest defence? What's that?"

"You've got ten outfield players. You attack with six, leaving four in a defensive zone for counterattacks. Those four are your rest defence. It's literally the 'rest' of the team."

"I've never heard that one."

"It's common sense but giving it a name helps players remember their jobs. You know. Ian Evans can go up to Sam Topps and say, 'If Aff has the ball you're part of the rest defence. For the managers, it's not just about the number of defenders. It's about how you use them. I'm actually confused by what's happening right now. We just saw Aff progress down the left, and he saw three players were forward with him, but he turned back. I *think* they've been told not to attack with only six in the rest defence. Evans wants seven defenders! Against Telford." I sighed, then remembered I wasn't supposed to slag Evans off in public. "He's probably going to get more adventurous in the second half."

"There's a first time for everything," said Boggy, and he, too, remembered he wasn't supposed to say such things.

I smiled at him. I liked Boggy!

He grinned back, then resumed commentary.

A while later, I got a text.

Emma: So far so good! You are definitely intriguing. The serial killer laugh is okay I guess? Stay positive. Don't swear. Say something nice about Mike Dean. He's wandering around with a face like thunder. Quite sexy.

Me: How's Crackers?

Emma: Cracking.

Doing co-comms was fun. A few times I got too specific and too into the weeds, but Boggy asked me what I was talking about and I explained it more clearly. Turning a wild jumble of movements and numbers into coherent, easily understandable sentences was hard. The guys from *Match of the Day* and *Monday Night Football* made it look easy. It wasn't.

Boggy pressed a button to turn off the ON AIR icon. He took off his headphones and exhaled. "Max! That was mustard! I don't know about DoF, but you can do co-comms with me anytime!"

"Sure! You'll have to pay for my petrol. I might be unemployed again soon. I'm off to check on my girlfriend. If Mike Dean comes to stop you interviewing me, stand up for yourself. Press freedom!"

Boggy boggled. "Would he do that?"

"Not if I was here. So if he starts, just say, 'Oh, hi Max.' MD will turn around in shock, at which point you laugh at him and tell him to get fucked."

"Are you sure you want this job? You don't seem to get on with any of the senior figures."

"Not get on with Mike? What makes you think that? We get on great. He's a top guy. And I like Ian Evans a surprising amount. All right, see you in fifteen."

I went to find Emma, without success. I called her. She was up in a corporate hospitality box with some business randos who were very happy to have her there. She slipped out of the warmth of the box to talk to me. "I did a Max," she said.

"What does that mean?"

"I thought about what I wanted—to be warm and to be not cold—and went the most direct route, regardless of the consequences. See that guy with the sweaty armpits? I'm engaged to him now. Can you find out his name, please? What are you smiling at?"

I was smiling because I'd earned 90 XP and had turned the worst football match in history into solid gold entertainment. "Boggy's going to get an award for this broadcast. I'm thinking a quick five-minute sermon, then answer questions. What do you reckon?"

"What's in the sermon?"

I stuck my bottom lip out. "Basically tell people about me and what I can do."

Emma shook her head. "That's not when you're at your best. Tell them about *them*."

"Storytime?"

"Exactly. Don't make rash promises."

"Got it. Can I get a kiss?"

"No. My fiancé might kick me out. Max, it's warm in there. They said they paid extra for the heating to be turned on. I like you but I would absolutely dump you on the spot if it meant I didn't have to stay out here."

I laughed. "Fair. Can you send me a kiss emoji?"

She thought about it. "I can send you a lowercase X."

"Yes, please."

"Okay. Bye. Enjoy your burger."

"But there's loads of food in there! Get me a butty."

She gave me a sorry look as she pushed me away. "You haven't been invited, Max. You can't just barge in everywhere. Bye."

I queued like a normo and ordered extra onions and triple cheese. The add-ons ruined the burger, which I ate alone in a corridor with people shuffling past me. The universe was punishing me. I didn't care; by the end of the match I'd know where I stood.

"No changes to the teams for the second half," said Boggy, back on air. "Let's hope things liven up on the pitch. Here in the media centre we've got our special guest, Max Best. Max, we've got three thousand people tuned in! That's huge."

"I think some of those are the Telford fans who have let my girl-friend into their warm and cosy executive box." I chuckled. "Hi guys! Everyone else, if you need a full-service marketing solution, I can hook you up."

"Early signs in the second half are that the action will be much the same as the first." I could hear Boggy add scare quotes around "action."

"This will be the first match in the history of English football where the highlights package includes a man trying to plug a second microphone into his laptop."

Boggy laughed. "I hope I'm *not* on the feed. I've got a face for radio. So. Max Best. For those just tuning in, tell us what's going on."

"Sure. I'm Max Best. I want to be Chester's director of football. I'll tell you what that means in a minute. A bit more about me. Hopefully most people listening have watched some footage of me playing right mid for Darlington, but if not, the local press there call me a mystery winger. Imagine if Mbappé played in the National League North. Er . . . oh."

"What?"

"I was expecting you to laugh. So that the listeners would know it was a joke."

"Sorry, Max! It's hard to tell when you're joking and when you're being Mancunian. The Mbappé comparison is not that far off, though, is it? The pace. The power. The skill. Though it's only been five games, so whether you can keep it up is another thing."

"Let's keep this family-friendly, Boggy. Let's just say I'm pretty good and an asset to any team at this level. But I see myself having more impact *off* the pitch. I've got an eye for a player. I'm good tactically. I know the business side of a club is the foundation for the sporting side. Buy low, sell high. I want to flood the club with talent at all levels and turn it into something like Benfica."

"Benfica? From Portugal?"

"Right. They've made a transfer profit of a billion pounds since 2000."

"A billion? Am I hearing that right?"

"A billion pounds, Boggy. Now you're thinking, we can't do that at Chester. But would you take ten million?"

A haunted look crossed his face. "I'd do a lot for ten million. A lot."

"Boggy, come into my time machine. Let me take you into the future. How far do you want to go?"

"Ten million years."

"Let's start with five. The year is 2027. You're controlling a drone, flying it around Cheshire."

"Strange way to use this time machine, but okay."

"You hover around some random football pitch. There's a Sunday League game underway. Who's that handsome chap on the sideline? Why, it's Chester's director of football, Max Best! You fly the drone to a five-a-side match. There's Max again! There's a school match going on. Max is watching that, too!"

"A quick reminder that nothing is happening in Telford versus Chester."

"That's right. Telford are picking up some yellow cards. That might pay off for us in the latter stages. So now let's fly to the Deva stadium. There's a little queue of people buying tickets. They look excited and happy. There's a cup game coming up this weekend! The website says it's sold out, but they're hoping if they turn up in person . . . Now, go through that little window. We're in the medical room. Dean and Livia are there with a couple of injured players. We've bought our own X-ray machine so we can get results faster and save money. That's how we think now. Long-term."

"Sorry, Max. Are Dean and Livia real people?"

"Yeah. Dean's the head physio."

"So you know people at the club already. That's handy."

"Everyone in this little story is real. Go through the double doors into the gym. It used to be small and useless, but we knocked through some walls and now it's huge and fully equipped. Magnus Evergreen is there, showing a new signing the best technique for lifting weights. He's our top expert on the subject. No more letting people find their own way. Every aspect of a player's development is monitored. They're always pushed. Always challenged.

"Into the new IT room. The goalkeepers are with Spectrum, one of our long-serving coaches, watching clips of next week's opponents. Where do they take free kicks? Penalties? It's fun in there, but they take it seriously because if Max asks them a question and they don't know the answer, something bad will happen. You know, to their careers.

"Heads up. Chester have a corner."

"Oh, what drama!" said Boggy. "Chester with a wonderful chance to open the scoring here. They've sent the big centre backs up but there are four in the rest defence." He glanced at me to check he'd said it right. "Aff with the outswinger. To the far post. Ryder heads it in and up . . . but the keeper claims it. Will he launch the ball forward? No, he collapses to the ground. Waits for everyone to retake their positions. Ahhh." That last noise was an angry exhalation. He ripped his headphones off.

"Our little drone continues its tour of the stadium. It goes into the dressing room. The new manager pushes it back out. It doesn't go in there."

"The *new* manager? Do you mean—"

"I don't mean anything. This is five years in the future, right? Ian Evans won't be the manager then. But the point still stands. The director of football doesn't pick the team, set the tactics, call the substitutions. It's my job to give Ian Evans and the next manager good players that he can use. You can say, 'Oh you're too young' and all that, but Evans is seventy-two. I offered him Henri Lyons and Raffi Brown and he bit my hand off. We agree on a lot. We both want quality players here. It's not complicated.

"Let's take the drone out to the training ground. This is new. We've bought the land and laid an all-weather pitch. There's an indoor pitch, too. Chester's men's team, women's, all the age groups, can train three hundred and sixty-five days a year. The new women's team that Max Best set up are going through some drills. One more promotion and they'll be playing with the big dogs.

"Now back to the stadium. Game's about to kick off. Stadium's full, and it's bouncing. Special round of applause here for Zoe from our pan-disability team—she's just played her first match as an England international. Big cheers as she waves her England cap around. We're all made up for her. Terry, her coach for many years, wipes a tear from his eye. It's not the first international he's brought through, and it won't be the last. Now hover that drone in front of Crackers. He's a lifelong Chester fan, goes to as many games as he can. He's blind, so for him the atmosphere is important. Now, I'm not going to pretend I know what it's like because I don't. But that sound before and after a goal—that has to be the best part. So we need more goals. I'll tell you what, though. You know what *my* favourite is? It's that noise when I'm running through at the keeper and I can hear everyone in the stadium standing up. What's he gonna do? I live for the excitement. When's the last time you had that on the regular? Smasho and Nice One? I want to bring that back.

"Now pan to the dugout. The manager's making a change."

"This is in Max Best's fantasy world, by the way," said Boggy. "Not in the actual match."

"That's right, though I'm sure we'll see some like-for-like changes around the seventy-minute mark. So who's this waiting on the touchline? It's a sixteen-year-old, yet another product of the famous Chester academy. Hey, Boggy."

"Yes?"

"Have you heard of the Lisbon Lions?"

"Yes. Isn't that the Celtic team who won the European Cup?"

"Yeah. I keep going back to the Wikipedia page. 1967. They were all born within thirty miles of Celtic's stadium. Imagine that! It was different back then, but if I can get eleven academy kids on the pitch at the same time, I'll die of pride. I'm not here to make rash promises— all I can promise is hard graft—but I'll scour Cheshire for talent, and if it's there, I'll do everything I can to get it into the first team."

"Is the drone tour finished?"

"I think so. I could go on for hours. I think people would get bored."

"I'm not so sure about that. It's a long time since I heard anyone mention Chester and the European Cup in the same sentence. On that note, message from the chat: 'Love the positivity!'"

The message was on the screen in front of me, including the part Boggy had left out. "Read the rest of it."

"I don't . . ."

"Go on."

"'*Love the positivity even if he's an obvious charlatan.*'"

I laughed. "Yeah. Let's start taking questions from the fans. How about that one? Am I a charlatan? No. I'm told I'll be the National League North Player of the Month for December. I'm the eighth top scorer in the division and number one in goals per minute. I'm racing through my coaching certificates. I know everything about football except how to lose." I chuckled again. "That's a terrible line. Cut that."

"We're live."

"Okay, let's keep it then. Give me the job and I'll work on my jokes. That's a promise. Next question, hit me."

"From Trev in Austria. '*You say your USB is scouting.*' I think he means USP. '*How do you find players? Watch a lot of clips? Data?*'"

"All that stuff is good. I'm comfortable with data. But I need to see players play. In the flesh. Which means watching a lot of dreary football."

"Like today."

"I didn't say that. I'm sure a thrilling final five minutes will make the rest worth it. My opinion is you can only really assess a player by seeing him live. Now, what I *can* promise is that I'll find loads of unpolished gems. What I *can't* promise is that they'll make it. I've seen incredible players who haven't lived up to their talent. I don't want to be cruel by naming names but when I brought my client Ziggy to FC United—that's where I met Jackie Reaper, by the way—there was a player there who was incredible. An absolute wizard. And so far it hasn't clicked. So, you know, there's no guarantees. But I think if you have ten talented eighteen-year-olds, five of them will have good careers. Right?"

"You've brought up two interesting points there. You're an agent."

"Yes. If I have this talent for finding good players it'd be mad not to use it, right?"

"I think people will have a lot of questions about that side of things."

"Really? It's quite dull."

"Things like conflict of interest. If you're in charge of football matters, you'll look after your clients' interests above everyone else's."

"Why would I do that?"

"Because they are your clients."

"But what could I possibly do? You know Henri Lyons is my client? He's here till the end of the season. If I go to Ian Evans and say, 'Put Henri in the team,' he'll say, '*Yeah, duh, I was planning to.*' Then Raffi Brown. He's going to be a great player. 'Ian, put Raffi in the team!' '*No.*' Oh. Okay, then." I laughed. "Evans likes those players. Everyone does. I didn't turn up one day and sneak two adult men into the dressing room." I fake laughed at the thought. "If you mean I might give them contracts they don't deserve, that's not in my interest financially. Henri should be playing League One. Raffi will catch the eye of a big team and move on. You'll be sorry to see both guys go. If you think I'm up to something dodgy you can fire me. My contract will make that very, very easy."

"Won't it be weird if you're playing right wing on Saturday and on Monday you have to discuss the right back's contract extension?"

"No. Football's hard. Tough business. It's emotional on match day and clinical the rest of the time. If I offer a guy a contract and he doesn't sign it, that's his decision. He has to do what's best for him and his family. Same's true in reverse. Most players understand they're part of a business and sometimes that means they get cut. Sometimes the club can't afford them anymore. Or they've had too many injuries and they have to be released at the end of their contract. Can I tell a guy that and then line up with him at the weekend? Think what you want, but when the tackles start flying in, you get lost in the action. It's band-of-brothers stuff. Fans might not be able to wrap their heads around it, but players will. I wouldn't worry about it this season, anyway. I won't be playing much, or at all."

"You won't play much?"

"There's no point, is there? We can't make the playoffs. My time's better spent improving things behind the scenes."

"Playoffs? We're battling relegation."

"The league table doesn't look good now. But Henri Lyons will be available for the next game. You won't be worried for long. You wait and see."

"But, I mean . . . you're a top player. You'd come to Chester and not play? It makes no sense."

"I can only be in one place at a time. Trust me, if it looks like the team need a points injection, I'll play a few matches. I'll tell you what, Raffi, Henri, and I are a *phenomenal* combo. But look, I'm getting carried away. I don't pick the team. But if things get really desperate, that's the cure right there. This eleven on the pitch here in Telford is *not* a relegation team. You add Henri and it's one of the best in the league. Give me the job, let me get stuck into the scouting and the whatnot, and sleep easy. I'm not worried about this season. I want us to have a proper fling at the title next year."

"The title?"

"Absolutely. I'm in a title-winning team right now. Darlington. I know what one looks like."

"You mentioned Jackie Reaper. How well do you know him?"

"Friends, I hope. Bit of a friendly rivalry between us to see who can grow the most hair. He's winning."

"He's bald."

"I know. But have you seen his back?" I made a shuddering noise that I was exceedingly pleased with.

"Question from Andrew. 'Why Chester?'"

I'd been expecting this one. "I don't want to play for a big club with a rich owner. You know who Darlington are playing today? Scarborough. Before every game I research the opposition. Not the team—I do that as well, of course. I mean the *club*. I want to get a sense of who and what they are. Scarborough are a phoenix club. Bad owners crash the club, boom, a hundred and twenty-five years of history down the drain. Why does this sound so familiar? Because it's the same every week. Telford. Hereford, Bury, Accrington. And, of course, Darlington. And Chester. I'll be honest, ownership models weren't something that used to get me out of bed in the morning. But now they do. The idea of taking one of these fan-owned clubs and bringing it up the divisions is highly, highly, motivational for me.

"So why Chester out of so many? Because of Jackie Reaper."

"Jackie Reaper?"

"Yeah. He saw I was a good player before anyone, and he wanted me to sign for Chester. He brought me in when I was injured and got me checked out by the medical staff. You always think better of a place when you get a bit of attention there, right? They made a bit of a fuss about me and you know what? I liked it. Then I signed on to do some scouting work and that was my first income from football. I did great reports, by the way. Used different colour pens and everything.

"Then I had a morning where I coached the Chester Knights. That's your pan-disability youth team, in case you didn't know. That was wild. So much fun. I was seriously impressed that a club of Chester's size was investing in all kinds of football. After that I had a go at coaching a boys' youth team. I've been on either side of the fence on that one—I was in charge of their opposition last Sunday. I know the kids. I know how well they're coached and I know some things that need to be improved. I could get the Telford job today, but I wouldn't know anybody. Fixing things, improving things, it wouldn't mean as much."

"You could get the Telford job?"

"Yeah. Player-manager. I'm interested. Look at this stadium. It's mint. Imagine it full, noisy, roaring on a fast, dynamic team! But I don't know anybody here. I know loads of people at Chester. I've got friends right there in the dugout. But there's a deadline. Or I should say, there needs to be a deadline. I've got three choices. One, I can stay at Darlington, win the league, and be well-paid. Oh! And the cup! We're still in the cup. We could get to Wembley. Imagine that! The Max Best Final! But I don't get to build anything there. Two, I could come to Telford and save them from relegation. They aren't going to have an open position forever. A few more days at most? Three, Chester. But if Chester really want me, they need to get a move on. If you don't, fine, no hard feelings."

"You have a fourth option. Go to a bigger club. I heard you had offers already."

"Oh, yeah. I suppose. But Chester's fan-owned. It's not like I wouldn't play for a megaclub for three hundred thousand pounds a week. I probably would! I'm not quite at that level as a player. No, my first choice is Chester. I'll do it for cheap and hope to boost my income on the side. Boggy, how am I doing?"

"Personally I love the sound of it. But it's quite odd and unexpected."

"Odd and unexpected? Those are my middle names. I'll answer a few more questions and then leave you alone. The last twenty minutes of the match might be worth commentating on!"

"Right. Quickfire round from the chatbox. 'How do you take those free kicks?'"

"Hit the ball really hard and have perfect technique."

"I'll try that next time I'm playing a journos versus ex-pros match. Next. Question from Derek. 'Is anything happening in the bloody match?'"

We both said, "No!"

"Question. What about buying the stadium?"

"What about it?"

"You know we lease the Deva from the council?"

"I did know that."

"A lot of fans dream of owning it one day. That would be a sign we have well and truly risen from the ashes. If you think you can make millions from transfer wheeler-dealing . . ."

"Yeah. I don't think I want to own the stadium."

"Whyever not?"

I clicked the corner of my mouth. "The common theme on all these phoenix clubs and clubs that nearly go bankrupt—almost all, anyway—is the stadium. You've got prime land in the city centre. Some guy buys the club for half a million, sells the land for ten million, does a runner. That's how it goes, right? A hundred years from now, Chester should still be going. And to make sure of that, you need to still be fan-owned. You know what depresses me? Portsmouth. They were fan-owned but they sold the club to the guy who runs Disney. Now he might be the best owner ever, but what about the next guy? Or the next? Eventually, you're going to get one who asset strips the club or—almost as bad—spends beyond its means shooting for the moon. The inevitability of bad owners is a historical fact.

"Obviously if you own the stadium you can expand it, make it more profitable, all that good stuff. But you're putting a big target on your back. Come and rip me off! I don't know. It's not my club. It's your club. I don't get a say. My instinct says don't do it. Don't even think about it. When it comes to expanding the stadium and whatnot, we'll have to talk to the council. Work hand-in-hand. Would they split the cost of undersoil heating with us? Let's start there. With that in place, we wouldn't get many matches postponed."

"Lots of questions about the current players and who you'd bring in and so on."

"I can't answer questions like that."

"Question from Emma. 'What do you think of Mike Dean?'"

"Top guy. Great guy. He's got the skills and experience to take the club forward. But what I love about him is that he won't do anything that puts the club at risk. If I find a million-pound player we can buy for fifty grand, if we don't have it he'll say no. It's that simple."

"Sounds like it'd be frustrating."

"Only if he's being overly conservative. If we really don't have the money, fine! No point going broke over a player. There's loads of play-ers! Move onto the next one. No, Mike will keep things stable. You're in good hands."

"Okay the chat now is mostly a discussion about the stadium. Some people agree with you, some don't. For a lot of people, buying the stadium really would mean the club was fully, fully back."

I sat upright. Something I'd wanted to mention at the start. "Bog-gy! You reminded me. One last reason why Chester. I had some time off in the last week and I took my girlfriend to your fair city and we walked around and it was lovely. It's really nice there and we had great pies. We loved that indoor food court near the town hall and the Christmas market was fun. Expensive! But the whole time I had a bit of a sour taste in my mouth. Because one of the first things I saw there on the high street was a club shop. Selling replica kits and mugs and scarves and all the rest of it. Right there on the high street in the centre of Chester."

Boggy shook his head. "Liverpool FC."

"Right. Liverpool. Why is there a *Liverpool* club shop in a prime location in your city? Nah. Nah, mate. That has to go. My goal will be to make Chester so dynamic, so fun, so exciting, that every kid in the county wants to be a Chester fan and that godawful shop gets shut down. And when it does, I'll hire an open-top bus with my own money and drive it around the city. I'm not even joking. Yeah we'll win leagues and cups and break records. No doubt. For sure. I mean, no promises, but come on! I'm really good at this. Cups are for the fans. But the day we purify the high street will be the day I know *I've* achieved something. Ugh! A Liverpool shop. I really want to swear Boggy. I haven't gone this long without swearing in years."

"I know. I can hear the frustration in your voice."

"Liverpool, though! Come *on*. Vote for me and I'll make Chester the biggest club in Chester. That, Boggy, *Seals Live* listeners, Crackers, Mike, and the rest of the fucking world, is a fucking *promise*."

SEVEN FUNERALS AND A WEDDING

My appearance on *Seals Live* lit a fuse and the Chester fans were the powder keg. Their team were eighteenth—a mere three places above the relegation zone. They were playing diabolical, drab, defensive football. October's thrilling FA Cup qualifier against Oldham felt like a tale handed down from a bygone age. My offer of a brighter future had opened old wounds and created new ones. I was a big shiny red bus with an optimistic slogan painted on the side, rumbling around, splitting families.

Mike Dean was unhappy. He still had calls pouring in about the loss to Broughton, the lack of ambition shown against Telford, and now there were more flooding in about every aspect of the club. For him, at this time, sunlight was not the best disinfectant.

Mike Dean having problems sounded like a Mike Dean problem. My exuberance achieved its aim—I forced the board into getting together to vote on the issue of creating a director of football position. When I got the job, I'd unite the fan base. I'd hire Miss Fox as my personal PR consultant. Angry phone calls would be a thing of the past.

I'd scheduled meetings with most of the board for the day of the vote. It was only polite. A couple didn't reply to my calls. Avoiding me? Good luck with that. I know where you live, mate.

Hanging over their heads like the Sword of Damocles was the curious scheduling anomaly that Chester would play Telford again on the first of January. If Chester's board didn't give me what I wanted, I'd be Telford's player-manager. The match would be a shootout between me and Henri. Somewhere between my third and fifth goals, the home crowd would go absolutely feral.

The thought made me less willing to take shit. From anybody.

That said, I tried to approach the day with a twinkle in my eye. I might not get every vote, might not win every heart and mind, but let's all have some fun along the way. Yeah?

i. Bulldog

At 7:45 I was in my Subaru in the car park next to Bulldog's office. Bulldog, you remember, was the foul-mouthed father of Tyson, the shitty kid whose petulance was ruining Chester's under-fourteens. I'd done my research—he owned a cybersecurity company. Not sure what job would have been more surprising. Tailor? Grief counsellor?

I was using my phone as a hotspot, burning through my precious data plan, so that I could gauge the mood of the Chester fans. The most common reaction to my interview with Boggy was ecstasy. That was rooted mostly in the idea that Chester might sign me as a player, but there were many who'd actually listened and were hyped by my vision for the club: my commitment to the ownership concept, my worries about buying the stadium, my desire to build the academy, my annoyance at the Liverpool FC club shop that blighted Chester's main street near the cathedral.

But while that was all amazing and motivational, I couldn't deal with the negative comments. Anonymous idiots who'd never achieved anything and had never set out to try were saying things like, "He should stick to playing." Other comments: *What does this twat know about scouting? About building a club? How do we know he wasn't dropped by Darlington and that's why he was at the Telford match? Pimping himself out to teams down on their luck? Pathetic.* Still others: *He's smug. He's a con man. Anyone who trusts this fraud is a lunatic. This is the guy who broke our youth system. And now we're going to hire him to fix it?*

I skimmed the positive comments and dwelt on the bad ones. There's no other way to say it—they got under my skin.

One popular fans forum put up a poll asking people to rate my "job interview" out of five. I came away with a 4.7 rating. Ten five-star ratings barely moved the needle, but a single half-star was cataclysmic. Reducing all my skills and effort into one single number . . . it was hard.

Too hard. This is why I wasn't on social media. Everything about it made me hate the human race.

It was in this foul mood—no twinkle in either eye—that I saw Bulldog pull into his office's car park. He was wearing a crisp white shirt, freshly ironed, and a waistcoat. It struck me then—he was a salesman! His product was cybersecurity, but it could have been anything. I leapt out of the car and paced towards him. I was on course to arrive at the door at the same time as him, but he saw me storming towards him and he bent and came up holding a big rock.

"What the fuck are you doing?" I yelled, pushing myself back so fast my arms waved around to help me balance.

"You came at me!" he said, his rottweiler voice briefly going Chihuahua.

I looked up—it was still dark. Winter morning in the north of England. Good time for a murder. "We aren't ever going to be BFFs, but I don't think it'll come to smashing rocks over each other's heads. What do you think?"

He put the rock down. "I won't vote for you."

I narrowed my eyes. I realised I was scanning his speech patterns, trying to match them with the most vociferous anti-Max voices online. Cybersecurity? Bulldog was probably running a botnet, downvoting me from hundreds of computers around the world. "Good for you. One man one vote. That's democracy, right?" His face was blanker than a fresh piece of paper. Maybe he *hadn't* infected an army of computers to skew a local online poll. A grin came to my mouth, unbidden. I was being absolutely demented. I'm not saying I got a twinkle in my eye, but I was a little bit more centred. "Okay, look. You can't say I didn't come to see you, right? How about I say what I need to say and then I'll fuck off?"

He nodded. "All right. Make it quick."

"If I get the job, I'll try to turn your son into a player. He's got the talent but there's one big thing holding him back."

"What's that?"

"You. I'll ban you from coming to training. And to matches."

He seemed genuinely upset. "That's your pitch? That's how you get my vote? With threats?"

"No. I don't want your vote. I want you to vote against me so every win, every title, every cup, is a dagger through your heart. But I'll do my best for Tyson. *That's* a promise." That seemed pretty succinct. I decided to leave it at that and began retreating to my car.

He called out after me. "For how long?"

"What?"

"How long am I banned for? When can I watch him again?"

"When he makes the first team."

"Get fucked."

For: 0

Against: 1

ii. Crackers

Crackers was an architect. My mind absolutely boggled trying to understand how a blind guy could do the job, but I was clueless about at least ninety-nine percent of all human activity. Probably everyone he ever met asked him to explain how he did it.

I was at his flat at 8:30 and was told by his wife that he always went for a long walk in the morning and wouldn't be back until after 9. There wasn't much to do in the vicinity. How could I pass the time? My choices were doomscrolling through the fan forums or making small talk with the wife for half an hour. Hmm. I checked how much mana I had, then opened my spellbook. I was about to yell "SUMMON TWINKLE" (which in this imaginary RPG would give me plus 1 d6 Charisma for twenty-five minutes) when her mouth fell into a downward curve. "You're that boy aren't you, what wants to be in charge?"

"Yes."

The curve trended downwards. "I heard you left Crackers alone. He was looking forward to having someone to talk to."

"Yeah. I did."

Well, now. This was . . . this was grim. The two members of the board I'd had prior dealings with were two firm no votes. What did that say about me? Nothing good.

The curve flattened. "Are you okay, love?"

"Yes," I lied. So Crackers had taken against me. Two–nil down, so early in the game. Bitten on the ass by my own assery. Forget doom-scrolling. I'd get started on my Telford research. "Can you give this to him, please?"

I handed over a small USB stick. She gave it an uncertain look. "Oh. A thumb drive." I scanned the room to see if they even had a computer. Of course he did. He was an architect. "What's on it?"

"Noise," I said.

"What kind of noise?"

"The kind we live for."

For: 0

Against: 2

iii and iv. Sean and Ollie

This meeting was a pub lunch. Sean and Ollie faced me from their side of a little table, with their wives or girlfriends on the next, separate table. They were all in a line—so bizarre. I was facing the guys. They were in their fifties or sixties—hard to tell because they didn't look after themselves.

I cast SUMMON MAJOR TWINKLE—or would have if it was real—and was doing a BIG smile so that my teeth might twinkle at them, too. The waitress got a full dose and she smiled back, so it was definitely working. I *was* being charming.

I guess what I'm saying is: it's not my fault.

Things went to shit as soon as I ordered mineral water.

"Ah, never mind that!" said Sean. "It's Christmas! Bring him a beer." I clarified to the waitress that I wanted water. Sean grimaced. "Mulled wine, then! Don't be so unfriendly. Have a drink with us."

Being told I was unfriendly by two strangers who were trying to boss me around? Mate, I should get a medal for my restraint. "I'm a professional footballer so obviously I don't drink at twelve noon. I do have a big glass of wine every time I score a hat trick. My doctor says I need to cut down because I'm killing my liver."

This harmless, mildly amusing banter was met with a baffled silence, but soon enough, Sean and Ollie were once again badgering me to drink something alcoholic. Being told to drink is one of the most annoying things in the world. Being forced to repeat a rejection is nails on a chalkboard to me.

Before long, I was simply glaring at them, wondering if I should leave. I became convinced this was Old Nick's doing. Truly, hell is other people.

One of the wives stepped in. "Max, I liked what you said on the radio. I'd love to see some good attacking football with young players. We need to get Ian Evans out of the club. If you get the job, will you do it? Bin him off?"

"That's one thing I absolutely won't do. That whole thing is between Ian and Mike Dean. My only interaction with Ian will be asking what players he needs this January."

"But we're shit," said Ollie.

"Ian was hired to keep Chester in the division. It's not pretty, but he's doing that, and will do that." I did believe that, but only because Henri was at the club. Without him, it was possible Chester would be in a real dogfight.

The two men looked at each other and the two women looked at each other. That wasn't what they wanted to hear. The second wife spoke. "You don't sound like the guy from the radio."

"The guy from the radio was talking about next season. This year, I'll be busy enough scouting new players and monitoring the youth teams and all that. I promised Mike Dean I wouldn't interfere in the first team. Next season, if the football's still shit, this will be a very different conversation."

"Which of the players do you see staying in the team next year?"

Finally an appropriate conversation! I blinked heavily so my eyes would glisten dreamily as I spoke. I tried to fire a bit more energy into my hand gestures. Tried to be more dynamic. Upbeat. "I don't know who's got how long left on their contracts and things like that, but next season I'd imagine the first team will feature Ben Cavanagh in goal, Glenn Ryder at centre back, Carl Carlile as the other CB or right back. Magnus Evergreen can cover a lot of positions, but I'd love to find a dynamic left back. I've got six months to find one. Midfield picks itself. Aff on the left. Raffi and Sam Topps in the centre. Me on the right—if I'm picked. Henri up front. So we need a left back, a right-mid version of Aff for when I can't play, and a second striker. That's the basis of an amazing team. Once that's on the pitch, it's a question of upgrading when opportunities arise." Twinkle. "But that's already a title-winning team."

I thought it was a pretty decent speech, but it was met with stony silence. Sean folded his arms and shook his head. "We don't like Aff."

"You don't like Aff? He's almost the most important player in the team. He's almost unique in the league in terms of what he can do. He's an attacking powerhouse and he defends like a terrier. There's no one in the league who comes close. What's the problem?"

"He doesn't wear a poppy."

I suddenly wished I'd ordered a beer. I was too sober for this. Around November 11, Remembrance Day, people wear little poppies to commemorate the nation's war dead. Football players and managers do the same. It is a nice, simple gesture and a way to raise money for veteran's charities. "Okay?"

"It's disrespectful," said Sean. "My great-granddad fought for his freedom."

"He should wear one. The club should make him wear one," said Ollie.

I massaged my temples and stared at a ceiling beam. The wood had cracked in a few places. Was it still strong? Could it still bear a load? No one else seemed worried about it. I blinked when I realised I was still in the pub with this awful pair. "Maybe he doesn't want to wear a poppy because he doesn't think the British behaved very well in his home country. Maybe it reminds him of all the famines and massacres and shit." Zero twinkles from Maxy boy right then, I can tell you.

"Let him go back if he doesn't like it here."

"It's disrespectful. The club should make him wear it."

I nodded a few times. A politician would know how to handle this. How to slip through the gaps without agreeing but also without annoying the bigots. And who knows? Maybe I'd learn it one day. "Tell you what, Sean and Ollie, let's do it like this. You vote for me and the four of us, including Aff, will have a sit down and we'll make a list. A list, yeah? We'll write down all the ways you want him to behave. All the things he has to start doing and stop doing. Yeah? We'll tell him he has to wear a poppy three hundred sixty-five days a year, and has to sing the English national anthem like he means it, and you'll tell him what you want him to do and say and think. And then, yeah, when we've made that list, we'll explain to him that this is what freedom looks like. Okay? That good for you? Now, I'm going to pay for my mineral water. Okay? I'm going to pay, and I'm going to leave, and you and I are never going to speak again."

One of the women said, "We've already paid!"

I took my wallet out and picked out ten pounds. I dropped it onto the table. "I don't want you telling people you bought me a drink."

For: 0

Against: 4

v. Sumo

I knew I didn't have the votes but I had this stubborn need to see things through to the bitter end. Also, I'd booked two nights in the Airbnb and if I didn't spend the rest of the day in Chester, it would have been throwing money away. So I turned up for my meeting with Sumo at his house—in his bedroom—and realised I'd walked into a trap.

Sumo was a large young man who was probably one of the hundred most famous people in Chester. He did Twitch streams. Imagine a Zoom call but only one person can speak and he's playing video games and you're allowed to send him money. That's Twitch. Sumo mostly played *FIFA* and his name recognition was high enough that he won election to the board every time he ran, which was once every two years, for a term of one year. The limitation kept things fresh and gave new faces a chance to get involved.

He'd adjusted his setup so that he could play me at *FIFA*. Thanks to a clever camera and a massive greenscreen, Sumo had placed me on the bottom of the stream next to him while our little men ran around chasing the little ball.

Sumo barely looked at me. I thought he did a couple of times, but I never actually caught him doing it. There were thousands of people watching—there was a chatbox that streamed past faster than I could read it, but Sumo somehow played the game while responding to the messages.

In other circumstances, I might have been interested in the technology and the business model and whatnot. But he'd basically done a Max on me—come up with a mad scheme and dropped someone into it without their permission. I put the controller down and tried to get to the bottom of why he'd done it like this.

Sumo wasn't used to being called out for his behaviour and couldn't put his ideas into words. He just kept putting the controller back into my hands because if I wasn't competing, the stream was moribund.

"But Sumo," I insisted, putting the controller out of his reach. "I came to talk about my vision for your club and how we'd do it. Why did you think this was an appropriate setting for that?"

"You did it on *Seals Live*," he said, flushing red.

"*Seals Live* is a football broadcast and the audience is one hundred percent Chester fans. It was perfect. How many people are watching us right now?"

He squinted. "About eight thousand."

"And how many are Chester fans? How many live in Chester?"

"Probably just me."

I tilted my head and looked at him. He had built this community of people who liked what he did. He was obviously interesting in some way that I couldn't perceive.

There was an awkward silence that stretched into infinity.

One comment came up in the chat that got a lot of emoji attention from other viewers. It was aimed at me and it said: *You're an actual star and you're intimidating. Sumo has brought you to the one place he really feels comfortable. He's not trying to show you up by beating you at FIFA. The green button is pass by the way. He isn't going to ask you questions because he knows you know more than him. You already got his vote just by showing up. Also I love your accent can we give you things to say?*

I laughed. I gave Sumo a little dig on the arm. "Why didn't *you* say that?" I picked up the controller again. "Green is pass. Green is pass. Right. You can unpause."

We played for a minute. When my little player got the ball, I tried to pass it around, but Sumo tackled, did a twinkle-toed skill, and was in a shooting position almost immediately. His shot went wide and I told my goalkeeper to smack the ball up the pitch.

Sumo paused the match. "Why did you do that?"

"What?"

"You're a good player. You're doing coaching badges. All the top coaches and managers want the goalie to play it short. Build passing moves in the defensive third, wait for the other team to press and then have more space for the attack."

"Absolutely."

"But you went long. And Chester, all the other teams, they kick it long."

"Sumo, mate," I said. "Come down to the pitch one day. I'll show you what it's like. It looks good from the stands but up close it's like a road full of potholes. There are pitches in this league that slope like a rollercoaster. No one's playing out from the back when the ball might jump up at any second."

"Oh," he said. And he gave me half a second of eye contact before looking away.

And then he thrashed me at *FIFA* in front of thousands of people around the world while I read things from the chat in a Manchester accent.

For: 1

Against: 4

vi. Barnesy

Barnesy was a former player from the era of Smasho and Nice One. I went to his house, starting in his kitchen where he made a tea to my exact specifications. Then we retired to his living room where he had pages of neat notes. Questions to ask me. Some were highlighted, some were triple underlined.

He cleared his throat. "Max. Can we start with what you said about football teams being a band of brothers? I've got friends in the game and we've heard mixed reports about you when it comes to teamwork and team spirit."

Talk about things escalating quickly! I smiled and looked around his living room. It was neat. Orderly. Photos of his playing career, a couple of football tops, watercolours of racehorses. "Do you miss it?"

He followed my eye. "Yeah. Course I do. Where else do you get the buzz?"

I picked up his notepad and skimmed through the questions. "Were you in the army?"

"Yeah. When I was young. Played footy with the other squaddies, but I got scouted and ended up playing for Aldershot." Aldershot was home to a big military base and there probably wasn't a family there that wasn't connected to the army in some way.

I gripped his notepad in my right hand and slapped it against my left. "Barnesy. I like you. You're the only one taking this as seriously as me. Do the youth team kids know who you are?"

"Oh! What a question. I suppose they do."

"Amazing. Let's do a field trip."

"What? Where?"

"I'm not getting the votes. But that little fucker Tyson doesn't know that. You know where they train, right? Let's drop by, unannounced, and I'll see if I scare some fucking football intelligence into him."

"Max, that's . . . that's . . ." He was shaking his head looking for the right word. Unprofessional? Unethical?

"I slapped his arm with his notebook. You drive. I'll answer your questions. We'll try to rescue a career. Come on! It'll be fun."

For: 1

Against: 4

Undecided: 1

vii. Ruth

I pulled into the driveway and was confused about where to park. I got out and walked around, and it was only when a huge floodlight attached to a motion sensor turned on that I realised there was a whole entirely separate driveway. I was on some kind of overspill. A place for the riff-raff to park without being seen from the house.

Imagine Downton Abbey. Now delete that from your thoughts, and imagine a large house. Thanks to my clever psychological anchoring you will now be picturing the exact right size. But wait, there's more! Add a big barn and an even bigger covered riding arena.

This was the home of Ruth, who I'm guessing wasn't on call centre money. I knocked on the front door—no reply. I started wandering around the grounds. There weren't any humans, but there were a lot of horses.

While I pottered around, sneaking ninja-style between horse box-es so the gigantic creatures didn't kick my brains out, I thought about the Chester under-fourteens training session I'd just gatecrashed.

The coach, Spectrum, had been as appalled to see me as Tyson was, but neither considered for a second the possibility that I had spent the day annoying people into not voting for me. I told Spectrum I was there to observe and maybe to help out with some ideas. He took my friendly tone for the threat that it was.

Has a man ever had more fun than me during that session? I doubt it.

I watched as they played some small-sided games. Every time Tyson shot, I covered my mouth with the notebook and pretended to complain to Barnesy. The third time, I went over to Spectrum and asked if he had a spare whistle. He said no. I said I'd take his, then.

The moment he handed it over was thrilling. I felt like an emperor or something.

Back in the giant stable, I heard a noise. A kind of rustling. I went towards it.

I brought the under-fourteens towards me. "Lads, listen up. We're doing a new drill. It's almost exactly the same as that drill you were just doing. But it's got a new name. Can everyone hear me? Good. The new name of the drill is 'Every Time Tyson Shoots He Gets Subbed Off.'"

"Max," complained Barnesy.

"Kin hell," complained Spectrum.

I put my whistle between my lips, smiled at them, and peeped.

"Hello?" I said. The rustling noise stopped.

"This is private property," came a woman's voice.

"I'm from the council," I called out. "There's been complaints about the horses. Animal welfare stuff."

I heard a rapidly escalating string of invective. Ruth came into view. She was wearing horse clobber. Jodhpurs, boots, navy blue riding top. She pushed some blonde hair behind her ears and gave me a magnificently indignant scowl. This meeting was bound to go wrong in some way, but my eyes, at least, were having a good time.

"Complaints?"

"This one's got leggings. But his mate doesn't. And it's random who's got hay."

She relaxed. "Ah. You're the boy."

"The boy?"

"The troublemaker."

"Sounds about right."

"You don't know anything about horses, do you?"

"Ha!" I said, pointing my finger in triumph. "That's a trick question. Some of these aren't horses. They're *ponies*."

She didn't smile. "They're all horses. Why are you here?"

I shrugged. "To discuss my candidacy. See if you have any questions to ask me."

"Questions like what?"

"Is four-four-two making a comeback amongst elite teams? When is it appropriate to use a double pivot? Do Mexican Waves go round the stadium the opposite way in the southern hemisphere?"

This brought a smile, and the smile brought a little thrill of victory. This . . . could end badly. Meaning it could end well.

"I have no such questions; I don't like football."

"Oh. Probably a good idea. You stood for election to the board, though?"

"Yes."

She showed no signs of explaining. I was pretty exhausted. It hadn't been a good day or a physically demanding day, but it had been a long day. I looked around at the horses. They were all different colours and the smallest was quite a lot shorter than the biggest. Presumably they were all different somehow. The big ones were for . . . knights and carts. And the little ones were for . . . making little girls fall in love with horses so that when you were old there'd be someone to sell your horses to.

Whatever the differences were, if I was hiring someone to brush my pony—not a euphemism—I wouldn't even know where to begin. And the same was true in reverse. What could Ruth possibly ask someone like me about being a director of football? It was pretty crazy that someone with no interest in the sport would be in a position to decide my future.

"There's a lot of poop in these boxes."

"Horses poop once per hour."

"Jesus fuck." I waved my hands around at all the buildings. In my head, this gesture meant *but you are rich*. "Why don't you hire some people instead of doing it yourself?"

"No matter how many people you employ, there's always more work. And you always end up doing it yourself. I am doing this now because I had to rearrange my entire stable's shifts so that I could attend an emergency meeting later tonight."

She was trying to shame me. I returned her eye contact and gave her a cocky smirk. Thanks for trying! "Yeah?" I said. "Well, the good news is that after tonight, you'll never have to worry about the club ever again."

She raised an eyebrow. "From what I hear, you shouldn't be so confident."

I felt my eyelids squeeze together as the truth burst out of my face. "Okay, you got me. I have no chance." I laughed. "I don't have the votes."

"Have you tried begging?"

"I'm not familiar with that word. Do you mean bragging? Yes, I've tried bragging. Sometimes it works." I was leaning against a horse box and one of the residents poked its head out and gave me the side-eye.

"Rusty likes you," said Ruth.

"One stallion to another."

"Rusty is female."

"All ginger horses are boys. Did I hear that?"

"That's cats. So you don't have the votes. You're not as charming as you thought?"

I rubbed my chin. I was starting to get some stubble. I hoped it wouldn't get so itchy I couldn't sleep. "One guy and I had pre-existing beef. That's unlucky that he's on the board. One I accidentally annoyed. Two are fucking mad racists. They probably build prototype wave machines in their sheds to protect us against refugee boats. Fucking ghouls. If they vote for me I'll die of shame. The streamer's living in a digital fantasy world but he's a nice guy. He'd vote for anyone who gave him some time. Barnesy is a prince among men. He's dubious about me. Thinks I'm too young. His is the only vote I give a shit about. I'll win him over, though. Retrospectively. We'll meet again in five years and he'll say, Max, I was wrong. I like him, though. He's wrong in the right way."

Ruth looked me up and down. The hairs on my neck stood erect. "His is the only vote you give a shit about?"

Being able to talk felt like passing a mental resistance check. "You don't like football. I want to be director of *football*."

"My vote's worth as much as his."

"Not to me."

"I see," she said, the light in her eyes fading. "Will you be there later?"

"Mike wants me to be around so I can sign things." I stuck my tongue in my cheek trying to minimise my grin. "He thinks I'm a shoo-in."

I shook my head and started back to my car.

Ruth called after me. "Are you as good as they say?"

"As a player?"

She nodded.

"No. I'm much, much better."

"They're on a diet."

That blew my mind. What the fuck was she talking about? "What?"

"The horses with no hay. They had some, and they've eaten it. They have to wait now. They're on a diet."

I looked around at all the horses I could see. They all looked the same, virtually identical, but apparently some were overweight. The more you learn, the more you realise you know nothing. Next time I met a horse woman, I'd have a conversation starter. The twinkle came to my eye of its own accord. I gave Ruth a Maxy two-thumbs and swaggered away.

For: 1

Against: 4

Undecided: 2

I had nowhere better to be, so I waited in the main reception at the Deva stadium. The board filed past. The only one who looked at me was Crackers—maybe I made some tiny noise that let him know there was a person where he wasn't expecting one.

After five minutes I got bored and went to find the groundsman to ask him to turn the floodlights on so I could thrash balls into the goals. But there was no groundsman—the place was deserted. In the entire stadium there was just me, the seven members of the board, Mike Dean, and Joe, the club secretary.

I turned my phone back on so that I could play *Merge Mountain* or do a sudoku. But I quickly remembered why I'd turned it off.

Emma: So? So? So? What's happening? You are the WORST at keeping in touch.

Raffi: You my boss yet lol

Ziggy: Can you get me a boot deal? The other lads are always going on about getting boot deals. Also I'm not having luck with ladies. I need you to wingman me.

Kisi: omgomgomg I caught James reading a Bible commentary but inside was Zonal Marking by Michael Cox!!! Busted! Should I tell him I know? No best not. lol though

Henri: My tenant. My playing partner. My agent. My former manager. My future director? If you are the director, I will be the leading man. *Chester: The Great Escape.* I will look for a suitable screenwriter.

Emma: Reply with a thumbs up or thumbs down. That's all. Come on.

Unknown number: Hi this is [person] from [a certain media outlet]. Can we talk about the job you're applying for? Seems odd?

Unknown number: Hi this is [another person] from [a less local media outlet]. Is it true you're going for Chester DoF? Please let me know when we can talk about it on the record.

AFC Telford Bigwig: Any news?

Emma: If you are not replying because you died in a car crash, I will literally murder you.

And so on. How could I explain to my friends that I didn't have the votes? And that in the morning I'd be driving to Telford to start my new life?

"Max?" It was Mike Dean. "Can you come in?"

I stood, stretched, and yawned. Had I actually fallen asleep on the shitty plastic chair?

I followed him into the boardroom. The seven members were scattered around. I didn't look at them. I had the strangest feeling that I was going to get the job. Why else would they invite me in here? Would they seriously invite me in to tell me they had decided *against* me? Maybe to tell me why, face to face.

"I'll keep this quick," said MD, who wasn't giving anything away. Or maybe I was just so tired that I could no longer read his microexpressions. "We've decided to create the position of director of football and offer it to you, if you accept the terms we discussed. We've got the contract here on the laptop if you want to check through it. Joe will print it and we can get it done and dusted."

I scratched my head. "What was the vote?"

MD smiled. "Massively in your favour, of course. But I don't think it's productive to know the exact count."

I narrowed my eyes at him. Something was going on here. I had one vote. Maximum two. Very mysterious. Was this the curse? Old Nick said I only needed to apply for a football job to get it. I thought he'd meant as a manager. I thought about it—I didn't give a shit. I wanted to run a football club. This was it. I sat and skimmed the document. "What's this? Three-year contract? I said month to month."

MD licked his lips. "Well, yes, but Max. We want you to build for the long-term. This is a show of faith."

"Switch it back. I don't do fixed contracts. I'll be here as long as you guys support my vision."

"Ah . . . okay." MD looked at the board. Whose opinion was most important to him? Bulldog? Ruth? Why did those two names jump to the top of the list? "Yes. Okay."

I kept reading. The rest was fine, except for one small detail. "Please change the start date to January third."

"Oh? I thought you wanted to get started right away."

"I do. And I will. But Darlington are playing the reverse fixture against Scarborough on the second. I want to give Cutter the chance to play me in one final game. Say goodbye to the Darlo fans. Properly. Try to do one classy thing in my fucking life."

"Fine, fine." MD pointed to Joe, the club secretary, who took the laptop and ran out of the room with it.

I checked the time. It was just after 8. It felt like 11. The night was still young. I pointed to a side table. "What's all that?"

"Champagne. To celebrate!"

I shook my head. "I'm going."

MD's face fell. "Where? If you say Telford I'll crack your skull open with that bottle. Do you know how many bags of ice I lugged up here?"

I allowed myself a little smile. "There's a five-a-side league in Blacon. They're playing tonight. If I leave now, I can start scouting."

"You're joking."

"Mike! I told you. I'm going to scout every football player in Cheshire, or come as near as makes no odds."

"But we should celebrate."

I inhaled. Maybe there wasn't a mystery here after all. The board had come in here to complain about me and MD, a better politician than me, had gone all *Twelve Angry Men* on them, turned them one by one through skill and persistence. This victory wasn't a triumph of Max Best and his storytelling. This was old-school diplomacy, with maybe a little horse trading. A masterful display from a mature, emotionally stable grown-up.

"All right. I'll go there next week. But can I speak to you in private just for a second?" I wanted to tell him I wouldn't celebrate with the xenophobes. Wouldn't drink with them.

"Max," he laughed. "You're always asking to speak to me in private. It's such a weird habit. No, let me crack open the champers."

"I'll do it," said Barnesy. "Why don't you do . . . the other thing?"

"That can wait till the paperwork is done."

Pop! The first bottle was opened and the mood lightened about four thousand percent. Everyone in the room looked towards the fizzing liquid as it filled the wine flutes. People had started to get up from their seats and oh-so-innocently move towards the booze. Barnesy gave me my glass last. "To a great coach!" he said.

"Whoa whoa whoa," I said, before anyone could clink their glasses. "Coaching's one thing I'm not good at. Let's drink to my new parking spot, which used to be Mike's."

Barnesy looked serious. "I've seen a lot of coaches, Max. Some good, some bad. That ten minutes you did today was as good as any of it. Deadly serious, demanding, pushing the kids. And more laughs than an episode of *Mrs. Brown's Boys*."

"Well," I said, because that particular TV show was about as funny as a flat tyre.

"Tyson loved it," said Bulldog. "Spectrum's good but he's not a star." He looked away. "T will listen to you."

"Argh!" said MD. "I'm thirsty. Here's to Chester! Down the hatch."

I clinked glasses with the board members nearest to me and downed my glass so I wouldn't have to do the same with Sean and Ollie, the twats. But Barnesy was already opening another bottle.

Joe came rushing back in. No laptop this time, but my contract printed out. In triplicate. MD signed three times. Joe signed three times. I signed three times.

I dropped the pen as if to say, ta-da! But in fact, I was reacting to the massive pang of headache I'd just experienced. Once I'd signed on that last dotted line, the curse interface had gone wild. Mega static, crushed screens, stretched fonts. It lasted just a second, and no one seemed to notice. I had a quick poke around and there was a lot that had changed, and the curse shop was bulging. I closed the screens—I'd take a proper look later, when I was alone.

But no sooner had I thought that than my brain processed something it had seen. I brought the screen back up. The first item on the news feed said:

Chester FC have appointed Max Best as their new director of football.

"I listened to it," said Crackers.

"What?" My heart was racing. I felt a full-body warmth that might have been from the alcohol or it might have been the incredible desire that was coursing through my veins.

"The mp3 you made me. All your goals. That Darlington commentator, he likes to scream, doesn't he? Nearly bust my speakers, heh heh."

Right. I'd inexpertly cut together some clips from Darlo matches so that Crackers would get to experience Max Best football. Fussing with the editing software seemed like ages ago. "It's only nine goals and a few assists but it took ages."

"Thank you, Max."

"Yeah, no stress."

"No, I mean thank you." His eyelids bulged a lot as his eyeballs rolled around. "For listening."

The scene was a bit awkward because it sort of felt like I was supposed to hug him. Not for the first time, Mike Dean saved the day. He banged on his flute. "Attention. May I have your attention." He put his glass down and fumbled in a bag hidden on the floor behind a plant. He came up holding something. Something soft and fabric-y. He handed it to me. It fell open into the shape of a football shirt. Blue with two vertical white stripes on the front. A sponsor's logo and the club crest, featuring a wolf. I turned it round. Saw that it said *BEST 77*.

The two bigots were grabbing their phones. Sumo was eyeing me like I was his millionth subscriber. Barnesy was grinning from ear to ear. Ruth was sensually holding her cold flute against her warm lips.

So wait. Wait wait wait. Bulldog had voted for me after all? Because I'd spent ten minutes turning his son's teamwork from one to two? Crackers had voted for me because I'd sent him a recording of me scoring goals. The bigots had voted for me because they wanted me in the first team. Sumo because I showed up, and Barnesy because he wanted to believe in me. Ruth? She was pretty hard to read, but holy fuck. Had the decision been unanimous?

Had I achieved a unanimous decision while being Max Best?

I looked at the crest again. Chester Football Club. A lion emerging from a crown like a genie coming out of the bottle. These people had granted my wish. And now I'd grant theirs. With a little bit of a twinkle thrown in for good measure.

I took my hoodie off. I pulled my t-shirt over my head, pretending to slow down so I wouldn't mess up my hair, but actually just giving Ruth an eyeful.

Then, slowly, I pulled the Chester kit on.

I closed my eyes, looked up, extended my arms in a goalscorer's salute. I let them take their photos—which I made them swear not to post anywhere until the third.

"Whoo!" I said, hurrrrring my arms together like a wrestler. "That felt good. Now. Mike. Obviously I'm going to need the biggest office, which is yours. So while the board, Joe, and I polish off this booze, why don't you start packing your stuff?"

"Get fucked!" he said. "We'll find you a broom cupboard somewhere."

I laughed, and we fell into a big hug.

While I waited for my flute to be refilled, I took a second to open the curse again. Just to re-read it. Just to check.

Chester FC have appointed Max Best as their new director of football.

FLAMINGO LAND

Monday January 2, 2023.

A two-hour trip to North Yorkshire through some of the ugliest and most beautiful parts of the country.

Junior was next to me on the team bus, asking what it was like at Chester and didn't it feel weird that I was going to play for Darlington today?

"The only weird thing is Cutter didn't pick me against Scarborough on Boxing Day," I said. "And you chumps lost three–two. There's stubborn, there's very stubborn, and there's Cutter."

"I don't know, man. Maybe he's right."

"Right to throw away three points?"

Junior hunched down in his seat, leant round the headrest to check if the coaching staff could hear us. "You're a big personality. We have to get used to playing without you."

"Come on," I said. "You were top of the league before I came."

"You stirred things up. It's different now."

"What's different?"

"The vibe. Now when he says we're going to do a shuffle and slide drill, there's this little *oh?* moment. You know? We want to attack. You've messed us up," he added darkly, which was incongruous with his grin.

"Don't talk shit." I shook my head. "You need to win promotion this year. I don't want to play against you next season."

"Chester are playing us in a couple of weeks. You'll play us then."

"No chance. You won't see me for the rest of this season."

His eyes bulged. "Why not?"

I hovered my finger in front of my lips to indicate this was confidential. "The manager."

He processed that, then *tsked*. "You won't play for your *own team* . . . waste *six months* of your career . . . There's stubborn, there's very stubborn, there's Cutter . . . and there's you."

"Mate," I said.

"Mate," he said.

We drove into the Flamingo Land stadium, which was something to do with a local theme park slash zoo. I saw a roller coaster from the motorway, but no action. Maybe there was a winter break? The zoo would still be open though, right? The website said they had penguins. I'd never seen a penguin.

While Pat the driver turned into Pat the kit man, the players checked out the pitch—it was a 3G all-weather one. Flat as a pancake. I practically drooled as I bent to rub my hand across it. I was ninety-nine percent sure that an artificial pitch wouldn't be allowed in the top four leagues, but it was practical for this level and perfect for a highly skilled technical player! Boss, boss, let me at 'em!

So naturally, I wasn't in the starting lineup. Cutter thought the lads couldn't be as bad again as they were in the previous fixture. My last day at the club and I probably wouldn't get to play.

My ears were pounding, so it was only when I calmed down that I heard the so-called team talk.

"Get stuck in, lads! They turned you over on our patch. Match their intensity! Match their work rate!"

Titan, the assistant manager, added, "Get up their arses! Keep it tight first twenty."

First twenty! These periods of tightness were getting longer. When I started my career it used to be first ten. Inflation was rampant in all sectors of the economy.

I raised my hand. Cutter didn't want to engage, but more and more players turned towards me.

"What, Best?"

"If we win, can we go see the flamingos?"

"No. My grandkids went and said the animals looked sad. If we win, I'll take you to the beach and give you a closeup view of the bottom of the North Sea. How about that?"

"Sounds good. You taught me to shuffle and sink, boss."

He raised his eyebrows as he broke into a grin. I'd won that round, but the only thing sinking was my heart. It was going to be a long afternoon.

While the starting eleven did a proper warm-up, I pottered around, listening to the away fans and seeing if there was anyone I recognised in the VIP section. There was! I leaped the advert boards, climbed the terraces past a lot of confused Scarborough season ticket holders, and greeted Bradley Rymarquis.

"Brad! Good to see you."

"You too, Max!" He seemed to mean it, as well. He'd been the second person I'd called when I'd signed for Chester. The first being the main dude at AFC Telford.

"Are you scouting someone?"

"Just checking in on an old flame." Huh. The phrase was supposed to mean *me*, but for a second I wondered if he *really* meant David Cutter. Nah. Although I'd thought Brad was gay at first, the way he looked at Emma concluded that debate.

"Listen, I'm sorry about how all that went down."

"I know. You told me. You don't need to keep saying it."

"I wanted to say it in person."

He shook his head. "You don't apologise for that. Sticking it to the owners? Oh, I thought I'd died and gone to heaven. Heh heh."

"Yeah but it can't have done your reputation any good. With Craig Summers and that." Summers was the manager of Sheffield Wednesday, and he'd been present when I'd exploded at Old Nick and everyone nearby.

Brad put his hand on my arm. "Don't worry about that. It's all good. I'm like buttered toast—I always land on my feet."

The match kicked off and Darlo struggled from the start. Scarborough were decent—their win over us had lifted them to sixth. They would fancy their chances of getting into the playoffs and then promoted—at Darlo's expense. My face started to hurt from all the grimacing and scowling. I imagined a TV camera was pointed at me—I relaxed and tried to breathe normally. Tried not to look as mutinous as I felt.

While I kept one eye on the pitch—I was gaining 2 XP per minute—I took another look at all the changes to my curse interface. I tutted. The number of screens I had access to had trebled! I should have been given all this shit from the very start! Why wait for me to get a management position before giving me tools that would help me *become* a manager? Old Nick was fucking clueless. He really was.

Control your anger before it controls you.

I am Max Best and this is my mantra.

Hom . . .

Hom sweet hom.

And . . . relax.

The most important addition to the curse was the button on the left that said *Max Best.* Now when I clicked on it the first options were Chester Squad, Chester Reserves, Board Confidence, and Resign from Club. Underneath this new Chester section were all the submenus I was familiar with, including News, Player and Staff Search, and Retire. This section had also been extended with screens such as Manager Stats, Job Information, and Transfers.

By far the most important was Chester Squad, so I'll come back to that.

Clicking Board Confidence told me what the directors currently thought of me. At the moment, the screen said:

The Chester directors are looking forward to a long and successful era under your management.

The Manager Stats screen was amazing. It showed twenty-two pages of managers currently plying their trade in the English leagues. At the bottom of the last page, in 352nd place, was the name Max Best. Reputation in England: Unknown. I skipped to page one. The sixteenth-placed manager had a reputation of Good. The ones from ninth to fourth were Very Good. Third was the only one to say Superb. The top two, Pep Guardiola and Jurgen Klopp, were considered World Class.

I went through the list looking for Cutter and Ian Evans. Cutter was 169th with a reputation of Very Poor. Evans was 131st, also Very Poor.

Even if they weren't my favourite people, it seemed pretty harsh. The curse didn't sugarcoat things.

Who else had I met? I went looking for Craig Summers from Sheffield Wednesday. It took me a long time to find him. He wasn't in the Poors or Averages, but was actually on the top of page two in the Goods, close to the big dogs in a very respectable seventeenth place. According to the curse, he should have been managing in the Premier League.

As for me, I was behind the managers of teams I'd never heard of, like Cray, Whitehawk, Canvey Island, Bromsgrove Sporting, and Leeds United.

On the pitch, Scarborough scored. One–nil to the home team!

I checked the list again to see if Cutter, the prick, had lost a few places. No. The list didn't update in real time.

The Job Information screen was my new obsession. It showed management jobs that were available for teams in England. On the left it said *No Manager* in grey and in the next column *AFC Telford, England*, a code denoting which division the team played in, and then the word *available*.

Handy, right? Yeah, if I had been given access to this months ago! Before I'd pair-bonded with my soul-penguin, Chester Football Club!

But here was the really fun bit. The screen didn't only show positions that were *currently* vacant.

Graham Potter—Chelsea—England—PREM—Insecure

Frank Lampard—Everton—England—PREM—Insecure

Jesse Marsch—Leeds—England—PREM—Insecure

Nathan Jones—Southampton—England—PREM—Very Insecure

You'll remember that I vowed to stop being immature several chapters ago, but wow! If I was going to regress to the old me, I'd probably say something like LOL!

Nathan Jones had only just been appointed. How could his position be at risk already? Lampard had been a great player but didn't look like a manager. Jesse Marsch was the kind of person who kept his LinkedIn profile up to date. It was unfortunate to see Potter's name up there. He deserved more time to fix things at Chelsea. It was easy to maturely think, *oh that's a shame* when it came to him.

But while it was very satisfying to see so many badly run clubs in crisis, I wasn't sure how I could benefit from this info now that I had a stable job.

Scarborough scored again. Cutter's head dropped. I checked the Job Information screen to see if his name had appeared. I remembered the imaginary TV camera and wiped the grin off my face.

The Transfers screen showed any incoming and outgoing transfers clubs had made. Two entries looked like this:

Sun 1st Jan—Henri Lyons—Darlington—Chester—loan

Sun 1st Jan—Timo Jentzsch—Benfica B—Crawley Town—£75K

Mere hours after the deal was formally announced, Henri had made his debut in the home match against Telford. Another defensive borefest ended one–all. Two points from a possible six against the worst team in the league? Abysmal. I kept checking to see if Ian Evans appeared on the Insecure list—no such luck. But Henri seemed to be happy even if he hadn't scored, so there was that.

The Timo Jentzsch deal was one I wouldn't have ever heard about under normal circumstances (i.e., without the curse), but something about it caught my eye. It was quite a large transfer fee seeing as the guy was thirty-six and considering Crawley were languishing at the bottom of League Two.

I turned to Junior, who was on the bench with me. "Junior. Is Crawley the team owned by those Bitcoin dudes?"

"Yeah," he said. "They're mental."

"Like what?"

He *tsk*ed. "Imagine the best way to run a football team and do the opposite."

"Like leaving your best player on the bench making sure you have no chance of winning the title?"

He rolled his eyes. "Nah. Like letting fans pick the team on social media and paying bonuses for weird things."

"Such as?"

"I don't know. Strikers get a bonus for tackles instead of goals. Mad shit like that."

"Huh."

"No, Max! Don't tell me you think that's a good idea."

I spread my arms in apology. "I don't hate it! I want to know more. Maybe there's a good reason."

"You know who I feel sorry for? Chester. Anyway, trust me, Crawley's a *mess*."

We scored a goal, which was annoying because it gave Cutter hope that the first eleven would turn things around. Going into the break two–nil down would surely have been enough to get me on the pitch. Surely?

In the dressing room, the boss yelled at everyone for five minutes while I played with my new toys. January was a busy time for transfers, and there was a new one added to my list every ten minutes or so. Could I turn this knowledge into cash somehow? It seemed unlikely. Gambling on which transfers had already taken place? Nah. Managers, though. You could bet on which ones would be sacked. If the Very Insecure status correlated strongly with actual sackings, then it seemed like an obvious play, but now that I was an industry insider, I would never place a bet in my own name. Probably not in Emma's, either. So who? I shook my head. No gambling.

"Problem, Best?" Cutter had taken my head shake personally. He got up in my face, wanted to give me the hairdryer. "Don't like the tactics?"

"Sorry, boss, I was just thinking about Nathan Jones being under pressure at Southampton. He's only just got the job and he did well at Luton."

"Are you taking the piss?"

This was a weird situation now. Not just because he'd decided to chomp me unprovoked, like a naughty pet—he'd done that several times. But I wasn't just Max Best, wandering agitator. I was also Chester's soon-to-be director of football. Could I really let him talk to me like that? Not just for my reputation, and Chester's, but for his! What if he wanted a job at Chester one day? Who would pick up his application form?

"I'm not taking the piss. I have no idea why you're yelling at me. I'm sitting here minding my own business. If you need to vent, go ahead. You can have ten seconds. Any more after that, I'll take it personally."

Captain Caveman decided to act as peacemaker, which was his job, so it was surprising to see him doing it. "Were you really thinking about Southampton?"

"Yeah. And the rest of the Premier League. It's a madhouse."

Caveman nodded. "Let's think about Darlo for the rest of the match, though, yeah? You might come on second half. We need your head in the game."

I gave him a Maxy two-thumbs and walked over to the tactics board and started dicking around with the magnets. "Their defenders are lazy as shit. They don't back each other up. Isolate one, turn him, it's three-on-one. Every time. Their right back is slow. Build on our right, quick simple square ball, that's deadly. You're hitting crosses too long. Aim for their tall centre back. He's shit in the air. He can't jump. Blondie has him on toast. Don't be afraid to go long from defensive transitions. They play here every week but they still aren't used to how the ball bounces. Think like a fast bowler. Get it to bounce five yards in front of a defender."

"Caught behind," nodded Caveman, completing the cricket reference. He looked more of a rugby dude.

"Yeah. Long story short, you'll *waste* these. And maybe don't worry about me paying attention? All right?"

I went back to my spot on the bench and, not to put too fine a point on it, sulked.

Cutter almost never made changes in the first twenty minutes of a half, so I knew I'd get twenty-five minutes of playing time, max. The best thing for me now would be for Scarborough to score a third. That would force a reaction. I closed my eyes—I hated wishing bad things would happen to my team, but I wanted to put on one last show for the fans.

I realised it wasn't going to happen. I rubbed my scalp for a while, then opened my eyes to watch the action. Back to grinding for XP, like in the old days.

A shit cross from Webby—far too long—was too much for Cutter.

"Best. Get warmed up."

The Darlington fans knew it would be my last match for the club. They didn't know where I'd go, but plenty of rumours were out there. Top of the list? Sheffield Wednesday. Based on the reactions to the three goals we'd seen, half the stadium was Darlo. I wondered if they'd cheer me or boo me. You never knew with football fans.

I jogged up and down in front of them, giving them little waves and whatnot when they called my name.

Some wag called out, "Are you going to celebrate if you score?"

There were laughs. I'd become aware that my non-celebration celebrations were causing a stir. Some fans loved it; most hated it.

I grinned and jogged away, and when I jogged back I mimed kicking a ball. Goal! I ran towards the guy who'd shouted to me and mimed a James Ward-Prowse golf shot celebration.

There were more laughs.

I jogged away and raced back—scored another pantomime goal—raised my arm slightly higher than a Roman soldier and ran around like Alan Shearer.

I jogged away and raced back—another goal!—and did an homage to the famous 1994 Bebeto celebration—rocking a baby in my arms.

By now the crowd in that stand was going mental, roaring me on, ignoring the match behind me.

I jogged away, sprinted back—the crowd went *oooh* as I approached the fake ball and roared as I struck it—waay! I stood soldier-still and put my finger to my temple. Think! The new, iconic celebration from Man United's local hero, the greatest living Englishman, Marcus Rashford.

I could have gone on for ages: Ronaldo's *Siiuu!*, Robbie Fowler snorting lines from the grass, Cavani's archer pose.

"Fucking hell, Max!"

I turned and saw Cutter yelling at me. "What?"

"Fucking do that on the pitch. Jesus Christ you're such a prick."

I replaced Webby—6 out of 10, yellow card, no goal threat—to a huge roar from the away fans. My direct opponent—a twenty-eight-year-old CA 33 right back with decent pace—was eyeing me warily.

I jutted my chin towards him. "Hey, mate."

"What?"

"Did you know the collective noun for flamingos is a flamboyance?"

"I did know that, yeah. We get cheap tickets to the zoo. Not a day goes past without someone telling me about collective fucking nouns."

"Gotcha. How about I show you something you've never seen before?"

"Gobby Manc twat swanning around doing pointless stepovers? Seen it. Seen it all before, mate."

I felt myself smirking. This would be my last match for ages. The pitch was perfect and I had a worthy opponent.

I intended to enjoy it.

5

HE BANGS
THE DRUMS

In 1989 my hometown was known as Madchester. It was a drug-fuelled era of dancing, raves, and great tunes. The fridges full of ecstasy are mostly a thing of the past, but the swagger lives on. And so does the music.

As the ref blew his whistle to resume the match, I took a few steps, scanning left and right for enemy weaknesses, deciding what my first line of attack would be. My mission: destroy Scarborough by making high-percentage decisions as part of a well-balanced, well-drilled unit. As I moved, though, my heels sprung up from the artificial pitch. So bouncy! The terminator persona *boing*ed away and I was reminded of the start of "She Bangs the Drums" by The Stone Roses. Intriguing snares, playful bass line, then a guitar chord that lets you know you're in for a hell of a ride. The lyrics arrive and you quickly realise it's about a cocky Manc twat who's doing things his way, and nothing can stop him.

I'd hyped myself up. Fuck scanning, fuck control, fuck shuffling and sliding. I wanted to *play*.

I jogged towards the ball and got a pass from Glynn. I played it back to him and pointed where I wanted it next—over on the right, where I was supposed to be. He played it perfectly into my path and I'd got the chance to attack my marker. See what he was made of. But I liked the guy! I dropped him a shoulder, just to keep him on his toes, but dribbled sideways, to the left, into traffic. Traffic? I'm a hovercar, mate! I hit a long pass straight onto Tim's feet, way over on the left, and followed it like a rugby player chasing his own kick. I made up half the distance in four seconds and then burst upfield. Tim was shit, but he was smart, so he played a simple pass forwards, hoping I could do something with it.

I could. I was in space, running in a place Scarborough didn't expect to find me. It was similar to my first goal for the club, when I knocked Glynn off the ball and sprinted eighty yards. This time, though, there were still three defenders I had to deal with.

The first came roaring towards me. The ball was in between us. He threw his shoulder at me—shoulder-barge, it's legal—expecting to knock me, a will-o-the-wisp man-baby winger, flying. Time for him to learn what strength 20 meant!

I matched his barge and he was lifted off his feet for a second, like when cars crash into each other. There was no time to savour the moment, because now I was bearing down on goal. The second defender was coming from my right and the goalie was moving towards me. The third defender, the guy who knew about flamingos, was running towards the goal line to try to block any shot I got off. Smart player!

Based on how fast I was going and the angles, the defenders were red herrings. I ignored everyone except the keeper, moved towards him at pace, did a stepover that brought his balance to my right, let the ball drift diagonally forward, then redirected it towards goal with my left foot. Just the faintest of half-touches.

It was such a subtle move that the Darlo fans didn't celebrate for several seconds. When they saw me coming towards them, smirking, that's when they went wild. Two–two, and maybe they could win the league after all!

My needle was hitting the groove all right; it was clearly one of those days when the ball obeyed my every thought. The challenge was twofold: how to celebrate my goals, and how to stop myself doing something I'd later have to coach out of Benny and the other kids.

I jogged closer to the Darlo fans. Their arms were everywhere—they were jumping around like monkeys, screaming inchoate noises.

Imagine Old Nick trying to get me to stop doing this. Bringing *this* joy into the world. Well, as the song puts it rather more poetically, Old Nick could get bent; what I was doing was heaven-sent.

That was it! A Christian celebration would annoy the fuck out of him. I positioned myself in front of the nearest match photographer and made the sign of the cross. *Spectacles, testicles, wallet, and watch.* Then I bowed my head, pushed my palms together with my fingers facing heaven, and smirked.

While we finished praying and the team dispersed to their positions, I stayed in Scarborough's half so that they couldn't kick off until I got to the other side of the pitch. I walked slowly to catch my breath after my big sprints, but also to think about more aspects of the curse that had been unlocked. We'd gone from losing to being all-square. How would that affect the league table?

There was a feature in the curse that would tell me just that, and it was available in the shop. For 1,000 XP I'd get access to live league tables during matches, plus a table section in the Squad screen. For another 500 I could also unlock Live Scores, which would tell me what was going on in the other games being played.

Useful, obviously, but the prices seemed to reflect a time before smartphones. These days I could get that info on hundreds of websites, making these perks the lowest items on my shopping list. If we were in a relegation or promotion fight near the end of the season, they *could* become more valuable.

I imagined myself managing a match in which I was playing a risky attacking formation because we had to win. But then the Live Scores would tell me that a rival were losing and if things stayed the same, a draw would be enough. I could switch to Men Behind Ball in the blink of an eye. Change the tactics before the score was even updated on the other stadium's scoreboard.

Yeah, good to have. One day. After I'd bought literally everything else.

I crossed the halfway line and closed my interface.

My feet itched for the ball. The drums were still banging.

It looks like Scarborough have adopted a more cautious approach.

Hey, ho! What's this? They were already pretty defensive. It didn't take long to find out what they'd changed—their left back, the flamingo expert, was no longer allowed to go forwards, and neither was the left midfielder. The Scarborough manager wanted them to stay back and deal with me.

Hmm. Yeah. Good luck with that.

I turned to Colin, the defender who played behind me. He was in the caveman club, which made him a twat, but we'd developed the beginnings of an understanding, built on mutual trust and—no, wait. The beginnings of an understanding based on him knowing his fucking place. "Colin. Stay flat."

"Flat?"

"Yes. Clear?"

"Yes, Max."

By flat, I meant for him to stick to the defensive line with Caveman and Shrek. In other words, not to go forward. I checked our tactics page and he was showing with a big black circle around him. These circles denoted tactical tweaks to the default formation and were pretty common, especially late in the game when managers threw caution to the wind or tried to shut down a particular opponent.

With him staying back and with our opponents doing the same, my side of the pitch would be virtually stagnant. Why? Because I had no intention of being there. Instead, I ran around like a toddler chasing the ball. I won headers as a defensive midfielder, played one-touch passes through midfield, and joined Tim on the left before making my way back across to the right. With the match like this, Scarborough couldn't get a kick of the ball and they were starting to buckle under the pressure. Starting to get frazzled and make bad decisions. Like me at a dinner party.

Grinning, I took a pass and burst past a weak tackle. The wind resistance, the bouncy pitch, my speed of movement and thought, even the way the goals were pushed right up against the stand behind them, making the net seem enormous—it all slotted into place like a jigsaw. I blew past another defender, kicks came that I didn't feel, my shirt was tugged but my momentum was undisturbed. I shaped to shoot and the goalie had a small panic attack. I straightened and jabbed the ball to Blondie. He held it up while I ran to his left, behind him; he rolled it backwards—beautiful idea, beautiful execution—and I was one-on-one with the goalie.

I decided to show off. As the goalie came charging out, with defenders scrambling to catch up to me, I rolled one foot on the top of the ball, dragging it halfway towards its destination, pirouetted mid-air, and continued the drag with my other foot. It's sometimes called the "Zidane Roulette," named after the French technocrat Zinedine Zidane. But Zidane never did it against Scarborough, so I think it should be called "Max Best's Scarborough Shuffle."

I suppose the name doesn't matter, because I actually made a mess of it. The second drag turned into more of a kick, and the ball raced away from me. I watched it head harmlessly towards the goal line, briefly annoyed with myself for dicking around with the scores level.

Then suddenly I was on my back, seeing clouds. I knew better than to try to move, and while I waited, the goalie and a defender untangled themselves from me. I thought about getting up then, but Junior told me to stay down and wait for the physio.

"What happened?" I said.

"Goalie took you out. Ref's given a penno."

That got my blood pumping. A penalty kick to take the lead in my last match! Yes, please. There was only one problem—Blondie was on pens, and he hadn't missed one for a while.

The physio came and checked me out. He helped me to my feet and did the concussion check. They are needed, and as a manager I planned to go ballistic at any player who didn't take them seriously, but as a player they were a nuisance. *Leave me alone! I'm trying to win a match here!*

"Who's the prime minister?" asked the dude.

"Some twat."

He smiled. "Can you be more specific?"

"Some fucking ghoulish twat. Hey, mate. Come with me."

"What?"

I grabbed his sleeve and pulled him towards Blondie. The physio was deeply confused.

"Blondie!" I said, nodding towards the physio. "Message just came from Cutter. He wants me to take this."

"No way," he said. He hid the ball behind his back.

"Yes way," I said childishly.

"Player who gets fouled shouldn't take the pen," he said, repeating a commonly held footballing superstition.

I turned to the physio. "Can you please tell Cutter that Blondie is refusing to give me the ball?" I spoke louder. "No win bonus today, lads. Soz."

Blondie threw the ball at me. "Fucking prick!"

I was grinning from ear to ear when I realised the physio was still hanging around. I waved him off. "Go on. I'm fine. The prime minister is Anthony Eden. See? All good." I placed the ball on the penalty spot. The goalie came towards me and kicked the ball a few inches back. Trying to put me off. The ref tried to reason with him. I said, "Ref! That's a yellow card. Get a grip." I checked the match commentary from the previous incident—the ref had booked the keeper for the foul. He didn't want to give two yellows and send the guy off. I thought about giving the keeper a blast of verbals, but he was a nobody.

The songs and chants subsided—Flamingo Land was abuzz with chatter, worry, speculation. Where's he going to hit it? What's he going to try?

Some thought I'd try to backheel the ball into the net—not without reason, because that had been my first impulse.

Some thought I'd try a panenka, a soft, slow lob down the middle of the goal. Very flashy. Very cocky. Yeah, maybe one day.

Today, though, I planned to hit the ball harder than it had ever been hit in a position that no goalkeeper would ever be able to save it. I wanted nothing less than to take the *perfect* penalty.

The ball was on its spot. The goalie was jiggling around. The ref was off to the side, watching everything. Behind me, fifteen players were lined up on the edge of the box, ready to compete for any rebounds.

The ref blew his whistle.

I smiled. I turned to the Darlington fans and pointed at them with a question on my face. Are you ready? A small eruption of noise said *yes*.

No more messing. I stepped forward, once, twice, third time faster, put my foot through the ball, intense focus showing on my face, massive follow-through, perfect balance at all times, hold the pose just long enough for the photographers.

Then off towards the screaming fans, off on my own . . . No! I waited as the other players caught up, picked out Blondie, and took him with me. All was forgiven! This time, there was no particular dance or theme. Just us players and subs hugging the fans, letting them bounce and sway and rock around us.

This time, as I walked slowly back across the pitch to the number seven slot, I rubbed the back of my head. I had a little bump there from where I'd smacked into the ground.

There was another new section of the curse, in the player profile area: Injuries and Bans. The bans part was simple—it told me if a player was suspended or not, for how long, and why. For example, Glynn was playing because the first-choice CM was banned for one match for picking up five yellow cards.

The curse gave me that section for free. The injuries bit I'd have to unlock, for a whopping 3,000 XP. The description said it would tell me what injury a player had and how long he'd be out for. That was something the medical staff should be able to tell me, but I suspected this perk would be well worth buying. For a start, players sometimes lied about their injury status, either because they wanted to play or, worse, because they didn't.

I was still committed to buying Playdar first. But it seemed to me that as a director of football I'd have to give any perks to do with injuries very, very high priority. I would look after my people very seriously.

I rubbed my head again, felt the bump.

Certainly a lot more seriously than I looked after myself.

While we celebrated, the Scarborough manager gave new instructions: he was going to take more risks and the flamingo guy and his mate were allowed to attack again.

"Colin! Back to normal."

"All right."

I spent a few minutes putting a defensive shift in. Slipping and sliding and shuffling and sinking along with my teammates. We absorbed the pressure from Scarborough and I watched as a loose ball fell to Colin.

"Go!" he called.

I obeyed, sprinting full pelt down the line. He smacked a ball over the top, like I'd suggested at half-time. Good lad! I was on it in a flash and hit it square. Blondie and Junior were there, along with one centre back. Blondie got to the ball first and tried another rolled backheel pass, but this time he got it all wrong and the chance was lost.

I enjoyed the move, though. It played to our strengths and was aimed at our opponent's weakness. I wasn't the manager but the team had listened when I spoke. Why had Henri Lyons left Darlington? Because he had such ideas all the time and no one ever asked him to share. There was no chance I'd make the same mistake as Cutter—I'd take ideas from absolutely anyone.

"Colin! Yes, mate. Do that again."

I stayed up by the halfway line so that I couldn't be offside, and waited. And waited. Cutter was throwing his arms around like a lunatic. Who cared? The next time there was a loose ball, it wasn't Colin but Shrek who booted it towards me. I spread my arms to stop the defender getting in front of me, and pushed him backwards as though I would let the ball hit my chest. But suddenly I stopped competing and ran around the player. He had a moment of excitement where he moved towards the ball—it was right there!—but that was replaced by cringe as he remembered how high the ball bounced. It flew over the guy's head, skipping off the artificial turf, right into my path. Timing? Almost as good as an ecstasy-fuelled drummer wearing a bucket hat.

This time I surged towards goal myself. The goalie moved to his near post. The defenders ignored Junior and focused on me and Blondie. I cocked my right leg. Time stopped. They'd all seen my cannonballs and the power of my penalty. In slow motion, while they all made despairing dives, I moved the ball onto my left foot and played a slow pass square. Junior tapped the ball into an open goal.

It was virtually the first thing I'd practised as a professional player. Darlo's goalies helped me get the timing down. This celebration was for them—I ran to the bench and hugged the GK coach Taff, and backup goalies Paul Larkin and Sky. Smokes understood what was happening and he joined us instead of the rest of the team. We bounced around in a private little bubble. I have to say it made me emotional. We'd come full circle, and this was the start of goodbye.

I needed to squash those feelings down. There were ten minutes left of showing the good people of Darlington what Max Best football looked like. Ten more minutes of gobby Manc swagger.

The Darlo fans, loving that I had the Midas touch—everything I did turned to goals—sang my song on a loop, relentlessly.

It's Max Best, you know. Never believe it's Darlo!

While I ambled over to the right-mid slot, I tried to remember how I'd ended up there. I'd hacked *Champion Manager* to let Max Best play anywhere, hadn't I? I'd tried different positions in my trial at Chester and right mid had been the easiest. I'd done okay in midfield and very well as a DM. But I'd failed miserably as a central attacking midfielder. It needed a speed of thought I couldn't offer and at the time I'd doubted I had the wide range of skills the position demanded. Now that I was up to speed, confident, and didn't have a crack in my skull, could I do it?

I lined up on the right because my threat there had forced Scarborough back again. They were 4–2 down and keen to stop it getting embarrassing. Once play got underway I drifted centrally, lining up behind the two strikers.

On the side of the pitch, Cutter was going tonto, waving his arms at me. One of the other coaches pulled him away. I laughed. I don't work for you anymore!

In the centre of the pitch, there was a much bigger chance of getting involved in the game. Passes came more frequently. Long balls went over my head. Any deflection or miscontrol could result in the ball popping right into my path.

I kinda liked it.

Once, my legs started pumping before I'd even spotted an opportunity. A pass bounced off a defender's shin, right into my path. I smacked the ball hard without thinking and it dipped and swerved. The goalie brought his hands together just in time and the ball burst off his gloves and away like a misfiring rocket.

That got Scarborough's attention. I got their aggro on me.

There's a famous photo of Diego Maradona against Belgium. It's misleading, but who cares? In the pic, Maradona has the ball and six Belgians are in a narrow cone in front of him. It looks exactly like their manager had tried marking Maradona with increasing numbers of players and settled on six. Six players needed to stop one! Wonderful photo. Check it out.

My case wasn't so extreme, but it wasn't a million miles off. The tactics screens showed that no one had been assigned to mark me, but wherever I went, so did the nearest three Scarborough guys. The aim was to stop me firing cannonballs at will, but it twisted their formation into a big pretzel. Or a doughnut, maybe, inviting me to fill that space with the cream of through balls, the jam of cheeky lobs, and the hot, melted cheese of no-look backheel nutmegs.

It was carnage.

I would wait for them to press me. I'd flirt with the edges of their zones and draw them towards me like a Wilson magnet. And then—

the magic. I'd conjure an impossible pass. A mathematically precise piece of triangulation. And when they started to back off me and keep their shape, I'd take another shot.

There was a word for people like me: unplayable.

During this phase, a fan tried a new song and it caught on. All English football fans are familiar with it. They sang, to the tune of "Love Will Tear Us Apart Again" by Joy Division:

Best! Best will tear you apart again.

Best! Best will tear you apart again.

More emotions. More energy needed this time to squash them down.

But my favourite moment in the entire match, maybe in my entire playing career thus far, happened in the second minute of injury time. Glynn, Tim, and Chumpy were passing the ball to each other on the left. I moved for a short ball, but Glynn turned away from me. So I turned and sprinted forward and right. Three opponents tracked me, opening a big gap for Colin to move forward into. He took a pass and played it forward to Blondie. I sprinted even harder, square across the pitch, causing mayhem as different opponents tracked and stopped tracking me. Blondie passed to Junior, who paused and played it short down the line for the overlapping Chumpy. He squared it across goal for Blondie to have a tap-in.

Five–two. The best goal of the season, I hadn't touched the ball, and I couldn't have been happier. I followed Blondie and the rest, and for the first time I felt like I was in a truly functioning team.

At the final whistle I spent time signing autographs and being in selfies. One little Darlo kid cried, begging me not to leave the club.

"I'm not leaving," I said. "I'm just going somewhere else."

I stayed until one of the coaches told me I had to get a shower so we could get going.

The mood on the bus was jubilant. We were three points behind King's Lynn, having played a game more. There was still loads of the season left. Still a good chance of winning the league. If they did, I wouldn't get a medal. It wouldn't say "National League North Winner" on my Wikipedia page.

But maybe the fans who'd seen me would remember that I'd contributed.

Junior bumped me and showed me his Twitter timeline. Posts from the away fans ranging from rapturous to ecstatic. One had got hold of the photo of me praying and added the text: BIGGER THAN JESUS.

"That's going to bite me on the arse, isn't it?"

"What do you mean?"

"Never mind."

I looked out of the window and grinned. Everyone was happy because of me. Ten out of ten match rating. Two goals, one assist. Two thousand pounds in twenty-five minutes.

Yeah, I could play CAM. Which meant I could play anywhere. Good to know . . . for next season.

There was one last thing to do.

The team bus pulled into the Eastbourne training complex where I'd spent most mornings since I'd arrived at the club. While Pat and the coaches unloaded the equipment, Cutter called us into the meeting room.

Unusual, and made even stranger when Bradley Rymarquis slinked into the room. He sat at the back and gave me a wave when I spotted him. I waved back.

It soon became clear this was a tiny little leaving do. Cutter didn't want me to simply leave with no mention of it. He encouraged everyone to grab a paper cup from a trestle table and fill it with a non-alcoholic drink of our choice.

"Max," he said, once he'd got the pumped-up players to shut up and sit down. I had to sit facing everyone. "You're a weird guy, but you're not a bad guy. We're sorry to see you go, and even more sorry to see you go lower down the pyramid." That earned him lots of confused looks. The squad had assumed I'd be going to League One. "Max is going to be Chester's director of football," Cutter explained. He struggled to regain control of the room. The explosion of laughter was bigger than at any comedy show. Cutter stuck the tip of his tongue out the side of his mouth and wheezed. "Yeah. Funny, ain't it? Lads, listen. Lads! It's not a joke. Max, do you want to say anything?"

I leapt to my feet. I hadn't expected anything like this, so I hadn't prepared a speech. But sure. I knew what to say. "It's true. It'll be announced tomorrow. When people mock Chester on social media I expect you to leap to their defence. Just remember Chester are playing you in a couple of weeks. Defy me and I'll do to you what I did to Scarborough." This brought some jeers and people threw empty paper cups at me. Good natured, but it reminded me of my first day. Something dark inside me bubbled. I rose above it. Mostly.

"So," I said, adjusting my posture to be more like a schoolteacher's. "I've promised the boss I won't tap up any of his players," meaning I wouldn't talk to them about a transfer while they were under contract. "But if Darlo let any of you go this summer, don't be surprised if you get a call from me. Now, I know what you're thinking. Do I have to wait until June to get in touch? No. Chester are always looking for articles for the matchday programme. I know that some of you are able to read and write, so maybe you'd like to submit an article for consideration? Topic ideas: How to become a footballer. My top ten memories of Max Best. Why do footballers cut holes in their socks? Payment. I'll replace the paper you used and buy you a new crayon, and of course, send a copy of the programme your article appears in." I retook my seat.

The mood was so positive that my suggestion some of them couldn't read bounced off, and my speech was met with giggles and amusement. Cutter shook his head. "Aye, well. Nice to be young and carefree."

I bounced back up again. "If you want serious, I can do that." I put my hand on his shoulder and looked at him for a few seconds. "You gave me a chance to play and believed in me and I'll always be grateful for that. You've put together a good squad and you get the best out of them. A pretty good model for me in my new job, right? And for the coaches, I appreciate the time you spent with me. The little tips and tricks. All the times you were a bit more patient than maybe I deserved. And look, this might sound sarcastic based on how I just played, but I really did enjoy learning how to shuffle and slide. I'd like to thank you all very much."

"Aye, well," said Cutter, startled by my change in tone. "We'd like to thank you an' all. Pat?"

Pat the driver, Pat the kit man, Pat the bearer of gifts. He had a brightly wrapped box in his hands. About the size of a shoebox. He handed it to me. "Should I open it now?"

"Yes," said Pat. "No time like the present."

"What, do you want to wait for your birthday?" laughed Cutter. "Get it open. I don't know what it is, myself. Pat said he knew the perfect gift. I am agog." He looked around. "We all are."

The wrapping was held in place by one piece of Sellotape. When I removed it, the paper gently fell apart. Quite satisfying.

The box was, indeed, a shoebox. I smiled with a frown. I could just imagine Pat thinking I needed a proper pair of shoes—I almost always wore trainers and no doubt for the older generation it was a bit strange. Maybe now that I had a managerial position, I'd need to—

I froze. The shock was total. I think I started to sway because both Pat and Cutter took a half-step towards me. I swallowed.

I reached into the box and pulled out one of the football boots my mother had bought for me. The last gift. The piss boots. I'd told Pat to leave them in the showers as a message to the other players. At some point, they'd vanished. Now, here they were again. Symbolising . . . what?

Pat was talking. "They've been deep cleaned. There's a place in Glasgow that does it. They're the best in the business. Now you trust me, Max Best, they're good as new. Your old boots. Good as new. You put them on when you play for Chester and you score your goals in them. Tell your mum. Make her proud."

That was it. Waterworks. I blubbed like a baby while various grown men tried to talk me down. I don't remember anything else that happened. At some point, someone unlocked the booze, and much, much later I found myself at Henri's house, which would remain my base until I found somewhere cheap to stay in Cheshire.

My career at Darlington was over. Tomorrow I'd be unveiled as a Chester employee. There was no point getting emotional about it. Pat, Margot from admin, the cooks, the cleaners, Junior, Bark, Benzo, Miss Fox, Longstaff. They'd still be there. I'd send them a Christmas card for a few years, and one day I'd forget about them completely.

Simple, right? You leave one job and start another. Simple.

Actually, not quite so simple.

Bradley Rymarquis had other ideas.

6

MARATHON NOT A SPRINT

Tuesday, January 3.

"Fanciful ornamentation in art and furniture originating in eighteenth-century France."

"Pretentiousness."

"Six letters."

"Any crossings?"

"Yellow sauce served on desserts . . . custard . . . so six letters, third's a C."

"Rococo."

"Fits. And that gives us crypt going down. How do you know words like *rococo*?"

"Agatha Christie books? Lil Nas lyrics? I don't know. Just one of those words you hear or read. I don't know what it means. Hang on, I'm getting a call." I pulled my phone out of a pocket and saw it was Mike Dean. I accepted the intrusion and said, so that MD would hear, "One of my employees." Longstaff put down the newspaper and pen and grabbed his laptop. If I knew him, he'd be researching rococo. He did the crossword both as a challenge and to learn things. "MD!" I said with a big smile. "What can I do for you?"

"You could come into work," he said.

I laughed. "What? Why would I do that?"

"I don't know. It's just sort of . . . implied that you would do so."

"That was a mistake on your part, wasn't it? We didn't agree on any metrics. Any key performance indicators. We didn't even agree how many hours a week I'd do. Do you know what rococo is?"

"Yes. An example would be overly ornate cornicing."

"Great. Now save me a minute and tell me what cornicing is."

"I'll show you. In the office I made for you. Which I am standing in and you are not."

"Well, I was pretty busy yesterday doing a Superman impression down in Yorkshire. And I set my own hours, don't I? I'm having a chill morning. It's called work-life balance. You should try it."

Longstaff looked up from his laptop and shook his head at me. "Max."

Fine. I checked the time. "MD, I'm having breakfast with my mate. In Darlo. I was going to set off early, but what's the point? Most of my work will be in the evenings."

"I understand. You're right. I just thought you'd be excited to start."

"I am. But it's going to be a long day. I'm pacing myself. I'll be scouting till ten or eleven p.m., then a long drive home. I need a house in Chester. Big mansion for five hundred quid a month. Know anything like that? My plan is, I'll leave Darlington about quarter past nine, miss the worst of the traffic. I'll be there before training ends."

"All right. Training. But come here first to talk about the budget. Then we'll meet Ian and talk about transfers and contracts. Plan what we can do in the transfer window and what we expect for the rest of the season. A lot of players are out of contract in the summer. We need to start discussing who we want to keep and tie them down."

"Hmm." Keeping players that the next manager—Jackie Reaper— would want, and binning everyone else without crushing morale . . . could be tricky.

"And I've got reporters who want to come meet the youngest DoF in Europe. What time will I tell them?"

"Eight thirty at Goals."

"Goals?"

"It's a five-a-side place near the stadium. You should come, too. Watch the magic happen."

"I'll tell the reporters. I don't know if they work nights. We'll probably have to slot them in during the day."

"Nope. Eight thirty. They can take it or leave it."

A pause. I counted five seconds. "Let me know when you're arriving."

"Is that a command? Are you trying to boss me around, MD? Are we starting our power struggle already?" Longstaff stiffened. He thought I was being serious and didn't want to hear me bicker.

"Max," said MD. "I'm hanging up. Please let me know when you'll arrive." My screen went black.

"Yeah, that's right," I said, with heat, jabbing my finger at the phone. "You'd *better* back down!"

I grinned. Being my own boss was pretty fantastic. I'd woken up at 5 a.m. thinking I had to be insanely productive from the word go. But why? Most of my weekday scouting would be in the evenings. So I went to a bakery and surprised Longstaff with some butties and two *pains au chocolat.* "Longstaff, why are half the lights still out? I thought you had a bumper Christmas?"

He looked up. "Yeah. We did. Thanks to you." He rummaged behind his counter and came up with an envelope. It was sealed. "This is for you. From a customer here. I think I know what it says. Don't open it here. Yeah, the lights. Even being careful, the bills are way up. If I kept things as normal, it'd be triple. It's murder."

"I wonder how much electricity a football club uses," I mused.

"Seems like your job to find out."

"Shit. Yeah. I have to get on top of every little thing. Players first, I think. We've only got January to make changes. I urgently need to see the eighteens. See if there's any talent there."

"Rococo is a style without rules," he said, looking at his screen. "What would rococo football look like?"

"Leeds United under Bielsa. Loads of guys running around, seemingly at random."

Longstaff nodded, continued reading. "It's often asymmetric. The halves of the piece don't match." He showed me a photo of a cabinet with one big, curvy horn and one small one.

"I know what asymmetric means. Stop cornicing me."

"I'm only reading this article. Halves don't match. That's interesting. You told me once you like symmetrical formations. You're a director of football now. You get to choose the formation the club uses. Right? And every age group will play the same one."

"That's one way," I said. "But it's not the Max Best way."

"Oh," he said, with a chuckle. "So what's the Max Best way?"

I pointed my *pain au chocolat* at him. "You'll see it. Next season. You'll be my guest of honour at any match you choose." I tilted my head. "Except ones my girlfriend wants to go to. Or someone famous or cool."

"Who's an example of someone cool but not famous who would take precedence over me?"

I munched on my pastry. "The one guy who had the same IT problem as me and left a question on a forum, but then he came back three weeks later and said never mind, I fixed it, here's how."

"Fair enough. Can't argue with that. That guy's a ledge." He picked the newspaper back up and clicked his pen significantly. "Seriously, though. This is your dream job. Aren't you excited?"

I grinned. "Course I am. But I didn't get here by burning all my stamina in the first ten minutes of a game. Days like these are marathons, not sprints. Next clue. Hit me."

In the car on the way to Chester, I thought about what Longstaff had said. His question was good. Which formation did I want to see? Ian Evans would play 4-4-2 until the end of the season, and the next manager would have his own ideas. But I could decide what the rest of the teams played, from the reserves down to the under-twelves.

The COPA MUNDIAL thing hadn't *seemed* like preparation for being a club manager, but I was starting to realise that it was. National teams couldn't buy or sell players. They had to work with what they had. That meant lots of asymmetrical formations. A lot of make do and mend.

Meanwhile, the big six teams in England had enough money to buy multiple thirty-million-pound players for every position, and when a new manager came in and switched to a new formation, they would simply buy more players for him. It was possible for a manager to have a philosophy. A style of playing that he would force onto his club. Philosophy first, players second.

Not me. At a tiny club with no resources, I'd have to cook with the ingredients that were in my pantry—plus whatever I could forage. If I couldn't find a dynamic left back before the next season started, I'd probably play a formation that didn't need one. If I found two incredible left backs, I'd obviously use a formation that leaned into their skills.

I scratched my chin. There I was again, thinking like a manager. It seemed like a curiosity of my role that I'd have to do just that—think like a manager—so that I could give the *actual* manager what he needed. But if he used the tools I gave him wrong, or we had a difference of opinion about a player's ability, there would be friction. Friction was, frankly, inevitable.

For now, though, I'd focus on bringing players with high potential to the club. Ideally, they wouldn't all play the same position, but there was no chance the first eleven players I found would perfectly fit my dream formation. No, I'd have to make compromises. Get asymmetrical. Break the rules.

Yeah. I'd have to get rococo.

XP balance: 4,767

Debt repaid: 259/3,000

Playdar cost: 8,000

The stadium was on the way to the training ground, so I went there first. I pulled into my parking space (they wanted to paint *DoF* on the ground, but I insisted they write *BEST*), and went to meet MD. When he saw me, a huge weight was lifted off his shoulders and a gigawatt of nervous energy shot out in every direction. His vibe was weird. Very out of character.

"Max! Finally! Come in here, come on." He dragged me into a supply cupboard. "That was unreal. Scarborough. Five goals in twenty minutes! How did you do it? I can't believe what I saw. There's no one that good who's ever played this level. Ever. And I've just watched Chester play five of the worst games in our history. We stink. I did a tour of one of our chemical plants, back in my old job, and the pong was beyond belief. What Chester are doing smells worse."

"Hmm," I said. Something was poking into my back.

"Max, let's get you in the team as a priority. If you play the rest of the season, I'll sack Ian Evans. Okay? Play like that, for Chester, get us out of trouble, get the vibes going, get the sponsors hyped, sell season tickets, I'll do anything you want. Holy shit. It was like watching da Vinci invent helicopters with his left hand while whipping up a quick masterpiece with his right. Holy shit. And the Scarborough MD told me you whipped the crowd up into a fervour he'd never seen before. I want it. I want it at the Deva, Max. Why are you looking at me like that?"

I glanced around the room. It was full of those stacks of paper that come wrapped up in other paper, which always feels cannibalistic to me. "First, a fact check. We only scored four when I was on the pitch."

"Oh!" he said, slapping himself on the forehead. "Only four! 'Only four,' he says."

"Okayyy . . . Mate, I don't *want* you to sack Evans. This season is dead. There's no chance of relegation. Not with Henri here. And no chance of promotion. Why would I play? What's the point? To get a broken leg? When Chester are playing I'll be out scouting. Do you hear me? I'm not available for selection right now. And by the way, the difference between the shit Evans is serving up and what the fans will get next season is so enormous that, narratively speaking, I see every dull moment now as a building block for even greater excitement later."

"What the fuck are you talking about?"

"So put all thoughts of sackings out of your mind. Our season is over. We've got six months to learn things. You can learn not to snort ALL the coke in one go. Save some for the weekend! Spectrum can learn what vertebrate means and whether he is one. Tyson can learn to count to two. And I," I said, with a slight grimace, "will learn to be kind and gentle and tolerant and how to get on with a sixty-five-million-year-old reptilian whose primary impulse is to keep things tight and score off corners. I've got six months to get good at dealing with people."

"But the money, Max! We need the money. With you causing havoc on the wing, we'll have sponsors queuing up to give us money."

"This season?"

"No. We sold the slots for this season. I'm talking about next season."

"So you want me to run around being a dick, one of those dancing horses, risking my leg being snapped in half, to get the sponsors excited for *next* season? Mate. They'll *be* excited. Don't worry. They'll be excited by the players I find *while Chester are playing football.* Now, look. We're about to have a budget meeting and you're going to tell me we have no money, right? So we have to use what we have and not waste anything. Even Ian Evans. Every player I bring to the club needs to learn to shuffle and slide and to win duels. Evans can teach that better than most. Now let's get out of the storeroom and go and be grown-up businessmen."

He showed me my office. It was small and bare with no windows. It'd do for now. I didn't expect to be in there much. "I'm going to put up your favourite art," he said. I expected him to make a quip about rococo. "Lots of mirrors."

"Ha ha. Let's get numbering." I walked out of my office, then walked back in again. "We could fit a bed in here."

"You're not serious."

"There's a toilet right there. Showers downstairs. A gym. Didn't you always want to live in a football stadium?"

"No. No one has ever wanted that. Anyway, you're not allowed." He checked my expression. "Shit. You've already decided. Just . . . don't get caught."

"Hmm," I said. The only evidence I was inside would be my car. I'd have to find somewhere to park it. Any night I slept in my office I'd have to wake up, go outside, and repark my car in my official slot. And in the evening, drive it away and sneak back in. Like a bad sitcom!

Pretty funny, but MD soon drained my good humour.

We went through the budget for Chester Football Club. It was grim reading. The club spent about a hundred thousand pounds a month. I asked MD to give me numbers in weekly amounts, since that's how we thought about player contracts. "It's about twenty-three thousand a week, with more than half going to player wages." He paused for effect. "This is *after* the cutbacks."

"What cutbacks?"

"Hundreds of small things. We've stopped heating the dressing rooms. Cold showers all the way. That doesn't make *much* of a dent, but we have to turn off every tap, switch off every light. We cancelled a tournament trip for the Knights to save four hundred pounds. Every expense is questioned. Despite my best efforts, the club runs at a loss and every year we do a fundraiser to make up the shortfall. Last year we needed, and got, eighty-five K. This year worries me. Have you seen what eggs cost? Who has spare cash? That's why I don't want you to rule out playing a few home games. Boost the mood. A little excitement would go a long way."

I nodded. The situation was much worse than I could have imagined. "I'll think about it. How's our credit?"

"Our credit? Um . . . yeah, it's okay. We undid a lot of damage from the collapse of Chester City. Mended a lot of fences. I don't want to add to the debt, Max. I told you that."

"I know. Can I bring in four first team squad players this window?"

"Four?" MD looked unhappy. "I don't know."

"If I find four Messis we can sign for five hundred pounds a week, mate. Do you know what I mean? Two grand of extra pain. Can we push the boat?" His face showed the absolute agony that was taking place in his mind. Eldritch spreadsheets attacking him from all sides, cells turning blood red. I smiled. "I won't let the club go bust. Worst-case scenario, we sell me to Liverpool for a million quid."

"Liverpool?"

"Yeah. First match I score ten own goals, they release me from my contract, I come back. Easy money."

He chuckled, half-heartedly, wrung his hands. "I don't know."

"All right, don't fuss. Let's see what I find out there. Now," I said, looking at the stream of numbers one last time, "what I'm seeing here is a club that can't afford a women's team."

"You'll need to fundraise for that. Not from the general fans, please. We'll need those donations to keep the club going. You'll need to, ah, persuade a rich person to part with her money."

"Her?"

"Slip of the tongue. I can put you in some rooms with some high-net-worth individuals. I've asked Inga to look into what's required for getting into a league next season. The quick answer is you need to play some matches and show you can compete. Show it's a serious project."

That sounded doable. Arrange friendlies against increasingly hard teams. Win the last one in front of a bumper crowd, get invited to join a real league. "Inbuilt narrative. Cool. All right, I think I get the theme of the morning. Money's too tight to mention."

"What about Youngster?"

"Yeah. I need to go and see him at Alty, see how he's progressing. Ziggy, too. That'll be good info about how fast these guys off the street can progress once they're in the right environment. Ziggy's at a low-level club but he's got a top coach. Youngster is at a higher-level club. His coaches might be worse, but he's got a much higher ceiling. There are so many variables. I really need to keep a close eye on them both. How they develop will teach me a lot."

MD smiled. I'd gone off on a big tangent. "I meant as a signing. You seem to think the world of him."

"He's going to be amazing. But he lives almost on Alty's doorstep. The only reasons to take him from there are if the setup there is bad, which I doubt, or if there's a chance he could get some first team min-utes here. What are the chances of Evans putting a seventeen-year-old on the pitch?" I sighed. Evans was such a disaster. "We're not doing this again. The next manager will have to *seriously* commit to developing young players. At the start of the season we'll agree on targets for the hot prospects. Player X makes his debut by Christmas, is a regular sub by February, plays two halves in May. Something like that."

"Players don't progress in such a predictable way."

"Don't they?" I said. I'd know their exact rate of progression from tracking everyone's CA on a daily basis. "We need a system where what we want is in writing and if the managers are too chickenshit to put the kids on the pitch, they know they're getting fired. They might not get fired for losing, but they'll definitely get fired for blocking potential. If it's really Jackie Reaper you've got lined up, tell him I said that. Talking about blocking potential and not getting fired for losing . . . let's go see the big man."

We left the stadium and MD drove us to the business park where Chester FC's first team trained. Buying some land to build our own facility seemed a long way in the distance. Most players and fans would settle for having the hot water turned back on. I had to rein my dreams in. For now.

The normal workers were on holiday—there were a few cars in the car park, presumably employees of the credit card company who needed to be around to help international customers. We went through the building to the pitches around the back.

There I watched the end of the training session while Henri and Raffi grinned at me. I didn't grin back—I saw a lot of red in the squad's player profiles. That was highly disturbing.

Training finished, and while the players went for a shower, the decision-makers went to the second floor. Evans had an office there overlooking the football pitches. I hadn't seen him since the Yellow Card party at Shona's. I expected a rough ride with lots of goading and provocation, but when we entered his office, I saw a man diminished. Where once he had been hewn from concrete, now he seemed dusty and cracked. A copy from a failed mould. The hair was as defiant as ever, the eyes as blue and sharp, but the snarl was timid. It carried as much threat to me as a charging hedgehog.

"Ian, you've met Max," said MD. "And Max, you know Vimsy." Vimsy was Evans's right-hand man. His main coach and unofficial assistant manager. Bit of a dick, but the kind of dick I could get on with.

"Yeah, yeah," said Evans. "Let's get on with it. We've got an appointment."

Thinking about various wisecracks I could make brought a twinkle to my eye, but it would be a long six months if I fell back into old habits on the first morning. I stood at the flipchart and took a marker. I went to my awesome new Chester Squad screen. It showed me the first team squad and which positions they could play. It was basically a portal to lots of other cool stuff. I wrote the first three names. "Goalies. Robbo, Ben, Angles."

Combining data from the player profiles and what MD had told me about their wages, the goalie options looked like this:

		AGE	WAGE	CA	PA
Robbie "Robbo" Robson	GK	33	500	39	45
Ben Cavanagh	GK	25	425	31	67
Steve "Angles" English	GK	35	500	26	80

Angles had a PA of 80, meaning he might have been a decent player at his peak. The fact he was a player-coach at his age suggested he'd had a bad injury that had stopped him achieving his potential. Ben's CA was red. He needed first team action to keep improving. I put the marker lid back on and tapped the names. "Robbo and Angles are over thirty. Robbo's good. Solid. Ben hasn't played for ages so he's rusty but he's got a higher ceiling. I'd want him in the team next year."

Evans scoffed and folded his arms. In his view, ceiling was a word used by wanky podcasters. "Ben lacks concentration. Keepers mature in their late twenties. Ben's still a babe in arms. Robbo's in his prime. He's got years left in him."

I mentally clicked on Robbo's profile. He was CA 39, PA 45. No injuries or suspensions. There was another new tab called Contract, which would tell me his basic wage, his bonuses, and any clauses he'd negotiated. As director of football I'd have access to all that on my computer, so unlocking that screen would be a quality-of-life upgrade. I was keen to buy it soon, though, because if the curse gave me that info for players *from other teams*, that would be yet another hilariously unfair advantage. Seeing the contracts other teams were giving out? Knowing who might become available at the end of the season? The possibilities were mouth-watering. For now I was able to memorise most of the important numbers, and MD said that Evans and Vimsy knew everyone's wages so there was no need to be coy about discussing those.

MD was even more of a walking database than me. "They're all out of contract this summer."

I looked at Evans. He shrugged. "Keep them all. It's a good group. Robbo's solid and Ben will take over in a season or two."

"Angles?" said MD.

"He's the goalie coach as well as being third choice," I said. "We'll see how he takes to the new regime before deciding on his future."

"The new regime?" scoffed Evans. "What's that?"

"That's where I go round Cheshire in my creepy car, scooping up hot talents, and dumping them into training sessions."

"The Child Catcher," said Vimsy.

"Don't know what that is, but yes. We don't have much here, but we have professional, experienced coaches. I'll bring rough diamonds and you guys will turn them into gleaming emeralds."

Vimsy eyed Evans. The latter said, "We discuss that later. Get this over with."

"You're happy with the keeper options for the rest of the season, though?" I said.

"Yes."

"Do you mind if I train with them?"

Evans's hair grew an inch. "Excuse me?"

"I'll train with the keepers every now and then, unless you object." Baffled, angry silence. "No objections. Okay, defenders."

"Wait. I don't get it. What's the angle? You got what you wanted. What are you playing at now?"

I kept my face as neutral as poss. "No angle, Ian. I want to understand what all of my employees do. I think we can all agree that I've mastered most positions on the football pitch, so it makes sense to spend more time with the goalies. And while I'm indulging my curiosity, it'll keep me out of your hair. That's the kind of win–win scenario the new Chester is all about." My smugness was rubbing up against his suspicion, causing sparks. The flame could ignite at any moment. I wrote the names of the defenders.

		AGE	WAGE	CA	PA
Glenn Ryder	DC	29	750	47	54
Carl Carlile	DCR	24	400	37	77
Magnus Evergreen	D, DM, M	25	500	23	-2
Gerald May	DC	28	700	34	38
Doug Walker	DCL	33	450	35	38
Trick Williams	DL	32	500	29	31

"All out of contract this summer," said MD. That was something, at least. I'd only have to look at this mess for six more months.

"MD, do you think I can give Ian a compliment without human resources getting involved?"

"Proceed with caution."

"Mate," I said, shaking my head at the names on the flipchart. "You're doing well to stop us getting mullered every match. Ryder is exceptional, and a good guy. I'd love to keep him another year, even on those wages. If he'll take little pay cuts as he ages, he can stay, what, four years?" I shook my head again. "May is . . ." I didn't want to slag players off in front of people I didn't trust. "May is less good."

"He wins headers," said Vimsy.

May played the Caveman/Shrek role, so winning headers was very important for the team. "For seven hundred quid a week he should be winning the headers and designing the kits *and* serving frothy coffees before and after training."

MD and Evans bristled. They'd both signed off on May's contract. Both thought he was worth it. The former spoke. "He's an important player."

He was, but he shouldn't have been. Still, there was no point bickering about every little thing. "So you're happy with the cavemen?" Blank faces. "The centre backs." Nods. "At right back there's two options. Both are unconventional players, but I'd like us to try to get more out of them. Have you any idea why Carlile is playing shit?"

Evans shrugged. "He's a wholehearted player. Never hides. Gets stuck in. Follows the plan. He's got the attributes but when something goes wrong it gets to him. He lacks concentration. We've talked to him. He says he's fine. We got in touch—didn't we Vimsy?—with his old coach. Said he was like a rock. Same with the scout who recommended him. That was before my time here, but I called the lad, he's retired now, and he said he was sure Carl was a triple lock."

"Triple lock?" I said.

"A sure thing," said MD.

"Yeah," I said. "He's got that high ceiling Ian keeps going on about." I looked out the window, then back at Evans. "Can I talk to him? Try something, maybe."

"Here we go," said Evans, shuffling in his chair.

I kept my cool like a champ-i-on. "Thing is, Ian mate, if he doesn't improve a lot, and fast, his time at Chester is over. I vote we do whatever it takes to help him out. If you can't get through to him, maybe I can. Or maybe it'll be MD. Or Henri, or Emma, or the girl who sells highlighter pens. I don't care where the solution comes from, but I can't take all these six out of ten performances from him. If you want to try again, great! Amazing. But time's running out. If I find a replacement before he gets his act together, he's out. I don't have the skills or experience to give him a kick up the arse. But I have the time. You have the skills but not the time. Better to try something, right? Because otherwise he's donezo. And that's a waste."

Vimsy spoke. "We'll have another go."

"Amazing. Now, bearing in mind our respective roles that we all understand clearly, it would be beneficial for the club if you gave Magnus Evergreen minutes."

Evans narrowed his eyes. "Why?"

"He can play anywhere across the defence or midfield. You can slot him in somewhere for five or ten minutes at the end of some matches."

"But why?"

I walked around a bit. Any info the curse gave me was hard to explain, but even more so in the case of Magnus. "I just think he has something." I pointed to the list of defenders. "I would crush all these guys, including Ryder, but Magnus is the one who'd give me pause." Evans and Vimsy gave each other that look again—it was starting to boil my piss. I sent my spirit into the stratosphere and looked down on the scene with a healthy dose of perspective. Magnus was a curiosity. He'd never have transfer value, so he wasn't worth spending my political capital on. "Whatever. Do what you want. What about left back?"

"What about it?"

"Would you like a new one?"

Evans laughed. "Aye, go on. Roberto Carlos, please. The 1998 model."

"I'll get right on that," I said, not bothering to smile. "I was thinking that if we could upgrade our left back, that would release Aff to play a more attacking role."

"Funny you should say that," said Evans. "I've been telling MD about a lad I could get in on loan. He's at Swindon Town but he's not getting in the first team. He'd do a job for us here."

"We've got two left backs," said MD. "We can survive without a third."

"What's he on?" I asked.

"More than we could afford," said Evans. "But the manager's a mate. He'll give us a deal so the lad can get gametime. We'll pay what we can pay."

"I'll go and scout him," I said.

Evans didn't know what to make of that. "I told you. He'd do us a job."

There was no way I was going to defend my role. I had decision-making powers. Not him. I focused on the loan aspect. "I don't want players on loan. We do that, we're developing guys for other teams. But I'll take a look at him and if he's good we'll talk turkey."

Evans's grimace hardened and I felt trouble brewing. Vimsy's phone beeped. "Boss, it's time."

Evans stood up. "We have to go."

"Club business?" I said.

"Mind-your-own-business business," said Evans.

"How was I?"

"You behaved beautifully," MD said.

"You see how he jabs at me all the time. Wasting all my energy on anger management. I never understood why dictators surround themselves with yes men. Until now."

"Have you got lunch plans?"

"No. I need to talk to Inga. Ask her to arrange trips for me. Including Swindon reserves, apparently."

"We'll take her with us. She loves eating on expenses. Don't overdo it with her. She's not your personal assistant. So, Max. Where does a director of football slash trainee goalkeeper eat?"

I shrugged. I didn't really know the options. "Nando's?"

MD rocked his head back. "You can take the man out of Manchester, but you can't take Manchester out of the man."

I Tysonned my arms. "What do you suggest?"

"I'll choose. Somewhere with a wine list."

"I'd rather get a new centre back than have a fancy meal."

"Shit defenders are a lot more expensive than nice steaks. Come on, relax. You get one treat, then it's back to nickel and diming everything."

The restaurant was fine. A bit too stuffy to really enjoy it. It was a place for old people. MD and Inga kept going on about how nice the food was, how attentive the service.

After our main courses, I peppered Inga with requests. Mostly for tickets to games, but also discussing the strategy for the women's team. I wanted to reserve January for scouting, so we could start playing friendlies against shit teams in February, building up to playing some big names in May or June. "I need to go to Swindon reserves, FC United, Altrincham. I get big boy tickets for our away games, right? I'll take them this week against Brackley."

"We won't ever give them away," said MD, "just in case you decide to turn up at short notice. You'll always be able to make a late decision. If I know the fans, and I do, they'll like it when you show your face. When you're visible."

I took a spoonful of my banana split and stared at it. I'd gain experience points by watching Chester, same as any other team in the division. In theory, my role was quite political. It would be good for me to be seen at most Chester matches. But being seen to do the right thing was less of a priority than actually doing the right thing. "I want to see every team in the league ASAP. Inga, I'll give you a list of the teams I've seen and played against. Try to get me to see the rest as fast as poss." MD coughed. "Er . . . please," I added.

Inga had an ability to flit between mental states and back again. She put her dessert spoon down, got serious, and said, "If you share your calendar with me I'll fill it with matches and organise your tickets. Go ahead and block dates when you don't want to go anywhere." She picked her spoon up and went back to indulging herself.

"Will do. Consider January wide open," I said. "I'll grind like a metalworker. Inga, my scouting is pretty important for the club, but feel free to say no if I ask you to do too much."

She smiled and waved her spoon in assent.

"Should we keep going through the squad?" said MD.

"Without Ian?"

"Yeah. He wasn't very committed to the process."

I was about to ask a waiter for a pen, but no sooner did I think it than Inga produced one. I gave her an impressed smile, which she took with a tiny moment of smugness. A kindred spirit! "The midfielders," I said, writing out their names and ages.

		AGE	WAGE	CA	PA
Sam Topps	MC	27	750	50	60
Aff	ML	26	500	50	70
Raffi Brown	MC	21	500	18	139
Max Best	Omni	22	500		
Joe Anka	MR	27	600	35	40
Chad Flintoff	MCR	31	450	32	41
Donny "D-Day" Dorigo	AMLR	32	500	36	55

"Some more absolute tosh here," I said. "MD, can I slag the players off in front of Inga?"

"Oh, yes. You should see her at the matches. Filthy mouth, she has."

"Don't believe a word," said Inga. "But go ahead. I love gossip and don't get nearly enough of it."

"It's not really gossip," I said. "It's nothing about them as people. It's a question of value for money. Topps and Aff are essential."

"Topps has another year left on his deal," said MD.

"Oh. One less decision to make. His wages are high but he's good and he puts it in on the pitch. No worries there. We need to keep Aff. I expect we'll have to increase his pay. But he's got room to improve as a player. It'll be worth it. Raffi is obviously a star in the making but shouldn't be used too much just yet. He's got a nice long contract."

"With pay increases every year," said MD, as though I hadn't negotiated the bloody thing.

"This Max Best guy seems like a bit of a superstar. Let's talk about him for, conservatively, twenty minutes. We'll do our best to keep him, right, MD?"

"If you're going to be like this I want more wine."

"Joe, Chad, and D-Day are pretty pointless and some are on good money."

"They're all out of contract in summer."

"Can we move them on already? If someone will take them off our hands that's budget I can use to bring in some hot prospects."

MD pushed a blob of ice cream against a wall of honeycomb. Trying to organise his plate. "But Raffi's not ready, right? You said it's going to take time before he's a real first teamer. If we replace these three midfielders with new Raffis, just hypothetically, we'd have four guys who aren't up to speed. And *you* don't want to play. So the midfield would be desperately weak."

"We can't do it all in one go, sure. But if we can ship out one or two, we should. It might cost us a few points but it'll pay off next season."

"A few points?" said MD, abandoning his meal. "We're already close to the drop zone. Relegation would be catastrophic."

I shrugged. "We have to take some risks to catch up to where we should be. Have you seen the ages of these players? They're so old. There should already be young guys breaking into the team to replace the oldsters. No offence, MD."

"Offence? I'm forty-two, you little shit. Wait till you're forty-two and see how you like being called old."

"How long can we leave the players with expiring contracts in the dark about next season? When will they start looking for other clubs?"

"They've probably already started. They'll take the first serious offer they get. They need stability. But in my experience almost all of them will still be here on May thirty-first. You can wait till then, if you're dead inside and have no consideration for their emotional well-being."

"We'll sign the key guys. The rest will depend on if I can replace them without losing too much starting eleven CA."

"CA?"

Oops. "Just a stupid phrase I use. Coach's assessment. Don't worry, MD. I know what I'm doing. We can't have a team of jam tomorrows. We need enough jam on our toast to win matches. It's good so many players are coming to the end of their contract, though. I should be able to replace some with better players for the same money. As long as we keep a good spine, we'll always have a chance of winning."

"The spine?" said Inga. "You mean Ryder, Topps, and Henri."

"I do. One strong, talented player with good leadership skills in each part of the pitch. Robbo in goal, too, though he's not as outstanding as the others. It's a good spine."

"We're talking about next season, though," said MD, who was back to nibbling his dessert. "Will Henri stay?"

"We can't afford him. We have to look for someone else."

"What about the ones who were already here?" said Inga.

		AGE	WAGE	CA	PA
Len Kearns	S	33	500	38	39
Henri Lyons	S	27	800	47	90
Tony Hetherington	S	25	600	40	44

Henri's CA had been 55 when I'd met him. He'd lost 8 points! That was shocking, but I hoped that now he was back playing regular first team football, he'd reverse the decline. If not—well, it didn't bear thinking about.

"Henri's a cut above but we can't include him in our long-term plans. Len and Tony, MD? Contracts?"

"Len's finishes this summer. Tony next."

I sighed. It wasn't as bad as the defence, but it wasn't great either. "Why do we only have three strikers? What about injuries? Suspensions?"

"Tony's never injured. That's one reason he got a long-term contract. But Ian uses D-Day as a second striker. I was wondering why you had him in the midfielders section."

I rubbed my head. "That's the squad, then, MD. It could be worse, but there's lots of inefficiency there and not much in future transfer fees. We've got a few reserve team players. Part-timers, right? On about ninety quid a week? Just in case there's a big injury crisis. I'll check them out. Tomorrow I'll watch the eighteens and see if there's any talent there." I rubbed my face. "Oh, God."

"What?"

"This is a big job."

"Running a football club with the hopes and dreams of an entire community resting on your shoulders. Ya think?" He chugged his wine. "Remember, it's a marathon, not a sprint. Pace yersel'."

"Right back at you, buddy," I said.

That afternoon, I went to watch the under-twelves train. There were a couple of okay kids. One had PA 25, another was PA 22. I told Spectrum to move them to the fourteens next week. I would need to find some talented toddlers, and fast, or the current crop of under-twelves would stink up the gaff for years to come.

After telling Spectrum the session was going well, I went to a café for a tea and to read the papers until the clock hit the top of the hour. I snuck back to watch Spectrum coach the fourteens. I hid behind a newspaper like a bad spy. The first ten minutes were infuriating, so I came out of hiding—i.e., rolled up my paper—and went over to remind Spectrum of what I wanted. Sullivan was not allowed to play it safe, and Tyson was not allowed to shoot. Furthermore, Tyson was not allowed to flap his arms around. Any time he shot or flapped he had to take a five-minute timeout.

It was annoying to have to micromanage Spectrum in this way, but I clearly couldn't trust him to follow my instructions, and if he didn't follow my instructions these kids had no chance of a future. Spectrum wanted to be seen as the cool coach who made training fun. Mirthlessly hammering bad behaviour out of some brat didn't come naturally to him.

Incredibly, even while I was right there, he didn't punish Tyson for flapping. I told the kids to do a million push-ups and pulled Spectrum far, far away to the other side of the training pitch. "Mate," I said. "I can't understand what you're doing. That pair have a short window to turn themselves around. If you don't help them, they're out. You're not helping them by letting them play like shit."

He swallowed the first thing he wanted to say. I was his boss now. "They aren't playing like shit. We're developing technical skills. They'll learn teamwork and the rest later."

"No. They'll learn it now. Or they're out. And if you don't give me what I want, you'll be out, too."

He nodded. "So it was all fake. All that stuff about me in the IT room working with the goalkeepers."

It took me a second to remember I'd namechecked him on my *Seals Live* appearance. "No. But you have to *want* to be part of this project. This youth system has zero output. Nobody is making it to the first team. The pipeline is blocked, and it isn't only blocked at the top. There's a huge fatberg right here in the fourteens. Things will change. Fuck that. Things *have* changed. You just don't realise it yet. This is me, for the last time, demanding change. You *will* stand up to parents, and I will support you. You *will* fast-track players into higher groups, and I will support you. You *will* fix character defects that stop players progressing, and I will support you."

I cracked my neck. Confrontation on my first day. I should have expected it. The simple fact was Spectrum had had it cosy for far too long. No one monitored him. Vimsy maybe knew a *couple* of the young players' names. I knew *everything* about the players, and even though I was the DoF and a star in my own right, here I was spending my afternoon making sure the training was up to scratch. I'm sure it came as a shock.

"I want Sullivan to play with freedom. Which means giving him permission to take risks and make mistakes. And I want Tyson to learn that it's a team game. Right now. I don't think I can make myself any clearer. This isn't me saying you need to be cruel to be kind. This is me saying give me what I want or get fucked. This is me saying this isn't a marathon, it's a sprint." I looked around. The kids were waiting for us to finish talking so the session could continue. "If I have to stand here and watch you do the session, I might as well do it myself."

I went back to the kids and blew the whistle. They went back to the drill. Two defenders. Two attackers—one trying to get the ball through the defenders into the path of his onrushing teammate. I hesitated—hadn't I done something like this back at FC United? The thought drifted away. The first kid started with a dribble and a trick to move the defenders apart. Nice. Tyson was next. He tried to do an elaborate shuffle pass, kicking the ball from one foot onto his other as part of the move. Moronic. And the little pleb looked at me for approval. He didn't get any. I wrinkled my nose like there was a bad smell. "Or you could keep it simple," I said. Simple was almost always best.

Then came Sullivan. He tried a forward pass. Weak. Easy for the defenders. I blew the whistle and went next to him. "See the defenders moved close together? It's because you telegraphed the pass. Made it too obvious. Can you practise this kind of thing?" I demonstrated a disguised pass—head angled away from the line the ball would travel. That kind of thing was pretty effective, especially in the hurly burly of a game where defenders didn't have time to think and sometimes reacted to small changes in body shape. "Or this." I did it again, but added a finger point. "You're literally saying, I'm passing that way! Lol! Psych!"

Sullivan was perplexed. "But how are you doing it? Your foot's the wrong way."

"Oh." I went through the motion again. "Ah. See, I'm making contact a bit farther down the side of my foot. Helps me get that disguise and boop—the angle's right."

"I'll mess it up," said Sullivan.

"I don't give a shiiit," I sang. "Your technique is fine. You'll get it. It's not that hard. Another thing you can do is . . ." I got the defenders back in their positions and shaped to play a pass between them. Both stepped towards the expected line of the ball. I chipped the ball past them, hip height. "Most people do *big* chips over the heads of defenders. Ball takes ages to come down, defenders have ages to get back into position, strikers have to do hard volleys. Low chips leading to half-volleys, that's the future. Sully, try that."

He did. And he messed it up. "Yesss," I said, even though it was the worst piece of garbage I'd ever seen. "But you can do it harder. That chip comes with backspin for free. You can put more heat on. All right, everyone try that. Low chips with a fuckton of spin."

Tyson, the prick, picked up the technique instantly. "Guys, if you're stuck, look at Hermione Granger over here." Tyson flushed red but kept doing the skill. "Tyson, five stars, five times out of five. Imagine being an elite passer and never doing it in games. What the fuck." I kept walking. "Sully, that's it. Gassy, it's a football, not a zombie. You don't need to smash its brains out."

And so on. Quite fun, and at the end the kids were buzzing, but no attributes turned green. Spectrum had slunk off.

While the kids gathered their stuff, I texted MD.

Me: Let me know if Spectrum whinges to you. I've got 200 coaches lined up to replace him. Thanks.

MD: Why would he whinge?

Me: *Shrug emoji.* Doesn't think he's doing anything wrong. Doesn't want to change. Thinks his job is safe. He's complacent. He might have to go. Please check his contract to see how easy that will be.

MD: I'm not sure if firing someone on your first day makes you look strong or weak.

Me: I don't give a shit. The pipes are blocked. I want them

unblocked. I want pipes so wide and smooth that Mario can pop in and out.

MD: Pipes. WTF. Explain it to me later.

From 6 p.m. I was at Goals, the five-a-side place. Picking up XP now that there were matches to watch, but also looking for talent. Christ, we needed talent. There were tons of things I wanted to buy in the curse shop, and some were pretty urgent. But nothing came close to Playdar. Anything to help me get some high-PA players into our system.

At the rate of one XP per minute, getting to 8,000 XP would take fifty-four hours. A couple of Premier League games would make a big dent in those numbers. I wondered if Newcastle would let me into the scouting section at St. James' Park now that I was kind of a big deal? I decided that if the journalists turned up, I would try to be charming. Getting my name in the newspaper might help get me into big games, which would let me progress my skills faster.

At half past eight, MD arrived with a couple of dudes who were fascinated by the appointment of such a young director of football. They followed me from pitch to pitch while I pointed out interesting things that were happening in the matches.

I remembered one thing I'd learned in Miss Fox's lessons: if you want attention, give them a good pull quote.

"There are two ways to play football," I said, with a smirk so they'd know this was the good stuff. "The Max Best way. And that's the only way."

They liked it and wrote it down in their alien squiggle language. But ten minutes later, the story seemed a lot less interesting to them. They were more confused than anything, and when I told them that turning the club around would be a marathon not a sprint, full of lots of tiny one percent improvements, they decided there wasn't much of a story here after all. Just a talented player who knew a thing or two and was helping out behind the scenes and was maybe a bit of a blowhard.

I could feel them mentally check out, and so could MD. He invited them for a pint in the bar, and I joined for an orange juice. With no story to report on—"maybe a few inches under your photo, my editor likes a bit of eye candy"—we started shooting the breeze and swapping anecdotes.

MD excused himself to take a phone call, and when he came back to the table, he looked like he'd just heard about a death in the family. The journos were instantly alert.

"What is it?"

"That was Joe," he said. "The club secretary," he added, for the benefit of the journos. "He's been on the phone to the FA for hours. They're refusing to register you."

"Register me?"

"As a player."

"Refusing?" My mind was treacle. Thoughts moving slowly. There was nothing solid about this conversation. "What?" I tried to work out what was happening. The process should have been simple. I was registered at Darlington. Joe would fax in a form and voilà! I'd be registered at Chester. My Darlo contract was so flexible there was no way to stop me leaving whenever I wanted. There was one major restriction on player transfers—you couldn't register for more than two clubs a season. Even that didn't seem to apply to non-league, as far as I could tell. Without a fixed contract, I was free to do whatever I wanted.

"We tried to register you but we couldn't. We can't use you in matches. If we do, we'll get a points deduction for fielding an ineligible player."

"Ineligible? No way. I'm eligible. Get a dictionary and look up eligible bachelor. There's a photo of me." I glanced at the journos. They were all ears. They'd stumbled into an even better story than the one they'd come for. "But Mike," I said, voice rising in a slight panic. "What are you talking about? Why can't you use me?"

"Because," he said, giving me a stern look, "your registration was transferred last night."

A chill ran up my spine. "What?"

"Max. According to the Football Association, last night, you signed for Sheffield Wednesday."

7

JANUARY SALES

Wednesday, January 4.

The office of the Chester FC manager, 9 a.m. sharp. Behind his desk, in the position of power, doing his usual impression of an Egyptian mummy stolen by the British, Ian Evans. Behind him, leaning against a window, his trusted lieutenant, Vimsy. To the right, on the hard-backed chair, Mike Dean, shooting off one-fingered texts at an impressive rate for a man his age. On the opposite side of the desk, Henri Lyons. The only man in the room looking relaxed. One of the rare times he wore no scarf. How did he manage to look like he'd just stepped out of a yacht club? Next to him, wildly uncomfortable, the club secretary, a generic but competent admin dude known only as Joe. By the door, pushing the handle down to check it will open whenever I want, me. Poor little Max Best. The big swinging dick who took a big swing and got dicked.

Evans's watch beeped. "We're all here. Let's do it."

"Good," said MD, standing up and stretching. He looked like he'd had a sleepless night. I knew the feeling. "Max. Why is Henri here?"

"He's my devil's advocate," I said. I didn't know what was happening to me, but I was sure Old Nick was behind it. He had insinuated himself into a famous old club well enough that he was on the verge of asking it to destroy itself. How hard would it be for him to worm his way into the Football Association? It would be a hundred times easier than scoring a penalty.

MD shook his head. "I don't think you're using that phrase right."

"He's my diplomat. My lawyer. My thingy. Friend in need."

"A friend in need is a friend indeed," said Joe.

"I'm not in need," said Henri. "Max is."

I tried to explain. "The saying means a friend who helps you when *you* are in need is, indeed, a friend."

"No," said Evans, revealing his glass-half-empty way of thinking. "It's the friend who's in need. And that's the only time he's your friend."

"Stop stop stop," said MD, doing the thing he sometimes did where he paused being in awe of the football experts and treated us like the cretins we mostly were. "We've got a big problem here. Henri, I'm all in favour of having extra witnesses. Max. You know what I have to ask." He took a big, dramatic breath. I could see him thinking: *This line will be in the trailer!* "Max. Did you sign for Sheffield Wednesday?"

I pushed the door handle, one quarter-inch at a time, all the way down, until it clicked and the door swung open one atom wide. "No?"

"Max," he said.

"No."

"Then why are you registered with them?"

I closed my eyes and went to the Latest Transfers menu. The transfers for this month were in chronological order. The name Max Best was nowhere to be found. How could the Football Association say one thing and the curse another? "I don't know."

"A-ha!" said Henri. He leapt to his feet. "Now I know why Max wanted me here. The French are the best detectives in the world!"

"Hercule Porro," said Evans, with a thin smile. "Good show, that. Used to watch it with me family. Every Sunday night. David Sachet. Magic."

"Poirot is Belgian," said Henri.

"Tintin's a detective," suggested Joe.

"Belgian," said Henri.

"So who's French, then?" said Vimsy.

"Inspector Clouseau," I said. The situation was serious but I couldn't help myself. And part of me was interested to see the reactions of the others. Who would believe in me? Who wouldn't? To find out, I wanted to try to be normal.

Henri stared daggers at me. "Maigret. Dupin. Lupin. And the first private detective was French!"

I pointed out one simple fact. "The greatest detective in the world is Coleen Rooney." That was a private joke between me and the 1.2 billion people who followed a certain court case. Mrs. Rooney had used her sleuthing powers to find out who was leaking her secrets to the media.

Henri had his hands on his hips. "I hate you, Max."

MD let out a frustrated noise. "This isn't funny. We have a big problem. Our best player can't play!"

Henri pulled his shirt down, straightening out any creases that might have developed as I threw spears of truth at him. "As I was saying. Allow *me* to investigate. Mister Joe, when was the transfer supposed to have happened?"

"According to the person I've been talking to, the paperwork arrived the evening of January second."

"Max, where were you then?"

I thought back. "That was when we played Scarborough. We played, I signed loads of autographs and shit because I was, hang on, what was the word Bingo used in his article? Can't remember *exactly* but it went a little something like . . . *'After the shock, the awe, after the awe, the sadness, after the sadness, the nostalgia. Mere moments after Max Best's scintillating display, his all-too-brief time at Darlington was uploaded to the North-East's collective consciousness alongside names such as Jackie Milburn and Brian Clough.'"*

"Jesus Christ," said Evans, but for once he was laughing *with* me.

"And then?" prompted Henri.

"Team bus home. Two hours, give or take. I think we got back around seven p.m. Bit of a leaving party kinda thing. Got a bit emotional, actually. We had some drinks. I had a couple more than I really should have and ended up walking home. But I'll tell you what I didn't do—I didn't go home and download the Darlo Fans Radio file for the match and then cut out all the bits that weren't about me. And I didn't listen to the last twenty minutes of the match on a loop while kicking a milk bottle top around the kitchen, recreating the goals. I did not do that and I would thank you to stop implying that I did."

MD shook his head. "Did you sign for Sheffield Wednesday to muddy the waters so that you wouldn't have to play for us this year?"

I slapped my hips. "Why would I sign for Wednesday? At what salary? What goal bonuses? What shirt number? I've spoken more to one of my client's pastors than I've spoken to Craig Summers. I've spent more time in *church* this past few months than I have in Sheffield in my lifetime! How can I sign for a club without ever seeing a contract? Having a negotiation?"

"He didn't do it," said Evans.

"What?" said MD, beating me to the punch by half a breath.

"It's not his style. Best doesn't want to play for me." The grimace was back, harder than ever. "He wants me to beg him to play. That's his drug. Five games to go. We need four wins. There's only one man who can save us. He refuses to play unless I beg him. Max Best, saviour. He wants to be the next Jack Reaper."

The eyes that were on Evans turned to me. "Yeah," I said. It had taken far too long, but he was finally off the only-in-it-for-the-money' line. "Pretty much that. Not begging, though. Just asking nicely would do it. It's your fault it feels like begging."

"*Eh bien*," said Henri. "I also don't think Max did it. He will make enough money out of football in his career. Playing in a big stadium fits his showman mentality, but the thrill would soon wear off as Craig Summers took credit for Max's tactical brilliance. No, Max is what the Germans call *ein Kontrollfreak*. The DoF job scratches many more itches than mere playing. Max's pathology is savage aggression tempered by crippling empathy." He paced around the room, clutching his chin. "Joe. What forms must be filled in for a transfer to happen?"

"They're standard. Fill them in, fax them to the FA. Easy. The contract between the player and the new club is the hard part."

"Forms are sent from both clubs? Buyer and seller?"

"Yes."

"So it's a two-man job. Someone in Sheffield sent a form. Someone in Darlington. The forms require a signature?"

"Yes."

"Max. You said you were signing autographs."

I exploded away from the wall. This investigation had just become a lot less amusing. "You don't think I accidentally signed a football contract instead of a match programme? Mate!"

Henri shrugged. "Strange things happen. You sign a blank piece of paper. Someone puts it into the printer. *Voilà*. It's a contract."

"Come on," I said. "That's mental. I didn't sign shit. Now look, this is all a red herring. We should be talking about why someone would do this. Cui bono and all that. That's what I can't get my head around. I can understand why someone would sabotage me getting the DoF position, but I've already got that. It's too late to dick me about. But me playing a few games for Chester? Who gives a shit? I mean—oh."

Henri, MD, and Vimsy all took steps closer to me. "What is it?" said Henri.

"I'll fucking murder him!"

"Who?"

"Bradley Rymarquis! This is him! He did this. This is his revenge for messing up a deal. He's fucking set me up! Nothing to do with Nick! Just plain old human pettiness. He was fucking *there,* Henri! That evening in Darlo. He was there. He was at the match and he followed the team bus. After I gave him a slice of my goodbye cake, he snuck off, sent the fax, drove to Sheffield, did that side of it. Wait—we were in Yorkshire. He sent the fax from Sheffield first. On a delay maybe. Can you do that on a fax? Holy fuck, I will literally murder him."

MD took my hand and prised my phone out of it. He stepped away while Henri and Vimsy sort of bustled me down onto a chair and stood guard over me.

MD looked around. "Calm down! You'll burst a blood vessel. Bloody hell. On behalf of Chester Football Club, I forbid you from having any contact with Bradley Rymarquis. We can't afford bad relations with agents. And I forbid you from contacting the FA. Their bad side is not a place you want to visit. Joe and I will deal with it. I want you to unlock your phone so I can delete Brad's number. Do you agree, Max?"

Bloody hell, he said. Blood. The world was made of blood, built on blood. Pyramids? Desert football stadiums? Drenched in blood. Bodies? Nothing more than six feet of red stuff, pumping complacently until one burst of rage sends it forth in a fury. Summon up the blood, stiffen the sinews. Brad? Tougher than he looked, but so was I. One punch and it would all come out. In the room, people were saying things. Why? Blood was all I could hear. I looked at my palms. I could see—and hear!—red cells rushing through my fingers.

The morning had started as a Kafkaesque situation. A lone, innocent man dealing with a vast, inhuman bureaucracy. But now I realised it wasn't that. It was one man trying to imprison another. I would lash out and the feud would escalate until one of us lay dead in a pool of claret. Bring it on. May the Best man win.

I'm not sure, but based on everyone's reactions, I think my lips had risen into a Draculan snarl. "What?"

MD repeated his request to delete Brad's number from my phone.

"I can get his number easily. What good is deleting it going to do?"

"It will stop you doing anything moronic in the next hour. And maybe you'll calm down when you've had a nice cup of tea."

Vimsy spoke. "Tea sorts you right out."

Tea. Right. I was British. We didn't tear people limb from limb. My revenge would have to be more subtle. More long-lasting. More complete. The pounding in my ears subsided. I started to feel human again. I scanned the room. Everyone looked slightly horrified—all except Evans. *He* approved. Being understood by Ian Evans was not how I wanted my life to go. I thought about some of the good things in my life. I knew about adblockers. I was a director of football. Emma wore my Darlington shirt in bed sometimes. "Tea."

Joe stood up. "I'll make you one. Come on, lad. This whole thing? It's probably just a mistake. Someone with a similar name. Or someone filled in the paperwork just in case you decided to sign. We do it sometimes around deadline day to move matters along. And this one time the papers got mixed up."

Henri scoffed. "From two different clubs?"

"Yeah, sure, it's unlikely. But there's got to be a rational explanation. Don't go killing your agent over it."

I cracked my knuckles; they popped like a pistol. "He's not my agent. And don't worry, I won't kill him. He's already dead."

While I fumed in the canteen, waiting for Joe to bring me a polystyrene cup of calming juice, Vimsy popped his head in. The rest of his body followed.

"Max. Sorry to be that guy."

"Go on."

"Spectrum called in sick."

I nodded. Typical. It never rains but it pours. "Okay."

"Spectrum was going to do the sixteens and eighteens this afternoon. What do you want to do about those?"

I stared at him, unable to comprehend what he was getting at. Was he asking if I wanted to cancel the sessions? "I'll do it."

He eyed Joe. "What about the, ah . . . ?"

Joe shrugged. "Max can't play a competitive match until we sort this registration mess out. He can do everything else. Coaching the youth teams? No problem there."

Vimsy hung around a bit longer than the conversation demanded.

I looked at him. "What?"

"Well," he mumbled. "Just thinking . . . you might not be in the right frame of mind for it."

"Me in a shit frame of mind is better than anyone else on top form," I said, rising from my stool of self-pity. "I'm the only one who gives a fuck about these kids. The worst hour with me will be the best hour of their careers so far. Count on it." I found myself looking into space. Thinking years into the future. "We're going to have the best youth teams in the world here. The world. I need builders. I need dreamers. I need people with the balls to believe the unbelievable."

Joe put the milk back in the mini fridge and pushed a cup towards me. "Tea's up."

I took a sip. "Terrible." I slapped him on the back. "I appreciate it, but that's garbage." I gestured towards the shitty polystyrene cups, the supermarket own-brand teabags, and the area where Joe had dropped the plastic stirrer. "Bad infrastructure, bad raw material, bad process. Huh. Is this analogy or metaphor? I can never get that straight." I slapped him again to show I wasn't having a go at him personally. "I'll make you a cup one day and you'll know what it's supposed to taste like." I put my hands on the counter and leaned against it. "I'm not going to let today get me down. It's not all steaks and fan mail. Bradley's never met anyone like me. I'll grind like a bullet train with the brakes on. Grind him to dust. I want to go scouting. January fourth. Everyone's back at work. Work means lunchtime games. Guys. Where can I find people who choose passes over pasta?"

I'd hoped Vimsy would know a match I could watch where I could pick up some XP and maybe find a star. But it was Joe who blew my mind by introducing me to an app called Footy Addicts. There, players of all ages and abilities met to organise games of football. You'd turn up, play for ninety minutes with a bunch of randos, go home. No stakes. No pain, no glory. Just football. Joe himself was an Addict—he went to one match a week and he loved the vibe.

"No one shouts at me when I play badly," he said, which was pretty heartbreaking, but also got my juices flowing. It sounded much more like my kind of football than watching two billion-pound clubs try to outcheat each other. And, best of all, there were women and kids who played. I could fill three squads in one go!

There was no way to find a match without signing up and asking to play, so within minutes, I was scheduled to play. I used a fake name.

"Kickoff's at twelve. I don't want to ruin the game for everyone else by being technically, physically, and tactically superhuman, but I doubt I'll be able to play shit on purpose. Do you think I should wear a fake beard?" I asked.

"Might be weird," said Joe. "Why don't you play left-footed?"

I stared at him. I was still being pretty secretive about my left foot. There's a Rocky movie where his new coach teaches him to box left-handed. I had vague notions of making my way through the football pyramid until I was picked for England, and in a World Cup final, with the entire defence set up to defend against my right foot, I'd suddenly switch to my left. 'Best is fighting southpaw!' the commentators would yell. "Yeah," I said, finally, way too late. "My left is decent. You know what? I'll go in goal. Vimsy. Let's head down to training! I need to borrow some expertise for a minute."

I kidnapped the goalies, loaded them into my Subaru, and drove to the nearest sports store. Judging by the lighting, it was doing better than Longstaff's shop, and it had a much bigger selection. They had a January sale going on.

We said hi to the store owner, who was bemused to find I had three ready-to-train goalkeepers as bodyguards. "Why have you got so much Wrexham kit in here? I thought Wrexham was a big rival of Chester."

"For the older generation, yeah," said the guy. "Try telling a ten-year-old that Deadpool isn't cool."

"Oh, for fuck's sake," I said. "I have to kick Liverpool out *and* be cooler than Ryan Reynolds? Give me a fucking break."

I stewed while my employees exchanged glances. The goalie coach, Angles, spoke first. "I think you're cooler than Ryan Reynolds, Mr. Best."

My mouth dropped open. "What the fuck are you—oh. You're taking the piss. Good! I needed that." I blinked. We were in the goal-keeping equipment section of the shop, which is normally one of the smallest areas. I turned to the shop guy, who had taken a few steps away and was full-facing the stock. "Why is the goalie section big here?"

"There's a goalie academy not that far."

"An academy for goalies? Goalies only?" I said, astonished.

"Yep. Run by an ex-pro. Got a bit of a name doing YouTube and Insta. Started doing clinics once a week, expanded. There's massive demand. He's got it sewn up in the area."

"Good for him," I said. "Guys. We should pop by and see what he gets up to. Yeah?"

My goalies looked uncertain. "Really?" said Ben. "What for?"

"Because I'm having a shit day and you saying yes to my whims is what I need right now."

Robbo nodded. "I'm always available for a field trip, Mr. Best."

"Right, good, that's settled. You'll be hearing from Inga. Attendance is completely voluntary. Changing the topic completely, I wish you luck in your contract negotiations . . . if they happen. On to the main event. I'm going to be training with you likeable dudes. Learning the ancient art of when to stay on your line for corners, when to punch, how to starfish, and how to kick the ball all the way to the other goalie to the apoplexy of your director of football."

"What!" spluttered Angles.

I gave him a hard look. I wasn't sure which part of my speech he was reacting to. "I want you to teach me to be a goalie. You can fit me into the sessions, I'm sure. A man of your experience."

"I only meant," he said, "that you're a winger. Why would you— oh. You've had complaints. Want to check on me." He rubbed a knuckle. The vibe was slightly off. Not in a really bad way, but none of us knew how to act. Should they call me Mr. Best or Max? How far could they joke with me? How much did I *want* them to be subservient? No doubt we'd smooth the edges over time but for now it was still a bit strange. One thing was clear—I didn't want people worrying about their jobs. Unduly.

"No," I said. "No complaints. Nothing like that. This is about me wanting to understand every part of the club. When I think about football, I don't really think about goalies. That's obviously not sustainable in my new role. And the training will keep me fit and give me something to do in the mornings when I want to feel involved without bringing loads of baggage to a first team session. Anyway, I have a sneaking suspicion I'll make a good keeper."

He stopped rubbing his knuckles and looked me up and down. That was normally something I found flattering. This time, not so much. "Could be."

I jutted my chin at him. "When it comes to football, you can speak your mind. Always."

He wasn't sure he believed me but decided to test the waters. "It's hard to imagine you in goal."

"Oh, is it?" I said. "Remember you said that next time I send you a trialist who appears to be total crap." I smiled, but he looked worried again. Bit of a nervous guy, this one. "Angles, stop worrying! You'll get to boss me around. You'll enjoy it. Think of *me* as a trialist. Actually, scrap that. My first day at Darlington there was a trialist and they didn't let him do anything. That still annoys me. If I send you a kid to check out, I expect you to involve him. And no initiations. We don't do that anymore."

Angles scratched his chin. I'd fired too many things at him, and he didn't know how to reply to any of them. "All right."

I picked up a glove. "If I'm going to be Chester's fourth-choice keeper, I'm going to need some kit. I'm here to buy gloves and whatever else I need. You three are going to explain the difference between all this gear. Wow me with science. Ready? Go."

I got to the all-weather pitch at ten to twelve and jogged around a bit. An organiser told us the teams, and we went into our groups and tried to come up with a formation. We had twelve—it was rolling subs—and five proclaimed themselves to be strikers, which made me laugh internally. Externally, I kept my mouth shut, except to introduce myself.

"I'm Cliff," I said, doing jazz hands to show my brand new gloves. "I'll take the sticks."

"Oh," said a dude. He pulled a worn pair of gloves out of his bag. "I wanted to go in goal."

This happened frequently, it seemed. More frequently than I would have expected. Normally, no one wanted to go in goal. The solution, in this world of pickup football, was compromise. "Cliff, you go in goal first. When you concede, you swap around."

"Are these normally high-scoring games?"

"Oh, yeah. You won't last long in net!"

I smiled. It was just a kickabout but his words triggered a need in me to prove him wrong.

We settled into a 4-4-2 with almost everyone in the wrong position. Fullbacks were strikers, midfielders were wingers, wingers were centre backs. No one seemed to care. It was football stripped of duty and animosity and spite, and everyone made a decent effort to enjoy themselves without ruining things for the others. Everyone except one guy on the other team who was taking it *very* seriously. He was yelling, claiming every throw-in, screaming that someone was offside. Read the room, mate!

Meanwhile, I spent the first five minutes with a big smile on my face. The morning had been absolute horse crap but now I was on a pitch playing football on the other end of the spectrum from guys out to smash me, kleptoclubs, multi-club models, superagents, FIFA, and the rest of the scum. This was football just for the love of it. No leagues, no tables, no fans. There wasn't even a referee—the game policed itself, guided by the fair-minded organiser who quietly but firmly did the opposite of whatever his screaming teammate wanted.

My smile widened as a guy on the other team leathered a shot towards my goal. As soon as it left his foot, he was already celebrating. He turned and pumped his arms as he ran towards . . . what? The ten thousand adoring fans of his imagination? Not quite Ziggy levels of cringe, but not far off. This guy loved getting an early goal!

Being the last line of defence, the dude whose job was to stop goals being scored, was not something I'd ever wanted. Goalies were akin to Secret Service agents—it was my job to throw myself in front of bullets whizzing towards the president. Who would that appeal to? I'd never understood it. But now that I had the confidence in my footwork, my speed, my reading of the game, and yes, even my handling, I actually quite enjoyed it.

While the striker turned away to receive the congratulations of his fellows, I took two lazy steps to my left and threw out a hand. The ball stuck in my palm. I stared at it for about five seconds, pulling it towards me until I was basically performing *Hamlet*.

Handling 20. I fucking knew it!

I held the pose until the striker saw that I'd saved his shot. I wouldn't want him to think it had been a close-run thing . . .

I threw the ball to the left back and tried to stop grinning—it was starting to hurt my cheeks.

Football, man! When it was good, it was so good.

The main reason for my smile was not that I was the new Gordon Banks, but the stats of two of my opponents. While virtually everyone on the pitch was CA 1 PA 1, there were two decent players. Kian, a fifteen-year-old who should have been in school. He was CA 1, of course, but had PA 30. Not good enough to play for Chester, but a talented youngster. Better than most in the Chester youth system, I was sure. I wasn't really interested in signing him, but I was happy to see random talent at a random game.

There was also Bonnie, a physically imposing centre back with PA 41. I didn't plan to approach her—with a blank slate and months before we played a difficult match, surely I could fill my women's squad with genuinely talented players? I was hoping to find an entire first eleven with PA over a hundred. But it was pleasing to find a solid player so early in the process.

That thunderbolt was the only shot on target in the first half. Every other time our opponents attacked, I'd leave my area to languidly intercept a pass (one-touching the ball through midfield so that we were instantly on the counter) or collect a long, high punt (where I'd stand still for a second before smashing a low, angled pass through the midfield to an attacking player). Low-level showing off, basically. This Kian kid saw me playing the sweeper-keeper role, which is where the goalie leaves his goal line and plays like a deep centre back, and he tried to lob me from distance. Intelligent, but also dumb.

At half-time, my captain asked me to swap places with the other goalie, and I said I'd sub off and let the others enjoy the game. The guy asked if I was upset and I said no, quite the opposite. I was trying to play within the spirit of the game. Talking of which, I looked for Bonnie and saw that she'd taken the screaming man to one side and was giving him something of a pep talk. The captain noticed me looking. "Yeah, that guy doesn't get it. We get a lot of that with first-timers. We're conditioned to conflate footy with rage. Normally I'd talk to him, or the organiser would. But Bonnie—she's different gravy. You get told by her, you stay told."

I grinned. "She's a good player, too."

"Takes one to know one," the guy said.

"Sorry, did I ruin the game? I tried to play within myself."

"That was you playing within yourself?"

"Honestly I just wanted to watch but there was no way to do that on the app. It wouldn't tell me exactly where the match was unless I signed up."

"Here, get your phone. I'll show you where it is."

He showed me how to find all the info without signing up. It really wasn't that hard. "Jesus. I was pretty out of it this morning. This has done me the world of good. Listen, that kid should be in school. Won't you get in trouble if someone dobs him in?"

The guy shrugged. "Did you never skip school to watch the cricket or something?"

"Miss school? Are you crazy? We played footy three times a day—break, lunch, afternoon break. If I had the choice, I'd never have left. You know what? I'm going to talk to him."

I wandered over to Kian. He was on his own, peeling an orange with great difficulty. I watched for a while—it seemed like he was afraid of pushing through the white bits into the pulp. "Kian," I said.

He looked up at me, alarmed. "That's not my name."

I laughed. "Isn't it?"

"No. I'm Michael."

"Cut the shit."

He sagged. "Michael's my dad. I use his account to sign up."

"Okay. I don't think I give a whatsit, to be honest. This is more fun than double French."

"We do German."

"You have my sympathies."

"It's all right when it helps me watch the Bundesliga. *Was für ein Tor!* But accusative dative?" He mimed vomiting.

"Why did you try to lob me, mate?"

He thought about refusing to answer because that would be giving his secrets to an opponent, but in the pickup footy spirit, decided to answer. Not before throwing a segment in his gob. "You was getting everything. I thought if I shot it might pin you back. Give us more space to build."

"But all you did was throw the ball away. Put pressure right back on yourself."

"It was worth a try."

"Statistically speaking, it wasn't. And you should have seen how dominant I am. How graceful, how serene. And you should have thought, maybe I'll stick to things that work instead of trying a one-in-a-million shot."

He thought about it. "What *works* against you?"

"Bureaucracy. Listen, I know it's just some fun, but you seem the type to try to get better. Nine times out of ten, pass to the guy nearest you. That's how you mess up our lines, how you keep control, how you get close enough to my goal to make me worry."

"Keep it simple, stupid."

"Absolutely. You think you need to do flashy things to get noticed, but you don't. Good players will see it. Bad players won't, but who cares what they think?"

"Short passes. I'll try."

"Kewl."

I started walking away when I noticed an envelope icon in my vision. Cursemail! I opened it.

Get 2023 off to a flying start with an experimental new mini game: January Sales!

Win mini games and complete challenges to gain up to three Coupon Codes.

Coupon Codes come in three amounts: 5, 10, and 20 percent off!

Redeem your coupons in the Perk Shop to reduce the price of any item you wish to purchase.

To redeem, simply shout the provided code before initiating your purchase.

Hooo-kay. So this seemed promising. Instead of offering me trash like Shocktober, the curse would let me win the chance to get discounts on the stuff I actually wanted. Perfect. I love a deal, and getting twenty percent off Playdar would save me 1,600 XP. Worth it, depending on the time involved. If it meant rewatching the entire World Cup, for example, then forget it.

The first challenge popped up right away.

Disruptors Assemble!

Build a team of newly scouted talents (minimum eleven players), arrange a friendly match, and lead the prospects to victo-

ry over their age-appropriate Chester FC counterparts.

Deadline: End of January

Rewards: Coupon codes, variable, according to the margin of victory

There was then a shit-ton of legalese and small print which firstly explained the task—I had to find a team of under-sixteens or whatever and use them to beat Chester's under-sixteens. Then there were lots of paragraphs warning me not to try to cheat because they'd thought of everything. For example, I couldn't stop the normal training of an age group, or tell them to lose, or try to "discover" players I'd already scouted like Bark, or pay kids from Liverpool's academy to pop down for a day. I had to keep doing what I was doing—scouting—and use what I found.

I was allowed to give them extra training. I was allowed to use other perks in the match, such as Free Hit.

The curse also made it clear that I could use Kian, which made sense because he had somehow been the trigger for the perk to arrive.

I rushed back over to him. "Kian. Dude. I was just thinking, how would you like to do something a bit more serious?"

"More serious? Like German?"

I smirked. "Not that serious. I like the way you play and the way you think. You've got a spark and you're open to coaching. Why don't you get yourself to the King George V playing fields at five?"

"What? Why?"

"You just won a trial at Chester Football Club." He choked on a segment of orange. "There's one condition. You have to go to school right away. The new boss won't tolerate this skipping school shit. It's bad for the brand. You with me?"

When he recovered, he took a few healing breaths and said, "But I can't let my team down. We'll be short a player if I leave."

"I'll stop, too. Then it's even." This was a scam I was very happy with, since I'd already decided not to play the second half.

"Oh. Well, I suppose." He wiped his mouth with his top. "Is this for real?"

"Yes."

"But who are you?"

I stared dramatically towards the future. "I'm Cliff Daps," I said, while a breeze pushed my hair around.

"Right," he said, and started typing into his phone.

The breeze stopped abruptly. The little shit was ruining my scene. "What are you doing?"

"I'm looking you up. I don't want to get abducted."

"Fucking hell. Okay fine. I'm Max Best. Keep that to yourself, though."

He looked me up and down, uncertain. Then he resumed typing. "Oh. You're a real person. You're—holy shit."

"Right. And we made a deal, didn't we?"

Kian looked at the search results on his phone, at me, then swapped his boots for trainers and jogged away. "Five p.m.," I called after him.

All right. Build a team capable of beating Chester's under-sixteens. One down, at least ten to go.

My smile turned into a frown. I had planned to scout loads of young players anyway. The curse had added a bit of spice. Given me some low-level stakes and a deadline. Why? The only reason I could think was to cheer me up.

I nodded. It didn't want me moping around. It wanted me grinding, working towards a goal. Because what made me stronger made Old Nick stronger. I nodded harder. This rare moment of actual help from the curse was simply more proof that Old Nick wasn't involved with the paperwork scam. It was all Brad. I stewed about the guy for a while. Thought of ways to get revenge.

Behind me, the match restarted, and even though I was getting ravenously hungry, I decided to stay and grab the 45 XP I'd get for watching the second half.

Skill levels were low, passes went awry, no one stuck to their roles. There was a moment when I started to get down on it, started to really focus on the negatives.

"Yes, Bonnie!" said a guy, and he sprinted ahead to receive a pass from her. She tried a high, slow lob—meat and drink for the defenders to clear. "Oh, nice try!" said the guy, laughing.

And that's when it hit me—he was the guy from the first half! The shouty whinge-head! Bonnie had talked to him, explained what these games were all about. Positivity. Relentless positivity.

Look at him now! Happy as a clam.

Fine. Forget Brad. I would stay positive. I whipped out my phone.

"Inga? It's Max Best. Your boss. No, I am! I need help. Yes, again. This one will be easier. I need to get invited to every school in Cheshire and I want to see every single kid playing football. No, I don't know how many there are. Are you looking it up? One hundred and fifteen secondary schools? That doesn't sound so bad. Eighty thousand children? Right well, yeah. That does sound like a lot. What was that word? Air-brained scheme? Oh, hare-brained. You know what? Let's start with one school. Ask if I can watch some kids play footy in P.E. Actually, forget it. This is what Playdar is for. In the meantime I'll focus on quality, not quantity. Hello?"

I slipped my phone away and focused on the match. The positivity started to draw shouts and yelps from me, too. "Yes, Gav! That's right, Ben! Man on, Des! Cover left, Govey! Great work, lads. Love it!"

But the positivity didn't last long. Yet another cloud came over my horizon.

My phone was ringing—Dave Cutter! Why would the manager of Darlington be calling me? Nothing good, I was sure. "Max," he said, flat-voiced.

"Dave."

"You still live in Darlo, right? Can you pop in before training tomorrow morning? I'd like to discuss something with you."

I thought about refusing. This was definitely part of Brad's attack on me. Still, better to get it over and done with. "Yeah. I'll be there. Let me check what my sched is for tomorrow. I'll text you what time I can make it."

"Great. See you."

He clicked off. The sound of his silence was ominous. I bit my nail. January was not going to be plain sailing.

8

SPACE INVADERS

After lunch, I moped around for a bit wondering what I'd got myself into. Work was piling up, and I was constantly finding ways to give myself more. Chester needed an injection of money. Of talent. And I wanted to change the culture. Each of these felt like a full-time job.

A tension in my shoulders came and went. I found myself unclenching my jaw every few minutes.

One thing that wasn't helping was the commute from Darlington. I needed a place in Chester. Something bigger than a windowless room, but smaller than an entire stadium. I went to a local furniture store and checked out their single beds. Nothing appealed, so in the end I bought two mattresses, some bedding, and a memory foam pillow. The pillow was as expensive as a mattress, but the amazing bed at Henri's had taught me the value of a good night's sleep.

I snuck the bedding into my office in the stadium, then drove to Shona and Raffi's house. They'd been house hunting in Chester recently; I could piggyback off their work. They graciously dropped their plans and we spent a few hours driving around looking at neighbourhoods. That was time well spent. I got a good idea about the local property market.

Raffi asked if I wanted him to help with the early-evening training sessions—word had got round that Spectrum was "wagging it." I thanked him for the offer and said I might take him up on it some other time. "Think about starting your coaching badges," I told him. "See if you've got the knack."

"I'll think about it," he said.

"I want smart players," I said. "Thoughtful. Analytical."

Shona said, "Eleven heads are better than one."

"Yup. Do the first course at least. It's a piece of piss and it'll pay off big time down the road. The club is skint but in theory we'll pay for it."

Shona shot Raffi a look. Some history there. I got the feeling she'd been pushing him to get back into night school or something, before I discovered him. She wanted her man to be educated. I decided to wait a few months before broaching the topic again. Shona would do most of the work.

Raffi getting a coaching badge had been a stray thought. But Shona's nudge got me thinking—I was still in the grindset of doing everything on my own. That's why I was so stressed. Three full-time jobs.

Fundraising—There was a universe where this meant running round local companies with a begging bowl while simultaneously applying for all kinds of grants and funding. Not appealing. I hoped money would come naturally through future transfers, although MD had said he'd put me in a room with some fat cats to raise money for my women's team. It'd have to be me doing the sales pitch—that couldn't be outsourced. Not a problem. It just meant going on the piss with some of MD's pharma friends.

Culture—This had to be me, too. No one else gave a shit about how things were done. My attempts at fixing the culture currently meant one of my staff was on strike and I was doing his work. Fine for a few days, since I needed to see the entire youth system anyway. I didn't want to fire people, but it would certainly fix the problem pretty damn quick.

Talent—The fact that I needed to see players in the flesh was the biggest bottleneck. Hopping from football pitch to football pitch all over Cheshire and hoping for the best was a brute force attack. Not very elegant. But that's how I'd always done it.

Now, though.

Now I ran a football club. I had employees, players, fans. How could I use these new resources?

I was in a pensive mood when the under-sixteens started arriving. I stood, rolling a ball under my foot, watching them warm up or dick around, according to their personality type. The standard was underwhelming. The lowest CA was 5, so someone somewhere had done a bare minimum amount of scouting. But the highest PA was 28. None of these guys would make it to the first team. Very, very disappointing. The most talented kid on the pitch was, incredibly, Kian, the kid who'd skipped school to play a lunchtime match, with his PA 30. No one was passing to him, so he did pointless stretches and tried to look like he fit in.

At 5 p.m., I gestured for him to come over. "Can you go over to that corner flag and check if I left my phone there? Thanks, mate."

Kian, obviously, was in dreamland, so he took my absurd request at face value and sprinted off. Wasting his energy! His speed meant I didn't have much time. I whistled and fifteen teenagers came towards me. Nervous energy was off the scale. They knew who I was. The new boss! The mystery winger! The guy who'd left the league almost-leaders to come and fix Chester. I very much doubt Ryan Reynolds would have impressed them more.

I pointed towards Kian, who was methodically searching the area around the corner of the pitch. "Who's the new kid?" Blank faces. "Anyone know his name?" Head shakes. The vibe was, who's this noob? Who invited him? It riled me up. "Last one to learn his name can fuck off home. Time starts now." I blew the whistle.

It was interesting, what happened next. You could *see* tranches of intelligence. There was the fox: a crafty midfielder who thought fastest and sprinted first. Then there were three flight animal guys smart enough to get their legs moving and think as they went. Then a general panic from the sheep class. One guy was left.

"Mate," I said.

"I froze. I tried to outthink the task."

"It's not a TV show."

"Do I really have to go?"

I shrugged. "I can't make threats I don't follow up on. Right?"

"Fuck. Sorry for swearing, Mr. Best."

The herd of kids came back, with Kian tagging along, all highly relieved to see there was such an obvious loser.

"He's called Kian!" shouted one douche.

"Let me ask you a question, Douche," I said, showing I knew his name in a formidable display of competence. Yes, I used his real name. Relax. Douche gulped. I glared at the group. "When I invite someone to come and join the session, why do I need to invent a fucking mini game for you twats to find out his fucking *name*? Why were you all ignoring him? What are you, supermodels at the world's most exclusive nightclub?"

I checked behind me.

"Is there a disco ball over the halfway line? No, all I see is an all-weather pitch serving the community three hundred sixty-five days a year." I brought my tone down from an eight to a six. "I know you're suspicious of new kids because they might take your place in the team. But that's no excuse for being a dick. If I invite someone to come and *you* don't make them feel welcome, I'll get rid of *you*." Pause for effect. "There will be a lot of new kids joining. Some might be good. Some might be to make up numbers for weird drills I want to try. If you're worried about some rando off the street taking your place, what does that say about you?"

I let them process that. Most of them had never thought of it from that perspective before.

"There's going to be a lot of change around here. Some of it you'll like. Some of it you won't. All of it will be for the benefit of Chester Football Club. If your hobbies include bullying and gatekeeping, start looking for a different club. A difficult part of your development will be dealing with new players who are better than you. What are you going to do? Whine and bitch and talk shit about them behind their backs? Or are you going to learn from them? Compete with them fair and square, drive each other to new heights, may the best man win?"

My hands were starting to get cold. I couldn't let the kids stay still too long or they'd pick up muscle injuries. Speech o'clock was over.

"Last word from me. If you want to be in a setup that is insanely obsessed with the idea of turning you into the absolute best player you can possibly be, get hyped. Get very hyped. Because that starts now." Many eyes widened at that. That resonated. And that was the moment three of the kids got a green teamwork attribute. "It's damn cold. Let's get you warmed up. Light jogs up and down."

"Mr. Best," said the loser kid. "What about me? Do I have to go?" Every other kid paused to listen to my judgement.

I laughed. "Mate, I'd forgotten about that. Way to dob yourself in. But yeah, you'll have to go home early. I read a website about dealing with kids. It said you have to always carry out your threats, no exceptions." I tapped my phone to bring up the time. "You have to go home . . . three minutes early."

"Oh." The noise came out of him like a sigh.

"Get fucking jogging!" I yelled.

He was so relieved that he burst into a sprint.

I tried to suppress a grin. These guys needed a real coach, but I could imagine taking some sessions now and then. If I shouted at them every three months, could I raise their teamwork by four points a year?

It'd be worth a try. And it'd be therapeutic.

I love a win–win scenario.

We did a few technical drills—passing, technique, dribbling. I got a bit absent-minded watching them. There was still this problem of me driving all over Cheshire hoping to stumble upon the best prospects. It was real needle-in-a-haystack stuff. If I went to a match between two schools, would that include the best players? Not in my experience. Were P.E. teachers good judges of talent? Were they fuck. They picked the tallest boys and the best runners.

What were my options, though? In an ideal world, I'd get the schools to come to me. Now that was interesting. What would that look like? Some kind of tournament, hosted by Chester, with every school sending multiple teams. If they sent an A, B, and C team, surely that would include ninety-eight percent of the players with basic hand-eye coordination.

Good concept, unlikely to ever happen. Maybe I'd mention it to Inga, though, just to see . . .

I blinked. Kian was talking to me. "Mr. Best. Should we change the drill?"

"Thanks, buddy." I blew my whistle and called them all in. "That's on me, lads. I spaced out. Maybe you can forgive me since I'm *running an entire football club.*" There were some goofy grins. They were starting to get used to my sense of humour. "Thing is, I've just had an idea. I want to find more good players. For complicated reasons, I need to play an A team—that's you lot—versus a B team, at the end of the month. Kian, you're the B team so far.

He put his palm flat. "Gooo Bs!" he said, throwing his hand up. A gesture that normally involved at least three people. The kids found it funny. Go, Kian!

"Don't be funnier than me, Kian. Thanks. Right. So here's the deal. Your teachers don't know shit about football. Your dads talk a good game but they don't really know. You know who I think can spot a good player? You. You pricks are actually quite good at this sport. So I'm going to incentivise you to find me some lads for my B team."

Some confused looks. "Incentivise? Are you shitting me? You don't know that word? Fucking read a book you little . . . ugh! Okay, focus, Max. What's a good player? Main thing: I don't want flashy show-offs who never pass."

From the fox kid, spreading through the herd to the sheep: sniggering.

"Right, yeah," I said, rubbing my chin. Of course they all knew about my beef with Tyson. "I shouldn't have started with that. What else? I don't want guys who always make bad decisions or don't understand their roles. I'm not interested in players who your dads think are good because they had a growth spurt and can win headers. I want players with a bit of technique, who can hit a pass, and who have a brain. Players where I can use really, really long words like incentivise. Think, *Would I like this guy on my team?* Right? You get me? Bring a player to training on Friday. Bring a different guy on Monday. You don't need to bring one dude every session. But if you bring a player and I like him and use him on the B team, I, Max Best, will give you one hundred English pounds."

Pandemonium.

Are you serious?

For real?

A hundred?

I blew my whistle. "I've never been more serious. Right. We'll do a quick match and I'll pick out some aspect to work on for the last ten minutes."

The session with the eighteens was similar, but without a Kian to justify my "welcome, new players" speech. I gave it anyway.

They were even more disappointing in terms of PA. I supposed any really talented kids had left when they realised they were never getting into the first team. That would explain why the talent we had was shaped like a pyramid—five or six first-team prospects in the fourteens (including the Broughton rebels), a couple of guys with an outside chance in the sixteens, and nothing in the eighteens.

The eighteens were less motivated by the offer of a hundred pounds—they knew it wouldn't go that far. But it was better than a kick in the teeth. I expected they'd be bringing their mates and their cousins and whatnot.

The project could get expensive—up to three thousand pounds in the worst-case scenario! But if we got a big infusion of talent into the system it would be worth it. The more I thought about this semi-outsourced scouting, the more stressed and excited I became.

I spent some time with Henri. Little did he know when he accepted my invitation to meet at Goals that I wanted to spend the entire evening there. When he realised I was serious about staying till late, he sighed, then settled into the role of assistant scout.

There was one player we disagreed about. Henri said he was cowardly, always running away from the ball. My opinion was wildly different—the guy was trying to draw opponents towards him and make space for the rest of the team. Problem was, there was no one on the same wavelength as him.

He was the only player of note. I didn't find any gems, but I picked up some XP. I was creeping towards my goal of unlocking Playdar.

Talking of creeping, Henri soon tired of watching the terrible matches and begged me to flirt with one of the women behind the bar. "A romantic competition," he said. "Like you promised me."

"What about Gemma?"

He let out an explosive sigh. "I am allowed to flirt! Jesus, Max. A man is allowed to live, is he not? How can I live if I cannot breathe? Do not assume I bind myself with chains every time I bed a woman. Metaphorical chains, Max. Remove your mind from the gutter."

I wasn't in the mood for a romantic challenge—even one I didn't take seriously. I was once again trying to combine grinding with spending time with a mate. It never worked! "Fine. How about you take the first turn? Pick a barmaid and give her your best shot. I'm sure you'll be the *highlight* of her evening."

"I may well just—what? What did you say?"

"I said go for it. But I don't want a reputation as a hound dog; I need a clean-cut image right now. Anyway, I'm off the market."

Another explosive sigh. "The market! You British with your love market. Human mating rituals reduced to the property ladder. Look at me! I upgraded from a red-brick council house to a semi-detached. Aren't I a successful man?"

He closed his eyes, apparently in genuine pain.

"Love isn't a market. It is a book of poetry, written in many languages but mostly French, a book you open in haste and read at leisure. Once or twice in a lifetime you find a phrase, an image, that speaks to the essence of who you are. It fills up your senses. It consumes you."

He held onto the netting that kept the ball on the pitch and swayed like a sailor.

"When you place the book by your bedside table and blow out the candle, you sleep, awaken changed, reborn, and next evening the poems are longer, more complex, more emotional. You can never read the same poem twice. You long to return to the simplicity of your youth, yet you must keep moving on. Forward. Ever forward."

"Right. So as I was saying, I'm off the market." I was trying to be funny, but also sensed that I was out of my depth. Henri was not quite himself. He seemed vaguely dissatisfied. Ennui Lyons. I thought I knew something that might cheer him up. "I need to start a women's team. Do you want to help with that? There might be some cute ones you can charm."

He waved the idea away. "Office romance? Stolen glances by the photocopier? *Popping to Tesco* to buy Meal Deal lunches together? Max. You disappoint me. I need a story. A real story. Thunder and lightning. My love life must be the human condition writ large." He sighed. "But I must admit, I am less opposed to office romances than previously. Livia continues to dazzle. She is stupendous. Did you see her ponytail today? She used a new scrunchie. How I envy Trick Williams and his gummi bear hamstrings."

"I didn't. I haven't spoken to the medical guys yet. Been busy."

"Too busy for Livia. Max. Please think about what you are saying. Get a grip. I implore you."

XP balance: 5,127

Target: 8,000

Debt repaid: 299/3,000

Thursday, January 5.

I went to see Cutter early—I had vague plans of going back to bed after the meeting, having a lazy morning, driving to Chester to take the under-twelves and -fourteens, then some scouting in the evening. The day done, I'd sleep in the stadium overnight and do a full shift before heading back to Darlo before rush hour. Seemed like a decent mix of grinding and taking care of myself.

Cutter met me in reception—no making me wait, no powerplays. He nodded at some kid sitting in one of the seats. The kid was so nondescript that I've actually just spent three sentences describing him and your brain has deleted the lot. Long story short, he was skinny with black hair and whenever I looked at him, he turned red and forgot how to blink.

The reception girl was there, also blushing furiously. I wondered if anyone had done research into long-term blushing the way they had with cracking your knuckles. Cracking knuckles was safe. Could you get so embarrassed so often you'd get bad skin?

I followed Cutter to his office. He was making small talk and I was doing the bare minimum to remain polite. His office looked like the last time I'd seen it. Cutter had a superstitious ritual where every month he remained in the job, he'd take one keepsake out of storage and display it. I scanned the room, trying to find the new items. There should have been at least one, right?

Another guy was in the room, sitting in front of Cutter's desk, tea mug in hand. I recognised him as one of Darlo's academy coaches.

I had no idea what this meeting would be about, but I doubted it would be anything good. Bradley Rymarquis was behind it. Cutter would benefit from me not being allowed to play for a few weeks because Chester were playing Darlington soon. Brad might have pitched the false registration scheme as a way to ensure I didn't play in that match. But then this meeting seemed superfluous—what else could they possibly do to hurt me? And anyway, I'd promised Cutter I wouldn't play against Darlo this season. It wasn't an issue. Unless, I thought, starting to sweat, he didn't believe me?

I wiped my palms on my trousers.

"Thanks for coming, Max." Cutter leaned back on his office chair and put his hands behind his head. He was enjoying himself. He smirked. "Max, I have a complaint. It wasn't that long ago that you promised not to tap up our players."

I froze. Of all the angles of attack I'd prepared for, me trying to steal Darlington's players had not come up. I tried to speak but my mouth was both too wet and too dry to open.

Cutter was still smirking. "You could get in a lot of trouble for this sort of thing, Max."

I exploded off my chair. It was too much. "No fucking way!" I walked away from the shocked men in case my anger spiralled out of control. I was feeding off it but not letting it feed off me. There was always a risk of my fury hitting critical mass and taking everyone in the room out with it. "I did no such fucking thing. I haven't spoken to anyone and you know it. I have too much respect for the club. I tried to leave with dignity, and this is my reward. If you think I'm going to sit back and take this shit, you haven't been paying attention. I will go fucking apeshit, mate."

I might not have been in *full* control of myself, because I realised my jabbing finger was close to the poor academy guy's face and he was trying to sink into his shoulders for protection. Like a turtle.

"Max," said Cutter, horrified. "What are you doing?"

"What am I doing? You just accused me of a fucking crime!"

He raised his palms from the desk. "I'm sorry."

"What?"

"I apologise. It was a joke. A bad joke, apparently." There was a standoff. I kept my finger directed at the coach while Cutter kept his palms up. "I know you didn't tap up our players." I eyed him. This was very confusing. "Max. Put the gun away. I'll explain."

I looked at my finger. I stepped away from the coach and picked my chair up. It had fallen during my outburst. "Okay. I'm calm. Pretty poor choice in jokes, Dave, considering the circumstances."

"What do you mean?" said Cutter, picking up an Italia 90 Ciao mascot and dividing his attention between me and it.

"I mean Brad!"

"What?"

I put my hands out. "Brad! What Brad did. Your mate Brad."

He seemed genuinely in the dark. "What did Brad do?"

My rageometer slid towards zero, and the coach guy visibly re-laxed. I took a breath. "All right. You don't know. I'm sure it'll come out soon enough." The journalists who'd been there when the story broke didn't seem to have published anything about it. Maybe they were digging deeper. Maybe they were saving it for a rainy day. But it *was* feasible that if Brad hadn't told Cutter his plan, Cutter wouldn't know anything about it. If he truly was in the dark, he could stay in the dark; ideally the mess would be sorted before the Chester fans even knew there was an issue. "Or you can get it straight from Brad. Let's just say my reaction will seem a bit less demented when you have all the info."

"Oh? That doesn't sound good. But why would Brad do something against you? He's quite a fan." He put Ciao back on his desk, stood, and moved to his little tea-making area. "Cup of tea?"

I knew what he was doing. Giving us a distraction. A chance to reset. I went over and chatted with him and the coach about the academy kids I knew, Bark and Benzo.

With the unpleasantness behind us, if not forgotten, Cutter went to the window. The first teamers were starting to appear, ready for training. "All right, now. You didn't tap anyone up, I know that, but we had a transfer request. One of our players wants to move . . . to Chester. That's why I made that little joke. I hope I seem a bit less demented now."

Stunning. Astonishing. I joined him at the window and tried to see who was out on the pitch—and who wasn't. "A transfer to Chester? That's mental. Who'd leave a title-winning team to join a basket case?"

Cutter looked down and did a three-quarter grin. "Good fucking question, lad."

"Junior?" I said, hopeful. "Larkin? Well, whoever it is, he's out of luck. We can't afford him."

Cutter nodded. "Pascal Bochum."

"Bless you," I said. My go-to joke when hearing unfamiliar names or words.

"Pascal is in our academy."

"I've never heard of him," I said. "I've been to a couple of training sessions. There was no one called Pascal."

"He's German. He's been home for a couple of months. Grandmother's sick. Came back this week, first thing he did was ask to be allowed to go to Chester."

I scratched my head. I tried to place this news in the hierarchy of crazy things that had happened in the last week. It was pretty near the top. "Wait. He's German. He's under eighteen. He can't get an English club. Brexit and all that."

"He couldn't join a *league* club. Non-league is easier."

I wracked my brain trying to remember an article I'd read ages ago. "Clubs can't sign foreign under-eighteens. It's pretty strict."

Cutter shook his head with a smile. "The kid got his parents to move to England and get jobs. If your parents move here and it's nothing to do with football, you're allowed to sign for a club. This kid," he said, with another fond shake of the head, "is an absolute maniac. He wanted to play in England and he convinced his parents to relocate so he could achieve his dream. He learned the rules and went through all the non-league clubs until he found someone willing to give him a chance. The idea of starting in the sixth tier and working his way up doesn't faze him in the slightest. Kid like that, when he says he wants to leave, he's going to make your life a misery until he gets what he wants. He's not selfish or difficult, just single-minded. If we talked to him and explained why we thought he should stay at Darlo, he'd stay and be good as gold."

"So?"

"So we can't do that. We're not the best place for him. We tried, we really did, but honestly, there's no club in England outside the Premier League where his style of play would work."

My head was spinning. So many questions! Cutter had to take training soon, so I wouldn't get time to ask them all. "What's his style of play?"

Cutter gestured to the coach, who unzipped a fabric folder and handed me a piece of paper.

SCOUTING REPORT: PASCAL BOCHUM

Pascal Bochum is a pressing monster, a dynamic miracle with absurdly good positional play, so much so that his teammates have nicknamed him the "Space Invader."

Pascal Bochum is a master of simplicity, the type of player who is often overlooked because he works more for the team than for his own success and thus has few moments of glory himself.

In other words, Pascal Bochum has a high level of understanding of the game, sees open spaces before they arise, and knows exactly how and where to run to tie defenders and open up paths for his teammates.

On offense, Pascal Bochum comes into his own when he can come out of space with depth, preferably down the flanks (combined with inverse runs, crosses, etc.), whether he's playing as a midfielder or winger.

Pascal Bochum has a wide passing range—simple passes, whether short or long, work fantastically. Bochum is fast, persistent, anticipatory, and can be used flexibly in midfield, although central positions are less his thing.

In terms of player type, Pascal Bochum is probably most comparable to Thomas Müller or Jakub Blaszczykowski (AKA Kuba).

I recommend a fast track to the first team squad.

I eyed the academy coach. "I know this is a weird joke given my overreaction earlier, but maybe I should be tapping *you* up. This report is incredible. I've never read anything like it."

The guy smiled. "Yeah. Isn't it fantastic? Only problem is, I didn't write it."

"Oh? Who did?"

"I'll give you two guesses."

I burst out laughing. The little shit had written a scouting report on *himself*. I re-read the document knowing it was autobiographical, laughing more with each repetition of the words *Pascal Bochum*. "This kid. What the fuck. Is it accurate?"

"In its way. He can do everything he says. He eats, drinks, sleeps football. He's off-the-scale competitive. In small-sided drills, he dicks everyone. No one calls him a Space Invader—that's wishful thinking. But you can sort of see what he means. He gets into space better than NASA."

"Nice line."

"Thanks. Pascal wrote it. Problem is, he's small. He gets lost in games. Headers? Forget it. Pressing? Yeah, he's high-level, but you can't press on your own. It's got to be coordinated. So that's a useless skill until he's playing for a big team, which he won't. He's playing on shit pitches, so his neat little moves don't lead to anything. He's no threat from a long shot, so teams learn to get goalside of him and let him pass sideways."

"He doesn't really fit anywhere in a four-four-two," said Cutter.

The coach nodded and continued. "He's too small to be a second striker. He can't dribble or do tricks well enough to be a winger. You can't use him as a CM because most of the match it's like you've only got one guy there. It's like Dave said: we've tried but we've hit a dead end. We can't help him much more."

"I've been telling him to go back to Germany," said Cutter, then winced. "Not like that. His style is valued there. Understood. They know how to use him."

"Makes sense," I said. "Why doesn't he listen?"

"He does. He knows that better than me. But in Germany, he's the hundredth best young player of his type. He's the best of his type in England. He's trying to carve out a niche."

I jabbed my thumb behind me. "Are we talking about that tiny little guy out there?" Nods. "Fuck me. I love everything you're saying. He's almost my dream youth team prospect. But I agree with you. There's no future for him here. In England, I mean. Footballistically, he'd be better off on the continent." They were smiling at me. "What?"

"We were starting to get through to him. It hasn't worked, his little adventure. We fucking admire him for trying, we really do. He's a weirdo, but he's our weirdo. There are academy kids learning German because he's always banging on about pathways through the Bundesliga. He's smart and well-liked. Anyway, we were getting through. His parents don't much like it here. Different work culture. Too informal. They'd stick it out for their kid, but he's not a complete psychopath. If it's not going to work, he'll be the first to start packing up. And we thought maybe this trip back would make him homesick. Speaking his own language and having currywurst on tap."

I'd never had currywurst. Maybe my career would take me to Germany one day. "Yeah. So you're making it sound like something changed."

Cutter scoffed and rubbed his forehead. "I'll tell you what changed. Some fucking prick turned up and started playing like the guy in Pascal Bochum's scouting report. A Space Invader. In the National League North. For the same club as him, in fact."

"Oh."

"Right. The kid's got it into his head that you're some sort of genius. So he wants to join Chester. Something about how you might understand him."

I tugged my earlobe. I wasn't going to look a gift horse in the mouth. If Cutter was offering me a player . . . Could it be a scam? "Before we go on, what are the conditions?"

"What do you mean?"

"Let's say we signed him. What would you want?"

Cutter shook his head. "He has no transfer value. No prospects for a career. I want what's best for him. It's crackers but he's right. If there's one person in non-league who can help him, it's you. He should probably stay in his school until the summer at least. He can stay in our academy and train there. But if you want him to go to Chester on weekends and play, something like that? Basically, you do whatever you want with him and we'll work around it."

"That's generous," I said, suspicious.

"Max. Most young players don't make it. Telling them you're letting them go is awful, and you know most will bounce out of football altogether. Some of the stories of what happens next . . . Mate. If I can give one of those kids a glimmer of hope, I will. And when you've been doing your job a few years more, you will, too."

That checked out. But if I had the budget for four more spaces in the squad, did I really want to sign a player who'd be hard to use? It depended on his PA. If it was high enough to let Bochum invade my precious space, then Darlington were handing me a prize asset. "If we sign him, I'll put a sell-on clause in his contract. You'll get five percent of any fee we get."

Cutter laughed. "Free money? Won't say no to that."

"It's not free. You gave him a chance. Trained him up. You get a cut. That five percent could be the most you ever make from a player. Then you'll give me more kids, right? We can all get paid. But that's putting the cart before the horse. Let's bring the spaceman in."

"We're going to training now. You have a talk to the lad on your own. Whatever you decide, go for it. Drop me a text or an email."

"I have a better idea," I said, pointing out the window. "Let him train with the first team. I'll stay and watch. It'll save me a lot of messing about organising a trial and stuff."

"Yeah," sighed Cutter. "Why not? I won't change the plan, though. Today's drills won't suit the lad."

"Pascal Bochum," I said, "never shirks from a challenge."

PASCAL BOCHUM		
Born 15.11.2005	(Age 17)	German
Acceleration 18		
	Handling 1	Stamina 13
	Heading 6	Strength 4
		Tackling 7

	Jumping 2	Teamwork 19
Bravery 17		Technique 18
	Pace 16	Preferred foot R
	Passing 14	
Dribbling 5		
Finishing 7		
CA 16	PA 133	
F (RLC)		

He was a forward with relatively poor finishing. He could run for days but a slight breeze would knock him over.

Fascinating player. I imagined him fully trained, in his peak, zooming around being an absolute fucking pest, intercepting, causing turnovers, combining with his teammates. But how could he get to his peak in England? Which club could give him enough game time? There were two problems. Most people wouldn't see the value in the work he did—as proven by my recent discussion with Henri. Jackie Reaper might get it . . . or he might not.

The second problem was Bochum was tiny. Tiny!

I watched as *Der Spaceman* struggled his way through the drills. He looked uncomfortable during a shuffle and slide drill, though he stuck to his work. He won zero headers in a set piece drill, and there wasn't even much point assigning him to protect a post on corners. He was easily the smallest player on the pitch. Passes to him had to be a little more precise than to other players; he was less able to hold the ball up, less able to win duels. Putting Bochum in the starting eleven would mean compromising elsewhere—you'd need more height in the rest of the team. Otherwise you'd get overwhelmed at set pieces.

I bit my nails imagining Chester's first team five years from now. If Future was in it, I couldn't have Bochum. Or could I? We could try to keep possession to the point where the height of the opposition didn't matter—like the Barcelona team of Xavi, Iniesta, and Messi. But we'd always have a weak point. We'd always be vulnerable from corners. Long throws. Agricultural football would work against us. Being beaten by a better team was one thing. Being beaten by *worse* teams was another.

Yeah, it was very obvious why Darlo's coaches found it hard to use this weird German kid.

On the other hand, his PA was higher than any five kids from Chester's under-eighteens *combined*. I'd be insane not to have a proper look at him.

I'd already organised the next steps by the time Cutter whistled to signal the end of the session.

I waved the kid over. "Pascal. Nice to meet you. I've heard a lot about you."

He didn't smile. He didn't blush, although it was hard to tell since he'd just done a very demanding session. "You have?"

"I have. How do you say incentivise in German?"

"*Einen Anreiz bieten.*"

"What's your favourite Max Best goal?"

For the first time, he smiled. "One you didn't score. The fifth against Scarborough. You made it possible by locking the left back and drawing players into your zone. In my match report I awarded you a pre-assist. You created the goal with your movement in the previous ten minutes."

"Match report?"

"I make detailed notes about every match I play or watch."

He was everything I wanted in a youth team player. So why did it feel like too much? Like, was he *too* football-mad? "I want to see you in a different environment. Put you through your paces the Max Best way." His eyes widened. Fear, excitement, determination. Such an interesting kid! "There are two ways to play football. There's the Max Best way. And that's the only way. You in?"

He swallowed. "I'm in."

"Good." I named two streets near Henri's house. "Be there at nine thirty Saturday morning. Bring your kit. One dark top, one light. Boots and astroturf trainers."

"Yes, of course."

"This will be a challenge unlike any other. A real test of character."

"I will pass it!" he said, eyes gleaming. I'd feared something of the sort.

"I wonder," I said, staring into space. He stayed there, waiting for me to keep talking. "That was the end of the conversation, Pascal."

He nodded and walked off. After twenty yards he turned back to look at me, like in a romantic comedy.

The poor kid. I was sure my test would mess with his head. I laughed. On the way to my car, I rubbed my jaw. All the tension was gone.

9

GOALS

Football glossary: Goal. The only method of scoring in association football. Goals are scored when the ball passes the goal line between the posts and under the crossbar.

After the pleasant discovery that Pascal existed and recognised my genius, I drove to Chester, where the good news kept coming. Spectrum had valiantly declared himself fit to work, so I supervised him while he coached the twelves and fourteens. He very deliberately didn't include any match-like scenarios that could provoke conflict between us. I couldn't decide if it was cowardly or smart, so I settled on diplomatic. A fragile peace had broken out.

Then there was my usual evening at Goals. I'd decided that its sheer convenience trumped all other considerations and I planned to keep going until I started seeing the same teams and players again. At that point, I'd have to branch out. As if to prove my luck had turned, I finally found a couple of players. A seventeen-year-old and a fifteen-year-old playing with their older relatives. Both had sub-30 PA, but I got their contact details in case I didn't find any better ones for my January Sales matches.

I stayed until the place closed, and that was healthy in terms of XP. More or less four solid hours of grinding, for 203 XP (plus 22 towards my debt). Then I parked in a side street and walked to the stadium. I let myself in with my special key and badge, which was astonishingly satisfying, and settled into my makeshift bed of two mattresses on top of one another.

It was fine—almost cosy—until I had to go to the toilet. That's when I realised how fucking cold an unheated English football stadium is on a winter's night. Wow. Back in bed, I called Emma so she could laugh at my stupidity. She asked if she could spend the night with me once so that we could bang in the penalty area at 2 a.m.

"Sure," I said, getting frisky at the thought, even though my teeth were chattering and my blood had retreated to my spleen or wherever in a desperate attempt to keep me alive. "But remember that football has its own vocabulary. Banging in defence is called Nobbing your Stiles. I'll be nobbing you for five, possibly six minutes."

"Can I nob you back?"

"We'd have to turn around so you could Crouch my Peter."

"Or you could Phil my Jones."

"Jesus Christ. How do you know about Phil Jones? He hasn't played for four years. Ugh. I'll see you on Saturday. It'll be a bit football heavy. Soz. I'll try to romance it up a bit before and after."

"And during?"

I laughed. "Sure. During the before and during the after. But not during the during."

After buying a toothbrush and making myself presentable, I did manager things.

I drove to the training ground to watch some of the first team training session. Partly to show my face, but mostly to keep tracking the daily changes in CA and attributes. So far, it seemed they didn't change much on a weekly basis. Slow inclines or declines through the season—that made sense. The player with the most green was Raffi, which was logical since he had the biggest gap between his CA and PA. Ian Evans already trusted him enough to put him on the bench for every match, and Raffi was responding by working hard in training. Soaking up the instructions and coaching, and progressing quickly. Roar!

I suspected his early exposure to the professional game was really helping him out. He'd had a long time to think about standards and expectations, and now that he had another chance, he was really going for it. Someone like Ziggy would progress more slowly. I planned to go and check on him, and ideally James and maybe even Kisi if I could fit them all into one day in Manchester. Maybe I'd also be able to go to the care home and get Anna addicted to *Merge Mansion* so she'd stop pestering me about *Soccer Supremo*. I think I preferred her when she only talked about gurus and meridians. Elderly Polish women shouldn't be fretting about high defensive lines, I was pretty sure about that.

After spending some time in the office helping Inga with random tasks—it only seemed fair since I kept adding to her workload—it was big boy time.

My induction day.

I'd put a twist on the concept. The purpose of my induction day was to introduce the old, established workers to my new way of doing things. To set expectations. To teach them the Max Best way.

First, I met the coaches. There was Vimsy—the most senior coach. Basically Ian Evans's assistant manager. If Evans was sent off in a match, Vimsy would take over. I liked him and I think he liked me, more or less, but he was also firmly in Camp Evans and had absolutely definitely been one of the guys who called me Maxy No-Thumbs. Which I only mention to show how much it didn't bother me and didn't prey on my mind every time I saw him.

Angles was the goalkeeping coach. I'd have to be careful with him, because he seemed quite insecure. Too many shots had squirmed through his hands over the years. One of them had broken his spirit.

Magnus Evergreen was there. I kept thinking of him as a physio because he spent most of his time doing medical things, but he was actually a coach. Floating above him was his player profile with that bizarre negative PA. And of course his coaching stats were all question marks. I really needed to unlock the real numbers by the end of the season. For all I knew, I had some super coaches here. Maybe Spectrum was the best coach in Europe and I shouldn't be so flippant about firing him.

Spectrum was present, trying to occupy as little space as possible and very much hoping I wouldn't start doing trust exercises and demanding he "tell us something about him" and all that corporate shit. Actually, it wasn't that. His vibe was more "how did I end up in the front row of this comedy club please don't interact with me."

Terry, the coach of the Chester Knights, was there. He was part-time and, sadly, the Knights were the lowest on my list of priorities. I knew Terry was doing well with those kids. When it came to the Knights, I would only need to check with him from time to time and make sure we had succession plans and whatnot.

That was the coaching staff. I hadn't invited the guys available as backups. Volunteers, retired guys. Dudes who could pick a team, do substitutions, yell at referees. It was enough to know that if I fired everyone in the room, the club would get by for a couple of weeks.

I told the five guys my coaching goals for the club—bringing in players to develop, selling them for a profit. Shepherding youth players from their starting age into the first team.

There's no point in retreading old ground—you can probably guess most of what I said. But I told them something I hadn't told many people, and that was what happened on my first morning at Darlington. I explained that I was busting a gut trying to find talented players and any incident that led to those players leaving the club at the earliest opportunity, like I had done, was unforgivable and unacceptable. And that it wasn't just the cavemen who I blamed, but the culture of the club that tolerated their antics. The honesty and emotion of the anecdote sold the point. Vimsy was stunned, Terry was close to tears, and even Spectrum was nodding.

I followed it with a sketch of a kind of Max Best utopia which combined fun and games with serious, methodical progress and winning football.

To finish, I invented a hypothetical player called Pascal Bochum and described him as the greatest challenge they'd ever face. (I hadn't decided if I wanted the real Pascal or not—I'd know better on Saturday.) I made the coaches come up with a plan for how to train this imaginary player. We didn't get very far until Spectrum, correctly, turned the topic to the kinds of formations Bochum could play in. Once they'd decided on a few options, the rest of the coaches felt more comfortable discussing a possible training plan for the player.

While that was happening, I found myself staring hard at Spectrum. He was smart. Analytical. I liked the way he thought. I liked the way he coached. Sacking him would be such a waste of talent. It pissed me off that I'd almost certainly have to do it.

After the coaches, I did a similar thing with the medical team. That was Physio Dean, Livia, and Magnus again, though his role there was informal.

I went through some scenarios and let them talk it out. Dean did ninety-five percent of the talking and one hundred percent of the deciding. Annoying, but not my main concern right now. Something to watch out for, if he kept his job long enough for it to matter.

The scenarios were these:

We've got a big game on Saturday against our relegation rivals. Defeat is not an option. Player A has just recovered from a hamstring injury. The manager really wants to use him. What do you do?

Thirty minutes into the match, Player B clashes heads in a duel. You do a concussion check and he passes, but he seems wobbly. You know the manager will be desperate for the player to keep playing. The player is saying he's fine. Do you let Player B stay on the pitch?

Player C is fatigued. He has played every minute of every game this season. You're worried about his ACL, but C wants to play in a big game against his former club, and his manager also wants him to play. What is your recommendation?

After consulting with himself, Dean announced his answers. He'd let Player A play. He'd let Player B play. He'd let Player C—get this—play.

"Interesting," I said. I held up fingers one at a time until I was showing three. "So . . . you're fired, you're fired, you're fired."

The temperature around his chair dropped to zero degrees Kelvin. "Excuse me?" said Dean.

"The manager currently has nineteen first team players," I said. "Plus eighteen eighteen-year-olds who'd run a thousand miles for him given half a chance. There is absolutely no scenario where one particular player MUST play one particular game. The manager might want to grind my players to dust, but my medical team isn't going to let him. Those players don't belong to him. They belong to Chester Football Club. This is me explicitly ordering you not to risk aggravating or causing an injury under any circumstances. I want access to all your data and records. I will investigate any long-term injury. If I think you're risking people's long-term health to get three points against Bradford Park Avenue, you'll be lucky to escape with just a sacking. Any questions?"

There weren't, mostly because Dean was frozen solid.

"One more thing. I want the atmosphere in the medical areas to be upbeat and positive at all times. Warm. Remember when I came in with my cracked skull and all that? The mood was fucking weird. It was off-putting. There's a word you don't want to hear when the future of the club depends on attracting new talent. I bring the Cheshire Messi here and he doesn't like the vibe? No. No way you're surviving that. Let me spell it out crystal clear: everyone who walks into this stadium is a potential star. Everyone gets VIP treatment."

This all came out a bit more direct than I'd been planning, but I blame Dean's smug face. He was a bit too full of himself. The guy was incredibly replaceable, and most physios didn't have a Napoleon complex.

"If I could give you one overriding goal . . . a sort of guiding principle . . . I think it would go something like: Everyone who works here leaves healthier than they arrive." I nodded. It was flawed and impossible but satisfyingly aspirational.

Before I left, I tried to see what kind of scrunchie Livia was wearing. It seemed the same as normal. Not for the first time, I worried about Henri.

Spectrum was still in a mood—the meeting had made things worse, if I was any judge—but he took training. He was exasperated by the rando players who'd turned up, but I was delighted.

My hunch that our players would have some talented friends had paid off. Of the five under-sixteens who'd been brought along, three were good.

One was a PA 35 striker, and we had a PA 23 right back. But the standout was a PA 66 centre back called Vivek. I watched him struggle through the hour. He was superficially useless—he didn't know what to do or where to be. As the session wound up, I took him and his mate aside and asked what the deal was.

Long story short, it was a stereotypical Indian family. Dad wanted him to be a doctor, mother didn't approve of violent sports. Such a cliché. Hence he'd barely played any footy, but he quite liked it.

I smiled my way through the story. "Right. I'm supposed to go and learn about Indian culture and slowly win your mum's trust? Yeah, no chance. The days when I had that kind of time are ho-verrr." I bit my nail for a minute, then laughed. "Vivek, who's the best at manipulating your mum?"

"My sister."

"Amazing. There's the solution. Outsource the storytelling. Can you bring her to training on Monday?"

"I can try."

"You, mate, are going to play for Chester Football Club. All right? You've got this weekend to daydream about it. Starting Monday you're going to learn football from scratch. It's going to be hard work."

"Play for Chester? Are you sure?"

"Course he's sure," said his mate. "That's Max fucking Best you're talking to. Youngest director of football in the world. And he owes me a hundo," he added.

I grinned. "I do."

As I walked off, I heard the mate say, "I told you you was mint."

The eighteens were less diligent. They only brought two guys. I suspected it wasn't cool to bring a mate to training, or at least the level of cool was uncertain. So I made a big fuss over the newcomers, including showing them my free kick technique. The young players were always asking me to bust out some moves, so this was a way of overtly rewarding the behaviour I wanted. The reactions to the cannonballs, I have to say, were gratifying.

I expected a bumper turnout on Monday.

Once I'd satisfied myself that I'd done all I could, I drove back to Darlington expecting a quiet night in.

Emma called and invited herself over.

Yeah, quiet night in.

My alarm went off. "No," I complained. "Just ten more houuurs."

"What are you doing?" said Emma. She'd woken up long before me and was lying there in the little spoon position playing *Clash of Spams*, the Monty Python–themed mobile strategy game.

"Hitting snooze."

"That," she said, "is not the snooze button."

"Oh? Soz."

"Very sincere." She patted my hand. "It's your turn to make breakfast. You need energy for that game you told me about. What are we doing after that?"

It took me a second to remember what day it was. Saturday. The schedule clicked into place. "Remember ages ago I promised to take you to St. James' Park? Well, today's the day!"

She wriggled round to face me. "We're going to see Newcastle United? Why didn't you tell me before? I'll let my dad know. We can meet him before the match and he can take us to the right pub."

"Whoa!" I said. "Slow down. Do me one tiny favour, please? Don't tell anyone. You'll see why."

Her face hardened. "Is this about Christmas dinner?"

She thought I didn't want to see her dad because of certain views he had expressed. I grinned. "I promise it isn't. Ems. Babes. Look at me. It's not that. I pwomise."

She cracked. "Oh, well, if you pwomise." She threw her phone onto the duvet. "Fine. I'll trust you. Now feed me."

I picked up Pascal at exactly 9:30. He got in the back and, when he saw Emma, forgot to close the door.

"Mate," I suggested.

"Sorry," he said, closing the door and belting up.

"This is Emma. My name," I said, "is Cliff Baps."

"Daps," said Emma.

"Right, right. Cliff Daps. And you are Joe." I'd asked Chester's club secretary to sign up for a match through the Footy Addicts app. I owed him six pounds.

"I am Joe?" said Pascal.

"Very good! Very believable. Let's do a quick role play. Hi, what's your name?"

"I am Joe."

"*Wunderbar!* All right, Joe. Begin your pre-match rituals. The meditation. The visualisation. Have you got any mantras?"

"Mantras? No. What like?"

"I sometimes look at myself in the mirror and whisper, 'Remember you are mortal. Remember you are mortal.' It helps to keep me humble."

"Joe," said Emma. "Max is joking. It's not that serious. You're going to play football with some amateurs. I complained on your behalf but Max promises me that he's not pulling your pudding and this is something he genuinely believes is good for you even though you're a professional."

"Oh," said Pascal, as he processed this. "Of course I will do whatever it takes."

I shook my head. "This was the fastest way to get a match."

"Max, you run a football club. You could have found all kinds of solutions."

I got a bit spiky. "I chose this way." Emma had been slightly sceptical of my methods with the young players ever since the Broughton match. She trusted that my heart was in the right place but worried I'd put people in embarrassing positions, such as playing with a bunch of random amateurs.

We pulled into the car park without a further word.

At quarter to ten, Pascal started a very lengthy, very serious warm-up routine that involved lots of stretching. I wondered if I was being fair to him. I thought so. I didn't like being challenged, but Emma had a point. I had a tendency to act first and rationalise it later. Which was exactly what had happened with this hastily arranged trial. Which is why I'd snapped. I'd fess up later and apologise.

At ten to, almost all the players had turned up. It was a bumper turnout. Loads of subs for both teams. I summoned Pascal.

"All right, Joe, listen up. This is pickup football." We looked around at the other players. Some were playing short passes to each other. Some were taking amusingly inaccurate shots. Imagine all the body shapes you've ever seen and populate an all-weather football pitch with three of each. Voilà. The scene is set. "Hopefully we'll get put on the same team. I asked the organiser and he said it should be poss. Have you ever heard of pickup football?"

"No."

"It's random people using the same app. A social experiment. They've all turned up hoping for a fun game. General rules—no bickering, complaining, cheating, or hard tackles. Special extra rule just for you—no pressing."

"No pressing?" Running at people trying to force them into making mistakes was his superpower—it was the first thing he'd mentioned in his scouting report.

"Yep."

"Why?"

"Are you going to ask why every time I give you an instruction? Is that my life now?"

"No."

"*Muy bien!* Tell you what, bonus point if you can work out why for yourself. Right. You interrupted me. Where was I? Er . . . the rules. Okay. Your mission is to impress me while following the rules and culture of pickup football. Is the task clear?"

He frowned. "The task is clear."

I smiled. This was actually tremendous fun, as I knew it would be. "Top. Let's go meet our teammates."

Our team had seventeen players, which meant we'd have to sub on and off fairly often. The subs would happen every five minutes. There was some disappointment that people wouldn't get to play a full ninety, but these were guys with 1 stamina. By the end of the match they'd be glad of the breaks.

I wasn't concerned with those guys—once I'd checked there were no rare talents in the throng, I turned my focus to Pascal. Like me, he would start the match as a sub.

The first five minutes were a chaotic mess of misplaced passes and people trying to work out what to do in their unfamiliar positions. Our captain signalled that Pascal should go on. He made a beeline for the left wing, where I'd told him to go. The rest of the midfield shuffled along to accommodate him.

I watched him for the next ten minutes.

"What's funny?" said Emma.

"It's not funny, really. It's just the humour of contrasts. Everyone's trying to enjoy themselves except Joe. He is lost. He doesn't know how to get involved in the game. I told him he can't press."

"Press. There's that word again. What is it?"

"You see the way the other team is passing the ball around? Normally, Joe would chase after them like a dog chasing a stick."

"Okay. And you told him not to because that's stupid."

"It has to be coordinated to really work. But that's not why I told him not to today."

"So why?" I didn't reply. "Cliff! Tell me."

"No. Because you'll tell Joe. Because you're a big softy."

"So what's funny, exactly? This is his big break, right? And you're being weird. I don't like it when you're like this. Pascal's a straight shooter, you said. You can't expect him to thrive in a Max Best world. Let him do normal things. Prove himself in a normal way."

"Babes," I said, with a slightly pleading tone. "He wants to *join* the Max Best world. *He* wants that." I put my hands on my hips and took in the scene. Football stripped of all its warts. "Can you feel that?" I said, eyes shining. I sucked in the cool morning air and breathed it skywards. Maybe it'd become part of a cloud. "He's a special player."

"Really?"

"I mean special like unique. If I find a striker, someone like Ziggy, I can train him up and sell him on in maybe two years. This kid, he's so unusual, it'll take five years. I've had marriages that lasted less than five years." I waited for the question to come; it didn't. She knew I was joking. "If I'm going to spend five years with someone, I think I need to like them. Do you know what I mean?"

"Of course I do." She sighed and came closer, gave me a hug. "So, do you like him?"

"Based on this, no. He's disconnected. He hates everything about what's happening. It's like he's had the fun cast out of him by a priest. Would you want to be on his team?"

"Yes."

"You're on Team Joe already! You're such a sucker."

"You've never complained before," she said, with that little smirk. She watched as Pascal once again failed to control a pass blasted in his general direction. "Is he *too* small?"

"No, but it makes things harder. That pass wasn't all that bad, really. I could have controlled it. You're asking the rest of the team to be a bit better. More precise passes. What I'd say," I said, carefully, "is that as we rose through the divisions and played with better players and against better players, he'd start to shine. But it'd be tough for him."

"Would be? So you've decided."

"No," I said. "There's an easy way to peek into the future. See how he looks when playing with great players. Legendary players."

Emma didn't get it. "What way is that?"

The match organiser looked down at a little clipboard he was carrying. "Cliff, you're in."

I went to the touchline, looked back at Emma, and smirked. "Legendary players, babes. Cliff Daps to the rescue."

Pascal had made this no-stakes amateur match look like torture. Without pressing his opponents, he couldn't get the ball—no one had the technical skills to pass the ball to him, except by accident. When he did get it, he'd make some quirky, unexpected run and try to combine with a teammate. It always ended in failure.

His shoulders slumped, his eyelids drooped, and yet he kept trying. Pascal Bochum never gave up. Pascal Bochum *never* gave up.

Based on what I'd seen, the patterns of play, where the ball spent the most time, I put myself in the DM slot. That would let me maximise my involvement while still letting me get forward.

My first intervention was a header—I rose like a majestic salmon, yelling "Cliff Baps!"—and laughed internally as Pascal's eyes widened. The ball had travelled twenty yards right to his foot. Right to his right foot, even. He took a touch away from the defender and saw me coming. He tapped the ball in my direction and sprinted infield. I touched it back into his path and rushed to take up his left-mid slot. He spun back towards me and played a simple pass to my feet, which I instantly tapped back to him. I sprinted down the line and heard the ball being struck. I knew where it would go—in front of me—so I looked around for support.

But our move had been so simple and so bewitching that the amateurs had stopped to admire it. I was on my own. The goalkeeper didn't know what to do. I moved closer and hit a gentle shot towards the goal. But it hit the post!

I jogged back, ignoring Pascal, who had his head in his hands. I kept my face blank.

The other team put a good move together, playing a few passes to move up the pitch. I didn't want to spoil their move with an explosive sprint or tackle, so I waited until one of them played a square ball. I simply stepped forward and claimed it as my own, the way you might take a bill from the postman just as he's about to put it in your letterbox. I took three steps forward, made a show of passing to the right, then swept the ball left to Pascal. He instantly touched it back to me and sprinted—copying my move from a moment before. I chipped the ball over the defender's head, a pass so full of spin it could work for any PR company, and double-timed it all the way around the left of the pitch so that Pascal could play yet another simple pass. This time I was the one who played it forward, and the German dashed onto it. He paused, then cut the ball back, more or less into the path of my latest dart upfield. From the edge of the penalty area, I opened my body and side-footed a slow shot past the feeble dive of the keeper. Amazing. But it hit the post!

"*Nein!*" yelled Pascal. I ignored him some more.

The goalie took a long kick, trying to keep it away from me. Unluckily for him, the ball curved near me anyway. The angles were wrong for a dominant header, so I had to show off a bit. No, really! I did!

While a striker competed with me, I angled my body towards the corner flag behind me to the left, took the ball on my chest, and let it drop towards my knee. From there it was the most natural thing to flick the ball diagonally right and up up up, over the striker's head. Have you ever seen a slow-motion clip of a dog trying to catch a frisbee but he's misjudged the flight? Anyway, there were *gasps* or whatever. No big deal. I took one step forward and clipped the ball over another defender to Bochum's feet. He played it back to me, along the ground. I passed it back to him, didn't move, and he wall passed it back to me. No frills, clean, nice and simple.

All these angled, line-breaking passes were starting to frazzle our opponents. Two were marking Bochum, and three were closing me down. As Bochum's pass came to me, I opened my body and played a long, left-footed, curving, luxuriant pass out to the right. All our recent play had been on our left so our dude on the other side was suddenly wide open. He was slow, though, so a defender caught up with him. My dude had enough sense to turn around and saw me coming to help at full pelt. He passed and I really let rip with a shot. Not full power, but not far off. It flew true and hit its mark—the crossbar.

Pascal yelled again. He couldn't believe this.

There was one more passage of play before half-time. A long shot from the opposition broke down. I moved to the left back position to get the ball from our goalie. I waited for opponents to come to me and prepared to chip the ball down the line. I went through the motion and two opponents moved that way. But Pascal had left his post and was now more central. I hit a diagonal pass to him and burst forward, slowing to receive his layoff. I turned to the right to pass that way, causing a midfielder to stick his leg out to block my attempt. One cheeky little nutmeg later, I was attacking and half the other team were already behind me. Pascal ran across me, drawing defenders that way. I rolled the ball diagonally the other way and chased it down. Then I slowed and flicked the ball up. It bounced, bounced, no defender could stop it, the goalie was stranded. But it hit the post!

Pascal didn't shout. I grinned.

That was half-time.

I trudged towards Emma, deep in thought. The little fucker could play, holy shit. For all his bookworming and attempts to break football down into what Ian Evans would call "wanky metrics," Pascal lived on instinct. He made great decisions, he was selfless, his feet were fast, his brain was faster. It wasn't quite like playing with Raffi, because Raffi was so physical it opened up many more ways to combine. But the clever passes and combinations with Pascal were satisfying and wildly destructive. I started to conjure up fantasy formations. Aff on the left, with Raffi and Sam Topps in the middle. Me on the right. Pascal as a space invader, off centre, the bridge between the midfield and Henri. Deadly. Coming at you from all angles with power, guile, craft, and imagination. It seemed almost cruel.

I stopped and looked back towards the goalposts. Five years, though. If I was going to lock myself into a five-year relationship with someone, I wanted to know a lot more about them.

I very seriously hoped Pascal had learned something from the first half.

10

SCENARIO B

I was so in my head, so internal, replaying Pascal's moves, wondering what made him go *there* and why that made me go *there*, that it took me ages to get back to the sidelines. It took me almost as long to realise that my girlfriend had her arms around a tiny German starlet. The scene was too bizarre to trigger what might be considered a standard Aggression 20 response. Instead, I sat cross-legged in front of them and waited for clarity.

While still hugging Pascal, Emma turned to me and raised her eyebrows the merest fraction. The meaning was crystal clear.

Italia 90, the World Cup that changed football forever, happened ten years before I was born. But certain images are seared into the minds of every English football fan. One of them, in particular, resonated at this moment.

Paul "Gazza" Gascoigne had been England's talisman, a player of rare imagination and vivacity in a country dominated by tedious long-ball tactics, by hooligans, by crumbling stadiums. English football was ninety-two teams managed by Ian Evanses. The Dark Ages. Gazza had somehow dragged England into the World Cup semifinal, so even people who hated football tuned in to watch. The obstacle? Germany. Gazza tore them a new one, England played their best game in decades, but those pesky foreigners kept fighting back. Why? Just let us win! Mate!

In extra time, Gazza had a rare bad touch, lunged to recover the ball, committed a foul, and got a yellow card. It was his second in the World Cup. The rules of the tournament meant, even if England won, he'd miss the final. The best player would miss the final. Thanks, FIFA.

Gazza, a grown man, a transcendent talent with the boundless energy and exuberant spirit of a child, burst into tears, and the reaction was titanic. Every housewife in the country wanted to mother him. Every dad wanted to give him a hug. Every boy wanted to be him. The nation—and this is no exaggeration—fell back in love with football. The Premier League was created soon after, football crushed all other sports, and every mediocre player who would become a millionaire owed his fortune to one man and one moment.

But back in the Stadio delle Alpi, Gary Lineker, another giant of the game, checked on his mate, and saw Gazza's head had gone. He turned to the manager and waved his hand—this was *muy muy no bueno*. Lineker pointed to his eye—keep an eye on this. Gazza was in no frame of mind to take a penalty in the shoot-out, and England lost.

Was it the German factor that brought the image of Gazza to mind that day, as I sat in front of Pascal? Partly, perhaps. But mostly it was because a talented player was crying, and my girlfriend was looking at me, playing the Lineker role. Keep an eye on this!

I waited until Pascal noticed me. He tried to get a grip. He wiped his eyes and made that *aaah* noise you make when you want to stop laughing or crying. "Aaah," he said.

It was time for me to tidy up my mess. "Why do you say Schleswig-Holstein?" I said.

Pascal blinked. "Pardon me?"

"I did history and I'm sure my books said Holstein-Schleswig. I'm sure of it. But now it's the other way round. What the fuck? It's like if everyone suddenly started saying *Ireland Northern* and there's only one man who remembers the old way." If this sounds demented, I'd read that saying weird and random things can sort of break someone's thought patterns and help them reset. And you know what? Sometimes it works.

"I have only ever known the region as Schleswig-Holstein," said Pascal.

"I suppose you guys would know best," I said reluctantly. "So, mate, I can't help but notice you're sort of squished into my girlfriend."

"Oh," he said, snot-laughing. "Yes. I apologise." He prised himself away from Emma, a move that involved no noise of any sort, but my brain supplied a big Velcro tear sound effect.

"Let me know when you're ready to talk," I said.

"I'm ready," he said, wiping his eyes again.

"Top. All right. I wouldn't normally ask this, but Emma thinks I'm a bit fast and loose, a bit careless with people and I'm worried she's thinking I made you cry or whatever. So . . . if you could maybe talk about what that's all about, that would be tremendously helpful."

Pascal made to stand up, but decided it was uncalled-for levels of dramatic and instantly threw himself back down. Which looked pretty painful. He turned to her. "No, Miss Emma. No! I swear it. It's not Mister Best. Sorry. It's not Cliff Daps. It's . . ." He sucked his lips in and out. "Actually, it *is* Mister Best. He is to blame." He smiled while sucking breaths in and out. Pretty weird. He never laughed like that again, as far as I could tell. "I came to England to further my career. I thought it was my best shot. You understand? But my style doesn't fit. I really thought it would, but . . . My style needs . . . companionship." He closed his eyes and I was sure the tears would return. Instead, there appeared a smile. "But now, I have it! I have it." He was silent for some time.

I looked away and tried to hide a grin. Who else in the football industry had to deal with this shit? Fuck me.

Emma's tone was perfect. "Joe. *Pascal.* Are you okay?"

Pascal seemed not to understand the question, but then his smile returned. "Yes! Very much so. Mister Best . . ." The tears were back. He looked up in an attempt to get ahead of his emotions. The gesture made things worse. "It was like a dream." His throat was throbbing—it looked very painful. "*Oh oh oh it is magic, you know.*" The throat started rocking sideways. Throats aren't supposed to do that, right? "*Never believe it's Darlo.*"

My smile widened. "Bro. Pascal. Mate." I took my phone out to check the time. "We've got half-time to decide your future. How about you bottle your emotions for a minute? You've been in England long enough to learn how. Stiff upper lip. Offer to put the kettle on."

Snot-grin. "Hurrr," he said, wiping his nose with his sleeve. "Who wants a cuppa?"

I'd decided to skip a lot of my questions. His show of emotion said more than a dozen carefully considered responses. "Time to talk turkey. Pascal. You've got talent. I like you. You're a foot shorter than I need you to be. You're weaker than the tea Chester's admins drink. Even though we can get you on minimum wage, the club is skint. There are millions of reasons to shake your hand and say goodbye. But the first question I ask when I look at players is: would I want to be on the same team as this guy? And I think, yeah. I can go places with

Pascal Bochum. Using you in the National League North would be insane. I can't wait to try it. I want to train you up and sell you for two million Euros to Fortuna Dusseldorf."

"Max!" said Emma.

"What?"

"Don't talk to him like that."

I looked at Pascal, and we both looked at Emma. "What?"

"It's not nice."

I nodded towards Pascal, indicating that he should explain. "Emma, it's okay. That would be fantastic. A sign that I have value as a player. It is called the football industry because it is an industry. We know that. Mr. Best isn't being disrespectful. The transfer fee is recompense for all the training. On a personal level, it would be fantastic. Maybe Mainz instead of Fortuna would be more fantastic."

"Oh." She seemed confused.

I scratched my scalp. "Er . . . anyway. This transfer window, Chester need a left back and a striker. I might wait till the summer to sign you properly. The current manager wouldn't use you. The next might not, either. Turning you into a two-million-Euro player is going to be a long, hard road. I was telling Emma it could be five years. You're smart. You know your abilities. Does that sound about right?"

He looked away. "I'd hoped less. But . . . yes. Five years." He shrank. "Perhaps longer."

"Yeah," I said. I leaned back and looked around at all the other players. So many smiles. So many jokes. Strange surroundings for a heavy conversation. "I won't be having this chat with guys who will be in and out in a couple of years. We'll need to give *you* a long contract. So let me put it like this. Whenever it happens, I'll try my best to get you what you want if you do what I want."

"What is it you want?"

"Fearless football."

He opened his mouth to reply but thought better of it. This kid was a lot smarter than me. "What is *your* definition of fearless football?"

I smiled. "Fucking incredible question, mate. Here's an example. We were three–nil down and we've clawed it back to three–three, last minute of the game. There's a two-on-two break and the opposition are incredible on counterattacks. Do you go for the corner and see out the clock? Take the draw and the point?"

"Mathematically speaking, yes. Of course. One point is better than zero."

"'Of course,' he says." I stood and paced around. "Why does everyone forget it's three points for a win?" I went internal, but snapped out almost immediately. "I want every kid in Cheshire to want to play for Chester. I want every kid who goes to a match for the first time to fall in love. Fall in love with Chester FC, with the match-going experience, with the sport. Football's a low-scoring game. Goals define how you feel. I want goals. We were three–nil down? Irrelevant. It's the last minute? Irrelevant. Every time we have the ball, we're trying to score. When we're defending, we're getting ready to score. The other team has a corner. How do we score? There's loads of ways; I should know. The other team has a penalty. How do *we* score from *their* penalty?"

I grinned. An image had popped out of nowhere.

"You know what I want? I want four players on the halfway line. Goalie saves the pen, boots it downfield, we've got four attackers there. First time we make that work, every team we play's going to have a team talk. It's going to go like this: 'Hey lads, if we get a penalty, Chester will try to score from it.' Imagine being told *that* before a game! It's *got* to mess with your head. Penalty taker can't shoot down the middle because the goalie might grab it and boot it to danger. So what does he do? Hit it high so the goalie can't catch it. You need Max Best technique to hit pens high."

I laughed.

"Mate, attacking football isn't just for the fans. It's how you stack the odds in your favour. Make people react to *you*. I want attacks. I want goals. I don't want stats or excuses. Goals is what I want. Attacks is what I want. You want to play the percentages and do the right things at all times? Yeah, I get it. It's smart. I'm not smart. I'm demented. I'm loopy. Twice a season I want our fans to go home fucking depressed because the other team scored a last-second equaliser or winner because we were going nuts trying to win. I *want* that. I want drama. I want emotion. I want to take ludicrous risks." I paused. I'd gone a bit over the top. "Fearless football. It's not for everyone. If it's not for you, we'll talk about Plan B. Maybe I can help you in a more conventional way."

Pascal closed his eyes and thought for a moment. He opened them, smiled, and said, "I can do fearless football."

"That was a fast decision."

"First of all, I will do anything if I can play with you. And second, if your ideas don't work out . . ." He smiled, showing lots of big, white teeth. "It is you who will be fired, not me." He grinned.

I went home, had a shower, and was torn between wearing my customary hoodie or my call centre suit. I went with the latter. For Emma.

We drove off. "Why didn't you stay for the second half? It's only half an hour to Newcastle. You could have made it easily."

"I got what I wanted. And Newcastle isn't our next stop. We have to go somewhere else er . . . first."

"Oh? Are you surprising me?"

"Yes."

Emma sighed. "So you're not taking me to St. James' Park. That's why the secrecy. So why even mention it? Never mind. Tell me about Pascal. What were you hoping to achieve with all that? Why no pressing? Why didn't you score? I feel like it was a message for him."

I overtook a lorry and pulled into the slow lane. Making excellent time, heading south. "Those aren't the right sort of matches for pressing. Those pickup games are supposed to be fun. If you're forty and shit at football, you know what isn't fun? Having a teenage German whip the ball off your toes before you've even counted your feet."

"It's fun for Joe."

"We can stop calling him Joe now. Maybe it is fun for him, but it's not fun for me if someone's ruining the game. Same reason I didn't score. Hitting the post four times *is* funny. They'll talk about it in the pub. It'll be a neat little anecdote. It might be one guy's first game in twenty years, and he's seen me do that and he'll tell people and everyone will love the story and he'll think, shit, I forgot how much I love this game. After school, most men make most of their friends from football." I sighed. I realised I was rambling, but I was simply following my neural pathways. It wasn't my fault if it was boring. "I went from being average to being incredible overnight. Incredible for this level, anyway. We'll get promoted next year, and the year after. That's two and a half years where I'll be the best player. So what if I score? Or do a nutmeg? It's no challenge. I miss being average, though I don't see how I could have got where I am as a nobody. This pickup football, I'd have loved it five years ago. I'd have been like Kian, skipping lessons to fit one more game in. Hitting the post four times in a row is much harder than scoring two or three. I'm quite pleased with myself."

"Oh," said Emma. "We're talking about you now."

"What?"

"I was asking about Pascal."

I thought about sulking, but she had a point. "Yeah, I was worried he was a bit too serious. I mean, that's good in principle. But I think it would get annoying after a couple of years, do you know what I mean? Anyway, he's all right. I think we'll get on. I hope he goes to the pub with the lads after the match." We'd fallen slightly behind the expected arrival time. Traffic up ahead? I sped up. "What did it look like to you? When he and I were combining?"

She blew a tiny raspberry. "Hard to describe. There wasn't much to it. You passed to each other. Is that good? Umm . . . it looked pretty basic. I didn't expect tears!"

"Oh, I get *that*. When he said it was magic. It's how I felt the first time I played with Raffi Brown. And when I hit crosses to Henri. You feel like there's someone who understands you. For me it was a nice surprise. A bonus. Pascal's been actively *searching* for that feeling for years." I added five miles per hour as I overtook a caravan. "It's interesting it didn't look dramatic. On the pitch, it is. You can feel the opposition being disrupted. Kind of a rising panic. It's fun."

Emma shifted. I knew her well enough to be alert. "Can we talk about promotion and relegation?"

"Sure."

"Remind me what promotion is."

"It's where we leave tier six and go to tier five. And then next season, tier four. When you go up a league, you play better teams in front of bigger crowds. Tier four is the start of what we call 'the league.' In the league you start getting proper TV money."

"And the opposite is relegation? You could go down to tier seven and play against Ziggy?"

"His team are doing well. They might be in tier six next season. I plan to bring him to Chester, though. But no, there's no chance Chester will be relegated. The team's too good. You'll notice that Chester fans, MD, all the rest, they all still use the word relegation. If they start to really, really worry, they'll switch to euphemisms. And you'll hear them say things like 'the team's too good to go down.'

It's a bit of a thingy. Opposite of curse. Ward? Something you say to ward off evil."

"But what would happen if it did happen?"

"Huh. Well . . . the minute relegation was mathematically certain, I'd be sacked. MD would be sacked. Ian Evans would definitely be sacked. Virtually no contracts would be renewed and the team would go semi-pro. Attendances next season would halve. Depending on the financial situation, they might scrap the Knights and all the youth teams. If I set up a women's team like I want, that'll be scrapped and all the investment lost."

"Fuck me."

"Yeah. Fairly cataclysmic." I glanced at her. "You're . . . unexpectedly stressed about it."

"Why aren't you?"

"Because I won't let it happen." I drove on another half a mile before checking. She seemed even less reassured. "Babes. What's up? Why are you asking about relegation? I never mention it."

"I was talking to . . . someone . . . and he said that Chester were heading towards relegation and putting a twenty-two-year-old hot head in charge was like stepping on the accelerator."

"Brakes. He said brakes."

"No."

"Then tell him he's a dick and I'll win the Premier League before Newcastle."

"I don't know what team he supports," she lied.

"By the time he was twenty-two," I said, "Alexander the Great had already won four Champions Leagues. Age is something for old men to obsess over. It won't be smooth sailing, but Chester's got me at the helm. Not even the devil could sink it."

I followed the roads towards Northamptonshire. Suddenly there seemed to be a lot more traffic.

Barely ten minutes before kickoff, I finally rolled into the reserved parking space at St. James Park. It felt small, but the capacity was 3,500. The outside was clad with corrugated iron, making it look like a closed shop in a rough area. Not very charming, if I'm being brutally honest.

"Voilà!" I said.

Emma looked around. "What?"

"St. James Park," I said. "As promised."

Emma leaned forward and looked at the sign. "What's this shit?"

"This is St. James Park. Home of Brackley Town. You said you wanted me to take you here. I remember you made a saucy joke about it."

Emma's face narrowed as she started to get pissed. "You've driven me three hours . . . for a weird joke? You found a place with the same name as the stadium in Newcastle?"

I swallowed. This wasn't going well. So much for long-term callbacks. My solution was to be very positive. Very upbeat. "Newcastle are playing in the FA Cup today. Against Sheffield Wednesday. Can you believe it?"

The distraction was interesting enough for her to stop blankly staring ahead. "Really? Don't *you* play for Sheffield Wednesday? If you really want to piss my dad off, you could knock his team out of the cup."

"I don't want to piss your dad off," I lied. "Chester are playing these guys. Brackley Town. We've got a fancy box with drinks and stuff. VIP treatment, as you deserve. Then I've got you a special, special moment planned. That's why I wore my best suit and everything."

"I do like it when you wear something other than the hoodie," she said. She unclipped her seatbelt and looked at all the metal sheeting that was protecting the stadium. "Who said romance is dead?"

Once we got into the VIP section, all was forgiven. It wasn't the unlimited free white wine, but the fact that I hadn't brought her all this way simply to make a bad joke. No, I was there doing my job. That meant catching up with MD and networking with my fellow C-suite executives.

"MD," I said, dragging him away from his Brackley equivalent for a second. He was always happy to spend more time with Emma. "What's the latest with the whole Sheffield Wednesday thing?"

He had been all smiles until then. "Not good. There's going to be a hearing on the fourteenth of February."

"Valentine's Day," said Emma. Weird when people do that.

"Hearing? To hear what?"

"Some guys from the Football Association will meet, look at the evidence, listen to the facts, and come to a decision. You'll be able to attend, though I'm tempted to say you shouldn't. It's going to be a formality. You standing up and giving an impassioned speech about justice and labour laws and how you'll smite them with the force of a hundred hurricanes . . . We don't need that."

"My dad will help," said Emma.

MD gawped at her. "Does he work for the FA?"

"He's a lawyer. He runs a big practice in Newcastle. He can help with the paperwork."

"We don't need a big company," I said. "*Anybody's* dad can handle this. It's a minor admin error."

"A proper lawyer does sound expensive," said MD. "Max has already sent thirty emails demanding we buy better tea bags and thicker toilet roll. I don't think we can afford big-firm legal fees as well."

"It'll be free," said Emma. "Max might have to drop a *tiny* apology for his behaviour at Christmas dinner, but it's really no big deal."

"Oh, tremendous! That's wonderful news. Why didn't you tell me, Max?"

Because I never want to be in the same room as Emma's dad ever again. "I think I did mention it. It was towards the bottom of one of the tea bag emails, I think. If we buy in bulk, I think we can stretch to Yorkshire Gold. I really do." I thought about my playing career. "All right," I said, scratching my chin. "Straightforward case, you said, no need for my theatrics, no need for a lawyer with no sense of right or wrong. Cool. Mid-February. Five weeks. That's . . . fine. Emma got me worried about Scenario B. But mid-February . . . there'll still be ten games left. That's thirty points. No probs. That'll blast us away from danger."

"Scenario B?" said Emma.

"It's a joke from an old Sunderland documentary," said MD. Impressive knowledge! "It's a way of talking about the R word without using the R word. You say Scenario B if you're really starting to worry about the dreaded *drop*." He laughed. "Max, I'm not worried. Are you worried?"

"About Scenario B? No. We're too good to go down." We clinked our glasses together at my joke. "So, I should be available around the middle of February," I said. "That's actually incredible if you think about it. You stop someone working for six weeks because you're too lazy to schedule a Zoom call? The meeting has to be in FA headquarters so they can get a six-course meal after. Laughable people. Empty blazers. But fine. It actually fits my plans. I can keep scouting. By the way, I found a player. Lad from Darlington wants to join. Let's talk about it on Monday?"

"Sure," said MD, brightening. "Good, is he?"

"No. But he will be."

"Oh. I'm sure that's . . . Look, would you spend some time with Ruth? I'm sure she'd enjoy the match with some younger people to talk to."

"Ruth's here?" I said. I must have said it in a strange way, because Emma's eyes snapped towards mine.

"Ruth's here?" she said, making MD wrongly assume I'd told Emma all about the sexy woman whose vote I'd won. "Let's go meet Ruth."

The Venue, as the hospitality space was called, was very pleasant. Wide spaces, hard laminate flooring, clean white walls, a spacious bar staffed by two friendly dudes, a big TV showing the latest FA Cup action for people who wanted to watch a slightly higher standard of match.

Ruth—dressed warm and stylish—had been networking—or flirting—with two guys who looked, to me, quite attractive. One looked hench. But Ruth dropped them both as soon as she laid eyes on me.

It seemed to me she glided across the room without her feet touching the floor, then suddenly she was there introducing herself to Emma.

Emma went bonkers. It might have been my fault. Since we met, we'd been doing tiny role plays and finding ways to make boring situations more fun. You remember the time she pretended to be my stalker, or the way she played along when I said she was in line to the throne of San Marino or whatever. This time, she took The Attention Game and tweaked it so that she'd be competing with Ruth for my attention. Normally, I'd have found this hot. Beyond hot, really.

For a few minutes I was into it. Did my best James Bond impression, made strong eye contact, said cheeky things. Ruth was into it, big time, and Emma was having fun trying to compete with her more experienced foe.

But I wasn't there to start a harem. The match had kicked off and I didn't like what I was seeing. When I had to give my attention to the women, I kept tracking the player ratings and the match commentary. Over the course of five minutes, which should have been among the most sexually exciting of my life, I edged closer and closer towards the pitch. When I was a couple of feet away from the high glass doors that kept us protected from the elements, Ruth stepped in front of me, daring me to look at her and not the football. She was gorgeous—a real minx.

The only thing that got hard, though, was my face. I glared at her. My jaw set. "Excuse me," I said, "I'm working."

Her reaction was subtle but tumultuous. Slowly, she turned, announced she needed another drink, and fucked off. Me choosing a shit game of football over her? I expected that would be the last we saw of Ruth.

I think Emma tried to talk to me, but I was staring down at the grass, a tiny pain somewhere in my stomach getting more intense by the second.

Brackley Town were good. Good enough to make me recalibrate my mental map of the division.

There were three very good teams in the league—King's Lynn, Darlington, and AFC Fylde were clearly the best, putting out teams with an average CA of 50. That was an estimate, by the way, because I hadn't seen two of those teams. But it fit mathematically based on the league table.

Then there were eight or nine with CAs between 40 and 50, who should have been competing for the next four positions in the league. With Henri in the team, I had blithely included Chester in that list, and now I added Brackley, too. They were a solid 45 CA team, playing a fairly normal 4-4-2. More attack-minded than average, and they were on a good run, climbing up the league table.

But I looked again at the pitch, and fumbled my phone's calculator app out. Sure enough, the Chester starting eleven had an average CA of 39.6. That was . . . shit.

The pain in my stomach got sharper.

Chester were a sub-40 CA team. How had that happened? I hadn't been paying very close attention to them in the months since I'd failed my trial there. I was *sure* the standard had been higher. They'd given Oldham a run for their money. Oldham were, what, CA 60? And that was before Chester got Henri. I was sure that adding him would turn them into a serious team.

So what the fuck?

MD bounded over to me. I snapped out of it and saw that Emma was gone. She was over at the bar with Ruth, and they were having what looked like a serious chat. MD was in fine form and didn't realise how out of place his energy was. "Max! How's your day going? Mine's great. Ruth's always a sight for sore eyes. And Emma? Wow. Ah! Life's good, sometimes." He lapsed into a reverie before chuckling. "You've had quite a start to your job. Going round, getting stuck in. I've had coaches in the office complaining about you, physios. No players. I suppose you haven't started on them yet." He laughed. "You're a disruptor, Max. Classic disruptor. I love it."

"You're not worried I'm being *too* disruptive?"

"Nah. Can't break an omelette without—ah, messed it up. Ha! Just keep me in the loop like you have been doing. I wouldn't mind if you slowed down, but then again, if people don't want to change, we'll have to change the people. I notice you, er, glaring at the pitch. Something wrong?"

"Yeah," I said, and was about to go into a rant when the ladies returned.

MD said, "Max was just about to tell me what's happening tactically."

"No, my hobby horse at the moment is injuries. Trick Williams is injured." His stamina was red, two points lower than normal. One lost point was fairly common—by the end of the match, five or six players would have a lost point in stamina. They'd have huge bruises, swollen ankles, sore hips, maybe a few stitches. But they'd recover the stamina point the next morning, and be considered by the curse ready to play. I wasn't a huge fan of that, but it's a tough sport, an uncaring business. I could stomach it. What I didn't like were two point drops. That signalled something potentially significant. "Playing with an injury is demented. He'll make it worse. Make it more expensive. He thinks he's being masculine. He's being a dick."

"Are you sure?" said MD. He shielded his eyes to better see the pitch. "He . . . he looks fine."

"He's not. MD, I need . . ." I glanced at the women. "I want to do something that might lead to two people leaving the club."

"Who?"

"Trick and Dean."

"Dean!" said Ruth. "He's a horrible little man. Yes, sack him. Sack Dean. I will make sure the board are on your side on this."

"The board," said Emma.

MD looked at Ruth, and that was the moment I realised he had a massive crush on her. He turned to me and shrugged. "Can you . . . be more tactful than usual?"

"What do you mean?"

He tutted and looked up with a smile. "Don't be rash. If you want to sack someone, you need to give them enough rope to hang themselves. So they can't take us to court for wrongful dismissal."

I thought about it. "I don't know. I only have one speed. I'll try to learn another one." While everyone watched, I phoned Physio Dean. "Little shit isn't answering. What did he do to you?"

Ruth crossed her arms, let her wine glass dangle alarmingly. "He acts like he owns the place."

Emma said, "So does Max."

"There's a difference. In quality."

I held up a finger. My second target had picked up. "Livia. It's Max Best. Please say *oh hi Max* nice and loud so that Dean knows it's me. Did he hear that? Great. Please ask him if he's noticed Trick picked up a knock, or if Trick mentioned anything before the match. No? Nothing. Okay, can you please give Dean the phone?" I licked my lips. MD had asked for tact. "Dean. Thanks for agreeing to take my call."

"We're in the middle of a match, Max."

"I know. I'm here."

"You're in Brackley?"

"Dean, please listen very carefully. Take your physio bag and walk around to the far side of the pitch."

"Why?"

"If this was a war, the patient would be dead already. The bag. Go to your left. If you do a little scampering run it will seem less strange."

From a distance, I saw him press mute on the phone and have a little bicker with Livia. Him bringing her into it was a mistake. Finally, he threw his hands up, grabbed the bag, and walked quite slowly around the edge of the pitch.

"What a prick," said Emma. "If you're calling there must be someone hurt. He should run."

"MD, I'd like a physio who isn't repellent to women, please. Do you know where to find one?"

MD smiled but shook his head. "He's not a bad guy. Give him a chance." From the corner of his mouth he added, "Or at least make him quit so we don't have to pay him off."

Dean's voice came through the phone. "Yes? I'm where you said to go."

"At the next stoppage, tell Trick to sit down so you can check him out."

"Trick? He's fine."

"This guy!" I snapped, bringing the phone away from my mouth. With it back in place, I said, tactfully, "Next time the fucking ball goes out of play, stop the fucking game!"

The ref whistled for a throw-in, and Dean waved his arms around. Everyone ignored him and the match continued. Which showed how powerful Dean was outside his own domain, but also showed how little people in football cared about footballers. The ref should have been over there in a flash wondering what was going on.

"Dean," I said. "Shout to Ryder. Tell him what I said."

"I'll try."

Ruth rolled her eyes.

The match finally stopped, and Dean rushed onto the pitch to check on Trick. Even from this distance I could see Trick insisting he was fine. Dean picked up the phone and said, "He's okay. Nothing wrong. I'm going back."

"Listen to me, Dean. Listen very carefully. Look at Ian Evans and roll your arms to signal a sub. Then help Trick to walk—very slowly—to the dressing rooms. You have until half-time to tell me what's wrong with him. Do you understand? If I don't hear from you, Livia will be our medical team for the second half and I'll be sending your contract to a law firm in Newcastle to find out how I can bin you off as fast as poss. Would you like me to repeat any of that?"

"Ian will go ballistic when he realises there's nothing wrong with him!"

"Bye, Dean. Give Livia her phone back on your way."

I stood and fumed for a while, watching as a visibly annoyed Trick Williams trudged off the pitch. Ian Evans was, indeed, going mental. I could almost lip read. "He says he's fine. He says he's fine." Dean was insistent, and Evans had no choice but to replace Trick. He had lost a substitution for no benefit. In his mind, the team was weaker now.

I was grinding my teeth again, imagining the fight I'd have with Evans about this scenario. Snippets of conversation filtered into my brain, and then I was back in The Venue. My companions were staring at me. "What?"

Emma gave me a concerned look. "We asked what you'll do if Dean doesn't find anything."

"Sack him."

"But how do you know the guy's hurt?" said Ruth.

"Do you ever look at your horses and know something's wrong, even though you're far away?"

"Yes."

I wanted to make some wise-arse comment, show off. But the pain in my stomach was back. Emma knew me like Ruth knew an injured horse. "Max?"

"I'm, er . . . I'm feeling a bit . . . Emma, has Gemma said anything about Henri?"

"What?" That had been the last thing she'd expected. "Er . . . no. I think they're seeing less of each other. Is it his choice?"

"Max! You've never shown any interest in it before. Now you're pale and asking for the hot goss. Are you okay?"

I pointed. "Look at him." All eyes followed my finger.

"What are we looking at?" said MD.

"Henri. He looks . . . shit."

"Max! You love Henri. He's your mate. Your client."

"I know. He's top. But . . ." I tried to explain that my mate had lost 8 points of CA without getting myself sent to an asylum. "He's lost a yard of pace. He's . . . he's not there. On the pitch. This isn't the guy I saw at the Deva stadium that time. This isn't the guy who came to my trial. I'm wondering if he's depressed."

"Huh," said MD. "I've seen him around. All the staff are happy he's joined. He seems . . . fine?"

"Whatever it is, it's hurting his performance. I need him happy and reaching his potential. Otherwise . . ."

"What?"

"Nothing. Maybe he just needs his first goal." But I was biting my nails, and MD didn't need to dig deeper. He knew I was thinking of Scenario B.

The rest of the half was torture. Agony. Made even worse because Emma was asking me if I was all right every few minutes, and Ruth had taken a step back and was appraising me.

That morning, Pascal and I had played perhaps twenty passes to each other, creating four chances across four elaborate passages of play. In St. James Park, Chester found it almost impossible to put three passes together. There'd be a throw-in that someone would boof up the pitch. There would be some head tennis, then another throw-in. Repeat. It was excruciating. The fans fell into a stupor—they wanted to cheer but there was nothing to respond to.

The match ratings made my pain worse. The four central defenders on the pitch had 8 out of 10. Winning all their headers, keeping things tight. Aff was on 6. Reward for his defensive diligence. Henri was on 5 out of 10. He was shuffling and sliding like a good pro, but he wasn't winning his headers. His only contribution to the first half was to get a yellow card for booting a defender. He was lucky it wasn't red.

Ian Evans was having the time of his life. He was loving this contest. If it stayed like this, he'd be delighted. He'd call it "a good point."

"MD," I said, sweating slightly. "You know this league way better than me. What would happen if we drew every match for the rest of the season? Would we be safe?"

"No," he said. "Very unlikely. Brackley are a good team, though, right? Near the top of the table. A draw's good today."

I shook my head. "If we have to win some matches, why aren't we trying to win matches?" I rubbed my thumbs in the space above my eyelids but below my eyebrows. "Is he . . . ?"

"Is who what?"

"Nothing."

"Say it."

"No. I said I wouldn't get involved in the first team."

"You just did! You dragged a player off the pitch."

"That's different. That's duty of care. That doesn't count."

"Spit it out, Max," said Ruth.

I was wondering if Ian Evans was consciously trying to get Chester relegated . . . Revenge for being given a boss fifty years younger than him. Revenge for the humiliation MD had heaped upon him. I licked my lips—they were dry. "Emma, babes. Can you get me something to drink?"

"Yeah." She rushed off to the bar.

I looked from Ruth to MD and back. "Is he *trying* to get sacked? The Max Best project makes him look bad. He thinks people are laughing at him. If we sack him, he's vindicated. *'They're crazy over there! I'm well out of it.'* See what I mean?"

MD considered it. "I doubt it. He's saved a lot of clubs from situations like these. He won't want to end his career on a low note. Do you think the tactics are bad? The players aren't trying?"

"No," I said. "The tactics are the same as always. And I can't fault their effort. Look, it was just a passing thought. I've got Scenario B on the mind now. I'm seeing demons in every shadow." The pain in my stomach turned into a single, excruciating jab. I was forced to sit down on a leather sofa. As soon as I stopped looking at the match, I felt better.

Emma brought me a drink—fresh apple juice, good choice—and I sipped at it.

MD took a seat in front of me. "You're unwell. Are you pushing yourself too hard? You were right the first morning. You were pacing yourself. That was good. Go back to that."

"It's not that, MD. I love the work." I looked around. I didn't really want to talk openly in front of a relative stranger in Ruth. But I had to let it out. I pushed the apple juice in the direction of the pitch. "That out there? That's fucking garbage. Today I played a match with this kid I told you about and we played more passes in a few minutes than that entire midfield has done in half an hour. I want passion. I want Gazza moments. I want our matches given the tag *swoon-worthy*." The sweat was dribbling through my hair now, but I was calming down. Talking was good. "I'm stressed because as DoF, I'm responsible for that. Fans will listen to what I said on *Seals Live* and look at what's on the pitch and think, 'Oh, so he was full of shit.' I know I said I wouldn't interfere in the first team and I'm fine with that. I'll stick to it. It's just . . . harder than I expected. And it'll get worse before it gets better. And my mate is sad and I don't know what to do about it anyway and it's weird because he's my landlord and I'm his boss. And the, ah, reality of how close we are to Scenario B is really starting to eat away at me. Fuck."

"But it's like you said, Max. You'll come in the team, win us fifteen quickfire points, no problem."

I nodded. That was true. So why was I breaking out into stress sweats? Why was I incubating a literal ulcer? Maybe my body was trying to tell me something my mind was too chickenshit to admit to.

"MD," I croaked. "This . . . this FA panel. Do you have the names of the judges or whatever they're called?"

"Yes, yes, I do." He fiddled with his phone and came next to me. He showed me each name and I did an image search for each. The first four were generic gammony randos. The fifth, though.

The fifth was one of Old Nick's imps.

How the fuck had he arranged *that*?

The stress came rushing back, harder than ever. I knew where this was going: Nick was trying to stop me playing the *entire rest of the season*. If I couldn't swoop in to save Chester, and Henri's inexplicable decline continued . . . We wouldn't be too good to go down. We'd be too shit to stay up.

There was no choice but to fight Nick in court.

I turned the phone and showed it to Emma. She recognised the imp from the day I'd ranted at Sheffield Wednesday. "Oh, shit," she said.

"Ruth, do you know any floating legal megabrains who'll work for free?"

"I do not."

I exhaled and looked at the ceiling. My lips twitched. I looked at Emma. "What was it again? Your dad will help us out . . . if he apologises to me?"

"Something like that."

I rubbed my head and face. I was starting to feel sick again. I'd rather be the laughing stock of the entire football world than offer a fake apology to Emma's dad. My phone beeped. I read the message and held it up for the others to see.

Physio Dean: Quad strain. Out 3 weeks subject to scan.

MD's mind was blown. "Holy fuck, you've done it again, Max. Jesus Christ."

Ruth said, "That . . . was impressive." She gave me another of those long, uninhibited looks, then checked her watch. "I have a proposal. Would you care to join me for an early dinner?"

Emma accepted before I even had time to think. Getting out of the stadium would probably be good for my mental health, and the meal would probably be high quality. The only question was, what did Ruth want to propose?

I thought I knew. It seemed obvious what she wanted. But as it turned out, I couldn't have been more wrong.

NOTHING ODD WILL DO LONG

The three of us left the stadium and paused in the car park. The thrill of going on a tiny adventure paused while we negotiated the logistics. "What was your plan?" said Ruth.

"Plan?"

"Emma told me you'd be making some grand romantic gesture."

I scoffed. "Did she? Well, maybe." Under the appraising eye of a mature woman, my idea seemed pretty feeble. "Maybe? Maybe. Maybe not." I gestured. "I was going to drive about a minute *that* way, to the Mercedes Formula One team's headquarters. And I was going to give a speech about incremental improvement and working as a team and how a team wasn't all about a few floating megabrains but everyone, everyone in all those buildings, pulling together. Emma would have been bored, but she'd have peeked in the windows to try to see Lewis Hamilton. And next season I'd have brought the squad here and given them the same speech, now perfected. So yeah, a romantic rehearsal for a motivational team talk."

Ruth didn't blink. "Let's do *my* thing. Hop in."

"You drive a Mercedes!" I said. "Small world."

Emma and I got in the back, and after shooting off some texts, Ruth zoomed away.

"You know these roads pretty well," said Emma.

"I do. I come here quite often. Here we are."

The drive had been approximately two minutes; I hadn't even had time to check out all the features in the car. Ruth had taken us to the second destination I had scouted for my evening with Emma: Turweston Flight Centre. "*I* was going to do this!" I said.

"That so? Great minds think alike. Come on."

I wanted to say she was going the wrong way, that the entrance was to the right, but she was pacing away to the left. I couldn't think why. All that was there were some small planes and some mechanics rushing around.

Moments later we were climbing the steps into a Piper PA-28 Cherokee. Ruth helped us into helmets, apologised for the lack of champagne, then got in the pilot's seat. The tiny little plane rolled forwards, taxied onto the runway, and took off.

There's an incredible passage in Patrick O'Brian's *Master and Commander*, where Stephen Maturin, a landlubber, describes the feeling of impending annihilation he experienced during his first ocean-churning storm. It came to mind during the rough, violent ascent. The Piper thing had a fucking propeller! I'd only ever seen planes with propellers in *Indiana Jones* movies. Modern planes should have jet engines, and every passenger should get a front and back parachute, plus a jetpack.

Ten minutes earlier, I had been watching a flying winger grounded, a Frenchman with his head in the clouds, a team born for murmuration forced into rigid, static blocks by an ancient flightless lizard. Ten minutes from there to here, in a little plane, soaring above all my troubles (or almost all, since I tended to keep a few with me). The change in your state came so rapidly it was dizzying.

Once we were at a stable height, I was able to enjoy it. The views were amazing. The feeling of freedom was . . . no, wait. We were stuck in a tiny coffin miles in the air. No, no sense of freedom. But it was fun in its own way. Just not how I'd imagined my first time in a plane.

"We're coming up to Silverstone," said Ruth. "That's a Formula One track, Emma. Home of British motor racing. I'm a speed freak. I love the feeling of powerful machines under me. There it is: northeast."

"I wasn't born with a silver compass in my mouth," I said, joking that Ruth had been born rich while saying I didn't know where north was.

"To your right, Max. Do you like Formula One?"

"Not really. Not as a sport. Maybe as a spectacle. I'd love to go once for the sounds and the smells. It must be amazing. Polar opposite of an ASMR video." I imagined a hundred thousand spectators in the arena below me, with all the little cars bombing around going *nee-ow*! Yeah, I'd like to see it once.

"It *is* amazing. I go every year. That's why I have friends in Tur-weston. I'm going to bank and go back. Emma, would you like me to do a loop-de-loop?"

"No, thanks," I said, mimicking Emma's voice. I trusted Ruth to fly as much as I trusted Spectrum to coach—a lot, but with reservations.

Ruth grinned and flipped something on one of her many control panels. Not the intro to a daring manoeuvre, thank fuck. Just the plane equivalent of putting your fog lights on.

The descent was terrifying. We could hear Ruth talking to air traffic control through our helmets. She was extremely calm, ATC was extremely professional. But every time anyone spoke, I thought, *Oh my God, what's gone wrong? Climb to level one-one-zero? Why? Why, mate?* Then the final approach—Ruth seemed to be flying diagonally at the runway, the way Ziggy would approach a girl at the bar. I slipped my hand into Emma's so that we'd die together. Then, at least, I'd have kept my promise to do something romantic.

And then we hit the runway . . . and it was so smooth. The little plane *aah*ed along the tarmac, making no more noise than an e-bike. Americans love to whoop and holler when a plane lands, and for the first time I understood the impulse.

"This is your captain speaking," said Ruth through the headset. "We hope you enjoyed the flight. Max, hope that helped with your stress. It's so terribly peaceful, isn't it? Emma, you don't need a man to take you to heaven and back. I hope you're hungry. Dinner's in fifteen."

Emma and I milled around with huge grins on our faces. Emma had enjoyed the whole thing from start to finish, but for me it was exciting in retrospect. Still, now that we were back on land, we were both on cloud nine.

Ruth shuttled us to a pub called The Chequered Flag, which had a fairly standard British menu. Not expensive at all. Completely, if you'll forgive the phrase, down to earth.

Ruth was chatty—we all were. "My dad used to take me here be-fore races. We'd fly in, come here, then go and watch Michael Schum-acher (him) and Jenson Button (me). It's not the best food in Bucks but it's very nostalgic. I feel at home here." She looked around the place;

it was such a typical modern pub that it was hard to imagine a woman as classy as Ruth going there on the regular. "But Max. You said you planned to take Emma to the flight centre. I didn't know you could fly. So many talents!"

I desperately wanted a burger but didn't want to eat messy food in front of Ruth. I had recently eaten my first burger in front of Emma and hadn't enjoyed it. I was still trying to impress her, and finishing a meal covered in ketchup and meat juice was not sexy. So I'd eaten it one atom at a time, which achieved my goal of not looking like a slob, but the process had detracted somewhat from the pleasure of shoving food into my mouth as fast as poss so that I could enjoy a constant stream of sensory input. I looked up from the menu. "Fly? No. I saw the flight centre had a knife and fork icon on the map. I investigated and decided to bring Emma to the café. Scones and a view of the runway."

Ruth frowned. "So your romantic day with your girlfriend was watching non-league football, walking to the *outside* of the Mercedes building, then having a scone?"

"I also made a teenager cry."

"I'm sure you've made a lot of teenagers cry, Max."

"Pretty sure that was the first ever."

"The day was lovely," said Emma, hugging my arm. "And I like scones. But the flight was breathtaking."

I growled at Ruth. "You won *this* round . . ."

She laughed and leaned forward. "You're such a good match. Some couples are strange; you know it won't last. You two have a chance. I want to know how you met."

We were so relaxed and still bubbly from our near-death experience slash gravity-defying adventure that we didn't even make up some tall tale. Together we told the story, from Ziggy and the deli in Manchester through to our double date with Henri and Gemma. Ruth kept me talking. Somehow I was telling them about beating Man City under-sixteens. I hadn't told Emma much about the Beth Heads arc, but it came out. Most of it. Halfway through I paused and wondered if I'd been drugged. I shook off the thought and continued.

"Wait," said Ruth. "You had Jackie Reaper as your assistant in an indoor seven-a-side match involving amateur players? Jackie *Reaper*?"

"Bald chap. Talks about The Beatles all the time. Doesn't like being nutmegged. What? What's so surprising about that?"

"I can't quite imagine it. How . . . how did you get him to do that?"

"I asked him. He volunteered. I don't remember. He got sucked into the story. We all did. What's the big deal? It was a few paid Wednesdays and a couple of unpaid Fridays."

She didn't seem convinced, but she wanted to go back to Ziggy. How I'd found him, how I knew he was good. I gave her my spiel about comparing players, which was less abstract now because they'd seen me diagnose a quad tear from the hospitality box. If I could spot an injury, why couldn't I spot a talent?

Ruth pushed some vegetables into her mouth and chewed. When she was ready, she said, "The men's team are hurtling towards relegation. They're only five points from safety. If things get out of hand, will you step in and save them?"

"I can't play."

"I mean as manager."

"Ooh," I said. "Of course I would, but it won't happen. MD would need to decide to sack Ian Evans, which seems unlikely, and he'd need to choose me as replacement. Even if MD thinks I'm talented, he's never going to give me the job on the basis of beating Man City's girls' team. No, that's not going to happen."

"So you need more practice. A place to show what you can do."

"Right."

"Which is why you want to start the women's team. So you can show that you're a serious candidate for the manager's job."

"One reason, yeah."

"You'd better get on with it, then."

"Right." That's when it hit me: Ruth was going to offer to finance the team. "I just need to save up first. I've stopped eating avocado on toast and I'm saving money on clothes. Aren't I, Emma?"

She pulled a face. "Max bought like five of the same cheap black hoodie. Said it helped with decision fatigue. He refuses to upgrade his look."

"Aah," I said, delighted that she'd fallen into my trap. "Ruth, could you help me out? I have this letter from someone, but my eyes are very tired. Could you read it out loud?"

Ruth rolled her eyes but took the note. It was the one Longstaff had forwarded to me when we were doing crosswords together. The writer didn't know what address to use. "Dear Max. I've got twins and they're big Darlo fans, and you're their hero. Money's hard to come by but I try to get them what they want. This Christmas they said they wanted Max Best drips. I took them to Longstaff's and I couldn't believe my eyes when they ran to the cheapest tops. They were made up, and I even had a bit left over for a little rebound board so they could practise their skills. You've saved Christmas. Thank you so much." Ruth had slowed down as she was reading.

"Oh, Max," said Emma, as she leaned in to hug me.

I accepted the hug. Then, without making eye contact, I said, "I was delighted when I got that, because it would help me win this dispute. But, er . . ." One side of my mouth curled upwards. "I would have liked to buy something *slightly* nicer one day soon. With a more premium zip and toggles that stay the same shape. I'm, er . . . imprisoned by my own sainthood. The idea of some brat seeing me in a fucking sarong and asking his penniless mum for one . . . Nah. The moral of the story is, I'm frugal to a fault. I don't splash money around on fripperies. Whichever kind, generous, ravishing benefactor comes along to finance the women's team, her money will go a long way."

Boom! Two birds killed with one stone. Beat that, Daedalus!

Ruth dapped her lips with a napkin, maybe to hide a smile? But then she was all business. "MD has told me what you want. Two hundred K. How did you come to that figure?"

"I plucked it out of thin air."

"That's not what a woman who's the target for every conman in the North-West likes to hear, Max."

I shrugged. "I know it's more than enough for two seasons. It could go a long way, actually. I want a full-time women's coach. Let's say twenty-five grand a year. Then it's renting a pitch to train on, buying some new equipment, kit, transport to matches. The players won't get paid at first. Just starting the team and competing in the league next year shouldn't add up to more than a hundred. Two hundred is so that I don't have to think about it and don't get an ulcer every time we lose. It will take time to start a whole new team from scratch. People don't have vision. Round one funding has to include round two as well. And by the time the two hundred runs out, the men's team should be selling players and starting to make serious profits."

"The men's team will subsidise the women's?"

"If needed. There's more money coming into the women's game. Women's transfer fees are slowly rising. If it keeps going like that, the women's team will be profitable, too."

Ruth stared at something. Some guy she knew, maybe. "A few years ago, Sunderland had a great women's team. The men were relegated and the women lost their contracts. If I were to finance your project, I'd want assurances that wouldn't happen."

I speared a piece of pasta. "Could be arranged, I guess. Siloed money. Trusts and things. MD's the man for that."

"The thing is, Max, talent isn't enough. You need a business plan. You need to think things through from all angles. Two hundred thousand is a lot of money. When MD told me your idea, I thought: no way. Ask someone else. I don't like football. I don't care if local girls have a place to play. If the women's team would be run like the men's, I'd say it's a net positive that it doesn't exist. But you're compelling. You'd give them an opportunity to do what they love, and you'd make sure they were treated with respect. Female players get injured a lot more than men; the medical room needs to be welcoming."

"I told Dean I want it to feel like a spa."

Ruth broke into a grin. "Charming boy. Now, despite my misgivings, I've been doing some research. Research you should have been doing, by the way. Have you been following the transfers this week?"

"This week? No, I've been rammed. I know Chelsea are buying every player going."

"That's the men's team. Chelsea Women sold Bethany England to Tottenham for two hundred and fifty thousand. That's a new British record. And here's an interesting one: Jordan Nobbs, who is thirty years old, moved from Arsenal to Aston Villa for thirty thousand pounds."

"Huh," I said, blood starting to pump.

"What? That's low, isn't it?" asked Emma.

"You expect star players to go for bigger and bigger fees," I mused. "But what's sort of missing in the women's game, as far as I can tell, is all the transfers underneath. Ninety-nine percent seem to move at the end of their contract, for free. There isn't a *market* as such. But this move suggests that one is developing; Nobbs is near the end of her career. Being able to sell okay players for okay money is a bit of a game-changer for a club like Chester. That makes starting a women's team way more desirable. Urgent, even."

Ruth nodded. "I've heard from my contacts that Arsenal are plotting to buy Alessia Russo from Manchester United. Her contract expires in the summer. Which means her fee *should* be low, Emma. But the numbers I've heard are astronomical. They'd smash the transfer record for a player they could get for free in a few months. You know what this is? The start of the bubble. If you can find the next Alessia Russo, there's profit to be had."

I nodded. "I know. That's why it's good I'm an agent, too. I'm going to spend all of January scouting. I'm sure I'll find loads of good players, and if I can't get them started at Chester I will still be their agent. I'll do all right either way."

Ruth placed her cutlery down. "No. You will bring them to Chester. You *will* start this team. And you can't be their agent. It's a conflict of interest."

"I can."

"You can't. I will shoot it down. And even if you could argue your case in the court of public opinion, it's going to be pretty surreal when the Chester manager turns up to negotiate a transfer between Hull and QPR. It's odd. Nothing odd will do long. No, you'll manage the women and live out your tactical fantasies. Chester will get talented players that the club can sell for a profit. And you will tell me the ones likely to be sold for big fees, and I will be their agent." She smiled.

"You?" said Emma.

"Yes. Me. That way, I'll be a local hero for funding the team, *and* I'll get my money back. This country is run on cakeism. I plan to buck the trend. I'll have my cake and eat it, too." She summoned a waiter. "We're ready for dessert." She turned to Emma to explain why she was being such a capitalist. "Planes, trains, and automobiles are expensive. Horses? Horses are ruinous."

I lapsed into silence for a while, thinking things through while I spooned a banana split into my mouth.

On the one hand, Ruth would give me the money I needed to start the women's team. With a big chunk of cash propelling me, the team could really take off. On the other hand, I'd accepted a flat wage at Chester, expecting to make a bit of side-hustle money along the way. Giving Ruth her fair share was fair, sort of, but also, I wanted it for myself. How was I ever going to get past the walks-and-scones spending level if I couldn't profit from my talent?

There were other rich people in Cheshire . . . But I didn't know them.

I watched Ruth and Emma as they chatted. Emma was great at getting to know people. "Are you dressage or eventing?"

"Eventing. For me it's all about the jumps. But I have a dressage trainer for my seat."

"Oh, very sensible. Max told me you have an amazing stable. No fat horses, he said."

"Did he now?"

"Now, what do you think about working equitation?"

And so it went while I worked from right to left across my plate.

"I've had an idea," I said, halfway across. The women seemed startled that I was there. They gave each other a look like "who's this guy?" I waited for their faces to return to normal. "I've had an idea," I repeated.

"Yes, Max," said Emma, turning to me and sitting up straight like a diligent schoolgirl. This was a sign she was mildly annoyed that I'd interrupted. But I was too enthusiastic to wait.

"Ruth has money and intimidates managing directors. I'm a floating megabrain. You're one of those lawyer people."

"The lawyer people. Sounds like one of those old bands you listen to."

"Why don't we . . ." I leaned forward and spoke more softly. "Why don't we start an agency? I'll find players and say what kinds of teams they should play for. *You'll* deal with the contracts. *You'll* be the one who turns up to meetings and squeezes another couple of mill out of Fulham. No conflict of interest for me anymore." Ruth made a little throat-clearing noise. "Yeah, okay, there sort of would be. But not really. Not *really*. And all I'll be doing is choosing who the agency takes care of. I'll be hidden. I won't be in *rooms*. My name won't be on paperwork. It's . . . I'll be a couple of steps removed."

"Um, Max," said Emma.

"Yes, babes?"

"We were trying to have a conversation over here. Before you interrupted. We'll get back to it, if that's all right with you?"

"Sure."

Emma took a spoonful of my melting ice cream and pushed it past those lips of hers.

"I knew it," said Ruth. "I knew he'd tried to get us into a three-way."

I still had the Match Overview and saw that Chester scraped through with a draw. One point. Still five points clear of relegation. A few minutes on the pitch for Raffi Brown, but no goal for Henri. I thought back to when he'd started dating Gemma. I'd thought they were an odd couple. What had Ruth said? Nothing odd can last?

I looked at some other scores. Darlington drew. Bad result for them. Meanwhile, in the FA Cup, Sheffield Wednesday beat Newcastle. What a shame for Emma's dad.

The next morning, I drove to Chester to watch the twelves and fourteens and grab some of the XP I lost by leaving the first team's match early. When I arrived, Spectrum fished in his backpack and handed me an envelope.

"What's this?"

"Handing in my notice," he said.

"All right. Does it slag me off and that?"

"No? No! It's copied from a template. I've never . . ."

"What's your notice period?"

"I don't know." He looked away. "I thought you'd tell me."

What was I feeling? I would have expected relief that a problem had resolved itself, or disappointment. Mostly I was just worried about him. "I'll check with Joe. Have you got something else lined up?"

"No."

"Well don't go before you've got a job. I don't want you freezing to death."

"Er . . . kay."

"Can I ask why?" I said, flapping the envelope around.

He shook his head, rapidly, then changed to nodding. "It's just weird. It's too weird. Kian? He's a lovely kid but he's awful. Vivek is literally the worst player I've ever coached. You're asking us to coach kids who've literally come in off the street. Is it because they're your clients? Why *else* would you do it? Tyson's a striker but you tell him not to shoot. I heard you were making substitutions from the corporate boxes. You've got some good ideas but a lot more bad ones. You don't know how to run a football club. How could you? You've been a player for two months. It's mad. It makes no sense. I don't want to be blamed for what happens. I can't face the kids. I don't want to be part of this relegation. I don't like you breathing down my neck all the time. I have to look after myself. My career and my mental health. Sorry." He added the last word because I was staring in amazement at him. He must have mistaken my surprise for hostility.

"All right," I said. My first reaction was defensive—ready to push back, explain how wrong he was, fight my corner. But what was the point? He'd already decided to leave. And he did have some valid arguments. I swallowed my initial burst of rage and focused on what was important. "Please do not communicate your low opinion of them to Kian, Vivek, and the other new kids who will come."

"No, I—"

"I was going to ask if I could take the second half with the fourteens. It's not a punishment or me trying to show you up. I need to practise my skills and try things for my coaching badges. Is that okay with you?"

"Well, yeah."

"Good." I looked up. There were some dark, angry clouds gathering. You had to be a pretty dedicated parent to stand on the touchline and watch your kid splash around in that kind of weather. I reset my face and went off to have some chats with them. First, because they were a big part of the Chester FC community. And second, because maybe some of them had daughters . . . and I had a women's team to start.

12

WISH LIST

XP balance: 5,434

Debt repaid: 332/3,000

Spectrum set the fourteens up in a daring 4-2-4, which took us to a two-goal lead. The other team knew Tyson was our danger man, so they overreacted every time the ball went near him. Helpful, but Tyson was still making the same runs. I wanted him to *adapt* his game to his new de-fanged circumstances. I wanted him to make dummy runs, lead defenders astray, create overloads. Huh. I wanted him to play like *Pascal*.

Meanwhile, Sullivan, the kid who was too conservative, didn't respond well to being used high up the pitch. I was starting to wonder if his problem was his dad yelling at him or if he was really just that cautious.

Shortly before half-time I asked Spectrum to switch to a 3-5-2. More Max weirdness, he thought, but he did it and I took over during the break. I'd asked him to make the change because I couldn't. I had access to 4-4-2, 4-4-2 diamond, and 4-3-3. The next formation would be 4-5-1, which was in the curse shop for 400 XP.

Of course I wanted to buy it, if only to see what the next one would be. More formations meant more flexibility, which meant more fun. But by my reckoning, 4-5-1 was the seventh most desirable item in the curse shop (out of fifteen). I wasn't managing enough matches to justify spending XP on in-game upgrades.

The same went for Match Stats 3: Action Zones. That was 300 XP and would add a little bit more data to the Match Overview screens.

Fine, but I didn't need it. It was ninth in my rankings, but it was only that high because it was in a chain and sometimes it was the *next* one in the chain that was the killer app. Maybe the curse knew about expected goals, expected threat, and heat maps. If it gave me data like how far players had run in a match, I could save real-life money buying GPS vests.

"Guys, nice job," I said, as the kids gathered around for half-time drinks. We were much fresher than our opponents—we'd been letting the ball do the work. "Spectrum's letting me do the second half. I want to get weird with it. Who's ready to get *weird*?" One hand went up—the goalkeeper's. "One vote? Fine. Not weird, then. You guys are *booring*. 3-5-2, then. Sully, you're left mid. You're allowed to pass backwards but I'll be counting how many passes you make in either direction. They should be about the same by the end of the half, right? Tyson, you're right mid. When I shout 'Go Go Gadget Legs,' get forward and smash the ball square as hard as you can. Cause some havoc out there. When I shout 'Tiny Dancer,' give me some tiki-taka. Hundreds of tiny, short-range passes. All good?"

He rolled his eyes. "What do you really want?"

"You know what I want. I want a team. Here's what we do. Every time we get the ball, I'm going to start a timer. If we get to one minute of passing without that lot touching the ball, you get a bonus."

"What's the bonus?"

"I don't know. I'll think of something. Maybe I'll let you clean the boots of the best player in non-league." There were some groans and more eye rolls. "Ungrateful little shits. What do you want, then?"

Tyson knew. "Next goal you score for the first team, you have to do a dance we teach you."

I scoffed. They thought they were being clever, but Old Nick was going to stop me playing the rest of the season. By the time I scored for Chester, most of these kids would be out of the system, and the ones who were left would have forgotten this conversation. "Fine. One minute of passing them to death. Passing to the goalie and back doesn't count. Impress me."

They ran back onto the pitch, full of beans. As soon as they'd turned away, my mask slipped. No goals this season. Which meant my first goal for the club could be in August. In the seventh tier of English football.

I spent Sunday evening with Henri at Raffi and Shona's place. Henri had also invited Glenn Ryder, our best defender and the player he liked to spar with in training matches. At first, I felt weirdly jealous. Or maybe it wasn't weird, I don't know.

Raffi was in great spirits. His career was on the up and he could feel it. Ryder was a very solid guy. He knew he was one of our better players, he knew we relied on him, and he knew his value. That made him confident and relaxed. Good company.

Henri, meanwhile, was very charming, very funny. But I knew him quite well. He was trying too hard. Reaching. Every time he thought no-one was looking, I checked him out. I never caught him sighing or staring into the abyss, but something was off.

And the worst part was, the curse shop was selling a perk called Morale. The description went like this:

"In football the moral is to the physical as three is to one." Winston Bogarde

Then it said the price. 2,000 XP. Big time. My guess was that it would reveal how players were feeling. Obviously a stunningly important thing for me to have. I mean, if it said something like:

Henri Lyons. Depressed. Lovesick.

That would be incredibly useful, right?

God, imagine if it told me how long he'd be depressed for! Maybe there'd be another perk that would tell me how to fix it.

Henri Lyons. Depressed (3 weeks). Lovesick. Buy flowers and tell him you envy his hair.

Yeah. Morale was number two in my wish list. I wanted to spend time with Henri, but being with him was hard. I nearly bought the perk a thousand times. What was wrong with him? What could I do? I had to be rational. I needed Playdar first.

I slept at the stadium so I could go to training in the morning. It was my first day learning to be a goalkeeper.

At first I wasn't really into it. I'd had the idea when everything was going great, but now that the walls were caving in my flights of fancy seemed . . . silly. Small.

Another reason I lacked motivation was that I knew I had 20 in all my attributes and the letters *GK* were included in my list of positions. I was probably one of the best goalkeepers in the country. Why train?

Angles had prepared an Introduction to Goalkeeping session for me. In my experience, most pros would have made the drills super hard to put me in my place. The objective would have been to finish the session by saying, "Not so easy is it, Max?"

But Angles wasn't like that. He'd really put some thought into it. His goal was to take me through all the skills in a ninety-minute session, so that I'd know what the goalies were working on and how hard and varied the job was.

He started with some light shots that I was supposed to basket catch. Easy. Then diamond catches where you jump up and catch the ball above your head. Then we ran into our first problem—shots along the ground. He wanted me to bend, get my knees behind the line of the ball, then let the ball roll into my gloves.

"Angles, mate. It's like you're passing to me. I'll just stop it with my foot."

"What if it bounces away? You'll give up a shot."

I smiled. Most goalies don't have good ball control. "Tell you what. You ever see a ball bounce off me, you can make me do a dance next time I score." The fourteens hadn't made it to a full minute of keeping the ball, but I suspected they'd be extra motivated by this week's passing and technique drills.

Angles, Robbo, and Ben fired low shots towards me, but I controlled each of them. Dropped the ball dead every time.

"But Max," whinged Angles. "What if the ball bobbles?" He meant, what if the ball hit a hole or a bump and bounced weird.

"Then I'm going to look like a dick," I said. It happened sometimes that a goalie would go to kick a ball and it would run under his foot, or bounce over, and because that could lead to a goal it was more noticeable than when it happened to anyone else. I was bored of this drill. Just because I bought some gloves didn't mean I wanted to wriggle on the ground like a worm. "Let's move on."

"Well," said Angles. "You'd give me kittens every time you stopped a shot like that, but if it works, it works. I guess we can skip the long passes and dropkicks and so on? Okay. Lads, corners and crosses."

Robbo and Ben stood on either side of the penalty box and fired high, curving balls into my zone. I had to catch the ball or punch it away. With no strikers bothering me, it was easy. "Angles," I said. "Go over there."

"Where?"

"Way out there, like you're Aff."

"You want me to coach you from left midfield?"

"Yes, please."

He didn't want to, but I was his boss. I got ready. Robbo fired in a cross. I shouted, "Keeper!" because that was the most fun part of the job, leapt, and punched the ball, letting it continue from right to left but redirecting it forward thirty-five yards. It bounced a couple of times and rebounded off Angles's shin.

"Fuck me," he murmured.

"Let's try the other side!" I called out. I expected it to be much harder, as I would be going against the grain, so to speak. Ben hit a cross and this time I double-fisted it to make sure the direction was good. "Yeah!" I yelled, as Angles took a few steps to the side to gather it. The ball hadn't gone quite so accurately, but in a real match situation it would probably have been good enough. "Right onto the counterattack. Glorious!"

"Let me try," said Robbo. I swapped places with him and hit a cross. He punched it, but couldn't get enough distance.

"Go again," I called, sending in another.

This time, he really swung his arm at it, punched with all his might. The ball spurted away behind him, spinning madly, and just barely missed going into the goal.

"Er . . . veto!" I called out, laughing. "I got lucky, I guess." We all knew I hadn't, but I didn't want them doing mad shit in games to impress me.

The next section was fascinating. Angles placed the ball on the edge of the D, twenty-two yards from goal. He told me to watch the shots as they travelled. "You'll learn to tell where the ball's going based on how far it is from the penalty spot."

I watched as the guys took shots from distance. I started to see what he meant—if you had a good mental map of the six-yard box and penalty spot, you could tell where the ball would go. *That* one was too far from the spot, so it would go wide left. *That* one was going to be close.

It was good to know, but I had a question. "But you have to dive anyway, right?"

"Yeah," said Angles. "But my coach taught me that tip, and I think it helped me save a lot of shots down the years. If you're running side to side, you can get lost. Training yourself to spot the spot is like someone's took your blindfold off."

I nodded. "Got it."

"Have you, now? All right. We're going to take shots from all sides. Save, recover, reset. Ready?"

"I was born re—hey!" Ben had taken a shot when I was halfway through my retort. "I was born ready. Fucking hell. *Now* you can start."

They took shots from the left, the right, the middle. They got closer and closer, until I was fending off shots from three opponents across the six-yard line.

A few minutes later, I was on my back, sprawled like a dead cockroach and feeling like one, too. "Fuck," I said. "That's brutal."

"It's not supposed to go on that long, Max," said Robbo. "You're er . . . you're pretty good!"

"Pretty good," said Ben. "He's better than us!"

"Come on," I said.

Angles was thoughtful. "If you weren't better used as a winger, I'd say you could make it as a keeper. You've got the reflexes, the anticipation. Obviously you're great with your feet."

"Handling," said Robbo. "Jumping."

"Yeah. The only thing I'd worry about is your positioning. I think you'd be too aggressive. Trying to play as a sweeper, trying to stay involved in the game. Mad Max, right? And your concentration, maybe. Would you get bored if you had nothing to do for five minutes? You seem the type."

Reflexes. Anticipation. Positioning. Concentration. Those sounded like attributes I would find on the completed player profiles. Attributes 4 was in the shop, available for 1,567 XP. I had it as fifth on my wish list. The more I knew about a player, the better. I had all my eggs in the PA basket. But what if I found a high-PA goalie and later found he had bad reflexes and concentration? Would he still be useful?

My phone beeped. "I've got a meeting. Thanks a lot, guys. That was awesome. Enjoy the rest of your sesh!"

We had a quick planning meeting. Me, MD, Joe, Ian Evans, and Vimsy.

Items on the agenda: Ian's thoughts on the team; my news.

Ian said he was happy with how the lads had been training and playing. I asked if he wanted to discuss the incident with Trick Williams and his injury.

Evans was clearly still pissed about it but knew he didn't have a leg to stand on. "He was injured. Better for him to come off before it got worse." It wasn't convincing, but it allowed us to move on. Fine by me.

I asked if they'd talked to Carlile. They hadn't. I pulled a face before I even knew what I was doing. Control came too late. Vimsy noticed and promised he'd try this week. I didn't want to push it too hard, because I was asking Vimsy and the coaches to do extra.

"Right," I said. "Spectrum has quit. I'll be looking for a coach to replace him. And I'll need another one for the women's team. We got the financing."

"What!" said MD.

"Yeah. That's happening. There was something else . . . Oh, yeah. I'm going to Swindon tonight. I'll check out that left back. I'm going to Newcastle tomorrow to schmooze a lawyer. That'll help with the FA situation. I'll be out and about in Manchester checking on some potential summer signings. And I want to sign a German kid."

Evans spoke. "Cutter told me about the kid. He's too small for the English game."

"He's a great prospect we can sign for free. Beggars can't be choosers."

"He's too small."

"Ian, we had this conversation. You said Lisandro Martinez was too small, and he won the World Cup a few days later. If Pascal's too small for you, you don't have to pick him. He'll train with the first team and play for the under-eighteens."

Evans looked like a bull about to start snorting, but he was much better at dialling the aggression down than me. "What's the hurry? I heard you can get him in the summer."

"Yeah," I said. "I want him now. Because of Chelsea."

"Chelsea?" said MD, his voice rising in surprise.

"You know they're buying every twenty-two-year old star in Europe? They're all getting eight-year contracts." Since the dinner with Ruth, I'd been a bit more diligent in tracking what was going on in the wider world of football. There was so much news! But Chelsea's latest spending spree was attention-grabbing. It was like watching a slow-motion car crash where the drivers were paying hundreds of millions of pounds to be in the middle of all the collisions.

"Eight?" Vimsy blinked. "Eight-year contracts? Is that legal?"

"It is for now. No one's ever thought to do it before. It's madness, or genius." Everyone in the room understood the issue. A lot could happen in eight years. Your mediocre non-league player could develop into Jamie Vardy and you'd be able to sell him or keep him depending on your needs. Or he might decide he doesn't like chasing balls around and you're stuck with an unmotivated player for almost a decade. The longest football contracts were normally five years. Six was newsworthy. The new American owners of Chelsea were doing things their own way. The main benefit of the extra-long contracts was Chelsea being able to bend certain financial rules. "UEFA are already talking about closing this loophole. So if we want to sign Pascal to a long contract, we need to move."

"Why do we want that, Max?" said MD, his voice neutral. I got the sense he didn't like this plan, but that he'd reserve judgement until he'd heard more.

"Brexit. Work permits. If we sign him right now, I don't think he'll need a work permit. He's here because of his parents, right? If I understand the rules, we can sign him before he's eighteen, no problem. But if we did a two-year deal, when we renewed his contract, the government would say no way, this guy hasn't played enough games for the first team. It's going to be a hassle. So if we want him, and we do, we sign him on a long contract."

"Long?" said MD.

"Eight," I said. Evans scoffed.

MD sighed and looked at the floor. "Can I at least see him play?"

I found my mouth being pulled into a cheeky grin. "If you see him play, you'll say no. Better if you just trust me."

"Kin hell," mumbled Evans.

That was too much. To be fair, I'd lasted longer than normal. I got to my feet and paced around. "All right," I said. "Hold your horses. I know I'm putting my neck on the line with this one. He's a player that most people in England won't *get*. He doesn't win headers, doesn't make tackles, doesn't score goals. But Vimsy, you'll love him. He's a coach's dream. You won't want him in the team, but you'll respect what he can do. Ian, this is your type of player! You want determination? Resolve? Fight? Fuck me, this kid's been fighting every day since he landed here. We're going to train him up and sell him for a profit. It's free money. All we have to do is hold our nerve when people start laughing. And who'll they be laughing at? Me. So what's the problem? I want him. He's going to pay for our training ground."

MD had his tongue playing with the side of his lips. "We've got budget for two first-team players and you want to use half on a kid who definitely won't play?"

This comment reminded me of another perk I could buy. Finances, it was called. It promised to show me some basic information about the club's income and expenditure, plus our current team salary and such data. Very nice to have all that in my head, but I could just ask MD or Joe and save the 2,000 XP. It'd be very useful to buy that if I ever thought the guys were lying to me. But for now it was near the bottom of my ever-expanding wish list.

I tried to remind MD and whoever wanted to listen that talented players could be sold for money.

"MD. Guys. Think of the squad as a meal releasing energy at different speeds. For energy, think money. Raffi Brown's a dollop of ketchup. The sugar hits fast. Mmm! Eight hundred thousand pounds, yes please, as soon as poss. Carl Carlile is a slice of buffalo meat. We need to learn how to cook it, but when we do, mmm! That'll bring in a few quid. Medium-rare, medium-term. And then, oops, what's this? Bowl of muesli. Bochum-muesli, as they call it over there. I don't really want this for dinner, not with a steak, but it's slow-release calories. Four, five years from now, ooh, look at all the money. Guys. We went through the squad. They're fucking *old*. There's about four knees and five hips between them. We have almost no assets. Who can we sell for money? Meaningful money? Almost everything you do is short-term. The next Tuesday, the next Saturday. I need to plan ahead. Signing a tiny German who might not play for three years is long-term thinking. That's why we should sign him. That's why we *have* to sign him."

This speech, one for the ages, was met with a stony silence. I'd get what I wanted, but no one would be enthusiastic about it.

I hung around to watch the sixteens and eighteens. More kids brought more kids, and there were more successes: a PA 43 left back, a PA 39 centre midfielder, a PA 36 centre back, and a PA 30 goalie. The problem was, only one of these was the right age. I hadn't said how old the visitors should be, so guys were bringing their little brothers and cousins and whatnot. Anyone who had some moves. It didn't help much with my quest to win a coupon code, but anything that brought the average PA up was most welcome.

The left back was already the most talented one we had in the entire Chester system. He was ten years old, so by the time he made it to the first team he wouldn't be good enough for the first team. But did I make a fuss of him? You bet your fucking *arse* I did.

And I met Vivek's sister. She was intrigued at the idea of her little brother playing football, and I made sure to twinkle at her. She agreed to work on her mother if any problems arose. I felt like Vivek's future was in good hands.

There was an unexpected problem, though. After two sessions, his CA was still 1. Normally, anyone with high-ish PA, like Vivek's 66, got an increase in CA in the first session. James Yalley's CA had risen after a few *seconds* of a Jackie Reaper masterclass.

Odd, but I didn't dwell on it, because I got cursemail. The curse awarded me an experience point for unlocking the achievement Overbearing Boss.

Overbearing Boss (formerly Benevolent Dictator). Watch 100 training sessions.

As you've noticed, I'd almost completely given up on the achievements system. The rewards were virtually nil and it was all geared towards management, which I'd done precious little of. So this was an eye-opener. Because when I got this one, another perk became available in the shop.

Staff Search. 500 XP. Find assistant managers, coaches, scouts, and medical staff.

Finally a purpose behind the achievements system! It signalled why certain things were happening.

Right there at the start of the eighteens session, I rushed to one side and pretended to be on a call. In fact I was thinking through the possibilities. I soon decided this was the seventh-most desirable item. On its own it had the *potential* to be useful—it was always hard to tell exactly what new screens and features would come. But what really excited me was the possibility that this would finally help me unlock the staff profiles. If I could turn all those question marks into numbers before Spectrum left the building, I'd be able to beg him to stay if he was a genius or boot him up the arse if he wasn't. And I really, really needed those numbers before I invested twenty-five K in a coach for the women's team.

That thought convinced me it had to be higher on my shopping list, but the more I thought about the alternatives, the more Staff Search got nudged back down into seventh.

I needed a lot of XP, and I needed it soon.

That night I drove to Swindon. Three hours. Three hours to watch part of a reserve team match to scout a left back we could get on loan. No transfer fee; we'd just need to cover part of his wages. John Thickes was his name.

I pulled into the car park of The County Ground. A proper stadium, 15,000, with covered terraces everywhere except the away end. The four corners were empty; there were plans to extend the stadium into two of them. Progress at Swindon!

I'd missed half an hour. The attendance, I would later learn, was thirty-five.

Some guy in the car park asked who I was. "Oh, you're here to see Thickes?" he said.

"Yep. Is he not playing?"

"He was in the starting lineup, I know that," the guy said. "Go right in. Sit where you want. Most prefer the Don Rogers Stand. We're attacking the New Town End, so you'll want to sit right of centre to get a good view of Thickes. Enjoy it, laddie!"

I did as he suggested and settled in. Thickes was a beefy boy. Obviously from good farming stock. But he was surprisingly good. I'd expected this to be a wild goose chase, some kind of joke arranged by Evans. Thickes had CA 33, but PA 47. He really could come in and do a job for us, especially if Evans had negotiated a deal on his wages.

I slipped into a pleasant daydream about this guy shoring up our left side and letting Aff be more adventurous.

Thumping challenge from Thickes! The winger bounces off him.

Thickes plays a simple pass forward to Aff.

Aff slips past his marker and presses forward. He speeds up.

Aff looks up and spots Lyons darting to the far post. But the move is a feint! Lyons charges to the near post.

The cross is delightful. Lyons leaps . . .

GOOOAAALLL!

Chester have done it! In the last minute!

It's twenty–nil against whoever their local rivals are! Warrington maybe!!

But no sooner had I thought all this than someone raced to the dugout and whispered in the reserve team manager's ear.

Within seconds, a substitute started warming up, and at the next pause in play, Thickes came off the pitch.

What. The. Fuck.

I sat there, dumbfounded, until half-time.

I'd driven three hours—one way—to see less than two minutes of my boy. No manager would willingly sub off a left back after half an hour. He wasn't injured. This manager had been instructed to do so. Why? Maybe that was Evans's revenge. Showing me what it felt like to lose a left back early in the game. But that was way too poetic for him. He wouldn't have thought it. So what was the point of asking me to watch a player and then making sure I couldn't see him? None of these clowns knew I only needed a moment to know everything about a player. This was . . . this was a plot.

I got up and wandered around to see if there were any kebabs lying around.

"You Max?"

I turned. A guy with question marks over his head was eyeing me. The name matched that of Swindon's manager. "Yep."

"You got a good look at Thickes, then? Half an hour under his belt. We're keeping him raring to go for you."

"Oh, thanks." I almost left it at that. Let the guy think I was stupid. "Actually, I just got here. There was a lot of traffic. I was lucky the chap was still in the car park."

"Simian? Yeah, he's a good lad. Looks after us. So apparently you need a left back up there. Do you want to talk about it?"

Did I want to talk about the player he literally ripped from the pitch the minute I turned up? You're fucking right I did! Whatever this game was, I wanted to learn the rules. "Yeah, course," I said, doing my best simpleton face. Which some people would probably say is my normal face.

We went to his office—clean, calm space, no view of the pitch but very nicely decorated—and chatted shit for a while. He was actually complimentary about my brief playing career. I'd done some research about him but nowhere near enough to maintain a conversation—I hadn't expected to meet him.

"So," he said. "John Thickes."

"Does he?"

The guy chuckled. "I know Ian is very keen to bring him in. Very keen, and that was *before* you got your first-choice left back injured."

"I've played against half the left backs in my division, and believe me, none of them are first choice."

That shut him up. For a second. But the guy was old school. They were born looking down on people. He couldn't help but feel superior to me despite all evidence to the contrary. "Very keen to bring him in. Now, Thickes is on big money here, obviously."

"Obviously," I said. Swindon were in League Two, a couple of divisions higher than us. I reckoned the average wage was about a thousand a week. Twice what I was getting from Chester, but a third of the offer I'd had from League One Sheffield Wednesday. Thickes was almost certainly at the lower end of the salary scale.

"But we'd be willing to let you have him for half price. Nine hundred a week."

"You would?" I said, faux ecstatic. I jumped from my seat and paced around. "Wow!" I rubbed my mouth to stop myself from laughing. If Thickes was on 1,800 a week I'd eat a hat. Then I realised my position. Yes, people were dicking me around, trying to take advantage of me. But I was still a representative of Chester FC, and it was possible I'd have dealings with Swindon as an agent.

As a player, even!

So I excused myself, saying I had to make a phone call. I went outside and found a dark crevice. I hid there until my rage and sarcasm meters had dropped to zero. I went back to the office and tried to be pleasant to the guy. I asked if I could talk to Thickes.

"He'll be getting a massage and he needs to be switched on for the post-match debrief and all that. He's a good lad, though. Don't worry about that. Wouldn't normally drop down to National League but for Ian Evans, he will."

"Fair enough," I said. "We'll let you know." I shook the guy's hand and pretended to leave. But I snuck back up into the back of the stand and watched the rest of the second half. The place suddenly seemed vaguely sinister, but I needed that XP. It was only one per minute, but I'd driven fucking miles. I wanted every drop of the stuff.

I'd decide what to do about this John Thickes debacle when I had a clear head. But I knew one thing. Someone was going to get dicked on this deal, and it wasn't going to be me.

On Tuesday morning, I slept in. I needed it. Lying in Henri's incredible bed helped me see the light. I really, really needed to unlock the Contracts tab. A perk called Contracts 1 would do just that, and the tab would show me a player's basic wage, bonuses, and clauses, but only for players from my team. And I already knew all that. But, and this was always the hope, if Contracts 2 told me what *other* teams were paying their players, that would be worth almost any price. A trillion XP? Yeah. I'd start saving up.

What was John Thickes being paid? If the curse told me he was on 1,800 a week, then Ian Evans had really got us a fifty percent discount. And I'd almost be tempted to go for it and fundraise for the money. The guy could help us prevent Scenario B.

But if John Thickes was *actually* on something like five hundred a week, as I suspected, and we were being charged nine hundred, then

Ian Evans was party to a monumental rip-off that Chester couldn't afford. What was his cut? A hundred a week? With five months of the season left, that'd be about two grand for Evans. Would he rip us off for two thousand pounds? I suppose he thought there was no way he could get caught.

I squirmed around on the freshly washed sheets. Conspiracies felt far away. The soft mattress, the barely-there pillow. I felt like a king.

That's when it came to me. I could use this Thickes fiasco to put a noose around Ian Evans's head. And if I got Contracts 2 fast enough, I'd knock the stool from under his feet. I could get Evans fired while keeping my promise not to interfere in the first team.

I stretched like a well-fed cat.

Come at the king, you best not miss.

Tuesday continued with a tiny trip to Darlington's training ground. I'd invited Bingo from the local newspaper and he took a photo of me and David Cutter. I was holding my Player of the Month trophy for December—a small glass disc with the sponsor's name above my own.

I wanted Cutter in the pic because he'd given me my chance, and because I'd earned the award playing for Darlington. In public I'd say it was a team award, but fuck that, it was all me. Still, it never hurts someone like me to be classy . . . when the option is available.

"A few years from now," I said to Cutter, who was really delighted I'd set this up, "when you're in League Two and you've emptied the rest of your boxes, you'll hang this photo up. Behind that plant, maybe."

"I'll put it behind my cactus," said Cutter. He pointed. "Right there. You and me in pricks corner, where we belong."

I went home and did some work for my coaching courses. I was sailing through it all—the only obstacle would be doing the practical work, since I'd signed up in Durham and my main opportunities for coaching were in Cheshire. This happened quite a lot, though, since footballers and coaches got moved around like military families or diplomats. It wasn't going to be an issue.

Once I'd done what I could, I rested. I needed it.

I'd suggested to Emma that if her dad got us tickets to see Newcastle United versus Leicester City in the EFL Cup that evening, I'd try to be nice to him. And the guy had come through—of course. It seemed I'd be spending my evening with Emma's dad. Trying to smile and not get sucked into controversies. It should be a rich source of XP, but it was going to take a lot of social energy.

While I watched mind-numbing daytime TV, I checked the perk shop and my wish list rankings.

RANK	PERK	XP COST
1	Playdar	8,000
2	Morale	2,000
3	Injuries	3,000
4	Contracts 1	1,000
5	Attributes 4	1,567
6	Condition	2,000
7	Staff Search	500
8	4-5-1	400
9	Player Profile 3: Nerdlonger	500
10	Match Stats 3: Action Zones	300
11	Bibliotekkers 1	1,000
12	Live Tables	1,000
13	Live Scores	500
14	Form	500
15	Finances	2,000
16	Player Comparison	630

Playdar was top because I needed to find players, fast. Like, six teams worth of players. That had to be the absolute priority.

In second place was the Morale perk, because I wanted to check on Henri. Carlile, too. From a cold, hard, business perspective, getting the most out of the players we had was crucial. I couldn't have them moping around the place. Being moody, sulking, and making every-one walk on eggshells was *my* prerogative.

Similarly, Injuries would tell me what was ailing my players. It could help me spot small problems before they turned into big ones. Across the course of a season it could easily be worth five to ten points, with obvi-ous benefits for when dealing with Physio Dean . . . or his replacement.

Attributes 4 was way up there. I needed to flesh out those player profiles.

Condition said it would tell me how fit players were. Very, very desirable, probably, but primarily useful for the first team. And if I asked Ian Evans to rest a certain player "because he looked a bit peaky," well, you can imagine. Still, I wanted it very much.

Then came Staff Search, mostly because I wanted to unlock the staff profiles. 4-5-1 was another formation, and I always wanted more formations. Nerdlonger extended a player's history page, so I wouldn't only see what they achieved last season. I mean, nice, but Wikipedia exists. Action Zones was an extra bit of data I wouldn't say no to. It seemed very slightly more useful than Bibliotekkers, which would show me the last twenty match reports from a team I was about to play. If it showed me the last twenty from *any* team, it would shoot almost to the top of the list. But with that narrow scope, I was able to wait for it.

Live Tables and Live Scores came into play when I was managing a team in a league—it would show me the "as it stands" league table and what other teams were doing. Not that urgent. Form was intriguing—it would add a field to a player profile that showed a player's last five match ratings. For example, on the profile of Max Best it would say 10-10-10-10-10 to reflect my flawless exhibition of all facets of the sport, while for Henri it would probably say 7-6-6-5-4. I knew some of the numbers because I'd seen the matches. Form was interesting and good to know but would it change my behaviour? I mean, I might pick Messi in good form over Mbappe in bad form, but I'd never pick Tim in good form over Aff in bad form.

Finally, Finances and Player Comparison were quality of life improvements. I could get the same info with a little elbow grease.

All these perks would cost me 25,000 XP. Over four hundred hours of basic grinding.

That XP would come naturally as I did my job. But time was running out for Chester's season. I needed to accelerate my XP income, and I needed to make good decisions. Rational decisions. Long-term decisions.

And above all, I needed to stick to my plan and not deviate from it. Under any circumstances.

13

FOOD CHAIN

The Premier League. The world's best and best-loved football league. Twenty teams playing each other twice to determine the winner. To win, you needed to perform better than Man City, Arsenal, Chelsea, and Liverpool. The American equivalent would be winning the Super Bowl.

Each season, the top four in the Premier League automatically qualified for the next season's Champions League. That was contested by the top teams from all the leagues in Europe. To win that, you'd have to beat the cream of the English teams, plus Real Madrid, Barcelona, Juventus, Bayern Munich, and many more. The American equivalent would be winning the Super Bowl.

Which Super Bowl would you want to win? Man City fans desperately wanted to win the Champions League. Liverpool fans would prefer to win the Premier League. It's a mad sport, innit? For most teams and most fans, winning the Champions League was the pinnacle.

The third most important trophy for English clubs was the FA Cup. That's the one where every team in England (and some from Wales) could take part. It was in the early stages of the FA Cup, when Chester lost on penalties to Oldham, that I decided to try to become a player.

Most European countries had a similar setup—League, Cup, European trophy—but England also had a fourth major cup. It was called the League Cup, and it was only for the ninety-two teams who played in the top four divisions. Chester weren't in that one. Chester were still non-league. For now.

Many clubs at the top of the food chain didn't use their best players in the League Cup. They used League Cup matches as an opportunity to give their young players a runout, or help an injured player get back from injury, and so on. For those fans, the League Cup wasn't a big deal until they found themselves in a semi-final.

But this season, two big teams had been taking the League Cup very seriously from the start: Manchester United and Newcastle United. The first to show they were serious again after years of mismanagement, and the second because they'd got serious new owners.

Serious new owners.

St. James' Park was jam-packed: 52,009 fans, almost all supporting the home team. It had probably cost Emma's dad a pretty penny, but he'd got hold of the two seats next to where he and his mate went to every home game. Whatever he paid, it was worth it. He'd tried and failed to get his daughter to go to a Newcastle match since she was old enough to say, "Can I have a pony instead?"

The four of us were positioned thusly: friend, dad, Emma, me. It was probably the best I could have hoped for. Being on the right gave me a bit more space to react how I wanted. I wasn't totally sure how I'd react. There was a lot going on in my head.

There was the wider geopolitical mess. The fact that this club had been bought by Saudi actual Arabia. Keep politics out of sport? Yeah, good luck with that. This stadium had become one of the most political places in the world. If Amnesty International wanted to highlight human rights abuses in Riyadh, they could best do that in St. James' Park.

There was the Weaver family and my relationship to it. I didn't much like the dad, mostly because he was all-in on the Saudi ownership. He didn't have any reservations about it whatsoever. It's not like anyone gave him a vote. It's not like he could have stopped the deal. But his enthusiasm. His glee. At the Christmas dinner, he'd tried to rub my nose in his team's new position at the top of the food chain. It was depressing. Normally I only encountered people like that online, in comments sections. They could be clicked away. But if I married Emma, this guy would give a *speech*. He would "give" her to me. No thanks. And I was supposed to be here charming him so that he'd help with my case with the Football Association. Fuck me, what a mess. Keep politics out of sport? I fucking wish.

And then there was me and what I felt. The politics of the takeover were grim. Sinister, even. But mostly I cared about the sport and how it had changed. Newcastle had gone from being one of the worst teams in the Premier League to being its apex predator. Six hundred billion dollars in the bank. Whatever I did with Chester, however skilfully I turned nothing into a million pounds, and one million into two, I'd always be six hundred billion behind.

But most of all, it was yet another Premier League club owned by someone with no connection to the sport, the local area, the history of the game. They were already surging ahead with the multi-club model, looking at clubs in Italy, Spain, Belgium, France. Feeder clubs in Ireland and Scotland. They were even talking about "closer ties" with Gateshead FC, a fifth-tier team. Newcastle sending all their best youth prospects to play a season in Gateshead would seriously fuck up my plans to blitz through the divisions, while simultaneously turning that club into a vassal state.

The takeover was a massive step in the direction of raising the drawbridge. If your primary reason for buying a football club was geo-political, why the fuck would you want to play against Chester, or Darlington, or even your long-standing rivals, Sunderland? Fuck that. You'd want to play against Barcelona and Bayern Munich every week.

Yep. There was another massive hand on the drawbridge lever. I could feel it.

There were 52,008 others who couldn't.

Or worse, they could, but didn't give a shit. Burn down the pyramid, so long as we're on top. That was the vibe I got. Still, I tried not to let that show on my face. For Emma's sake.

A few minutes before kickoff, Emma was primed. She was willing to be thrilled, to be swept off her feet, to be converted to football super-fandom. She was wearing a Newcastle kit, scarf, and bobble hat. She wanted the full experience.

And what an experience it was.

It was the quarter-final of the League Cup against a woefully out-of-form Leicester City. Smash these guys and Newcastle would get to their second League Cup semi-final . . . ever. They had a chance to win something for the first time since 1955.

And this was just the start. Newcastle's previous owner had been a frugal, fractious billionaire. The fans hated him with a rare passion. English football teams have been owned by despicable rich men since before the invention of the offside law, but that owner-fan relationship was especially hostile. After years of mutual loathing, the prick had finally sold up. Thanks to their new owners, nights like these would be the rule, not the exception. Going from a relationship state of minus one hundred with the old guy to plus one hundred with the new owner meant that the Newcastle fans were in a state approaching religious ecstasy.

So the noise when the players strode onto the pitch was seismic. More than half of the home fans had brought black-and-white scarves, many were waving black-and-white flags, and almost all were wearing the black-and-white home kit. While "Hey Jude" blasted around the vast stands and almost everyone sang along, an enormous banner was passed around. It must have been twenty by forty metres. In the centre was a blue star, and two cartoon ducks in tuxedos were standing on either side. Where the actual duck does all this stuff come from?

Despite the ducks, the spectacle was about as impressive as displays get in English grounds. A proper assault on the senses; Crackers would have loved it. Emma was definitely caught up in the moment, and she turned to say something to her favourite man about it. Which, yeah, didn't help my mood.

The match kicked off and I found I was getting 7 XP per minute. I wasn't quite sure what I'd expected for a League Cup match—maybe a lower amount because it was only the fourth most important trophy? Or did the curse award XP based on the highest level of the partici-pants? For example, if a Premier League team played Chester, would I still get 7 XP from that? It made a certain kind of sense. I'd still be learning from an elite team, right?

"What are you thinking?" said Emma, who had finally remem-bered that I existed.

"I was thinking that if a crow was a mafia boss, his underlings would be his *cronies*."

She didn't laugh. "Right. Who's going to win?"

I checked the tactics screens and the match ratings. Even after two minutes, some of Leicester's players had dropped to 5 out of 10, while several Newcastle guys were already up to 7. "Depends what you mean by win," I said. It wasn't the right time to blab on about the future of football—Emma merely wanted to know some things to look out for in the match. I pointed to the blue team. "Leicester are a bit of a mess at the moment. Not a very connected team. But see that guy in midfield? Number eight. Tielemans. I love him."

"Why?"

"He's the player I'd want to be if I couldn't be the player I am."

"What does that mean? What player is he?"

"He's a dream-weaver. He sculpts passes out of . . ." I tried and failed to think of what materials could be found on a football pitch. "Out of ether. He's a conjurer. You know those puzzles with matchsticks and you have to move one matchstick to make it say eighty-eight or whatever?"

"Yeah, I've seen them on Facebook."

"Right. Well, there's one where you have to draw two lines to get the same number of bananas in each section and when you first look at it, you think it's impossible. Tielemans does that with passes. He'll get the ball in the centre circle and there will be four defenders in front of him. And he'll pass the ball and it'll curve past one and then curve the other direction past two, *boop!*, perfectly into the stride of the striker and I just go 'ahh!'"

She smiled. "You just go 'ahh'?"

"Just 'ahh.' It's the most beautiful thing we can hope to see today."

But no sooner had I finished talking than a Newcastle player got the ball in the Max Best position, as it's known, and ran forward.

"Oh!" said Emma, hands by her mouth. She was taken aback by the speed of the guy. His pace (18) was impressive, but even more so was the tricky pass he played behind a defender—it cut Leicester's defence into slices. The guy on the other end of the pass struck the ball across goal—it landed at the feet of a midfielder. He had a simple chance to score but blazed his shot over the bar.

The stadium went nuts. I thought the volume was at maximum before kickoff, but somehow, they took it up a notch.

And the chances kept coming and the volume kept finding places to go. The match was one-way traffic. There's nothing worse than a one-sided contest. Okay, there's one thing worse: a one-sided contest where the team that's going to win has fans like Sebastian Weaver.

Football reveals character.

What do you do when you've got the ball? Are you a selfish prima donna (Tyson), a scaredy-cat (Sullivan), an optimiser (Pascal), or a guy who'll do a piece of skill that puts a full back flat on his arse, then help him up (me)?

What do you do when the other team's got the ball? Nothing (Tyson), run around a lot (Sullivan), follow the manager's instructions exactly (Pascal), or whatever you want because you know best (me)?

That's your character.

And the way you support your team says something about you, too. There are lots of types of fan.

The Conspiracy Theorist—believes every referee in the world, including ones not yet born, are involved in a plot to deny their team a throw-in on the halfway line in a match they're winning 2–0.

The Transfer Nut—loves gossip and rumours about transfers. Signing a player shows you're high in the food chain. Failing to sign a player shows you're slipping into irrelevance. Loves to talk about "net spend."

The Fatalist—believes their team will always find a way to lose, to screw things up. Is usually right.

The Optimist—believes their team will do well. Will come back from a two-goal deficit. Will win the game in hand. Will beat relegation. Is usually wrong.

The Analyst—pores over data looking for patterns that will back up his esoteric theories. Will say things like, "Yeah we lost three–nil but we battered them in final third entries."

And of course . . .

The Sebastian Weaver—dangle the prospect of a third-place league finish and a cup win and he'll sell you his own grandmother.

Sunday, December 25, 2022.

Christmas dinner in the palatial Weaver household. Primarily memorable for being the first time in my life I enjoyed Brussels sprouts. Had my tastebuds changed, or was Emma's mum just a way better cook than mine? I suppose the meal was also memorable, in some circles, for other things.

Quick tour of the space. A double-height, open-plan kitchen diner with big glass doors leading onto a patio, all with views of the garden. Emma's mum, Rachel, assured me it looked amazing in the spring, but I thought it was magnificent in the winter. "The trees have so much character. Henri has a tree. I've never spent so much time looking at one tree before. I think I like trees. That's new information."

"Max's dream house is a hobbit hole," said Emma. "He wants to live underground."

"Basements flood," said Sebastian, killing the conversation the way dictators kill journalists.

It might have been my imagination, but he seemed to have taken a dislike to me. If I had to guess, I'd say he thought I was flash, brash, and unserious. That I was some kind of international playboy who was banging his daughter and would soon break her heart.

I didn't mind that. It must be shit having a hot daughter and meeting the boyfriends. Or worse, *not* meeting them and having your imagination run wild. I was inclined to wind him up, just slightly, just for a laugh, by hinting that deep down, I was exactly who he feared I was.

"So what's it like being a footballer?" he asked, while Emma and Rachel were out of the room doing things.

"Oh, it's got its ups and downs. There are perks."

"What like?"

I grinned like we both knew what I was talking about. "Perks," I said, with a slight forward nod. I left it at that. Let his imagination run riot. The women came back in, hauling vegetables. "Do you need help chopping?" I said. Sebastian slinked out of the kitchen.

When we sat to eat—stuffed turkey, meat, roast potatoes, mash, veg, gravy—Rachel was amused and horrified to learn that I normally had a frozen pizza for Christmas dinner. "On your own?"

"Yeah. With a few cold beers. It's actually really nice. I like spending time with myself. I'm a great conversationalist."

"Well, we're very honoured that you'd break your traditions," she said. Ten out of ten for charm. Did I mention she was gorgeous? She was an amazing advertisement for what Emma would look like twenty years into the future. "No beer today, though, right? You've got a match tomorrow."

"I'll stick to water but I won't be playing," I said. "The manager's mad at me. So I'm taking Emma to Telford."

"Where's that?"

"Buckinghamshire."

"Ooh. Sounds dead posh!"

"Posh is the nickname for Peterborough United," I said, in case that was helpful to her.

"Oh, that's strange. Is it a rich area? I'll have to check out Zoopla." She pushed some mash into her gravy. "Why Telford?"

"Might get a job there. They're bottom of the league, but I think I can rescue them. Emma says I'm a football romantic. The story is almost irresistible. Save them from relegation, get them promoted next year."

Sebastian was shaking his head. "Why are you wasting your time? If you're bottom of the food chain you don't go *lower*. You've proven your talent. You've got to move up. Like me. Like the Toon."

"Mmm," I said. It was pretty strange being told what to do with my life by a guy who was, essentially, a rando. "Like the Toon. Right." The Toon—Newcastle United—hadn't moved up the food chain through its own efforts. It had been picked up and dropped there in murky circumstances.

His one comment, three words, was enough to tell me what Sebastian thought about the Saudi ownership. He thought Newcastle had won the lottery, which in a way, they had. They would be top of the pile until English football ate itself. But the Saudi project was everything I'd complained about that day at Sheffield Wednesday, with added nightmare fuel. If he blindly supported the new owners in everything they did, Sebastian was on Team Nick.

Emma had stopped eating and was looking at me. She didn't care about takeovers and food chains, but she would care if I didn't make an effort with her dad.

"What did you mean, like you?" I asked, inviting him to talk about his favourite subject.

He put down his fork, signalling that the topic was of utmost importance. "I started with nothing. No experience, no name. A lot of ambition, a lot of hard work. Started at a small firm, got myself noticed. Moved up in the world. Found myself in one of the biggest companies in Newcastle. Most men are satisfied with that. Not me. I wanted to take it over. Do things my way. There was a fight. Got kicked out, so I bought a small firm, fought tooth and nail, turned it into a giant. Five years ago, we bought the firm that kicked me out. Hostile takeover. The best kind. Those men who took up arms against me, they work for me now."

"That's impressive," I said, mostly because I had to say something. The story was actually horrific. Not that he'd turned himself into a major player, but that he thought I should have a similar career arc, one based on constant conflict. There was a danger my life could go that way. Sebastian was the Ghost of Christmas Future. "I don't want an ownership role, though. I know I'd lose all sense of perspective. I'd do crazy things like end relegation, turn smaller clubs into my servants, and buy hundreds of talented players just so no one else could have them. I'd vote for Super Leagues and maybe even move my club out of the country altogether!"

Sebastian, correctly, took this statement as an attack on his club's new owners and a rebuke of him, personally, for supporting them. The best part was that Emma and Rachel had no clue anything untoward had happened. He took a swig of wine. "No one," he said, and I'm sure I saw his eye twitch, "would ever take an English club out of England."

"Not that long ago, there was a very credible proposal to move a club to Dublin. Every year the Premier League tries to introduce a thirty-ninth game, one that'll be played abroad. Two NFL matches are played in London. It's not crazy. If I buy a club I have absolutely no connection to, why wouldn't I move it to the Middle East? It's my club. I can do what I want."

"Max," laughed Emma. "You wouldn't even discuss having a holiday in Italy. You said it was too hot there!" She laughed again. "The Middle East. You're so strange sometimes."

"You know what I used to like?" I said. "The Tyne-Wear Derby. Newcastle versus Sunderland. A hundred and fifty years of history, that fixture! The big rivalry. Two cities brimming with emotion, ninety minutes later, one's bursting with pride. Stories you pass down. Memories you cherish."

Sebastian squirmed. "We've still got that."

"No, you don't. That died the minute you got six hundred billion in the bank. Sunderland is like a worm to you now. It's conceivable they will never, ever beat you again. Even a draw would be beyond belief. No, that's gone. Poof. It was nice for a hundred and fifty years but nah, bin that."

"I'd rather have the Champions League than beat Sunderland."

"Ah, the famous rivalry between Newcastle and . . . Napoli. Not something you joke about with the Mackems in the local caff." Mackems are people from Sunderland.

Sebastian was top of the food chain now. He didn't have to take banter from some kid from the side-streets of Manchester. "You're jealous. We're above Man U and we'll stay there."

There it was. Team Nick confirmed.

"Maybe we shouldn't talk about politics," I said, turning away from him.

"Oh, yes, let's not," said Rachel.

"We weren't," said Sebastian, bristling. "We were talking about football."

I gave Rachel a full blast of attention. "Football's great sometimes. It's all about rivalries and competition, but it's a sport, a game, and when you love the game there's so much to love. A while ago, Borussia Dortmund had financial problems and their biggest rivals, Bayern, gave them a few million Euros to keep them going. Because even though they fight tooth and nail most of the time, they never lost sight of the big picture: there's nothing more important than the game itself." I was very pleased with my use of the tooth-and-nail idiom that Sebastian had used. He actually flinched when I said it. "Now Dortmund are healthy and a role model for other clubs, and every time I get annoyed that Bayern won the league again, I remember that they're a proper football club run by proper football people."

This was going great. I was talking earnestly, with the women eating up my words, while simultaneously throwing little jabs at Sebastian. Great fun. And because he thought he could get under my skin by talking about my boyhood team, I decided to use that. Bear in mind that while everything that comes next could, if we were being generous, be classed as the truth, I knew Sebastian would not see things that way.

"And there's a huge rivalry between Liverpool and Man United. You get in the stadium and it's thunderous. A whirlpool of rage. Crosses the line, big time. And you think, holy shit, this is dark. But come with me next time there's a match and I'll show you all those same nutjobs from both sides of the stadium, laughing and joking, collaborating to raise money for food banks. They go to the stadium to vent, it's escapism, but when there's a need, they get together. Couple of years ago there was this project to do a European Super League. Basically ripping the big clubs away from the rest, letting the small clubs die. It was sick. Liverpool and Man United were both in it, and *our* fans went nuts. They went mental. They said, you don't use *our* clubs to destroy the pyramid. No way. We have too much class for that. So they cooperated, along with fans from the other Super League teams. Fought tooth and nail for what was *morally* right. United fans invaded a match, got it cancelled. That was live on TV, hundreds of millions around the world watching. Boom. Liverpool fans, United fans, people who actually care about *football* more than their own clubs, they got together and made a *difference*. Made the world a better place. Yeah, it makes me proud, when I think about it, that most football fans can still tell the difference between right and wrong."

I'd got under Sebastian's skin, all right, and he spent most of my speech turning red. But then he did something surprising—he realised how easily he was being played and he got a grip. A steely glint came into his eye. Here was the lawyer who had built an empire. "I wonder how principled you'll feel when someone offers you a lot of money to forget your principles."

"Dad!" complained Emma, partly because his statement didn't appear to be connected to anything I'd said. "He turned down silly money at Sheffield Wednesday because he didn't like what they were planning. I *told* you."

"You told me he went for a trial and decided to stay where he was. I took it to mean he hadn't done well."

"Er . . . *no*. He slapped. Didn't you, Max?"

"I slapped," I confirmed. "Yeah, turns out, you can rent me, but I can't be bought." I gave Rachel my best twinkly eyed smile. "Who would have thought it?"

"Me," she said. "That doesn't surprise me at all, from what Emma has said." She offered me more sprouts. "Who's your favourite player?"

I was done poking the dad, so I answered honestly. "There's this guy at Leicester City. Tielemans. I love him. Looks like a schoolboy, has perfect technique. So when I was a kid, must have been about thirteen, I had my best ever minute as a player. There was a corner from over on the left. I was loitering near the edge of the box because I don't like getting involved in all that headers stuff. That's a bit, you know, agricultural. So the ball comes and it misses everyone. I step forward, bop! No, it wasn't even a bop. It's the time when you hit the ball and it doesn't even make a noise. It happens once a year. Ball flies." I demonstrated with a Brussels sprout. "Top-left corner. Perfect. Glorious. Round of applause for tiny Max. Thirty seconds later there's another corner. Guy hits the ball exactly the same. I'm in the same place. It's all the same. Bop! That once-a-year moment, twice in a minute. Top-left corner. No applause, because everyone's freaking out. Are we in a time loop? That was me against my mates in a park in Manchester. This guy at Leicester—he does it! He does what I did. In a top match! It felt so strange, like I was watching myself. Boop, top corner. Minute later, boop, top corner. It was unreal. Started to blur in my memory as soon as it happened. What was me, what was him? It was disconcerting, but beautiful. I don't want to think about human rights when I think about football. I just want to be happy. I want to be a boy again. A boy kicks a ball good and creates a memory. I wonder, sometimes, if any of the others even remember it. They all had their own little moments of glory. No, though, because I remember some of *theirs*. Ste K scored a scissor kick with his first touch for the school team after he'd just told me he didn't feel ready to play. Reece was so agile we used to have to think up different names for his saves. It was simple. It was pure. Tielemans is the closest I get to feeling that." I sighed and realised I'd forgotten where I was. I was surprised to see two hot blondes gawping at me.

Emma slapped her mother's arm. "See? I told you."

"I never thought I'd say this," said Rachel. "But can we talk more about football?"

"Let's talk about Christmas," I said. "I used to be so insane about the presents, my mum would let me open one the night before. Just to shut me up. How do you guys do it?"

Back in the present day, Newcastle didn't let Tielemans have a kick, and they battered Leicester. A combination of snatching at chances and great goalkeeping kept the score to 0–0 at half-time. I rushed off to the toilet so that I wouldn't have to speak to anyone.

While queueing to pee, I sighed.

It was perfectly natural for fans to be excited that their team would get the best players, have the best facilities. It would be weird if they didn't. Fans are tribal—they want their club to do well. But this take-over had scrambled the brains of these guys. The Newcastle fans had embraced the entire Kingdom of Saudi Arabia as part of their tribe, and that was next-level bonkers.

I'd never understand that mentality. But for the sake of Emma, I'd be willing to take a step towards her dad.

All he had to do was say something like, "Being a Newcastle fan was shit for a long time; it's a dream to have an ambitious owner; I wish it wasn't an authoritarian state; there are no good billionaires and these guys are no exception; all things considered I've been a Toon fan all my life and will be until the day I die; I'll support the team but not the owner."

If he said that I'd cross the bridge. No problem.

But he didn't.

Just before the second half kicked off, I slunk back into my seat, eyes hooded, expression fixed. I was thinking about three things.

First, Emma. I didn't need to like her dad, or ever see him again, except that I was supposed to ask for his help with my case. But what can I say? Being around him was a drag. How could I let Emma know without hurting her feelings?

Second, Tielemans. The entire Leicester team was playing like shit, and he was no exception. The tactics, 4-2-3-1 against Newcastle's 4-3-3, seemed right, based on the players they had. So why were they dogshit? Morale? Form? I *had* to unlock those perks. I'd get about 650 XP from this match. An enormous amount.

Finally, Chester. Whatever I did, however smart I was, Newcastle would always have six hundred billion dollars more. How could you compete with that?

I could start by being ruthless. Being there in the giant stadium had smashed home the point:

There. Was. No. Time.

Newcastle weren't spending money wildly. They weren't making mistakes. They'd picked a manager who would improve players. They were improving the first team and everything around it carefully and thoughtfully. It seemed like everyone at the club had bought into the new demand for excellence.

Getting people on board wasn't as easy as it seemed.

Physio Dean's bedside manner was abysmal. Tyson had cost me a coach and five good players. Sullivan was a dead end. Spectrum was lucky he'd already quit. Vimsy wasn't taking care of the players. Some of whom were money pits, while Carl Carlile was giving the team 6 out of 10. Henri was supposed to be the best striker in the league and hadn't even looked like scoring in his first two games. And Ian Evans?

I'd made a promise to Mike Dean and a promise to myself that I would stop agitating for Evans to be fired. There was still half the season left. Plenty of time for him to turn things round. Everyone else? Everyone else needed to get with the programme. Yes, even Henri.

And there was more. I was being too nice to the other teams in Cheshire. The small outfits like Broughton and Ellesmere. I'd hoped to find players at five-a-side and in random matches. But most likely, the best amateur players would be at some small club already. I'd been too social, too wishy-washy, hoping to avoid doing what I knew I needed to do.

I needed to go and teach these minnows about the food chain. I'd gobble up every ounce of muscle they had grown. Strip them bare. Turn their work into my profit. I had to fight tooth and nail for my club.

"Max," whispered Emma, leaning over me with her hand in my hair. "Are you all right?"

I stood, put my hand on her back, and admired her. How could a moral vacuum produce a daughter so beautiful? "Yeah, great, why?"

"You look . . . unhappy."

"No. Just got to make some hard decisions."

"Oh. Gotcha." She looked around the stadium and smiled. "Is this a good atmosphere?"

"Yeah. They'll blow the roof off when they score. Are you glad you came?"

"With my two favourite men? Absolutely. I'd even think about coming again."

My lips twitched. "That'll be you and your dad, then. Next time I come here, I'll be on the pitch."

She gave me an amused lip curl. She didn't know loads about football, but she knew Chester were many, many years from playing in this stadium. "Oh? And I suppose you'll score two identical goals and make us all swoon."

I grinned. She always managed to cheer me up. "You remember that story?"

"I didn't realise the guy from that story is the same number eight who's playing now. Dad reminded me when you ran off. When are you going to ask him about your case?"

"Maybe in the pub after you've won and he's happy."

"Okay!"

Newcastle scored twice and progressed into the semi-finals, where Man United and Newcastle would play teams from further down the food chain, meaning the most likely final would be between the two predators.

Sebastian was gloating already. He was drunk, on victory and on beer. "Man U are shit," he proclaimed. "You've got no strikers. You've got no midfield, no defence." He laughed. "First trophy since 1955. First of many. Way aye the lads!"

I remained impassive. Then I looked at Emma and asked if she wanted to come with me so the guys could stay out drinking. Emma was ecstatic that I was being so considerate to her dad, which was funny because I had just ruined his mood in a big way.

"I'll just powder me nose," she said, leaning in for a tiny lip smack. She went to do girl things.

Sebastian tried to poke me in the chest but missed. "This'll interest you, Max. Just heard from a friend that the Qataris are in pole position to buy your team."

"I don't think Chester's for sale, mate."

He managed a fake chuckle. "You're a Man U fan, Max. You've got shit owners, like we had. You've suffered, like we did. Now you'll get ones who'll put money in, instead of taking it out. They want to help United get back on its feet. You must be thrilled."

"No, it sounds like a waking nightmare."

"Oh, does it? Winning the league again, finally? Winning the Champions League?"

I shrugged. "Best if I don't talk politics with my girlfriend's dad."

He didn't like *that*. "It's not politics, you . . ." He got a grip again. A slight smile acknowledged that I'd landed a jab. *Good shot, young man!* "This takeover is going to happen. What are you going to do? Stop supporting your team? Sit with your hands under your arse while they're scoring goals?"

"Teams should be owned by the fans. United's big enough to stand without help." I remembered I was supposed to be asking *him* for help. Now was a shit moment, but it was the best I was ever going to get. Sebastian knew it was coming; he tensed—I realised that Emma had done all the work. I just needed to ask. If I asked, he'd agree. But he wouldn't *offer*. And, I realised, I wouldn't ask. I wouldn't ask *him*.

But.

It wasn't just about me. There was Emma—she'd like it if I acknowledged that her dad was, like, useful or whatever. She put up with so much weirdness from me. It would be a nice thing for me to do. Good for my relationship. Lose a little to gain a little. And it would be good for Chester. One tiny question could end this registration farce. And yes, it'd be a poke in the eye for Old Nick.

There. Three reasons. Fine.

Sebastian saw the moment I decided to ask, and now it was time for him to score a tiny victory. There was more than a slight twinkle in his eye as he said, "Everyone needs help, Max. Even Manchester United. That's why they've gone cap in hand to Qatar. They'll be good owners. They'll clear the debt, rebuild the stadium. It's nothing to be ashamed of, asking for help."

"While we're on the topic of help," I said, looking a bit downcast. "And since you're one of the biggest experts around here . . ." His eyes lit up. "Which way's the nearest exit? I'll wait outside."

On Wednesday morning, I watched training. Carlile was distracted. Henri was dogging it. Evans and Vimsy were standing next to each other on the touchline, doing almost nothing. The scene was so set up to provoke me that I looked around to check if Emma's dad was there, masterminding it.

We don't have time for this!

I called Vimsy and he came over. "Have you talked to Carlile?" I asked.

"No, not yet."

"Got it," I said, nodding. "You're planning to leave when Evans does, then."

He took a half-step back. "No! What? Why would you say that?"

I inhaled. Gave myself time to get past my first impulse, which was a lot of shouting. The thought came to me that the team's CA was in recession because the pair had checked out. They didn't care. No, they cared, but not enough to put in the extra work. Every second that they were idle, a hundred other teams pushed themselves a little bit further into the distance. "Got it," I said again. "Yeah. I see." I swallowed a lot of things I wanted to say, then strode over to Evans. "Ian, mate. Went down to look at the left back the other night. Didn't see anything of him, so obviously I'd need to go again. Six-hour round trip. Pretty unpleasant stuff."

"I'm in the middle of training, Best. What do you want?"

"The manager there said he'd give us the fifty percent discount that you talked him into. Great work. But, er, this is embarrassing. I was so tired from the endless drive that I can't remember the wage he said. Do you know what Thickes is on?"

"No," he said, suddenly shifty.

"Oh," I said, looking unhappy. I brightened up with a click of my fingers. "Just remembered! I asked Joe to get Swindon to send over the loan details. It'll be on there, won't it?"

"I imagine so."

"Yeah," I said, not pretending to be anything other than his boss looking sternly at him. "It'll all be there in black and white."

Evans's normal expression—hostility—didn't change. Except at the edges, inside the creases, where most people wouldn't notice. I saw it. He was guilty as fuck and he knew I knew. How would he get out of this mess?

On Thursday afternoon, the fourteens had training with Spectrum. I'd missed the Tuesday session because I was in Darlington.

When the kids started warming up, I saw Tyson's profile. His teamwork had dropped a point. With me constantly monitoring and badgering him, it'd risen to 4. Now after just one unsupervised session, it had fallen to 3. Unacceptable. It didn't matter if his hidden coaching numbers were high, Spectrum was having a negative impact on the only kid with a high enough PA to become an asset. It was time to clean house.

"Mate," I said, drawing Spectrum away from the kids. "On Tuesday, did you let Tyson do whatever the fuck he wanted?"

"What? No."

"Some sort of cool uncle thing? *Max isn't here. When the cat's away, the mice will play.* Something like that?"

"No."

"I believe you. Millions wouldn't. I think, to be on the safe side, we'll leave it there."

"Get on with the session, you mean?"

"No. That's *not* what I mean."

"Are you . . ." he scoffed. "Are you sacking me?"

"Can't sack you, mate. You already quit! No, why don't you take this time to go work on your job applications? That'll be a better use of your time than being somewhere you don't want to be."

"But—"

"Thanks for your service." I walked away and signalled that Tyson should join me. "Tyson. Let me ask you a question. Were you dicking around in the last training session?" He looked towards Spectrum. "Don't worry about him. He's out."

"What?"

"Were you dicking around, yes or no?"

"No."

"Okay. Why don't you gather your stuff and go home?"

"What about training?"

"You're not in it. That's what I'm trying to say."

"Not in it?"

"That's right. We should probably have a sit down with your dad where I can explain my decision. Won't take long. We all know the score."

"Can I finish the session?"

"No. This will be preparation for the match on Sunday. If there is one. We might have to forfeit."

"Forfeit?"

"Don't worry about it. Off you pop. Sullivan. Quick word, please."

While what was left of the under-fourteens processed the shock of seeing me ask people to leave, I made some phone calls.

My first was to Jude, the guy I was paying to coach Broughton. Now I'd pay him to coach Chester. Part-time, trial basis. He was beyond keen.

My second was to Nice One. He didn't pick up, so I left him a voice message. "It's time to bring Benny home," I said.

Finally, I called Terry, the guy who coached the Knights. "Can you help me out tomorrow? Take a couple of sessions?"

"I'll do it if you come on Sunday," he said.

"What's on Sunday?"

"Our tournament! In Crewe."

I pinched my nose, trying to remember. It clicked. "Ah, right. Wait, I thought that was off. Club didn't have the money to send you or something."

"Someone donated the four hundred quid," he said. "Anonymously."

"Huh," I said.

Terry laughed. "Max. I know it was you. You're the only person MD told. We don't go round announcing our poverty. Not when it makes us look heartless."

"Oh."

"Why did you do it?"

Why had I? Leaving the cash on Inga's desk with a printed note seemed like weeks ago. "You told me they need to compete to progress. You're the only part of the club that's competing and progressing."

"Yeah, but . . . Well, anyway. Thanks. It'd mean a lot if you came. There will be some frame football. Remember I told you about that?"

"I do." The Chester Knights, frame football, it was all great. But it wasn't going to help me shape the future of football. Wasn't going to help me cross the drawbridge while it was still there. "I don't think I'll have time," I said.

"Oh. I understand." He paused. "Still, the kids are buzzing about it. This Crewe tournament is like their Champions League final. It's a big deal."

"Awesome," I said, though I wasn't really listening. "Talk soon."

I looked around at the under-fourteens. There wasn't a lot of talent there. I could send them home or use them to do experiments. The smart thing would have been to send them home. Save my energy. When the five rebels were back, we'd have a team with pockets of potential. Future? Now *there* was a kid who could take me places. There was a kid worth spending time on.

"Guys . . ." I said, looking at their little faces. Their fearful, apprehensive faces. I'd just cut two of their teammates *and* their coach. I was *on one*. For some reason, I thought of Sebastian Weaver. The Ghost of Christmas Future. *He'd* send them home, no doubt about it. Gloat about his decisiveness, too.

But this lot were good as gold. They didn't have the talent, but they had the attitude. They wanted to learn. Wanted to give me what I asked for. No, they didn't get cut-throat Max. They got romantic Max, the guy who wanted to be a dream-weaver. "Guys. Who are you playing on Sunday?"

"Newton Athletic Eagles," said someone.

"What formation do they play?"

"Four-four-two, normally."

"They got any good players?"

"Couple."

Huh. Might be worth checking out. I nodded. "All right, listen up. I went to a match the other day to see one of my favourite players and he barely got a kick. So I want you dudes to show me what he didn't. Four volunteers? Great. Line up here. Couple of yards between each of you. When I say 'go,' run from side to side like you're doing widths. Not all the same speed, not all the same direction. Joey, go the other side of those four. When they're running, I'm going to try to pass the ball through the mayhem, to you. Yeah? Is it clear? Ah, it'll be clear once it starts."

I whistled and the four kids started running from side to side. I hesitated—this was an insanely dumb drill—then cleared my mind. I rolled the ball through the forest of legs. I stuck my tongue out. Dumb, but satisfying!

"Let me have another go," I said. While the kids formed a video game–style obstacle, I jinked my shoulders around, shifting my weight, then suddenly I wrapped one foot around the other and span the ball to the other side.

The kids went "Wroar!"

"Right," I said smugly. "After you pass, you become the first obstacle. And everyone else moves down one slot." I did the same, becoming the first side-to-side obstacle. "Dan, your turn. Feed the ball through to the other side."

Dan tried, failed, and we all moved one slot along. The guy at the back ran around to join the massive queue of players waiting to pass.

"Form another set!" I said, and half of them ran off to do that. The drill contained its own kinetic energy. Perpetual motion.

I blew my whistle. "Drill tweak! Add a pass at the start. Dan, pass to me here."

He passed to me and I had to turn, check the moving obstacles, and then play the long through-pass.

The drill got more and more elaborate. We did it for fifteen minutes, then took a break.

"That was class, guys, well done. Fifty quatloos to anyone who plays a pass like that on Sunday."

"Mr. Best!"

"What?"

"That drill was top! I've never seen it before. What's it called?"

I bit my bottom lip before smiling. "I just invented it. It's called The Dream-Weaver."

14

ROOT AND BRANCH

I was plagued by dreams of loneliness and turmoil, only remembering flashes when I threw the covers back and put my feet on the floor. An empty fridge when I was supposed to be hosting a party. The unsmiling, unfriendly faces of my guests—nobody I'd ever met. An inexplicably oppressive atmosphere. Confusion. Why had I invited them? Why couldn't I make them leave?

I plodded downstairs and made a tea. I planned to bring it back to bed and get a few more hours' rest. But I glimpsed Henri's tree, the one I'd been getting fixated on, and remembered some more dream.

I was climbing a big tree, but no matter how many times I stepped onto the next branch, I was always at the same height. There was something good above me, something I wanted. But I couldn't get closer.

I took my phone and cup and went outside to stare at the real thing. It was bare, of course—even I understood the seasons. About three metres tall, covered with wonderful knobs and bumps.

I FaceTimed Henri. He was frowning as he picked up. "Max? Is this a bootdial?"

"No. Listen—"

"We have training in a couple of minutes."

"Is Ryder there?"

"Yes."

"Hand over the phone."

He did. "Max?"

"Captain. I need to talk to Henri. Fine him for being late and we're going to have a problem. Good?"

"Good."

That reminded me of something I'd learned in Darlington but hadn't participated in. "You collect fines from the players and that? And you use it for nights out and stuff?"

"Yes."

Why was I dipping into my private accounts to pay for the Knights to go to their tournament when those first-team fuckers had a fat, juicy pot? "Can we discuss that sometime, please?"

"Yes, sure."

"Great. Any questions?"

"Are you naked?"

"No. Bye."

The phone was passed back. "Henri. Did you plant this tree?" I held up the camera.

"Yes. The garden as it was was paved. Practical, but conspicuous. Unyielding. Abrasive. Nature bends. Trees are strengthened by the storm. You like my crab apple, Max?"

"I do. Why . . ." I wasn't sure how to word my question. "Why is it here?"

"There? It is where I chose it to be. There, it will offer shade and privacy, should I ever lose my mind and wander around in God's pyjamas. And of course, it's the sunniest spot."

"Sun, right. You couldn't put it by the house. Not enough sun. They need sun."

Henri laughed. "You talk as though this is all news."

"I saw the pictures in school but I've never really thought about it before. I thought you could plant anything anywhere. Emma's mum tried to tell me some things but it's so complicated." I thought about my dream. The enormous tree that had swallowed me. "But what if the neighbour plants a bigger tree? And this one doesn't get light?"

"It will die. Max, are you okay? Would you like me to go there?"

"No . . . no. You need to train. But look, how do you . . . How can I . . . How do you help the tree? Can I give him some food or something?"

"The best you can do is plant the right tree in the right spot. The crab apple loves where I have chosen. A woman of my acquaintance told me to choose something more ornate, more showy. No, I said. Look around. The crab apple loves the area. As you see, I chose wisely. It is a wonderful specimen. Its beauty is a reflection of my own impeccable taste. When a tree is young, you may stake it. That helps it grow strong enough to survive all but the strongest of winds. You may nurse it through a drought. Mostly you leave it alone. Sometimes it appreciates a prune."

"Pruning. That's where you cut bits off."

"*Oui.* Branches that grow the wrong way." *Spectrum.* "Branches that compete with others." *Tyson.* "Branches you deem unaesthetic." *Physio Dean.*

"Branches that don't produce enough crabs," I suggested.

"If producing crabs is important to you, yes."

"Can you cut it all back to the start and grow a new tree?"

"No. And you must never prune more than thirty percent of a tree." Huh. Good to know.

"You know a lot about trees. Why?"

"The real question is, why don't you?" Henri smiled. Then he lowered the phone and peered downwards so it was like he was checking out my crotch. "No, the real question is: why are you naked?"

"I'm not," I said. "I'm wearing your crocs."

I went back inside and made another tea. The first one had frozen by the time I remembered to drink it.

I called the care home and asked if Anna was around and active. Soon I was asking her about my dream and what it meant.

"Dreams about climbing trees," she read aloud from some website, "show you are planning and using resources to achieve a goal. The dream reminds you that helping other people won't lead to personal benefit." I heard what sounded like her taking her reading glasses off. "Does that mean anything?"

"I gave somebody some money and it was a nice thing to do but realistically it's not going to do them any good. It's just a nice day out. And I'm not exactly loaded. The money could have bribed four kids to bring their mates. Or paid for eight hours of Jude. Or been used to get me a massage after grinding for a few days in a row. Let me get right back at it. Do you know what I mean? There was this kid. He said no good deed goes unpunished. Every time I try to do something nice, it usually bites me on my arse. And when I'm a dick, or selfish, that goes well."

"You have my permission to be a selfish dick," she said.

"Come on," I said, laughing. "That's not what I meant."

"Yes, it was. This nice day out you paid for. Why don't you sneak along and see how nice it is? See what effect your good deeds truly have. Humm?"

"Maybe," I said. "I'm quite busy on Sunday."

"Busy. Too busy to walk Solly, after all he did for you."

"What?"

"I *know*, young man. I know. Now, tell me. *Soccer Supremo*. How do I beat Newcastle? They buy the players I want."

"Ask me again in five years."

"I shall hold you to that." She hesitated. Her voice lost its usual strident tone. "Take care of yourself, Max. If you need a massage, get a massage. If you need to stop climbing the tree for a day or two, do so." She exhaled, gathering her strength for what she needed to say next. "And if you would like to spend some time with your mother and I, you are always welcome." She exhaled again, using all the energy she had stored in her roots. "Especially if you want to read out articles about *FBoy Island*."

"*FBoy Island!*" I laughed. "What the f . . . Oh. I think I just got the premise. Don't tell me my mother watches a show called *FBoy Island*."

"Max, she's obsessed. And Solly loves it. He thinks he can tell the FBoys from the Nice Guys. So you see. Whatever your problems are, they pale in comparison. They really do."

Henri didn't have a calendar on the wall. I asked him why, once, and he said, "Because I am not a Mayan."

So I whipped my phone out and went to the app. Noticed how the ends of months loom like cliff edges. It was mid-January. Henri had agreed to let me stay in this house rent-free until the end of January. He'd probably extend that, seeing as how I was working hard to create lots of football, but I needed to find an affordable place in Chester and let Henri get a paying tenant.

My bank balance was okay, and Darlington would be giving me 6,500 pounds soon—reward for my stupendous December. And in February they'd have to pay me two grand for my half hour of work in the Scarborough match. No doubt Darlo would be a lot more careful throwing around goal and assist bonuses in the future! (Thinking about it, if I'd stayed at Darlo, we'd have had to renegotiate my wages or I would have bankrupted them.)

So I had a buffer, but once my goal money was gone, it would be *gone*. I was on five hundred a week at Chester, plus 165 a week from being an agent. The only increase in those numbers likely to come in the near term was if Altrincham wanted to sign James Yalley. I was planning to ask them that evening.

But first, I was off to Broadhurst Park to watch FC United's training session. This was a kill-eight-birds-with-one-stone kinda scenario, and the biggest bird was getting to see Ziggy's updated player profile for the first time in ten weeks.

Ten weeks! It was crazy to think I hadn't seen him play for that long, but so much had happened, and Darlo trained and played at the same time as FCU.

So what did I expect? How much progress?

On the negative side, FC United were in the seventh tier. Based on what Jackie had told me about player progression plus my own observations and common sense, Youngster's training at tier-five Altrincham would add more CA per day than Ziggy's, with tier-six Chester being in the middle.

There was also the fact that Ziggy had played no games since the little burst he'd had around his debut. Most matches, he didn't even make the bench. Lack of game time would suppress his progress.

On the positive side, lack of game time meant he could work harder on his fitness. I expected a fair chunk of green in his physical attributes. I knew he'd been hitting the weights because every time I called him he was either coming or going from his local gym.

Facilities were a point in FCU's favour compared to Chester. FCU had a grass pitch *and* an all-weather one. Perfectly flat, great for passing drills, and as far as I could tell, they owned it. The stadium was right next to it, with its big *FC UNITED OF MANCHESTER* sign. It was impressive. Chester trained at a credit card company.

Finally, the most positive aspect of all: Ziggy was being trained by Jackie Reaper. Even without the curse numbers, I was growing increasingly convinced that Jackie was a top coach who should have been at a big club. Exactly how much CA per day he was worth I wasn't sure, but I knew he was miles ahead of Vimsy and the guys at Darlington.

So when I arrived in North Manchester, I wandered to the side of the pitch and watched. They were doing some transition drill, and it was so fast, so intense, so serious that it made me slightly depressed. This seventh-tier team was doing training sessions light-years ahead of what I was seeing at Chester.

But I didn't dwell on it—if Jackie Reaper was truly the Chosen One, then we'd have this kind of session at Chester from the summer.

And then I wouldn't feel like I was walking around with a ball and chain around my ankles.

Ziggy was zipping around, working hard, totally focused.

BARRETT "ZIGGY" GRAVES		
Born 13.1.1999	(Age 24)	English
Acceleration 6		
	Handling 1	Stamina 7
	Heading 8	Strength 8
		Tackling 4
	Jumping 7	Teamwork 16
Bravery 4		Technique 8
	Pace 6	Preferred foot R
	Passing 8	
Dribbling 5		
Finishing 17		
CA 24	PA 58	
Striker		

Constantly doing running drills had improved his acceleration and pace, although he was starting from such a low point that it would have been hard not to improve. He was still slow, but if you were asking him to chase long punts, you'd set your team up wrong.

His jumping had stopped improving, so maybe he'd hit a hard limit on that one. His heading was better, though. If I sent a perfect cross onto his head and he tried to redirect it into the goal, would the curse use his heading or his finishing? I still didn't know!

Because of the way he played, his improvements in his dribbling and tackling wouldn't be seen much in matches. But all green was good green. There would be one or two times a match when he'd try to tackle someone.

His passing and technique were still below average, but again, as a striker he wouldn't need to hit fifty-yard diagonals. He wasn't a dream-weaver.

Stamina and strength were important for a player in the Northern Premier League Premier. Those defenders tried to grapple you, grab your shirt, wrestle you. It didn't happen much to me because I was usually running at my opponent. Ziggy would spend most of the match facing the same way as the defender and referees allowed a bit of inter-team hugging. If he didn't want to be the little spoon, he needed to fight back.

And finally, his CA. Twenty-four! I vaguely remembered hoping he'd hit 20 by January, and now he had. He needed to get to 30 to become a viable option for the first team, but he wasn't far off. At 40 he'd be ready for Chester. I'd planted him in the right place. Pleasing. The raw numbers didn't tell the tale, though. He'd been given a chance and he was jumping at it with rare enthusiasm. I knew he'd had the odd beer, but adding more than 20 CA points in ten weeks struck me as proof of tremendous sacrifice and diligence.

But the best thing was seeing him score! Finally! These little drills ended with shots being struck towards half-sized goalposts. There weren't any goalkeepers, and in the drill it wasn't the shot that mattered; it was the build-up. After a goal, the drill simply restarted and they did it again. But Ziggy scored! A few times! Putting the ball in the net was as easy for him as putting on a Kappa tracksuit was for Jackie.

That said, my dude could have scored twice as many. If Ziggy had time to think, he'd control the ball and try to hit a good shot. He was most effective when he acted on instinct. His one-touch finishing seemed excellent. It reminded me of someone . . . some old video I'd seen.

My plan was to hang around until the end of training and take my dudes to lunch, but my dudes had other ideas. Ziggy left the session and ran over to me. "Max, did you bring your boots?"

"Hi, Ziggy."

"Yeah, hi. Boots?"

"I always have a pair in the car."

"Mint. Hurry up, will you? We need you for the next bit. Ta."

Jackie Reaper up to mischief, no doubt. Well, there wasn't enough mischief in my life. I went to get my kit bag.

"All right, lads," said the baldest of FCU's many bald coaches. Jackie, head both gleaming and steaming in the freezing cold air, seemed to be in charge of the session—there was no sign of Neil, the actual manager. "Everyone remembers Secret Agent? He's made quite a name for himself since I taught him the half-turn. Haven't you, Max?"

"Yeah, I'm massive."

The FC United lads liked that. They'd always liked my cocky attitude. Why hadn't Jackie got me involved *here*? Taking a fan-owned team based on the principles of Man United and making them more successful than the real Man United? That'd be a hell of a story.

"Let's just check you really learned it, though, yeah?"

"Yeah. Let me do your little drill. It's not like I have a whole fucking football club to run."

Jackie smiled and got everyone in position. It was the exact same scenario as the day I'd brought Ziggy to the club. I had to take the ball on the half-turn and pass between two defenders into the path of a fast attacker called Sandro.

I got into position, while Jackie grabbed a chunk of my tracksuit top. He'd try to stop me. "You're not going to kick me up the arse, are you?"

"Me? Never." He grinned.

So this was interesting. Last time, I was sure he wouldn't foul me. I was a rando in a suit. This time I was one of the best players in non-league football. He definitely *would* try something to stop me. Something he planned to teach to his players.

"Ready, Secret Agent?"

I yawned. "Mmm," I said, looking bored.

A coach passed the ball to me, and suddenly Jackie had two hands on my top, grabbing and pushing me as hard as he could. I twisted myself towards him as though resisting, but unseen by Jackie I was flicking the ball up once, twice, three times, then backwards over his head. At the exact right moment, I spun the other way, out of his grasp, dashed onto the ball, and finished the move with a disgustingly pretty rabona flick—one foot behind the other—sending the ball neatly through the defenders in front of Sandro.

You can imagine the reaction from the players.

I yawned again. "Wait. Were we supposed to be practising half-turns?"

Jackie glared at me. Nutmegging him in front of some university students was one thing. Doing whatever the fuck *that* was in front of all his players was . . . maybe too much. No—the smile arrived late, but it arrived. "I asked for it . . ." He turned to his players and jabbed a thumb at me. "I spent weeks trying to persuade this prick to go for a trial. He said he was dogshit." He shook his head and checked how interested the guys were. Very, it seemed. "Max, you're crushing the National League North. What is it, ten goals in five games?"

"Mate," I said dismissively. "I don't count my stats like some weirdo. But if I did, I'd say five starts, three subs, eleven goals, four assists."

It was easy to tell the guys who didn't know who I was—they were the ones whose heads were literally exploding. My stats were *up there.*

"All right, all right," said Jackie with a smile. "You've come a long way in a short time. What's one thing you've learned that might help our lads?"

"Jesus," I said, bravado gone. That question had done me in. Jackie was a great coach and a guy who was interested in learning more and being better. Who else did I know who would ask a question like that? Jackie's way of thinking was completely missing at Chester. Being thoughtful wasn't quite the right vibe in front of all these guys. I tried to step back into cocky confidence. "Do you want me to spout some guff about winning duels or keeping shape?"

Slightly exasperated smile. "No, Max. Be honest."

I thought about it. "I don't know if this is helpful, lads, but the first thing I did at my trial in Darlington was shoot. Goalie was coming off his line, stopping us playing through balls. He was getting everything. Suffocating us. So I got the ball, shot from forty, forty-five yards. I scored, but that wasn't the point, really. It was about stopping him coming off his line. He didn't try that again. We dominated. Bosch. I've been doing that ever since. My first one-on-one with any left-back. I normally just blow past him. Surprise him with my speed. Bosch. They don't go forward after that. They've got to stay with me as much as they can, otherwise I'm through on goal whenever I get the ball. Another thing's corners. First one in a game I normally shoot. And free kicks. First one's a shot. Keeps goalies pinned back the rest of the match. Know what I mean? Rest of the match I'm flexible. Do what's best in the situation. But the first thing is, I show you my best move. If you can deal with it, good for you. But if you're dealing with me, you're not doing anything else."

"The Max Best Way, ladies and gentlemen. But Max. What if you aren't fast, skilful, or have a shot like a mule's kick?"

"Do you mean: *what if I'm Ziggy?*"

"Ooh," said everyone. The guys nearest him gave him digs.

A grinning Ziggy gave me a pair of *V*s. I smiled at him; the memory I'd been searching for finally dropped from the recesses of my mental vending machine into the flap where I could reach in and grab it. My brain had just needed a good shake. "I told Jackie you could turn into the Manc Chicharito. But there's another Mexican you could play like: Hugo Sanchez." His reaction told me he'd never heard of the dude. Nobody else had, either, including Jackie. I bet Raffi Brown would have known him. "Top player," I explained. "Striker. Real Madrid. There's a video that did the rounds a while back. Quality's shit, but the title says it all. 'Hugo Sanchez, Thirty-Eight Goals from One Touch.'"

"What?" said one guy.

I nodded quickly, amused. "Yeah! That's what I thought. Thirty-eight from one touch, what does that mean? Here's what it means: thirty-eight goals in one season. And every goal was a first-touch finish. A few pens, a few free kicks, but mostly, ball comes into the box and he hits it first time. Bosch! Bosch! Bosch! Think about it. Goalie has no time to set himself. It's lethal."

"You think I can do that?" said Ziggy.

I gave him my best warm-wash voice and looked at him like we were alone on FBoy Island. "I know you can."

In fact, I *didn't* know that. I was pretty incredibly certain he *couldn't*. But from the look in his eye, I knew Ziggy would try.

After a tiny and rare moment of confusion, Jackie checked his watch. "All right. Go and cool down. Big game tomorrow."

I wanted to complain. He'd made me get my boots on, and all this talk of pinning goalies back and one-touch finishes had made me itch to get a game going. But I kept my mouth shut.

I went into town with Jackie and Ziggy. We wandered around for a bit, then chose a spot to have lunch. Food was the last thing on my mind. I think I ordered something brown.

"Oh, God," I said. "Manchester is quality. It feels good to be home."

"I met a player," said Jackie. "He was at a club out in Malaysia. Seemed like a nice gig, nice people, all that. But he told me he used to fly home four times a year."

"Four?" I thought about that. It seemed excessive.

"Yeah. He said he'd worked it out. If he went home any less than four times a year, he'd start cracking up. He's got a few half-friends, no family. No roots. Uproot a tree, it dies. He used to go home, soak up all the nutrients. *Bake Off.* Corra. Night at the bingo with his mum and a curry. Sort his head out."

"Interesting," I said. I wasn't sure it applied to me, but it was worth thinking about. "Ziggy, let's get straight down to business."

"Yes, Max." He'd been eyeing a waitress but was now all ears.

"What do you want for your birthday?"

"Oh!" he smiled. "You remembered."

"Your birthday is carved into my brain, mate. So. There's a ticket to see Altrincham versus Wrexham tonight in the FA Trophy."

"Will Ryan Reynolds be there?"

"I hope not. I want to be the hottest dude."

"You're going anyway? Without me?"

"Have to. Work stuff. You're not into it?"

"Not really."

"Fine. What about going out after? I'll be your wingman. Like in the old days."

He smirked. "I have plans for tonight."

Jackie said, "Didn't you know, Max? Ziggy is a legendary swordsman. He's got a girl in every port. Southport . . . Ellesmere Port . . ."

"Portmeirion," I suggested, naming a famous village in Wales.

"I *don't* have a girl in every port," said Ziggy. "But I appreciate the offer, Max. You can buy me lunch. How about that for a present?"

"Cool," I said.

"You can buy mine, too. Interest on the money you owe me."

"Deal. I can pay you now, Jackie. Send me your deets."

After some more chitchat, I brought up the mess that was Chester. It wasn't just for the rare opportunity to use Jackie as a sounding board, but because if he was going to be the next manager, then he had a stake in what I was doing. And, as I explained to him, he had helped to get the club on its feet. If he thought I was endangering it, that would mean a lot more than if Spectrum did.

"What exactly have you done?"

I told him about my initial attempts at pruning, and why I'd started there. "And Physio Dean is next unless he bucks up his act. Even fucking Vimsy is getting on my nerves, and I *like* him! He's fine. But that's the problem. Fine doesn't cut it. I'm pretty sure they do the same sessions in the same order every week. Your sessions are to Vimsy's what Manchester is to Liverpool."

Jackie chewed some more. He had paid careful attention to everything I'd said. "You weren't hired for your tact, Max. MD wants you to improve things. You're allowed to do that. But tell me," he said, dipping some food into some other food. "Do you rate him as a coach?"

"Spectrum? Yeah. I do. And he's smart. And he can set teams up in loads of formations. He's a loss. I want to spend Sunday watching League One matches or whatever, but I can't think who can do the under-fourteens. I thought Jude would do it, but the Rebels want to play one last match for Broughton, so he's decided to stick with them. Apparently they were inspired by my 'one last game for Darlo' thing. So that's another good deed that's come back to bite me on the arse. I'll have to do it myself."

"Is the situation terminal? Would you mind if I talked to him?"

"Huh." I took a bite of whatever it was I was eating. "Sure. Yeah, go for it. No, actually, no. Fucker lied to me."

"You don't actually *know* that."

"I do. I promise you, they had a fucking hairbrush karaoke session. Let's all sing *Grease* songs while Tyson prances around taking shots. Oh, shit. My blood's boiling again. No. I don't want him around. It's bad for my health."

Jackie tutted and laughed. "I'm going to talk to him. You can't expect him to know you're a scout as well as everything else. He hasn't seen Ziggy turn from a five-a-side left back into Hugo Chavez."

"Why are you always comparing me to Mexicans?" wondered Ziggy.

"Hugo *Sanchez*. I don't need him to believe in me, Jackie. I'm not starting a cult. I gave him two instructions. Encourage Sully to play forward. Don't let Tyson shoot. It's not much to ask."

"Just checking: You don't blame him for Sully?"

"I don't. But he undid a lot of hard work I'd done on Tyson."

"'Kay. I'll talk to him."

I shook my head. "Fine. But listen. If he doesn't admit that he let Tyson let his hair down, then that's that. No, Jackie, I'm serious. I was *livid*."

"All right."

"Another thing. I want to sign a tiny German on a long-term contract. The next manager will have to give him minutes to help his development."

"Will he?"

"Yes, he will."

"Why are you talking like that?" said Ziggy.

"Good, is he?" said Jackie.

"There's a long list of things he can't do, but he's the best player we're likely to get this year. For what it's worth, I played with him for twenty minutes and we slapped."

"You slapped?"

"Yeah. He's the right tree in the wrong place. So we'll give him extra sunlight. Put a coat around him in winter. That's a thing, right? It's a coaching challenge, Jackie. A big one. An ambitious coach would drool over the degree of difficulty. And I'll take the blame if it goes to shit." Jackie looked up at something, stared for a while, then gave me a little nod. That was it. The last chance for anyone to talk me out of going for Pascal. Back to the pruning. "What does Livia say about Dean?"

"Lots of things."

"Dean makes women's skin crawl, yes or no?"

"No."

"Dean needs to go to charm school, yes or no?"

"I think he went to the same one as you, la."

"It's easy to replace a physio, yes or no?"

"With a generalist, yes. Dean's got football experience. Football's not tennis. It's not rugby."

I sighed. "It's just legs. It can't be that hard. A vet could do it."

"He was fantastic during the pandemic. Talk to the players who were at the club then. I think you'll hear about a side of him you haven't seen."

The pandemic was a massive head-fuck and lots of people didn't come out with any credit. If Dean did, that was a massive point in his favour. "Fine. I'll ponder it. New topic. If you were manager of a team next season, what would your default formation be?"

"I don't know, Maxy boy. I'd probably do whatever my director of football told me to do. I hear they're all rageaholics."

He was saying that to wind me up, and it was working. I rubbed my temples. I wasn't sure why we were talking in code. Maybe because it's bad luck to assume you've got a job before you've got it. Or just bad form—the sale of the house hasn't completed but you're talking about ripping up the whole garden. "Let's imagine the guy has two weeks to bring in players that would be useful *this* season as well as next. See what I mean? He needs to fucking *know*."

Jackie thought about adding fuel to the flames but put the lid back on the canister. "Three-five-two."

"Really?"

"Yeah. Sorry."

"What are you sorry for?" said Ziggy. I thought he knew that Jackie was in line for the Chester job. Probably he'd been told and had forgotten.

"Max needs a left back for the rest of this season, but there's a chance the guy wouldn't fit the *next* manager's formation. And knowing Max, he'd want to bring in a talented kid. Who Ian Evans wouldn't use."

Ziggy wasn't really following, but he had a solution. "Get an experienced guy on loan till the end of the season. Problem solved."

He was right, but I didn't like it. "Loans are dead money. We're developing someone else's player. Using wages that should be going to talents we can sell. That's buying liabilities not assets. That's short-termism. Short-term thinking is why we're in this mess."

Jackie eyed me. "You'll have to compromise, la. It's not a dirty word."

"I agree. I compromise loads. One day we'll work together, Jackie, and you'll see I'm top of the league for compromises."

He grinned. "I bet you're always in compromising positions." That got Ziggy—he laughed so hard he had to cover his nose. Jackie was very pleased with himself. He basked in his triumph. "Can't help notice, Max, that you're not in the Chester team. Is that . . . your choice, or Ian's?"

"Admin issue. No biggie."

"Hmm." He gave me his best "man stares into abyss; doesn't like what he sees" look. "And you're happy with Ian in charge, are you?"

"That's MD's call," I said.

"You're the DoF," said Ziggy. "You don't like the manager and you have the power to sack him. Er . . . what am I missing?"

"I need to learn to work with dicks," I said. "In case the next guy is an even bigger dick."

A few hours later, I went to South Manchester to watch the Altrincham under-eighteens train. James Yalley would be there. I tried to think back to the last time I'd seen his live player profile. I'd seen it the very first time at Jackie's masterclass with the Beth Heads and the shithousery. Then he'd refused to play for a while, and when he caved, I got him the gig at Alty. Yeah, I'd literally only seen him play once.

Once!

Bonkers.

What I'd seen was a CA 2 defensive midfielder with lots of potential. Since then, he'd been training on a casual basis, a couple of times a week, for about six weeks. He hadn't played any matches, but Alty were tier five and it seemed like a good setup. I expected him to have improved in a few areas.

James, of course, exceeded expectations.

JAMES "YOUNGSTER" YALLEY		
Born 19.10.2005	(Age 17)	Ghanaian/English
Acceleration 8		
	Handling 1	Stamina 9
	Heading 4	Strength 4
		Tackling 10
	Jumping 4	Teamwork 20
Bravery 16		Technique 5
	Pace 9	Preferred foot R
	Passing 5	
Dribbling 6		
Finishing 6		
CA 20	PA 181	
Defensive Midfielder, Midfielder (Centre)		

Like Ziggy, lots of running was enough to improve his running numbers. Passing, technique, and finishing had improved, but were still low. The passing was a worry, long-term. If I saw the future correctly, James would make a lot of tackles and interceptions, which was awesome. But then he'd need to do something productive with the ball.

But he was only seventeen. If he added one point in passing a year, he'd eventually get good enough that people didn't mention it as a weakness.

His teamwork was outstanding. Literally perfect. And his CA? Chef's kiss! It was plausible that with a couple of sub appearances, and maybe a start in the last match of the season, that he'd get to CA 40 this year.

Well, that sold me. Of course I wanted him at Chester, but our facilities and coaches were shit. If he signed a deal with Altrincham, they'd play him in under-eighteens matches and then fast-track him into the first team. Chester would miss out on a future transfer fee, but letting him stay at Alty was clearly best for James's career, and they would get a nice transfer fee to justify their faith in him.

Almost a win-win-win. Close enough.

While the kids were being put through their paces, I sidled up to Gavvo. "Mate. This is impressive. Love the intensity, love the drills, love the facilities. I assume you guys are interested in signing Youngster to a proper deal?"

Gavvo gave me a weird look. "Why don't you talk to your client before we have this chat, Max?"

"Oh. Is he not happy?"

Gavvo shook his head. "Talk to him. But listen, when I agreed to let your boy come and train, you promised me a free kick masterclass."

"Oh! You want it now?"

"That okay? I notice you haven't been playing. You injured? It can wait."

"Even if I was injured it wouldn't stop me showing off. I'll get my boots."

That evening, I went with the Yalleys to watch the FA Trophy game. Mr. Yalley had to work at the airport, but Mrs. Yalley came. When the match kicked off, she whipped out a little book and started reading.

Wrexham made lots of changes to their team, generally a sign the manager doesn't care too much about the competition. They started poorly and went a goal down. Alty were quite impressive. Sharp and hungry. They were taking the competition seriously. But then Wrexham's greater quality started to tell. Even their reserve players had higher CA than Alty's 55. Wrexham took a 2–1 lead and looked comfortable. But a mad, last-minute scramble led to an equaliser and a penalty shoot-out.

Altrincham won. Great news for James! Having extra matches in the schedule would make it slightly more likely that he'd get game time. It remained a long shot that he'd feature for the first team this season, but sport's all about hope.

With six minutes of injury time and the curse crediting me with XP for watching the penalties (as if I'd look away—even Mrs. Yalley watched them), I picked up 281 XP with 31 going towards my debt.

We walked home to their house—super convenient!—and chatted.

Kisi told me all about her training with Man City and asked how I was getting on with the women's team.

"I need to unlock a perk from this curse I got from a demon," I didn't say, "to get this thing called Playdar which may or may not be useful. But don't worry," I didn't add, "tomorrow I'm going to break my record for most XP in a day. Boom."

"Max?" she said.

"Er, I haven't started yet," I said. "Had to get the money in place. Right. James talk. Everyone ready? James. I've decided you'll get a contract with Altrincham. I'm delighted with what I've seen there. It's the best place for you. When you're signed up you'll train every day, have full medical access, and get game time. This season, break into the first team squad. Next season, first team regular. So I'm thinking two-and-a-half-year contract so they can sell you in the last year and make some money. That's fair for the club, Mrs. Yalley. And yeah, we'll see who the next team is. Wrexham, maybe, if they move up the divisions like we all expect."

I clapped my hands together to end the speech. Job done. James was one step closer to being a hundred-million-pound player.

"No," said James.

"Er . . . you what?"

"I have decided to move to Chester."

"Well, that's dumb. So, veto."

"God has spoken to me."

My heart sank. I thought I was done with that guy. "What did he say?" I asked carefully.

"He told me to follow you, Mr. Best. He said you needed me."

"Right. Follow me on Instagram or what?"

"To Chester."

"Well, call him back and tell him he knows fuck all about football."

Kisi laughed—big laugh—but James cringed. "Please, Mr. Best."

"Oh, fine. Sorry." He accepted my apology. I stood and wandered around their living room. A few bare trees were visible in the next garden. I retook my seat. Like most people, James responded to stories. "James, listen. You . . . You are a tiny baby tree. I have gathered you in my arms like that Bible kid. Who'm I thinking of? Little Egyptian kid. Kisi?"

"Moses?"

"That's the one. Thanks. And I've wandered around looking for the right spot to plant you, mate. And I've chosen Altrincham. Because you're a native tree. You grow best in South Manchester, see? And you get sunlight. That's coaching. And the soil's good. That's the facilities. And . . . there are nice birds here. Aren't there, James?" His eyes flickered. Was I going to tell his mum about the girls who'd turned his head in the pub? "Birds are your teammates. The better the birds, the faster you grow. I'm sure that's how trees work. And they need worms, too, right? Worms are the opposition. The better the opposition, the faster you develop. See? The analogy is flawless. Altrincham, great soil, lots of sun. Chester? Ugh. We're renting soil from a credit card company. There's a massive dinosaur blocking the light. The worms are lazy and don't do as they're told. And the birds are . . . what did I say the birds were again? Look, do you get what I'm saying?"

James did his best Pastor Yaw impression, speaking as though to a great multitude. "I will plant the cedar in the wilderness." I'm not sure where it came from, but suddenly he had a Bible in his hand that he clutched to his Chester. I mean, to his chest. "Where I go, God will provide light and water." He rolled his eyes slightly. "And worms."

"Mrs. Yalley, can you help me, please? We can't mess around here. Alty have better facilities, better coaches, and play in a higher league. That means better players around James and better opponents. His development *demands* that he stay in Alty. He can walk there from his house! Chester have no money!" She gave me nothing. I turned back to James for one last attempt. "We literally can't pay you. Where would you live? No, mate. Come on. You must have misheard. God wants what's best for you—I hope we can both agree on that." He pursed his lips. Telling him there was no money strengthened his resolve. I literally couldn't have said anything less likely to persuade him. "What is happening? Kisi. Tell him."

She smiled. "Max, you're wasting your breath. He's decided. And you know what? I agree with him. Alty isn't the best place for his development. You are."

"I'm not a place, mate. I don't keep a three-G pitch in my back pocket. Ugh. Clients are supposed to listen to their agents. That's kinda the point. This," I announced, "is a disaster." I inhaled to stop myself from going on a rant.

"Would you like another cup of tea?" said Mrs. Yalley.

I stared forwards, blank and unblinking. James's decision had stupefied me. I'd need time to fully process it. Exhaling was like waking up from a cosy daydream. "Did you say . . . plant cedar in the wilderness?"

"Yes. It's from Isaiah."

"*I will plant cedar in the wilderness.* That's actually beautiful." James leaned forward, the book in his hand gliding towards me. "Hey," I said. "Easy now." James blinked with defeat and leaned back. A small smile played on his lips. "Planting trees in the wilderness," I murmured, pinching my top lip. That was my task. Plant players where it was hard to grow them. James's phrase was already haunting me; it would bug me if I couldn't remember the words right. "Show me the bit," I said, pointing to the Bible. James nearly had a spasm in his haste to launch himself forward.

Out of nowhere, Kisi's hand slammed onto it. "No." We looked at her in astonishment. She smirked. "I reckon Max is a KJV kinda boy."

James grinned his goofiest grin, while Mrs. Yalley complained, "Kisiiii."

"I think Mr. Best would prefer the King James version," said Kisi, all prim and proper. She came back to the table with an older, more frayed Bible. It had those golden edges on the page that I guess was supposed to make it seem more holy and less full of talking donkeys.

James opened it to the section and held his breath until I finished lining up a photo of the passage about the trees. Me liking the wording of one passage had made his day.

Weird kid.

I was glad to know him, though. I was glad to know them all. They were the kinds of people who'd help me grow my trees.

And I needed all the help I could get, because that very weekend I went out into the wilderness, found a tiny, fragile, delicate sapling in the only environment where it could reliably flourish, and made it my life's mission to uproot it.

15

A GLIMPSE OF THE BELOVED

All I expected from Saturday was a colossal injection of experience points, but the day gave me that and more.

I'd decided to hit the Championship, the division below the Premier League, because I hadn't scouted that level yet, and because with a bit of fast driving I could make two matches in one day. I wouldn't find any players we could buy or loan, but 6 XP per minute across a hundred and eighty minutes would be like buying a jetpack. Up we go! My problem was that I couldn't really justify going to loads of matches in the higher tiers, because any players likely to come to Chester wouldn't be there. Indeed, when I asked Inga to try to hook me up with tickets to see Rotherham and/or Burnley, she swallowed the obvious question: why?

Me being Chester's director of football was enough for Rotherham —they generously put aside a seat for me. Burnley was a much hotter ticket for scouts and media, and I ended up having to pay for that one myself.

I arrived bright and early to the New York Stadium in *Rotherham*. Rotherham is just outside Sheffield, so it was about ninety minutes of monotonous motorway. Classic FM was doing a bad job of relaxing me, and I was having dark thoughts. Teetering on the edge of catastrophising. The worst of many projects I was botching was finding new players for the first team, but the more I stewed on it, the more I got annoyed by MD and the board's delay in appointing me. If I'd been given the DoF job right after the World Cup in December, I could maybe have been more methodical, or had a plan, or something. I could have hit the ground running. What I was doing now felt like jogging slightly slower than the treadmill I was on—I was slipping, about to fall flat on my face.

All I could do was hope Playdar would be worth it—I was about to place eight thousand eggs in that basket.

That thought frustrated me even further. If I could wait till the end of the month, and if I could win a twenty percent coupon code, that would save me 1,600 XP. That was a lot of XP to waste.

I sighed. There wasn't an option, really. Improving my ability to scout was at emergency levels. I'd have to pay full whack for Playdar and save my coupons for something expensive in the future.

The first thing that cheered me up that day was seeing the New York Stadium from the motorway. It looked like a miniature version of Arsenal's beautiful Ashburton Grove. I was early enough that I had ample time to walk around the whole thing. From the other side, it was weird looking, like a kid had spent weeks building a football stadium out of Lego but had run out of bricks. It sort of tapered down from right to left in the style of terraced houses built on a slope. Bit strange, but once inside I went straight back to loving it. The capacity was twelve thousand, which is relatively small for the level they were playing at, but it had the vibe of being the right size for the club.

I stopped a few fans and asked what they thought of it. The reaction was universally positive. With some follow-up questions I asked about their owner, who received mostly positive ratings. He'd saved the club from bankruptcy and injected thirty million pounds, wisely, such that the club achieved two promotions, and he had delivered on his promise to build a stadium in the local postcode. The complaints about him were absurdly trivial, but they were given equal weight to the success and the stadium. Football fans are hard to please!

I was shown to my seat by Rotherham United's hospitality manager. Busy dude, rushing around like a blue-arsed fly, but he lingered to ask me some questions. For example, director of football? You? Really? Not in an obnoxious way.

"Yeah, really," I said. "It's weird but it turns out I'm a genius. I'll leave ten, fifteen minutes early. Got to get to Burnley for the three o'clock. You won't think it's rude?"

"No, a lot of scouts and whatnot do similar things. You're all right, cock."

"What are you expecting today?"

"Blackburn are third. Flying high. We're near the bottom. Been a bit of an ordeal, season so far. Most folk'd be made up with a draw, to be honest."

"All right," I said. "Fingers crossed. Hey, I'm fascinated by this stadium. If we ever develop ours, I think this would be a hell of a template. I don't suppose you know how much it cost?"

"Twelve million," he said.

"Twelve million," I repeated. That was a lot of money for a club like Chester. "Thanks." Yeah, twelve mill was a lot of Pascal Bochums.

The match was great. Highly enjoyable. Rotherham's average CA was 120, while Blackburn's was 135. Despite that, Rotherham battered them. Four–nil. Big win for the Yorkshire lads over their Lancashire rivals.

Even better, one of the goals was a Max Best-style fuck-this-I'll-do-it-myself cannonball from thirty-five yards out that thundered off the underside of the crossbar and bounced up into the roof of the net. Almost as visually and aurally satisfying as a solo goal can be. And another was hit direct from a corner. Perfect strike. I was jealous, but in a way, relieved. The more other people had moments like me, the less I seemed like a demonic freak. And while I played in the National League North, people would be able to dismiss what I was doing as "only against Scarborough" or whatever.

Yeah, great goals, great match.

I had been feeling a bit burned out, but my XP was rising so rapidly and Rotherham was such a friendly place and its small club was holding its own so well (in a very, very tough division) that my burnout receded. I wanted more. I spent half-time looking for options to really pack my weekend full of footy.

By leaving early and driving slightly more insanely than I would normally countenance, I arrived at Burnley only ten minutes late. There was five minutes of faffing around peeing and finding my seat, and I was a bit sweaty from sprinting up loads of flights of stairs, but I made it. Massive triumph. Back on the Championship XP train, whoo whoo!

Turf Moor is a great stadium. Two spoonsful of old, northern pie-and-a-pint tradition mixed with a pinch of modernity, most notably the massive, modern screens showing replays during the game.

But with Burnley, the interesting thing was the team.

For my whole life, Burnley had been synonymous with teams playing a direct 4-4-2. Keep it tight, set pieces, flick-ons, long throws. The whole Ian Evans experience. But what was almost unique was that Burnley were able to make this throwback style work in the Premier League against turbocharged superhumans coached by highly paid floating brains. It shouldn't have been possible, but they survived at elite level for six seasons.

When they were finally relegated, their new billionaire owners appointed a former Manchester City player who had done a mediocre job in his only previous stint as manager. Get ready for the lols!

And what he asked from his players was even more unlikely than Burnley's gravity-defying stay at the top. He asked them, these beefy boys, these bruisers, these willing runners, to play fantasy football. Fantasy football!

I watched in something approaching stupefaction as players I'd last seen crashing into late tackles were now zipping the ball to feet, playing it around in triangles, rectangles, rhombuses, before storming into space they'd opened up. They played short and long passes with equal accuracy. They were a menace from all areas of the pitch in aspects of the game. The changes in formation were so fluid I only noticed something had changed when it changed back to what it *had been*; 4-4-2 without the ball transformed instantaneously into 4-2-3-1 with it, but then the full backs would move into midfield and DMs would vanish and pop up elsewhere and suddenly it was 2-3-5 and then a truly mental 3-1-6. Six attackers in a horizontal line!

Watching my dreams play out before my very eyes was euphoric; I felt drunk.

You'll notice I haven't even mentioned the opposition. That was Coventry City, who were just about to go on a sensational march up the table. Their CA of 140ish was close to Burnley's 145. But Burnley swatted them aside. It was a frighteningly dismissive performance for fans of other Championship teams.

But for me, it was wonderful. A rebuilding job that would take a normal manager four years had been done in four minutes. I'd love to play in this team. I'd love to manage this team. This team was nothing short of glorious.

And yet.

Billionaire owners. Happy to get out of the Championship, no doubt, but what would they do to make sure they never went down again? They'd got lucky finding a legit genius, but lightning wouldn't strike twice.

And the team. There were still some big-name tough guys from the old squad. But when I checked the player history tabs and did some research, I found a huge number of players were at Burnley on loan. These talented players were helping Burnley get promoted, and that was worth almost any price. But there *was* a price—the opportunity cost of giving game time to Burnley's own youngsters. What would Burnley do next season when those loan players were back at their parent clubs? They'd have to buy ten new guys. The summer could be quite frantic.

Still, though. There couldn't have been a more effective demonstration of how loan players could help a club achieve its goals.

While the happy home fans drifted out of the stadium, I hung around and drank it all in.

It felt like I'd learned more in an hour than in the entire World Cup. But maybe I had needed to watch all that for this to make sense.

There was one thing I knew: if total football could flourish in Burnley, cedars could grow in the wilderness. I wouldn't accept excuses.

I sent Jackie a text.

Me: We need to go and watch Burnley together. He's doing total football. I want it.

Jackie: You can't play that style in the National League North.

Me: I know a tiny German who can.

Jackie: Great. Now find ten more. Ones who can win headers.

Me: I want it.

Jackie: I want doesn't get. By the way. Check the scores.

I wondered what he meant. I checked Man United, and they'd beaten Man City 2–1. Quite a turnaround from the last match where City had thrashed us 6–3! United had managed to close the gap after all. City were still way better, but United were now close enough that they could sometimes win. Progress. But Manchester rivals slugging it out wouldn't interest Jackie much. Nor would he want to draw my attention to the fact that Brighton had thrashed Liverpool 3–0. Brighton had a very interesting new manager. I'd have to get to one of their matches and check him out.

I skipped several divisions and checked Chester. We lost. Henri didn't score. That was four games without scoring for him. Not bueno in the slightest. Darlo also lost. They were in something of a mini slump, to the point that winning the league seemed out of reach. They were still favourites to finish second, but they'd have to fight their way through the playoffs if they wanted promotion. It would be a slog.

And then I found what Jackie had meant.

FC United of Manchester 4, Hyde United 4. FC United's unbeaten run preserved by an eightieth-minute equaliser from . . . drum roll . . . the Ziggster!

It was there in black and white:

Ziggy 80

So simple. A story in two words. I jumped for joy. Punched the air.

Punching the air was dumb, since I was holding my phone in that hand. It went flying and the screen shattered.

Worth it.

With bits of glass threatening to pierce my skin, I typed carefully.

Me: Ziggggggy! Please tell me this one wasn't an own-goal!

Ziggy: Through ball. First time shot. Lob. Hugo Boss, like you said.

Me: Hugo Sanchez. Oh, man. I can't wait to see the video. How did you celebrate?

Ziggy: No clue. Ball hit the net then I was back ready to play. Whatever went down in the meantime, *shrug emoji*

Oh-kay. Pretty sure I knew what that meant. He'd gone full Tardelli.

The day was thundering along at breakneck speed, but then it turned . . . strange. My friend slash underperforming employee slash landlord called me. He must have just stepped out of the shower after the defeat.

"Henri, what's up?"

"Did you see that?"

"No."

"Where are you?"

"Burnley."

"Ah. You wanted to see the unlikeliest total football."

"Henri, it was amazing. I'm buzzing. I feel like a kid who's seen footy for the first time. Ah!" I gasped. "I think I'm in love."

"For the lovesick, the only cure is a glimpse of the beloved."

"Oh, totally," I agreed, because Henri didn't like when I asked him to repeat himself.

"I must ask for a favour." Rare moment of hesitation from the guy. Maybe he was choosing which scarf to wear.

"Go on."

He sighed. He left a noisy room and was now in a silent, echoey one. "It is well you were not here. I played like *merde* today, Max. It must have been my worst match since I was learning the game as an adolescent."

Not what a DoF wants to hear. "Oh."

"I must glimpse my beloved. I need you to come. I must fall back in love."

"You've got it, *mon ami*. What do you need?"

"In the morning, come to me. There is a rumour you sleep in the stadium. *Haunt* the stadium, as one person put it. Plan to stay there tomorrow night; you will spend the day with me. Yes, that will do. Come as early as you can, Max."

So it didn't seem like I'd be getting more XP tomorrow. Was he taking me on a quick jaunt to France? Sort his homesickness out by eating bits of animals not intended for English mouths? I texted him that I didn't have a passport, in case that was relevant.

His reply was a link to the UK's passport office. I swiped it away. More paperwork and admin were the last things I needed.

Instead, I checked my stash.

XP balance: 7,263

Debt repaid: 503/3,000

All right! Playdar was one big push away! If I got no XP on Sunday, I could go to Stoke-on-Trent to watch Port Vale on Monday night. That would earn me something like 450 XP, plus give me my first taste of League One action. That would leave me about 300 short. If I juggled my schedule I'd have Playdar by close of business on Tuesday.

What was Henri planning?

Knowing him, we'd end up in a jazz bar or naked swimming in a reservoir or geocaching or just generally the last thing you'd expect. Which, thinking about it, ruled out the jazz bar and the nudity.

Later, I had a big "oh, shit" moment when I remembered I'd kicked out the guy who managed the youth teams on Sundays. If I couldn't get someone to volunteer, we'd have to forfeit the games.

"Hi, Max."

"Hi, Raffi. You well?"

"Not really."

"Good, good. Is Shona there?"

"Yeah."

"Put her on speaker."

"Hi, Max!"

"Hi! Raffi, listen. I need a favour . . ."

Sunday, January 15.

"Okay," I admitted. "I knew to expect the unexpected. But wow. This wouldn't have been in my top *thousand* guesses."

"What do you mean: *this*?" demanded Henri. "Why do you say *this* with such a supercilious expression?"

I lifted my phone a few inches from my mouth, taking care not to grate my face off with the cracked screen. "Computer, tell me what supercilious means. Later. Not in front of Henri." I put the phone away and waved at an object that came up to my waist. "This. I didn't expect this flavour of midlife crisis."

"Midlife?" he said. "Henri Lyons, dead at 54." He shoved his bottom lip out. "Could be."

"Same as Alain Delon."

"He isn't dead. But seriously, Max, are you not delighted?"

I sighed and took a step back. Walked around it.

It wasn't a motorbike. It wasn't a skateboard. It was something in between.

"Is it a Vespa?"

"No, Max. This is a scooter. Four hundred cc. It is made by the same company as Vespa. Look," he said, suddenly as happy as a child showing off his new toy. He tapped the place where the driver rested his feet. "Plenty of space for a passenger. Total comfort."

I eyed the machine with extreme scepticism. "Comfort?" I pushed the seat. It was pretty hard. "Mate, ten minutes on that and I'll never have kids."

"Do you want kids?"

"Not until I know if my brain is full of holes."

"Perfect. Please note the USB charging port. All the modern conveniences! Now look," he said, with another boyish grin. He summoned a helmet. It seemed pretty standard, except it had a pair of those old-fashioned flying goggles built in. "Do you like it? I always wanted one of these. When I *really* have my midlife crisis, I want to buy a biplane. No! I want to *build* one. I wonder if there are kits. I shall check later. Perhaps I should buy the kit now for when I need it, in case production stops."

I slapped my hips. "Henri, what's the plan? You've bought a scooter thing. And then?"

"What size is your head?"

"I don't know."

"Try this," he said, producing another helmet. It was totally boring.

"Yeah, fits well. Comfy. Good foamage."

"I estimated your head size as 'big.' *Eh bien*. Let us prepare ourselves for our journey."

"If you've got a lamb and an altar in your back garden, I'm not getting involved."

He shook his head sadly. "Go to the water closet. Once we are in motion, nothing can stop us." He pulled his goggles over his eyes. "Our flying time will be approximately one hour." He held the pose, grinned, then took off the goggles. "Can't see anything in them. Ah, well."

I had one decision to make—to hold on to the little handle behind me, or to hug Henri. I started with the first and switched to the latter.

And then we rode off and there was nothing for me to do but enjoy the scenery and think. And then I relaxed. I expected him to go into the countryside, but we stayed in Chester and pulled into a garden centre.

I don't think I'd ever been to a garden centre before. Why would I? It was surprisingly busy considering it was winter.

"This is on our way," he explained. "It is galling to be in a friendship with a tree-hugger who knows so little about trees." He glanced around. "Also there was an attractive woman working here the first time I came . . ."

Henri took me to the section with the trees and spent a few minutes telling me about the ones in stock and what he liked about them. Most people would have overdone it—bombarded me with info. But Henri pointed out a few botanical things (they grew to different heights, were interesting at different times of year) and some aesthetic ones (shapes, colours, what he called "texture") and left it at that.

Back out in the car park, I realised he'd pitched his lesson perfectly, and told him so.

He shrugged. "Less is more. I had many coaches as a youth. Most were knowledgeable and enthusiastic, and I learned a lot from them. But often they went overboard. One day, an old guy came, former player, and after our session he took me aside and said, 'You move too much.' And that was what I needed to hear at that time. *Voilà*. You know something about trees now. When you are ready to learn more, the teacher will appear. Or you will go on YouTube."

Then it was back on the scooter, and again I expected we would hit the countryside and again we didn't. We went on the motorway, which alarmed me. Henri sensed my reaction and gave me a thumbs-up. It's okay! I tried to relax, and when we didn't die or get arrested I decided he probably knew what he was doing.

Instead of obsessing about where we were going and trying to work it out based on the road signs, I let my mind wander. Daydreamed about buying a house big enough where I'd have to think about which trees to plant. Walking around a garden centre with my girlfriend, pointing at, I don't know, ferns? And . . . ponds?

I tensed. Henri reacted. I gave him a double tap to signal I was okay.

But why had my daydream been about me and *my girlfriend*? Why not me and *Emma*?

The relaxation benefits of the short ride were already gone. My subconscious had dredged something up, and now I had to decide what to do with it.

An hour and two very crushed testicles later, Henri pulled into some generic car park. I glanced around at the buildings—probably a swimming pool. Henri had taken me to a water park and we would spend an hour sliding and pushing in front of children in the queues. The idea cheered me up, actually.

"Good trip?" he asked.

"Mostly," I said, adjusting my junk in the least obscene way I could manage. "My unborn children will remain unborn."

"It's a myth. Studies from Rome suggest Vespa riders have the most children. Perhaps because riding one is the ultimate in masculinity." He looked around. "This way," he said.

We carried our helmets with us and went inside. Past a reception area, through some double doors, down a corridor, and into a large sports hall. On one side of the hall were long benches rising in a terrace. They overlooked one large pitch, suitable for a roomy seven-a-side match, or two smallish ones. That's what the setup was today.

Dozens of player profiles popped up above the players. There were lots of ones, lots of tens, lots of twenties.

Henri was scanning my face. When I smiled, he did, too. "Mate," I said. "Did you go through all that drama to take me to *Crewe*?"

He put his hand on my shoulder and came close to me. Somehow he felt closer than on the scooter. "Max. I told you about an old guy who came to coach our team. He was a former French national team player who had become an administrator. Like you, he spent his days ankle-deep in bullshit. You can imagine the politics of a French football club. The jealousies, rivalries, backstabbing, the affairs—and that's just the ticket office. When it got too much for him, he walked down to the training grounds and watched the youth teams. Wherever there was joy, he would seek it out. To remind him what he was fighting for. Do you follow? We *must* watch the Chester Knights compete. It will make us happy. It will be a glimpse of what we love." He let go and looked over his shoulder at the pan-disability football that was taking place. "This is where it all started for us, Max. Page one."

"I hope you're not expecting me to lose my mind again. I don't do that anymore."

He twitched his head towards the other end of the hall. "No expectations. Just being around uninhibited joy for a few hours. Does that sound good?"

"Yeah. It does." But also, dude. Watching football but earning no XP was the last thing I wanted. I wanted to spend the day either powering full throttle towards 8,000, or totally chill. A ride in the countryside! Show me some trees in the wilderness! This was half one, half the other, adding up to a whole load of nothing.

We found where the Chester parents were and to say they were happy to see us would be an understatement. Now that I was Chester's director of football, showing my face was even more meaningful.

Terry was also happy, but not surprised. I got the feeling he'd been manipulating Henri into manipulating me. "Do you want to manage one of the matches?" he asked.

"I'm good, thanks. Quite happy to sit and watch and not get into the weeds. I've been going at it pretty hard. No, this is a day off for me. You go right ahead."

"Well, you're welcome to step in if you change your mind. I'm going to go get them. The first game's coming up."

"Where are they?"

"Changing rooms. They're pretty giddy. Nervous. Excited. You know how it goes."

"Not really. I've never been in a tournament like this."

He thought I was joking until he checked my face. "You're a professional player. You've played in cups. Don't you get nervous?"

My playing career seemed like a long time ago. I scratched the back of my neck. How did I feel standing on the touchline, waiting to be subbed on? Pretty calm. Butterflies in the stomach? Yeah, when I was waiting for Emma. At the football? Nah. "I played one cup match for Darlo. The stress was knowing I had to fight my own team. Maybe," I said dreamily, "if I was in a real team, one that was really united, I'd be nervous. Because it wouldn't only be about me. I'd be worried for everyone else. But I've never had that—only glimpses, only a taste."

That damned silence again. Terry looked embarrassed, which I think I preferred to what Henri was doing. He was nodding along. I told myself he was translating what I'd said into a more poetic version, one he could use on a date. First date? Probably second-date material.

"I'll get the kids," said Terry, and he scuttled off.

Henri slapped me on the arm. "You want to glimpse your beloved, and your beloved is teamwork. Team spirit. Community ethos. Then why did you pay for this tournament and then abandon the children?"

The stress was back, big time. Left backs on loan. FA hearings. Scenario B. Spectrum, Tyson, Pascal, James. New coaches, new staff, new ways of working, new ways of playing. "I don't have time. I'm swamped. If I don't use every waking minute from now till the end of January, it could be a disaster."

"Come, Max. Talk to me. Let us really talk, no?"

We sat at the back, on the top bench, and watched the Knights. Wilson, Zoe, Chester the goalie, and Johnny Winger, now Johnny the box-to-box midfielder.

I told Henri about the coaches, the lack of talent in the youth teams, the contrast between what Evans and Vimsy were doing and what Jackie Reaper was doing, what I'd seen at Burnley, Rotherham's delightful stadium, and every other little thing that popped into my head. I talked pretty much nonstop for the whole first half.

The half-time whistle came as a surprise. I absently noted that the ref had a linesman's flag that she was carrying around. It made her seem like she was on her way to another match. She waved the flag around. Pretty weird. "Sorry," I said. "Been very egocentric. I didn't mean to monopolise. What about you, bro? How are you doing?" I wondered if my outpouring would lead to him fessing up about his ennui.

"No, Max. We are not done with you. When you spend time in France you will learn that we will devote hours to a single topic, examining it in detail from all angles. You will find it beyond tedious. *Mon dieu*, I *have* to put you in a room with some pseudointellectuals from *la Sorbonne*." He began cackling. "But seriously. You have spoken of many things, but you have not told me what is really troubling you."

I sighed. "Emma."

"Things are bad. You are on the verge of breaking up."

"No. Things are perfect. But . . . I don't like her dad."

Henri dipped his head in a big show of empathy. He rubbed his mouth. Yes, my words had really moved him.

I tilted my head, suddenly suspicious. "Are you laughing?"

"No, of course not."

"What the fuck, man?"

He gave up his pretence of empathy and openly mocked me. "You don't like your girlfriend's father. Oh, woe is me! I am undone!" He sniggered. "I am very disappointed in you. I thought you had a real problem."

I grabbed his arm. "I do. It's a real problem."

"Why?"

"He thinks if I were in his shoes, I'd act and react the same as him. He thinks he's acting rational, but he's not. He's been radicalised. He's extended his support of a football team to include another country. This guy supports a country now. Like, cheers it on at the Olympics and stuff."

"He doesn't. Be serious."

"He probably does. There are Newcastle fans defending Saudi foreign policy in reply to Tweets about what's the best tea. Loads of Man City fans are the same. A lot of Man United fans are excited about the possible Qatari takeover. Journalists who report on it from a human rights angle get jostled in the street, have to change hotels, mad shit. Actual mad shit is happening. People are losing their minds, Henri."

"What those people have is not a *mind*."

"We used to talk about the footballification of politics, when people started supporting their guy or their party no matter what, but now politics has gone so extreme, football's got to catch up, and fuck me, it's trying. But I don't have to talk to those nutjobs. I've avoided almost all political conversations for years, and I'm not on social media. I'm as insulated as I can possibly be, I think. But Emma's dad is one of them! I spent Christmas dinner with him, thought I was being dramatic maybe—"

"Surely not," mumbled Henri.

"And now what? He's the personification of everything that's wrong with this country. I don't want that guy in my life. I don't, Henri." I put my head in my hands. "So how do I tell Emma I don't like her dad? I . . . I've realised . . ." I looked down at the bench in front of me. "The other day she asked if I wanted her to come over. I said I'd be in Chester that night. I lied to her, Henri. I've never lied to her before. I hate it. I hate everything about this. I just want to be happy."

He nodded. Genuine empathy this time. "Max. You need to tell her soon. How about . . . Wednesday?"

"What?"

"Call her on Wednesday. About . . . five thirty."

"What the fuck are you talking about?"

He nodded and gave me a soothing one-handed back rub. "Tell her after she finishes work. If it goes well, great. Good for you. If it goes badly," he said, whipping out his phone and going to the maps app. He typed fast. "Yes . . . I could be there by half past eight."

"Where?"

"Newcastle. To comfort her."

I stared at him. "Are you seriously telling me you'll make a move on my dream woman three hours after we break up?"

"I'd wait longer out of respect for you, but I can't take that kind of risk. She is tantalising." He made a strange face that made my fists curl into balls. "And I will be very charming with her father. Yes. His lack of moral fibre is not going to stand in the way of me getting what I want from his daughter. Mmmm." He made a noise like a cook in a commercial tasting his soup. That's when I knew he was winding me up.

"Jesus Christ, what are you doing to me?"

"You are being preposterous. The fathers of my lovers are of no consequence. If you wish to avoid him, avoid him. *Mon dieu.* You are such a *waste.*" He stood and clapped. "Yes, Wilson! Very good! Go again, Chester!"

I exhaled. When he sat down again, I said, "So are you saying I shouldn't talk to Emma about it?"

"I am not saying anything. I do not give relationship advice to idiots." I must have continued to look miserable, for he finally relented. His energy levels rose. "Yes! Tell her. Jesus Christ. Be mature and talk through your emotions. She is a woman. She is much more used to processing her feelings with a friend or partner. Perhaps, Max, you might avoid saying her father is the personification of all that is wrong with the world! Perhaps you might have enough diplomatic skill to avoid *that*! Humm?" He went from an eight to a five. "But talk to her. It might be difficult for you, but the chances of this triviality ending your relationship, I'm sorry to say, are slim to none. Yes," he mused. "This might be good for you. Talk to her. Hold on to what is important and discard everything else. Go step by step. Hmm. This could be good practice. Good. That is decided."

I wanted his words to make me feel better, and they sort of did. Yes. I'd talk to her. Easy. No biggie. "Should I tell her I lied about sleeping in the stadium that night?"

He went all the way back to an eight. "Are you fucking stupid? What benefit could there be in that?"

"Right. God, you're right. But look. Would you really make a move on Emma? If I, if we, you know."

His energy dipped all the way back to the lowest setting. His eyes flickered around before centring. He rubbed his upper lip. "Of course I wouldn't."

The only possible benefit to me and the club from my being in Crewe was me schmoozing some parents, so I did that while Henri stood next to Terry and helped coach the team.

I was basically showing my face, taking selfies, asking questions. Getting to know what was going wrong in this part of Chester Football Club. But generally they were very happy. Terry was great and my dedication to the disabled program was energising the parents and the kids. The first team, on the other hand . . .

"I know," I said, once per parent. Actually, more than once per parent. A good season for their child that ended with relegation for the first team was, unequivocally, a bad season.

I finally had a proper chat with Chesterkid's mum and dad, and the night I slept in their son's bedroom was, in retrospect, the stuff of legend.

"We thought we were hosting a lad who'd play for the team, but now you're running the whole club!"

"We can't wait till you make your debut. Are you going to play soon? We could do with a few goals."

They were trying to be nice, but they spoke a bit too loud. I noticed Henri's shoulders slump, and when I looked exasperated, Chesterkid's mum looked aghast. She mouthed "sorry" and I stood there, helpless. What could I do to cheer him up? I'd tried nothing and was all out of ideas.

The Knights won, or lost, or drew. It didn't matter. All that mattered was that they were a team, they were competing, they were progressing along their individual pathways.

There were about twelve teams in this tournament, sponsored by a company called So Solid. There were two teams from Crewe, one from Wrexham, one from Stoke, one from Manchester, and so on. I glanced around but wasn't getting XP, and as the minutes ticked by, I realised I had been sitting on a bench staring at my trainers for at least one half of a match.

Just talk to her. So easy. So hard. Henri didn't know how much I needed Emma. Her lips, her laugh, her playfulness. If I married her, I wouldn't need to hear the name Weaver ever again. That was something. Unless she kept her name. Emma Best-Weaver. Weaverbest? No way. Come on. She wouldn't. Would she?

Someone snuck up and slipped his arms around me. I only saw a head and a kit, but because the curse was in tournament mode, the player profiles were displayed even when the kids were off the pitch. I wondered if the profiles would vanish as teams were mathematically eliminated. I doubted I'd stay to the end to find out, but I guessed not. The profiles would show until the last kick of the tournament. That's how I'd do it, so that's how the curse would do it.

"Wilson," I said. "What are you doing?"

"You need a hug," he said.

"Yeah, maybe. I also need twelve or thirteen million pounds. Help me out?"

"I don't get pocket money because I swallowed a pound coin."

"Dude."

"I had to go to hospital."

"Have you scored any goals today?"

"No. It's hard. The other teams are better."

"Better than you or better than usual?"

"Better than us and better than usual."

"Are you doing your best?"

He nodded lots and fast. "Yes!"

"Then I'm proud of you. One more hug, then go to your teammates."

"Yes, Max!"

I really wanted to know what happened to that pound coin, but also, I didn't want to know. I stood and stretched. I'd been moping around for too long. Yeah, I had some problems, but I'd solve them. One by one, I'd solve them.

Henri was waiting for me pitchside, one foot on the lowest step. He looked so cool all the time. It was pretty annoying how effortless he made everything seem. "Max, are you hungry?"

"Yeah. Didn't have breakfast."

"Let's go see what we can get. My treat."

"Absol . . ." I froze.

"Max?"

I pointed to the second pitch. There was a match going on. "What the shit is that?" Henri scanned the pitch. He saw nothing out of the ordinary and indicated as much with a gigantic shrug. How could he not see it? An enormous sporting fraud was going on. A shameful deception.

"No way," I said. "Not on my watch."

I took a huge, angry stride towards the pitch.

Henri grabbed me and pushed me back. "Max," he said, "are you quite calm? Remember who you are."

I am the Sword of Justice, mate! "I'm Chester's director of football," I said.

"Yes."

I nodded. Counted to three. "So you want me to start calm?"

"How about we make it a rule to *always* start calm? Think of this as practice for talking to Emma. And if you get it wrong, if you let your tantrums do the talking, you'll meet Emma's father again . . . at my wedding."

I let a fair amount of rage escape through my nostrils, but then took his advice. I stretched my neck so that I was looking all the way up, then all the way down. "Calm. I'm calmly going to humiliate some cheats. Henri, are you in?"

He smiled. "Emma and I will make a great couple, don't you think?"

"Right." I thought about what I'd said and reworded it. "I'm calmly going to calmly investigate a potential source of . . . misaligned . . . alignments."

"Oh, Max! You learn so fast. We are proud of you."

Somehow I knew his *we* included Emma. The bastard was helping me in a way that was infuriating. I walked towards the pitch to check out the sitch up close.

The sitch didn't change. The team in black had seven players of varying disabilities. So far, so good.

The other team, playing in red with vertical white stripes under the sleeves, had six players of varying disabilities. All very proper and correct so far.

But then they also had a non-disabled girl. Her name was Dani. She was thin, with light-brown hair tucked into a long ponytail. Her face didn't react much, making her seem shy. Or like she was *hiding something*. She had a totally normal player profile. I mean, it was extraordinary in its own way, but I thought I was seeing a comparative profile. Like, the curse was inflating her attributes relative to the disabled players, and if I took her outside to a non-disabled match, I'd see her *real* profile. Something like that, anyway. The specifics didn't matter to me at first. What mattered was that she was in the wrong sport. It wasn't a million miles different from if I had joined the Chester Knights pretending to be partially sighted.

I began to fume at the injustice of it all, but Henri's warning made me pause. As director of football for a well-known club, I couldn't go around having tantrums at disabled matches. I put two fingers against my neck to check my pulse, but I didn't know how to interpret the results. Maybe I'd ask Dean to teach me. Weird thing to think. Maybe I'd ask *Livia* to teach me.

"What is the matter, Max?" whispered Henri.

I glanced at him, really quite amazed. "Can't you see?"

"No. What? Stop being coy."

"That girl. She's . . ." I kept having to check my language. "She's not disabled. She's cheating."

"Are you sure?"

"Can't you see? She's millions of times better than the rest. It's absurdly unfair. It's a joke. I can't believe they think they can get away with this."

Again Henri grabbed me. "No. Stop. I am very serious now. The girl is in no way better. For once, you are wrong. Do not make a scene. I forbid it. I want a nice day. Do not bring your manias here, Max. No. No."

I coaxed his hands away from me. "Henri? I'm calm. Look at me. And I'm not wrong. Let us go and investigate. Okay? If my temperature starts to rise, take over. But it won't." I started to move away. "But mate." I gave him a sad look. "The girl is playing a different sport than the rest. It's crazy you can't see that."

Henri stared at the pitch again, trying to see what I saw. But then he noticed a Max-sized hole where I should have been, and scampered towards me before I did anything stupid.

I went to the red team's coach. His profile was over his head, and for once I used this knowledge to obtain an advantage. "Hi, Alex. Budge up." I was asking him to move along his bench. He did. Henri sat on his other side. "Alex, I'm Max. This is Henri. We were just having a lovely old chat about your player, there. Have you got a team sheet?"

"Oh, er . . ." He fussed around with his stuff, but clearly wanted to keep an eye on his team. He had only sat down to make a few notes for his half-time speech.

I helped him by calmly ripping the item I wanted from his grasp. "Thanks, bro."

"Er . . . welcome," he said, not looking at me. Henri was giving me daggers.

I ploughed forward. This was happening now. I scanned the document. *Now* it would be realistic that I knew everyone's names. I leaned back, crossed my right leg over my left, all nice and casual. "Alex, mate. Your girl Dani there. She's pretty good, isn't she?"

His smile went full beam. It would have lit a motorway for three hundred yards. "Yes! Very good player. Very popular. Very easy to coach."

"Oh, I bet she is." Henri didn't like that. I toned the passive aggressive shit down. "Listen, I . . . I can't help but think that she's maybe too good for this tournament."

"What do you mean?"

"I mean that she's too good. She's so much better than everyone else. Maybe there's like . . . a tournament for less disabled people or something like that?"

Massive confusion nearly leading to something worse. Alex gulped a few times, then said, "I don't think I understand. Is there a problem? Are you one of the organisers?"

"No," I said in a soothing voice. "It's all good. I just think she's a really good player."

"What Max is puzzled by," said Henri, keen for this to be over, "is that . . . Dani . . . is so much better than the typical player with her disability."

"Oh!" said Alex. "Oh! I see." He turned to me and beamed at me again, while Henri mouthed aggressively at me from over Alex's shoulder. When Alex turned back, Henri was smiling, too.

"Yeah, I haven't seen many CP players like her," I said, fishing for the answer. CP was cerebral palsy. If *I* was going to enter a pan-disability tournament under false pretences, I'd say I had a mild form of CP. But Alex had such a wholesome vibe. He didn't strike me as the cheating type. Which meant *Dani* was the liar. And again, *she* didn't seem the type.

"She's not CP," said Alex. "She's deaf."

Deaf? Absurd. I stood and paced up and down. How could she be deaf and have a complete profile? If she had a complete profile that would make her . . .

All at once, everything changed. This wasn't a scam. No one was cheating. And that meant . . .

I rushed back to the bench. "A little bit deaf? Like, she lost one percent hearing in one ear?"

"She's totally deaf. Completely deaf."

"What!" I spluttered. So many questions. I couldn't contain myself; I had to move. I went pacing again, up and down. I put my fingers on my neck. Pulse much faster, much stronger—I didn't need expertise to feel that! "Oh my God," I said, running my hands through my hair. "Oh my God."

"Max!" said Henri, jostling me. "What the fuck are you doing? Explain yourself. This is unattractive."

I grabbed his chest, two-handed. "Henri! Can you really not see how good she is?"

He tutted. "Max."

I turned him towards the pitch. "Look! Look, man! She's not just the best player here . . ." The enormity of what I was seeing finally hit me. "She's going to be one of the best players in England! We've found our first star, Henri. Our first superstar!"

He put his hand to his head. It seemed like he counted to ten but it didn't calm him, so he kept going. Finally, he said, "You're crazy. She has to be the worst player on the pitch. She is swamped. No passes, no tackles, no impact on the game. Can we please drop this? I am hungry." I put my arm around his shoulder and grinned. "Oh, no," he said. "Not that smile."

I nodded. "I know what you need."

"I need a pizzaburger."

I spread my left palm across the pitch, transforming it from a drab, grey corner of Crewe to an Alice in Wonderland feast for the senses. "You need a *demonstration*."

"Max, no," he whined. "Don't."

My mind was fizzing. I was mentally optimising the red team. Move that guy over there? No, because this guy couldn't cover the left. That guy was fast, but if he played centrally he wouldn't get to use his pace . . . I snapped out of it. Henri was eye-begging me. Eye-pleading with me. Like a hungry puppy, he rolled his head towards the exit. The food is that way, he said, non-verbally.

Non-verbally! Communicating without words would be a challenge.

But I knew the right thing to say to put an end to Henri's whining.

"Mate. You brought me here because you wanted to fall back in love with football. Right?" He couldn't disagree. "So," I said, letting go of him, spreading my arms wide. "Watch as I miraculously turn that tiny deaf girl who can't pass, can't tackle, can't impact the game . . . into England's future number seven. Are you watching closely? I'm about to turn her into Max fucking Best."

INVERTING THE PYRAMID

Football glossary: Inverting the Pyramid. *The seminal tactics book by Jonathan Wilson, in which he tracks the evolution of football formations from the pyramid-shaped 2-3-5 to the modern 5-3-2. Which is also a pyramid, but, you know . . . inverted. It's the first book Coach Beard reads in Ted Lasso.*

I was tempted to get stuck in straight away, to start giving orders, start fixing things. Old Max would have done just that. But this tournament was the team's big day out, and the team had a manager, and some of the people in the stands were parents of these players. If I was going to make a big mess, I wanted to do it thoughtfully. New Max. Still a bull in a China shop, but now with front and rear collision detectors, and third-party insurance.

I did a slow lap of the pitch, checking that my tactical plan would work. By the first corner, I was convinced it would. By the second, I was thinking of the consequences of diving in. As I turned the last corner, I knew what to do.

I went back to the bench and spoke to the red team's actual coach. "Alex, I love your formation."

"You do?"

"Yeah. Three-two-one. Very solid. You've got that guy Darnell up front, and he's really good. He's so good you can put an extra body in defence."

That made Alex happy. He very nearly made eye contact with me. "That was what I thought."

I picked up his notes and scanned them. "How are you doing? In the tournament?"

"If we win this, we go top of our group. Group A. First plays first in Group B to decide the overall winner."

"But the most important thing is to improve the players, right? Let them progress along their pathways. Right?"

"Yes, but you do that by winning the tournament. Scouts pay attention to the winners. The winners get more chances."

I took a few breaths. I was a tiny bit impatient—I wanted to get started on my project. I had my emotions under control, though. If Alex didn't want to work with me, I'd wait until he went to pee and then hijack his team. Something like that. The fact I had to wait to get what I wanted was actually making me more excited about the moment when it would happen. I smiled. "Normally you'd be right." I tapped on my phone and brought up the Team page on the Chester website. Whoever ran the site had finally put my photo there. It wasn't very flattering. "That's me. I'm the director of football for Chester Football Club. My friend here is Henri Lyons. Star striker. Oh! And I'm the reigning Player of the Month in the National League North. No big deal. Just saying. So, look. I'm very interested in Dani. She's got the potential to be an absolute star, but she's not in the right place on the pitch to show that."

"She's a midfielder," he said. He was impressive, actually, this Alex guy. He knew his players and he put them in logical positions while having a clear overall playing style. We watched as Dani competed for a pass over on the right of midfield, where she should have been bossing the game. Her opponent was twice her size, a really huge kid with Bravery 20 who rampaged all over the place, heedless of the danger to himself or others. He barged through her and she ended up on the floor, rubbing her shin.

"That guy," I said, annoyed. "He's reckless."

"He injured one of our players. He's in the medical room now, with his friend. I hope they come back for the second half."

"Yeah." I steamed at the bull for a minute, then returned to the topic. "You're right, of course," I said. "She's a natural midfielder. But right now she's lost. What I'd like to do is move her, give her some tips, get her into the game."

"Move her?"

"Yes. Just a tiny tweak."

"But I'm the manager."

"Alex, mate. You *are* the manager. *You* are the manager. But I'm the scout. I'm the director of football. I'm the pathway. Your job is to make the players impress *me*. Imagine a pyramid with this match at the bottom, and players who do well move up to the next level and then the next and the next and if they're really good and really lucky, they get to meet *me*. Yeah? But I'm here. I've flipped the pyramid."

"You're her pathway?" He blinked a few times. "You want to take her to the Chester Knights? That isn't logical. We are much better."

I gave him a friendly pat on the back. "Confidence. Love it. No. I don't want her for the Knights. I want her to play for the Chester Boudicas."

"Max," complained Henri.

"The name is TBC," I admitted. "Chester Women is a bit dry, isn't it? I want a legendary name like the Doncaster Belles. I'm going to let the players decide. I think. Point is, Alex, I'm pretty sure Dani will be our first female professional. I want to pay her hundreds and hundreds of pounds to play football. Think what that would do to your intake!"

I was making lots of good points, but Alex wouldn't hand over the keys to his kingdom so easily. Neither would I, if the roles were reversed. Plus, he had to consider the six other players. "What change?"

"Excuse me?"

"What change do you want to make? Tell me and I'll decide."

"Yeah," I said, rubbing my mouth. "The thing is, I do this thing where I get everybody hyped up. I'm great at half-time team talks. What I'll do, yeah, what I'll do is I'll give the team talk, get them all hyped, and that one tiny change I'll just sort of slip into the middle all nice and gentle."

"Dani can't hear you," said Henri. I think he *basically* approved of the approach I was taking. Like me, he didn't want to be making regular trips to Crewe to scout this girl. Two-thirds diplomat, one-third pushy salesman—it was acceptable. There was a problem, though. It wasn't working.

I clicked my fingers. "Right. Hey, when's half-time?"

Alex glanced up at a massive timer on the far wall. "One minute twenty seconds."

"Alex, can you help? Henri has a massive whiteboard in his car. It's incredible. Could you help him bring it in? Then I can sort of show Dani what I want. And tell you what, you can keep the whiteboard for the rest of the day. That's fair, isn't it?"

He frowned. "How big is it?"

"Big! And it comes with three colours of magnet."

"Max," said Henri. "Just to check. You want me to take Alex out to my *car*. To get the big whiteboard?"

"Yes, please. You'll be back before half-time, Alex. The car's right outside, if I remember right. Oh! And you can check on your injured player. You want to check on your injured player, don't you?"

Henri didn't like that last part. His head flicked up and I saw his lips moving quickly.

There was a brief silence. "Don't worry, Henri. It's not that heavy. Alex will make sure you don't hit the door on your way out."

Alex, understandably confused, was on the verge of refusing, but Henri put his arm around the guy's shoulders and gushed about how kind Alex was for helping and so on and so on. Their first few steps were a bit forced—literally—but then Alex went along on autopilot.

When he was far enough away, I danced up the hard wooden steps to one of the parents. He was wearing a red baseball cap. "Can I borrow that, please? It's important. Give it back in five minutes. Thanks!"

Wearing a red cap with a badge I didn't recognise, I bounced on the touchline hoping Henri would distract Alex for long enough and willing the half-time counter to hit zero.

When it did, I wouldn't have much time.

While I bounced, burning some of my manic energy, I checked the player profile that had made all this happen.

DANI SMITH-SMITHE		
Born 24.06.2007	(Age 15)	English
Acceleration 8		
	Handling 1	Stamina 5
	Heading 3	Strength 1
		Tackling 1
	Jumping 4	Teamwork 16
Bravery 3		Technique 9
	Pace 9	Preferred foot B
	Passing 9	
Dribbling 9		
Finishing 11		
CA 1	PA 177	
M,AM (RLC)		

The first thing that jumped out at me were all the low physical attributes. They were horrible, but I felt sure—really sure—that it was because she was deaf. Not *because* she was deaf, but because she'd either never taken sport really seriously or her parents were overprotective.

Her parents, by the way, holy shit. I hoped I'd be able to get her signed at Chester without having to meet them. Smith-Smithe, what the hell?

Anyway, once she started in our training sessions and hitting the gym and all that, her strength and stamina would fly up. Once we taught her how to tackle, that would fly up.

Numbers flying up seemed absolutely inevitable given her PA. Massive! I hadn't scouted the Women's Super League or seen any international matches live, but assuming it followed the same pattern as the men's game there would be five to ten players worldwide with PA 195, twenty or thirty over 190, and a few hundred over 180. There was a *lot* of assumption there, and I was also assuming that while virtually all world-class male footballers had been scouted, there would be a lot of superstar girls who'd never even played a competitive match because their schools only had netball or they lived in countries that didn't let girls play sports.

So surely Dani's PA 177 was high enough to play for England or be a very useful player to bring off the bench in tight games. She'd get a cap, at least, I was sure. One day, she would run onto the pitch at Wembley. Maybe even before I would! And that high PA meant years and years of improvement, which gave me confidence that most of her attributes would shoot up.

But the thing that really clinched my obsession was her two-footedness. One thing my playing career and the MUNDIAL mini game had really made me notice was the value of players who had that oh-so-rare B in the preferred foot cell. The ability to dribble left or right, pass left or right, oh! It was like gold dust. Would I take a bipedal PA 177 over a one-footed PA 187? If you'd asked me there and then, yeah, no contest.

Half-time.

The ref whistled and waved the flag. Ooh! The flag was for the deaf players! My God. So obvious.

"Guys, come in," I said, waving at the team.

They were confused, but they came. I was in the red hat, after all.

"My name is Max. I have to be quick, so listen up." This sounds dumb, now, but I wasn't talking to Dani. "You guys, you're a good team. I love what I'm seeing. But I want to change the formation so that Dani can impress a bigtime football director who is here now." They all looked around, scanning for the bigwig. Dani looked around to see what they were looking at. "What I'm saying is, will you help me? It might be strange at first, but if you do what I say, you'll probably win this match. Probably. But there's something more important than winning. And that's doing whatever it takes to help your friend. Am I right?"

"Yes!" said one.

"You're strange. Where's Alex?" said another.

"Guys. There's no time. Your friend needs you. Are you selfish? Or are you masters of friendship?"

"Friendship!"

"Amazing. Come here. I'll show you what I want." I brought them onto the empty pitch and told them where to go. "Darnell, you're in the same place. Simons, left wing. Harold, right wing. Go on. Go and stand there so we can all see. No, even farther. More. Get right up there! That's it!" I'd pushed the two wide guys even farther forward than Darnell.

This was exciting. The opposition manager was looking at me like I was crazy. He shook his head and continued his team talk.

I stuck my tongue out and coaxed the next two into position. "Bev, here. Ally here. You're a screen. A funnel. Block attacks."

"Are we the midfield?" said Ally. The position didn't make a lot of sense to her.

"No, you're defenders."

"Where's the midfield?"

"Midfield is so last century. Totally out of fashion, like skinny scarves. Am I right? No midfield. Just stay there and clobber people. Right. Now the fun part."

There was only one player left to position, and I couldn't communicate with her. I turned to face her, full on, and grinned. I knew she must have been totally bewildered, and I didn't mind that. We were starting from zero, I needed to get to a hundred, and I had the rest of the short half-time break plus fifteen minutes. The air was fizzing with static electricity. She couldn't hear, but surely she could feel it? The birth of a new superhero.

I was about to open my mouth to say something but bit my bottom lip. How did this work?

"Can you read lips?" I said, pointing to my mouth.

She shook her head and circled her finger around. I didn't get it.

"Not here," said Bev. "Not in the football."

That made sense. Like, how was she supposed to read lips when she was jogging around and I was shouting to the whole team and there were loads of distractions? Easier for her to say no. I nodded, and smiled again. This was so hard! I loved it! I stood to my full height, put my hands on Dani's shoulders, and pushed. One leg went backwards, then another. On the third step, I gently pushed downwards. Stop there. I stood next to her and imagined I was playing. Yes, this was the spot. I turned towards her and gave her a big Maxy two-thumbs.

She shook her head, pointed to the spot I'd positioned her, and wagged her finger.

I wondered what the curse would tell me about this relationship if I had the right perk. Something like:

Your current reputation with Dani: 0.

"She's not a defender," said Bev.

"I got that one, thanks." I laughed. I pointed at Dani, then mimed using a broom.

Dani frowned and did something with her hands.

"Sign language! I need to learn that," I said. I glanced at the Chester Knights. They were getting ready for their second match, huddled up on one section of the benches, laughing and joking. I hoped Wilson wouldn't run into one of the benches. He was a very determined player. Next to him was Zoe, our cyberpunk deaf midfielder. Zoe probably knew sign language, but I didn't want my project to mess up her day. Plus, I needed to make a connection with Dani for myself.

I went back into pantomime mode. I pointed for Dani to shoo away, and I took her place. While she watched, I stood on my tiptoes and shielded the sun from my eyes as I looked on the horizon—left, right. Ship ahoy! I mimed, pointing. I fell into a defensive half-turn and crabbed to the right. I imagined an attacker trying to dribble at me, then shepherded him away from the goal. Then the attacker made a mistake! I pounced on the ball, flicking it behind me to my left foot, where I played a gorgeous—and still completely imaginary—pass forward to Darnell.

Dani's reaction was pretty funny. She'd pulled her head back and slightly away, and her mouth was twisted. For a microsecond I thought she was appalled by my acting, but no.

She pointed to herself. *Me? You want me to do that?*

I pointed to her and nodded. Three BIG nods, my grin getting more maniacal with each pump of the neck. I walked away and left her space vacant. She didn't move. I raised my eyebrows and made a tiny "go left" gesture with my head. I did it again, but everything bigger. I did it a third time, including a stuck-out tongue.

Dani sighed and went to her spot.

The timing was on point—the referee came back onto the pitch just as Alex and Henri came in through the double doors. Henri was repressing a grin—God knows how he'd explained the fact that his car had transformed into a scooter—but as soon as Alex saw the match had restarted, he rushed over to his bench. We were positioned looking at our goalie's back, because in the morning, the reds had colonised the space behind the goal. It made sense—less trudging around carrying bags and equipment. But it wasn't the most optimal spot for coaching. That suited Alex fine, since he gave almost all his instructions during breaks.

He stood on the second tier of benches for a better view. "What have you done?" he said. Henri caught up with him and scanned the pitch, frown lines appearing on his forehead.

"Bog-standard half-time team talk," I said. "Keep it tight first five, get stuck in. The usual."

Alex gawped at me, then the pitch, and after a brief but intense stare, he said, "You've inverted it!"

"Fuck me, you're fast," I said, and for once I wasn't manipulating the guy when I said, "Send me your CV."

"I have to undo it," he said, stepping forward.

"Whoa whoa whoa," I said, partially blocking his path. "That wouldn't be fair to Dani."

"Why?"

"Because you can't make changes during the half because she can't read lips when she's playing. And you don't have any subs. So if you change things again she'd be stressed and confused. And you wouldn't do that to her, because you're a nice person."

Henri shook his head, but he was partially responsible. At this point I think he wanted to know how it would all play out.

"I don't know," said Alex. The guy was miserable. I'd ruined his whole month. Year, maybe.

"Tell you what," I said jauntily, but I never finished the sentence.

The reckless black team player bundled through my defensive shield and the ball sped towards Dani. It was fifty-fifty who would get there first. Actually, it was sixty-forty in Dani's favour, but she lacked confidence and the striker barged straight through her. He rammed the ball into the net.

Dani shrank.

"Henri, quick," I said, pushing him onto the pitch. I grabbed the ball out of the net and threw it to him. "Hard low pass." I looked at Dani and pointed to my eyes. *Watch.*

While the black team's manager and referee asked what the Clough we were doing, Henri kicked the ball towards me. With my entire body virtually motionless, I let it hit my right foot, and with the most microscopic flick the ball popped up and to the right. I took a dynamic stride towards the ball and then mimed dribbling away.

The referee waved the flag at us. I put my hands up and got off the pitch.

If you kick a ball at someone's foot, you expect it to bounce off in a more or less predictable way. It might roll left, or right, or come back to you. What it doesn't do is pop up and land a metre away, exactly where the opponent can push off into a dribble.

Dani was frowning, big time. Not at me. At my foot.

Your current reputation with Dani: 1%.

Henri and I exchanged glances. Electricity flew. He didn't know what I was up to, but he sensed the change in the air. My reality distortion field was up. Henri grinned and coaxed Alex back to the small manager's bench.

I couldn't sit; I paced around, blood pumping. For some reason, I kept nodding. I glanced at the spectators. There were about six parents there, most on their phones. The only ones really paying attention were the red cap guy and his wife. Dani's parents. Right. Of course.

The game continued. The black team streamed forwards, virtually unopposed, unable to believe their luck. Our three strikers were out of the game and the defenders were inept. It was six against one. I felt the manic grin return—by the time I was finished with Dani, they'd need a lot more than six.

This time, the two defenders got stuck in and slowed the attack. The ball fell to a midfielder who burst towards Dani. But like almost always happened in these games, the player overhit it. Dani's ball! But Dani didn't move. It was like she was frozen. Rabbit in the headlights. The midfielder was almost on top of her when she booped the ball exactly as I'd shown her. It went slightly less than a metre to her right and she pushed it away with her dribbling stride. Two more strides and she was free on the right. And then? She tried a pass but it hit a black player and went out for a kick in.

Dani did a quarter-smile, then went impassive again.

Your current reputation with Dani: 2%.

"Yes!" I hissed. "Come on!" I paced up and down some more. This was fucking amazing. If I could pause the match, I'd be able to teach her one move a minute and she'd finish the game playing like Beckenbauer. "Hey, Bev. Bev!"

"What?"

"Kick the ball over there."

"What?"

"Smash it away. Far as possible."

Bev pulled a face, but in the next passage of play she did just that. She absolutely twonked the ball down towards the farthest wall. I was ready with Henri and a ball. "Same again, mate."

I made sure Dani was watching and fell into the same position as before. Henri kicked the ball at me, and I adjusted so that it would hit my right foot again. But this time I moved my body weight so that it was obvious what I was about to do. And I did it. Boop, one metre right. I looked at Dani and gave her a thumbs-up with a questioning face behind it. Thumbs-up, she said. "Same again, please."

Henri repeated it, and I started to do the same boop. But with my weight trending *right*, I booped the ball *left* and went through the motion of sprinting away.

The referee came over and waved the flag quite aggressively.

I pulled an innocent face and stepped off.

"Don't come on the pitch," he said. "Or I'll yellow card you."

"You can't yellow card me," I laughed. "I don't work here."

"I know who you are, Max Best."

Fine. *Jesus.* Of course I'd bump into the one referee in Crewe who recognised me.

"Henri, come round here." He followed me to the left side of the pitch. Aggressively close to the other team's manager and subs, but Dani would be able to see us.

And we had a great view of what came next. The same pattern of play repeated—the blacks attacking down the middle, coming into contact with our screen, getting slowed down but bundling their way through. This time there was a genuine fifty-fifty and I was sure Dani wouldn't challenge for it. But she did—she got her foot to the ball first and popped it to the right. That bought her some space, but the reckless attacker was coming. She booped to the left—really smooth, really balanced—but the first attacker was alert. He pushed the ball more central and was lining up a shot when Dani stuck a foot out to try to kick the ball away. She kicked the guy instead, and he howled with pain.

It wasn't in the penalty box, but this tournament was playing a rule where if a foul stopped a shot, wherever it was on the pitch, a penalty would be given.

Dani looked distraught.

Your current reputation with Dani: Leave me alone!

I waved my red cap wildly. "Guys! Get Dani for me!" She finally turned. *Come over*, I waved. *Come on!* She sighed and trudged closer. *Watch.* "Henri, dribble at me." He did. I kicked him on the back of the calf.

"*S'il vous plaît*," he said.

I turned to Dani and wagged my finger. *No no no!* She threw her hands up. *I know! I know that!* The black team scored the pen. She slumped and walked away. I raced onto the pitch and tapped her on the shoulder. Demanded that she watch me.

"Henri, again."

"The match is starting."

I made a frustrated noise. "Who gives a shit?" He sighed and came at me. I half-turned away from him so that he'd naturally drift to my right. He moved at me and I kept my distance. He moved, I retreated. He moved, I shadowed. I looked at Dani. Two thumbs up. *Yes yes yes do this.* She looked over at Alex. Her expression said, *save me from this madman.* But Alex was in shock, staring up at the scoreboard, slapping his hands against his hips.

Dani needed a minute to process. "Let's go back behind the goal. We have to manage Alex for a minute." On the way, I decided positivity was best. I gave the guy a friendly pat on the back. "Isn't she great? She learns so fast. Wonderful player."

"We're losing," said Alex. "It's chaos."

I scoffed. "It's actually highly organised. A very effective formation."

"Effective at what, Max?" said Henri.

"It achieves multiple objectives," I said smugly.

"The main one being that all the action flows through Dani."

"Huh. I hadn't thought of it like that. Alex," I said, changing the subject, "what do you think of sweepers?" Sweepers sit behind the centre backs and mop up anything the other guys miss. It's not really compatible with the offside trap and I can't remember the last time I saw a professional team use a sweeper. The modern version is the sweeper-keeper, where the goalie has the technical qualities of a midfielder and can rush out of his box to clear danger.

"The sweeper position is dead," said Alex, but he wasn't really engaged in the conversation. He'd gone internal. We watched yet another break that Dani ended by racing to the ball and popping sideways. She was fouled and everyone took a breath. Alex stuck out a finger. "This . . . This concept is almost starting to make sense. But not with Dani. She can't play this role."

I clapped, once. "Yes! I love that you said that." I sighed contentedly. "I love meeting a fellow visionary."

"It doesn't actually make sense, though, does it, Max?" said Henri. "You have perhaps two players in the right positions, including the goalkeeper. Your outside forwards haven't touched the ball this whole half."

"They did!" I complained. "After the goal."

"The restart doesn't count. It's interesting to watch you teach Dani some strategies, but I fail to see how playing like this will lead to victory."

"Victory? What do you mean?"

"I mean winning."

I scoffed. Waved the word away. "Winning is for losers."

Henri cradled his nose with thumb and finger. "Do you mean to tell me that this formation isn't designed to win? It's all about aggrandising Dani?"

"No," I said. "I mean, yes. They'd win if the match was long enough and I had breaks to coach her. She's blocking almost all their attacks now. They *might* score another goal. I wouldn't count on it. Her positioning is really good and she sees danger. I told you—she's like me! The more tools we give her, the more she'll dominate her zone."

"Max! You've proven your point. Change the formation so they can win." Henri didn't like my reaction to that, so he took a step closer. "The team came to win. Dani came to win. She won't thank you if you focus on her to the detriment of her friends."

I thought about telling him the rest of the team had voted to be masters of friendship, but Henri could see through my bullshit. "Ugh," I said, energy flopping out of me. "Fine. We'll stop writing a story that will astonish the world and instead we'll put our pen down and spend an afternoon fucking rearranging all our library books. Jesus Christ, Henri, I didn't have you down as the Person from Porlock!" I fumed for a few seconds and checked out the pitch. Dani was shepherding the reckless defender to the side. He realised he was going nowhere and tried to dash towards the goal, barging into Dani. The ref gave a foul. I scanned the other players. Darnell was still impacting the game, as were the two defenders. The outside forwards were currently useless. The goalie stepped forward to take the free kick. That would be her first touch of the ball for a while.

I slapped my hands together, cracking a big smile. "Henri, you're a genius. I can get even more of what I want while letting the kids go for the win. Alex, have you got any more red tops?"

"Yes, there's a bag." He pointed.

Henri watched as I had a good old rummage. "Max, if you're thinking about playing, there are one or two impediments."

I surfaced with a large red shirt. I held it up over my torso. "Bit tight, do you think?"

Henri's mouth opened and closed like a goldfish. I darted to the side of the pitch and bounced around, waiting for a break. When it came, I waved the shirt around like one of the referees with their flags.

The ref paused the timer, rolled his eyes, and walked over. "What now?"

"We need to change keeper." I handed our goalie the red top. She looked at it. I waved at her. *Come on! Come on!* She frowned but took her gloves off and started to change. "You're second striker," I said, and her face lit up. Goalies love being strikers.

The referee was right next to us now. "Well, you can't."

"I've read the tournament rules and statute eight section eight says we can."

He was exasperated. "There's no such rule."

"Look," I said. "Changing goalies is completely normal. That yob over there smashed our player in the first half and you didn't even book him." That was a guess, but the ref's face suggested I was right. "We've got no subs. We're doing it. Sue me."

"So who's going in goal?" said our goalie, now wearing the red top.

"Yes, I'd like to know that," said Henri, but he must have already known. It was *obvious.*

I handed the gloves to Dani. There was a chain reaction of appalled noises from all around. Dani refused to take them. "Put the gloves on," I said in my sternest voice, then remembered she couldn't hear. She took a few steps back. Practically ran away. She made big, wide gestures. *I can't! I can't!*

"Henri, take a shot on me."

He zipped to the penalty spot. "Anywhere in particular? Face? The testicles?"

"Left of me, ankle height. Hold on. Wait till she's watching." Simons, our left winger guy, was trying to bring her back towards the pitch. When she saw me in goal, she froze. *Watch,* I gestured. "'Kay go."

While Henri approached the ball, I stuck my hands behind my back.

Henri shot, aiming halfway between me and the left side of the goal. I swung my right foot behind the left leg and killed the ball. I did an enormous yawn. Too easy.

"I'm sorry," said the ref, "but we can't wait. If you don't have a goalie, that's on you."

I kicked the ball back to Henri. "Knee-height, right," I said.

Henri did it. I stuck out my thigh and caught the ball on it. Then I leaned back and did the most enormous stretch anyone has ever done. Henri laughed, but the ref blew his whistle and rustled his flag.

We scampered off the pitch, and Dani, teamwork 16, saw the empty goal and ran to fill it. Henri and I exchanged a glance.

"No, Dani," I said, and then grunted. Her back was to me.

"Why have you done this?" said Alex. "She's worse as a keeper than as a sweeper."

"I don't want her to play in goal," I said.

"Oh, Max," said Henri. "This is exasperating." But he was cackling. I think he was starting to get it.

The ball came to Dani, and she had two attackers running at her. She thought about trying to pass through them, thought better of it, and moved the ball sideways. She looked for a pass but couldn't find one. She kicked the ball out of play and turned, stared at me, and threw her hands wide. I gave her a few big claps. "Yes! Good. Henri. Alex. If you want to win, how about you get those lazy fucks to run around a bit? Give us some passing options, yeah?"

Henri paused. "Before I waste my precious life force, is this a genuine attempt to win the match? Or not?"

"It is."

Henri's tongue appeared between his lips as he went through some internal calculation. "It had better be. Alex, you take the left side. I will go right. The goal is to get one of our . . . four . . . strikers into space for the pass." He looked for confirmation; I gave it. Henri glanced at Alex. "Actually, come with me. I'll show you what we mean."

They strode around the sidelines towards Harold, our right winger.

Dani turned to see what was going on. I made the sweeping brush gesture. She shook her head. I did it again. She rolled her eyes and took five steps forward. She stopped. Looked at me. I pointed. She took another step forward. I signalled for two more. She bent down and stared forwards, but when she finally turned back, I was still there, still holding up two fingers. She inhaled and finally obeyed.

Your current reputation with Dani: 3%.

We were now playing a 0-1-2-0-4 formation. Surely even Burnley wouldn't play something as insane.

I'd done most of what I could do now. I took a couple of steps back from the pitch and rested one foot on the enormously long wooden bench behind me. I idly noticed that all the original parents were watching, and a bunch of players and parents from other teams had sensed something was happening. They were giving me and Dani very curious glances.

I tuned it all out.

It made sense that Dani hadn't been spotted. She'd been coached like Terry coached Zoe—to be a good egg, to run around, to try. And yeah, even if she'd spontaneously decided to learn tricks and skills, only one in a thousand managers would want the hassle of dealing with her deafness in match scenarios.

But it wasn't a hassle for me. The curse was definitely a blessing in this scenario. In a match, I wouldn't ever need to say anything to her! At least not for any of the important things. I could switch her from left back to right wing at the speed of thought.

And coaching would be easier—I'd telepathically instruct her to do things in games which we'd then coach her to do! Using the video of her *already doing it*. Finally, a story with a logical time paradox!

I did a little moonwalk along the bottom of the benches. "Hee hee hee!"

No, Dani's deafness was not a problem if I was the manager. We'd still have to do a lot of hard work in training sessions, a lot of adapting. Some kind of signal board like in Formula One, perhaps. Because I wouldn't always be her manager. And if she really did make it to the national team, we'd need to be able to tell those guys what we did and why.

That was all in the future, though. For now, there was only this match. Staggeringly unimportant, except to those who were playing in it, and maybe the two managers. The reds were losing 4–2 and hadn't had a shot in the second half. Since the break, there had been wave after wave of black team attacks. But now . . .

Now another attack came, this time down the left. Dani hesitated —should she sweep or should she keep? She decided to go against her instinct and do what I'd told her. She followed the player over to the left, like I'd demonstrated with Henri. There was an opponent in the middle, unmarked. I berated the midfielders for not dropping back, but when I looked back at Dani, she'd stolen the ball and was dribbling back towards the goal. I waved my hat around like a crazy person. Henri did something, and Harold dashed diagonally towards Dani. She rolled the ball to him. He touched it to Darnell, who wanted to play it left but found no movement from Simons. So Darnell laid it off to Jackie, our former goalkeeper, and she lashed at the ball. It span well wide.

I celebrated like there had been a goal, bouncing up and down like the hard floor was a trampoline.

Your current reputation with Dani: 8%.

I saw Henri in deep conversation with Alex, and then Alex was rushing around to the left. Suddenly there was energy all around me. I couldn't help but pace around.

Your current reputation with Dani: 9%.

Another attack, and Dani's quick footsteps were in full retreat. She ended up on her goal line, and the black team were two on one. One simple pass later, the ball was slammed into the roof of the net. Five–two and much of the new energy was gone.

Your current reputation with Dani: 7%.

It was deeply frustrating, but I had to let her work out her new position. She glanced over and I pointed to the sweeper spot and mimed that she should *sweep*. She stood with her hands on her hips, staring at nothing, then trudged forward. She would do it my way.

Your current reputation with Dani: 10%.

We kicked off, and the ball was lost almost instantly. Another attack, but this time Dani didn't retreat. She found herself with two players coming—one shaped to shoot, but I knew he wouldn't. I tried to beam out a psychic signal warning her, but I needn't have worried. Dani read the move, intercepted the pass, and played it forward to Darnell. He turned and passed out wide to Harold. He shot—why? Bad angle; dumb choice—scuffed it, but Simons was on the move, close to goal, and he slammed the ball low and hard into the net. Five–three, and a big pop of energy.

Dani looked at me. I put my hand to my mouth, overacting that I was shocked. Shocked, I tell you!

She did a demure little grin. Now *she* was starting to get it.

Your current reputation with Dani: 20%.

The tide had turned. Time was running out, but we'd broken through. The black team's manager had been telling jokes with his coaches the whole half, apart from those moments where I was dicking around on the pitch. Now he looked worried. I lived for those moments! He didn't make any changes just yet, but I knew what he'd do. He'd go defensive. Try to hold on to the lead. And we would absolutely thrash him anyway. Yawn.

I walked around to the long side of the pitch, into the middle, and scanned the team. The electricity I'd summoned up was almost tangible. I bent to feel the air above the pitch, to see if I could feel it. There was nothing, but for a moment I thought about launching fully into the game. I could become an emotional presence on the sideline, blood and thunder, thunder and lightning, and the team would respond. God, they'd respond, and I was a few misfiring neurons away from doing it.

But that wasn't the mission. I stood and took a few paces back towards Dani and angled myself directly at her.

Over my shoulder I kept watch for the next black move. The goalie had the ball, and I knew they'd pass long to the right. I waved my hat and crabbed to the left. A dozen tiny leftwards shuffle movements in two seconds. Dani's eyes widened and she moved left herself, before the ball had even left the goalie's hand. The black team winger was racing forward, but Dani moved against the tide, took the ball on her chest, and passed to Simons. He burst forward, cut the ball back, and then there was chaos. While the ball bounced around, Dani was entranced. I waved my cap around. *Get back into position!*

With a start, she did. I did the "sailor watching the horizon" mime again, which made her roll her eyes. But she smiled—a blink-and-you'll-miss-it microsmile.

Your current reputation with Dani: 40%.

The scramble ended with the ball in the goalie's hands, and this time I crabbed to the right. Dani copied me, intercepted the ball, passed forwards, and retreated to her position.

I looked up at the timer. Loads of time left. We would absolutely crush this. No danger.

I took a second to enjoy the scene I'd created. Across the chasm, the other manager, begging his players to fall back. To my right, Alex and Henri rushing around giving tips to the strikers. Behind me, some kind of tournament organiser. She had a clipboard and a lanyard. She gave me a little hat tip. I saluted in return. Then over to the left, the five banks of benches. Solid, ancient, easily bearing the weight of the spectators. Almost all the Knights were there now, taking in the show before their match. Terry was watching me coach a rival team with multiple shakes of the head and a twinkle in his eye. Lots of players from other teams had come, too. Word had got around that something was happening. Many were pointing their phones at the pitch.

Dani was checking me every ten seconds or so now. Wondering what I'd teach her next. Instead, I pointed to the stands behind her. She looked at them, then back. I put my hand out, flat. Then I raised it. I was trying to say: *Let's take things up a notch. Let's put on a show.*

Dani raised her arms. *What?*

I thought about how to say it. Then I thought, *fuck it*. Show, don't tell, and all that. I went to get a ball, waited for a break in play, then flicked it up and did some mad tekkers. Basically what that means is crossing football skills with tricks a seal does to get a fish. After my tiny routine, I bowed to the spectators.

Dani laughed. *No way!*

Why?

She pointed to the scoreboard.

I rolled my eyes, highly exaggerated. *Fine! Create some fucking goals, then.* I Tysonned my arms in mock frustration.

Your current reputation with Dani: 60%.

The pair of defenders, Ally and Bev, had been pretty shit, tbh, but now that they were under less pressure they started to get a grip on their roles. Ally made a tackle, Bev picked the ball up and passed it to Dani. Although we had four strikers, she found it hard to pick a pass. She put her foot on the ball. I waved my hat until she looked at me. I mimed a golf shot. What's it called—a sand wedge? The loopiest one.

Dani rolled the ball forward and tried it. She made a big mess and the ball went flying. Nowhere near me, but I threw myself to the floor and covered my head. When I looked up, she was laughing pretty hard.

Your current reputation with Dani: 70%.

I took a ball and chipped it to her. She chipped it back. I extended my arms. *See? Easy.*

Oh, I was having the time of my life. Dicking around, showing off, making amazing football happen, while being socially useful? What more could I want? It was incredible. I was getting pretty hungry, though. I wandered back behind the goal to drink some of the sugar water stuff Alex had brought.

So I was handily located when my spider senses went wild. I took a few steps to the right before I even knew what I was seeing.

The reckless yob, the Bravery 20 bulldozer, wasn't used to being on the end of such a mauling, and he had taken it upon himself to sort things out. He dribbled down the wing, full pelt, and when Dani went to intercept she correctly decided to do . . . nothing. The enormous kid kicked the ball too far, but instead of leaving it, he chased it even harder.

"Shit," I said, pushing my legs in that direction.

The fucking wooden benches! The edges weren't sharp, but fuck me. The guy's head was literally going to crack open before my very eyes. I didn't want that haunting my dreams.

I got there in time, wrapped my arms around his waist, tried to arrest his momentum.

Then I was falling, trying to twist, fleetingly astonished by the guy's weight, and then I saw the bench shooting up towards me and then I was looking down, surprised to see blood. I took a second to check I could move all my limbs, but when I tried to stand up I felt weird.

The kid got up and ran back onto the pitch. Little prick didn't even thank me.

Terry was first on the scene. "Max, Christ, what."

Some parents. "Anyone a doctor?"

"Don't move."

"Sit down."

"No, he should stay standing."

And then Henri was there, and Alex, and they supported me across the hall. Before we went through, I found some strength and made them turn me back to the pitch.

"Attack!" I yelled. Henri looked alarmed. I misunderstood why. "Oh, yeah. Deaf. Well, shit. I was doing so well."

Henri later told me I'd babbled in baby gurgles or one of those languages you get in a random Swiss village.

Henri stayed with me in the hospital, flirting with nurses, making a fuss. I later learned it wasn't a hospital but a private clinic. Apparently I had private insurance through the club.

It was a nice, quiet place with lots of staff—I should have guessed it wasn't a normal hospital—and I was feeling just fine with the odd bout of wooziness.

"Did they win, then?"

"Who cares? Winning's for losers," he said. "I can't believe you said that. You're shameless in pursuit of something."

"Let's go for the same nurse," I said. He'd spent the whole day trying to cheer me up even though I'd been trying to find out what was wrong with *him*.

"No, Max. Please just rest." He got a text and shot to his feet. "I must fly. Be safe. I will talk to you tomorrow."

"What? Don't leave me," I said, suddenly pathetic. A mighty pharaoh become helpless invalid.

"Hush, Max."

"But . . . but did you like it?"

"I did. It was a great day. Page five of our story."

I wanted to ask what pages two to four were, but I had a little pang and when I opened my eyes, he was gone. And my hand was in someone's. I tried to turn but it hurt.

"Max," said Emma. "It's all right. Stay still."

"You came," I said.

"Of course. Henri called me right away." Huh. Spends the whole day threatening to steal her from me, then plays cupid.

"How? It's miles to Newcastle."

"Three hours. Dad drove me. I was in no state. Henri said you'd cracked your skull open saving a disabled kid."

That was exasperating. I mean, yeah, but also, no.

"Mr. Best?" said someone from the door. "You have visitors. Would you like to see them?"

Obviously Emma's dad. Well, shit. His daughter had called him in an Henri-induced panic and he'd dropped everything to drive her to me. "I thought Newcastle were playing today."

"They are. He left when I called. We listened to it on the radio."

"Mr. Best?"

"Yeah, send him in." I couldn't say no, could I? Guy was acting like a fucking hero. Anyway, if he got annoying I could just pretend to black out. If you think I wouldn't produce some grossly unattractive drool to get rid of someone, you haven't been paying attention.

While Emma gave me a little hand squeeze, I steeled myself. But in walked two randos . . . and Dani.

I tried to sit up straight, but it hurt and I collapsed.

"Where's your dad?" I said to Emma.

"Gone back."

Six-hour round trip and the ruination of his day. Wow. But it wasn't time to think about him. "Hi," I said to the newcomers, then remembered the whole deaf thing. It was a lot more of a problem now that there was no football.

"Hi," said the guy, so he was hearing. "I'm Dani's dad."

"Are you Smith or Smithe?" I asked, which made Emma squeeze my hand, worried for my sanity.

"Smith," he said with a smile. At least, I think that's what he said. "When we went to pick Dani up from the So Solid, we were, ah, pretty surprised to find that she had been named Player of the Tournament." He signed to her, and she shyly showed me a little football man on a small plinth. They'd engraved her name into the plaque. She also had a gold medal on a ribbon, with *2023 Crewe WINNER* engraved. So they'd won the whole thing.

"Mate," I said, resting my head back on my pillow.

"Well, we asked and quite a lot of people tried to tell us the story."

The mum started signing at me now. It was the first time anyone had ever signed at me. I was surprised how big and expressive some of the movements were, and how small and precise were some others.

The dad translated. "Alex said you wanted to recruit Dani for your team. Is that true?"

"Absolutely," I said.

"Tell us your phone number and we'll make a WhatsApp group with you."

This was it! The day was going to pay off. Signing a superstar from the comfort of my own bed. I smiled and closed my eyes, just for a moment.

When I opened them, the parents were gone, but Emma and Dani were facing each other across my bed, texting. I groaned and picked up my phone—there was a lot of chat history to go through. I typed.

Me: I'll read all that later. Dani. Really great to meet you. You are an amazing player. I'm starting a women's team in Chester. It will be the best in the country one day. I want you to be my first signing.

Dani: I liked meeting you, too. You are funny. And this is another joke.

Me: No joke. Very serious.

Dani: You mean a deaf team?

Me: Normal team. Can I say normal? I don't mean normal. I mean thingy. Non-disabled. (Bit woozy. Soz if I said bad.)

Dani: How can I play in a hearing team?

Me: Hearing. Right. I knew that word. Mate, it's not a hearing team. It's a team. It's Chester Somethings.

Emma: Somethings?

Me: I want a cool name but I can't think of one. Chester Medusas. Fans and players can choose. Dani will get a vote.

Dani: I can't play that kind of football.

Me: You can. You're top. I'll teach you. I don't look like it because I'm all humpty-dumptied right now, but I'm actually the best player in the world, probably. I know what I'm talking about.

Dani: I can't.

Me: Emma, type you can you can until Dani gets that she really really can. And will.

I put my phone on my chest and put my hands over my face. When I took them away, Dani looked at me. Thumbs up, thumbs down. *Are you okay?*

Wavy hand. *Bit woozy.*

She returned to typing. There were three dots for a while.

Dani: **Years ago, I played big pitch football with hearing girls. I made a noise to tell my team where I was and where I wanted the ball. I don't know what the noise sounds like but it must have been very stupid. The players on the other team always laughed at me. Some of the grown-ups, too. The people watching. Laughing. My friends told me the people copied the noises. It wasn't nice but I could cope with it. Later someone told me my teammates laughed at me, too, but I didn't believe them. So she showed me chats. And they were. They were laughing at me. My own team.**

Emma: **Oh, Dani, no.**

Me: **Holy fuck.**

Dani: **And the managers. I couldn't read their lips. They'd turn away and give instructions and I wouldn't know what to do. So they wouldn't pick me. I'd train and go to matches and after six games I'd have played ten minutes. And one time I got a yellow card for kicking the ball away but it was because I didn't hear the whistle. I tried to sign to the ref to explain but she didn't want to know.**

Me: **That is fucking bullshit and none of that will happen on my watch. I promise.**

Dani: **You can't stop it. It's people. People are shit. My team today, they get me, and I get them. We're a real team. You're fun and kind but you can't understand it. You don't know what it's like to want to shut out the world and only be with people you trust.**

I gave Emma a guilty glance that she didn't notice. I went to type but Dani was going again.

Dani: If I went to training with your team, I know you'd try your best. And you're the boss and the star so while you were there everything would be perfect. I know that. But when you're not there. When you're in hospital again because you saved some asshole's life . . .

Me: Dani! We don't talk like that here!

Dani: Sorry.

Me: This is England. We say arsehole.

She laughed—the biggest I'd got out of her yet. We had to be getting close to one hundred percent on the relationship tracker. Had to be.

Dani: When you're not there I'll have to struggle and to be brave. Like Harry.

I learned who Harry was later, and so will you.

Dani: "Normal" football is the worst thing that ever happened to me. I don't want to struggle for what everyone else gets for free. I don't want to be brave. I don't want my life to be a constant drama. I'm happy where I am. Thank you very much for believing in me and for teaching me. I will keep this trophy forever. It already means the world to me. Thank you very much Max Best, and goodbye.

Me: But did you like it?

Dani: Did I like what?

Me: Being the best.

Dani: I did.

Dani has left the chat.

17

CULTURE

Football glossary: *Cultured left foot*. *Reference to an aesthetically pleasing left-footed player whose ability to curve a pass around a defender is the closest most football fans get to watching live ballet. "He struck the free kick with that cultured left foot of his." Please note right feet are never cultured. Hey, I don't make the rules.*

I had a restless night and didn't sleep much. I'm not sure when it happened, but I'd convinced myself that the curse had given me rapid healing. Not quite Wolverine levels, but a definite boost. If it happened it happened when I slept, though, and if I didn't sleep I didn't get the benefit.

What was causing me to stare at the ceiling was the fact I couldn't turn left and right every twenty seconds like I normally did—the nurses had put me in a neck brace and when they saw me trying to manoeuvre it so I could side-sleep, they did something to make it harder.

But mostly it was Dani. And Pascal. And James. And Vivek. And all the other prospects I would find who didn't quite fit into the standard picture of a football player. I had vague aspirations of doing something dramatic that would persuade every talented player in the country that Chester was the place to go. But it wasn't, was it? It was the same kind of environment as Darlo, and I'd survived there by bullying the bullies and being talented enough to reshape the team in my image. Guess who isn't doing that? Every single one of the players I wanted to sign.

So it came down to culture. Like Dani said, culture wasn't only what happened when I was around, but what happened when I wasn't. How could I massively, rapidly improve the culture?

Yeah, a sleepless night obsessing over what I used to think of as a corporate buzzword. Football is about glory.

I wasn't the only one suffering. Emma stayed at some nearby hotel but didn't get much sleep. She said she was plagued by visions of me slipping into a coma and dying alone. She was in the clinic's reception at half five, begging to be let into my room. When she was allowed in, I promised her I felt much better, which was true, but I was so subdued she didn't believe me.

"Let's think about how we get home," I said, testing my injuries. The impact site was very sore and my neck hurt.

"No need. Henri's taken care of everything."

"He has?"

"Yeah. Mike Dean is going to come and take you to Chester. You'll be close if you need any tests. We'll stay there overnight and on Wednesday Henri will drive you to Darlo."

Nursed by Emma for a whole day? Top plan. Flawless. The only problem was that there were sixteen days left in January and I couldn't afford to spend two full days in hospital. At the very least, I needed to spend the evening grinding for XP. But if I kicked up a fuss, MD and Emma would conspire to inject me full of sedatives. I'd have to get what I wanted in slices. Salami tactics.

MD was stressed. He drove with one nail between his teeth. I could feel the times when he thought about the league table—he slowed down by five miles per hour.

"Are you thinking about Scenario B?" I asked. I hadn't spoken much that morning; rapid movements, excitement, noise, bright lights—everything made me slightly queasy.

"I think about it all the time." He glanced at me, but I was done talking. He checked his rearview mirror. I hadn't liked the way he angled it at Emma when he thought I wasn't looking, but I supposed loads of people did that no matter who was in the back seat. "I got a call from Crewe Alexandra asking why our DoF was running their Para team."

"What did you say?" said Emma, smiling.

"What *could* I say?" he said. "*Oh, yeah. He does that.*"

"Are they angry?"

"I don't know. It was hard to tell."

"They won, didn't they?"

"Yeah." He went back to biting his nail. "There's a post on the Chester fans' Facebook page. Link to a banter website. Title's something like, 'Hero Director Steps in to Lead Wrong Team to Victory.' Top comment is 'I had the wrong leg amputated and that was an easier mistake to understand—my legs both look the same.' Some fans think you helping Crewe is funny, some are upset. 'Why are we paying this guy to coach other teams?'"

"Fair point," I said.

"It's not a fair point!" said Emma. "You were scouting a player! Tell him, Max."

I closed my eyes and rested my head on the backrest. I didn't care about defending my name. Dani didn't want to come and if she did come she wouldn't stay. That's all that mattered. That had to be fixed—urgently.

"I heard the story from Henri and Terry. Henri's version seemed fanciful, but Terry's version was even more unbelievable. Henri had you creating an intricate tactical web in which a deaf girl was the spider. Terry said you took a tiny, frail girl and turned her into Al Capone. He said you played the most attacking formation conceivable, got bored of that, and got shot of the *goalkeeper*." He shook his head. "And they won the final, eight–one. Terry normally brings the Knights home after their last match, but yesterday they stayed right to the end to watch the whole thing. Almost everyone did. I have to confess, Max, I didn't know all that when I called Terry. I put some of the Facebook comments to him and he got quite angry with me." MD grinned. "I've never heard him angry. That's one employee we don't have to worry about. He is all in, and then some." MD sighed. "So who's this girl?"

Emma told MD what she knew, and added details she'd learned when I was unconscious. I hadn't read the chat history yet. I turned to give Emma my full attention; the nurses would have been furious.

"I asked her about football and that lasted about a minute. She wanted to know who Max was and so on, and how we met, but mostly she wanted to talk about Harry Styles."

"Harry is Harry *Styles*," I said.

"Yes."

"The singer dude. Not Harry Kane, the footballer."

"No."

"Shit."

"She's a massive Harrie. That's the name for the fandom."

I closed my eyes. To try to understand James Yalley I'd read the Bible and talked to loads of Christians. Conceptually, religion makes sense. Ancient humans needed it to cope with nasty, brutish, and short lives. My brain was just about on solid ground, there. Understanding a teenage girl was maybe a challenge too far. I closed my eyes to help concentrate. "She's deaf. He's a singer. She can't hear his songs. Does she like his videos or what? What is it?"

Emma did some gesture. A shrug, maybe. "She's a teenage girl. He's a hot boy. Hot but safe."

MD shocked me by making a valuable contribution. "He's from Cheshire."

"That's right, MD!" said Emma. "He's from Holmes Chapel. She grew up in the next village, more or less. He's one of the biggest stars in the world but he's legit the boy next door. There's a cardboard cutout of him in the bakery where he worked before he got his big break. Fans go on pilgrimages to the spots he's talked about. She's seen all that. Eased into the community. Facebook groups, websites, Twitter accounts that post daily pics of Harry with cats."

The way she said his name! I found the energy to smile and point accusingly. "*You* are a Harrie!"

She flushed. "I *was* a Harrie. I had my One Direction phase. Now I'm a . . ."

"Bestie," suggested MD.

"Maximalist," I said.

"Nevertheless," said Emma, copying one of my ways of changing the topic. "She's massively into Harry Styles. I doubt you can do anything with that, but there you go. It would help if you had a social media presence. Just saying."

"Nope. Still hate it. I'll find a way," I said. "A Max Best way. She's my top priority."

"Just how good is she?" said MD.

"When she signs," I said, "she'll be the best player at the club." Then I put my neck pillow on and closed my eyes.

When we got near Chester, I asked MD if we could stop off and watch training for a second. He tried to refuse, saying I was all smashed up and needed to rest, but I promised him I wasn't going to play or butt heads with Ian Evans.

"I just want to show Emma where the magic happens. You, as well. Point out a couple of cool things I've noticed. When will I get a chance to show you both at the same time? We should make the most of it. I'll go straight to bed afterwards." I deserved an Oscar for that little performance, let me tell you. Outside, I was breezy and upbeat. Inside, I was feeling . . . mutinous. A strange word, given that I was theoretically running the club. But that was just it. When it came right down to it, I wasn't running shit. I could sack Spectrum and kick Tyson out, but the club was still so far from what I wanted it to be that bile actually rose in my throat.

I kept up my calm, amiable charade all the way to the training pitch. As soon as I saw the drill, my pulse shot up, triggering a mild headache. I calmed myself, idly noting a red attribute in one of our key players and that Raffi had added a point of CA .

We strolled up to Ian Evans and Vimsy, who were sometimes barking out orders but mostly chatting. When they noticed us, Evans scowled and Vimsy's eyes widened. A normal reaction, you might think, when a ravishing blonde shows up. I knew better; it was guilt.

MD made the introductions and joked about someone finally giving me a whack on the head. Evans snorted, a single, unpleasant laugh, and turned away.

There was a hole in the scene, and that hole was me. Normally, I'd have chatted nonstop, explaining what we were seeing, what the point of the drills were, all that kind of thing. But with my whiplash and the queasy feeling in my gut, I stood silent, undercurrents of emotion not quite touching my face. I wanted MD and Emma to feel that something was wrong. The way Emma was side-eyeing me—mission accomplished.

After a long, awkward silence, I finally spoke.

"Vimsy. These are the same drills you did last Monday."

Evans's hair quivered, while Vimsy defended himself. He said routine was important and players liked it and blah blah blah.

"MD," I said, softly. "Tomorrow night's match has been called off?"

"Yeah. Pitch is waterlogged. Ours is holding up, just about. And from what I've heard from your former haunt, Saturday's home match will go ahead."

"Mmm," I said. I stared at the drill for a while. When Vimsy started to relax, I spoke again, trying to make sense of the contradictory facts. "No match tomorrow . . . Doing the same drills . . ."

Ian Evans turned, remembered Emma was there, and scaled back the attack he was planning. "You don't tell us how to train the players, Best. We've been doing this for a long time."

"Mmm," I said. I rubbed the sore spot on my skull. There was something about causing the pain that was almost addictive. "Mmm," I said again, checking that MD and Emma were trying to work out what was going on. They were. "Vimsy, could you get Aff?"

"Aff?"

Instead of repeating myself, I sucked in a big blob of air—kind of an inverse sigh—and waited. The guy called the left winger over.

The Irishman was lightly sweaty. "Hi, Max. Emma. MD. What can I do for you?"

I looked at his feet. "Are you injured, mate?"

"What? No." He gave Evans a worried glance.

"Huh," I said. And waited. It was good, this waiting thing. Way more effective than I would have thought.

"He said he's fine," snapped Evans.

"So if he aggravates an injury you'll pay his wages?" I said.

"What are you *talking* about? We're trying to *train*. These interruptions are *unprofessional*."

"Aff," I said. His acceleration had dropped a point and was in red. He had some injury he hadn't told anyone about. Disappointing. I scanned his legs, thinking an acceleration injury might be located in a muscle. Calf strain?

"Well," he said, watching as I tried to X-ray him. "I did feel a twinge in me hammy, but it's nothing. I'll run it off."

"No," I said. "We don't do that here. You'll go to medical. Right away. Because you're our best player and we can't be without you for two *fucking* months." That little exertion cost me. Pang of headache, nausea, dizziness. The whole shebang.

"Right," he said, looking from me to Evans to Vimsy and back to Evans. "Right so."

"We'll all go," I said and turned back towards the credit card building, leaving Evans to mutter obscenities under his breath.

In the mornings, Physio Dean and Livia were based in the credit card building. There they treated minor sprains and injuries and gave massages and all that. In the afternoons, they went to the stadium where the equipment was better, or they went off to do side jobs to help pay their bills.

Aff, Emma, and MD chatted all the way to the door of the building, but on the last step I blocked them from going through. I put my finger to my lips, waited until they got the message, then we walked into the medical room in near silence. We found different places to sit and waited. And waited.

MD pointed to his phone. He wanted to make a call. I shook my head. We waited some more.

Physio Dean finally slammed through a door, talking angrily on his phone, striding through into his little office room without even looking at us. As we listened to his conversation, MD got more and more angry. Now he knew what it was like to be an injured player at Chester Football Club. He understood what I meant when I complained about Dean's bedside manner. MD stood up, ready to go in and confront Dean. Again, I shook my head and silently asked him to sit down.

By the time Dean came out, pulling on a latex glove, the mood in the room was sour.

"Oh," he said. He tried to plaster a smile onto his face. "Max. MD. Er . . ."

I stood, went to the door, and gestured that Emma and MD should follow me out. As I closed the door behind me, I saw the face of someone who knew he'd just cost himself a job.

The three of us went to a little greasy spoon café. Those places normally have good tea, large breakfasts, and shit furniture. This was no exception. My plastic chair wobbled. The table was covered with crumbs, coffee stains, and what I hoped was a blob of mustard. Before she took our order, a waitress gave the table a wipe, replacing the debris with a harsh chemical smell.

"MD," I said. "I'm glad you saw that." I took a hit of tea. I was feeling much better. Much more like myself. "You, too, Emma. That's how it is. That's how it is, how it was, and if you listen to anyone in the football world, how it will always be." Outside, cars were going past at regular intervals. Normal people with normal jobs. Normal people told their bosses what they were doing. I spoke to MD. "I know it must seem like I'm popping up all over the place with no rhyme or reason. I'm working hard, though. I'm being serious."

"I know that, Max. It is baffling, sometimes, hearing that you've asked for tickets to Burnley, or when my phone starts blowing up because you're going bananas in Crewe or you're in critical condition in hospital."

"Yeah, well. Hospital. I was there in the bed last night thinking, what's the point of me?"

"Max," said Emma.

"I don't mean it like that," I said, smiling. "I mean for Chester. Like, am I supposed to go and find a very slightly better left back? Is that my purpose?"

"It wouldn't hurt," said MD.

My smile broadened. "Yeah. But what's my talent? Really? It's not finding incrementally better left backs. I mean, I'll do that, too. But no. My *real* superpower is finding talent no one else can find. But then what? What do we do with them?" I pointed back towards the training centre. "Ems. Would you bring Dani into that?"

She eyed MD. Didn't really want to say negative things in front of him. "Probably not, no."

I opened my arms a little as though I'd scored a big point. "I wouldn't bring *me* into that!"

MD opened the little biscuit he'd got with his tea. Brought it towards his mouth. "You're talking about culture."

"Yep."

"It's hard to change. A lot of companies try and fail." He popped the biscuit into his mouth, and we watched him munch it.

I said, "Those companies don't take it seriously."

MD then told us a long and fairly boring story from his life in the fast-paced, hard-nosed world of pharmaceuticals. It ended with him saying, "So you see. Sometimes it's not as easy as you think."

"It will be pretty easy, actually. Most players are out of contract in the summer. Anyone who's a dick gets kicked. From now on, we put behaviour clauses in everyone's contract. Make it easy to bin them. Emma, can you help with that?"

"Maybe. You'll have to get specific."

"Oh, I can get specific. But before we do anything . . . MD. Are you with me? You have to be with me all the way."

He looked into his cup—reading the tea leaves, maybe. "We need this to improve as a team?"

"No," I admitted. "We can get better players. But I'm talking about big jumps in quality. *Big* improvements. You saw what I did with one talented player yesterday. Give me a star striker and a midfield fulcrum and I will move the earth. You know who said that?"

"Archimedes," said Emma.

"No. It was Theo Zagorakis."

MD pushed his cup away. "I'd say about half the first team won't take any change. You'll create conflict with them. And, you know, Scenario B is looming. Can we do this in the summer? When we're safe?"

"No."

MD grinned. "Why did I even bother asking? I'm hungry. Let's talk about it over some food. Somewhere the tables don't wobble."

We went out to a nice lunch, MD's treat. I tried to ban football as a topic—I liked to have breaks from it so it didn't totally fill my days—but they kept checking the Facebook groups and TikTok.

MD said, "Someone's posted a new link. Thumbnail is you in a red hat doing a kick-up. Title: 'Tekkers to the Moon.' Tekkers is technique, Emma. Skills." Emma went round to watch along with him.

I exhaled. "Why do you never turn the sound off in public? Literally spent the last two hours talking about culture."

The clip was pretty short. Emma frowned. "I thought you didn't do this *performing seal stuff*."

"Show me," I said. MD rotated the phone. It was the clip of me doing tricks on the sideline. Pretty cringe. "I was trying to get Dani to entertain the fans. Hard to say that nonverbally. So I did that."

"But Max," said Emma. "You want kids to *want* to come to Chester, right?"

"Yeah."

"So even *I* think this is impressive. Imagine your mate sends you this video and it says Open Trial, Saturday, three p.m. And the guy doing the tekkers is the boss? That's awesome. Sign me up."

MD's eyebrows shot up. "You're talking about a social media-based recruitment drive? Let's workshop some slogans! Chester Welcomes Careful Dribblers. Er . . . Got Skills? Chester Wants You! Chester Wants *Youth*. No, keep it simple. Come to Chester."

I rolled my eyes. "Come to Chester. Max Best performs at ten a.m. and two p.m. Jesus Christ."

"Are you saying, Max," said MD, glancing at Emma, "that we have an incredible marketing tool that we're not allowed to use? Look at this! You're a natural. Listen." He gave me one of his serious faces. "If we do this. If we reach out to young people, show that we're modern and inclusive and diverse and cool, it'll do a lot. It'll show the first team we're serious about culture. It'll attract talent." He licked his lips. "And the sponsors will love it. This . . . I've been daydreaming about this for years. We're so far behind. We can combine your culture war—oh! I like that. Your culture war with my sponsor-friendly content. Perfect synergy. Really, Max. Come on, you know I'm right."

Emma gave him an Emsy Two-Thumbs. I looked towards the exit in a show of wanting to flee. "Team," she said, in a weird voice that made me twist so fast I nearly gave myself whiplash again. "Teamwork. *Teamwork.*"

"Is that an impression of *me*?"

"Teamworrrrrk."

I sat back, smiling. She'd done me. "It's a good idea. But what you're asking is three things, right? One. You want me to do tekkers on camera. And I'm not into that. I tell the kids to practise skills they use in matches. Flicking a ball onto the back of your neck is inane. And a crisp three-yard pass is not going to go viral. Two. If we're doing *content*, we might as well make it something for Dani. Which means I have to listen to loads of Harry Styles. And maybe he's my favourite singer and I just don't know it yet. But spoiler alert, probably not. And three. I don't like social media. It's toxic. This is like using anthrax to kill some germs in your sink."

"No, it isn't," said Emma, who loved that whole world. "You're so mental."

"Will you at least think about it, Max?"

"Yeah, sure, big think."

The tekkers clip provoked another wave of reaction from the Chester fans. Lots of positive voices saying things like, "What a player, can't wait till he's in the first team." And lots of negatives. "Show-off prick does nothing for the wages get rid."

I found myself scanning the negative comments looking for patterns, just as I'd done the morning before I went to meet Bulldog and the rest of the board. "MD. While we're doing all this culture stuff, let's go talk to Bulldog and Tyson. Then Spectrum. Then, bed and soup. I promise."

Bulldog's cybersecurity office. Around 4 p.m. Emma and MD made small talk with Bulldog until Tyson came zooming in, sweating from a rapid bike ride from school.

I clapped my hands. "All right. This shouldn't take long. This whole situation has been unpleasant for everyone, but I've come to realise we all want the same thing. We all want Tyson to improve and do well and, ideally, have a career. And the problem isn't talent, it's culture."

"Culture," said Bulldog, the way you might say "anthrax." As in: you've chosen to clean the sink with . . . anthrax?

"Yeah. Tyson's an individualist. What we're doing now in Chester is collectivist. It's that simple, really. It was never going to work. So . . ." I fussed in my pockets looking for a slip of paper. "The match against Broughton, there were scouts. They asked about Tyson before anyone else. I've written their phone numbers. They'd love to hear from you." I smiled at everyone.

"Is that it?" said Bulldog.

"Yep."

He turned to MD. "Max promised to try. I don't call this trying. What was that, a week?"

MD met his gaze. "If anything, Max tried too hard. Spectrum felt he was being micromanaged."

"And the minute I wasn't there, he was back to his old ways." I shook my head. "We're changing the culture at Chester. Massive focus on . . . what's a less wanky way of saying inclusivity?"

"What does that mean?" said Tyson. He was pretty sullen.

"In your case, it means passing to other players," I said, surprising myself by not lacing my voice with sarcasm.

"But what does it mean for everyone else?"

"It means don't be a dick. It means treat people with respect. It means if I bring some rando to training, be nice. They might be the next star player and we want to make them feel welcome at the club."

"Like that girl?"

"Which girl?"

"The disabled girl from the tournament. We've been watching the videos all day. You made her a goalkeeper but she had, like, twenty assists."

"She's not disabled. But yes."

Tyson suddenly seemed close to tears. "Are you saying you think I'd be a dick to her?"

"No, because your dad would batter me if I said that."

"Say what you think," said Tyson. Kind of brave, really.

I shrugged. "Imagine you're deaf. You get asked to go to play for Chester boys. Everyone's super nice. Super nice. You feel great. You start playing, but there's one boy who's always moving into your position, who never passes to you, who . . . expresses his displeasure in a way you understand very clearly. Then off the pitch, he's super nice again. What do you think? Is that a place you'd stay?"

"No," mumbled the kid. I nearly asked him to speak up, then remembered I wasn't his headmaster.

I tapped the paper. "You go to Tranmere. Wrexham. Alty. You'll fit in. You'll do well. It's fine."

Bulldog lifted a paperweight from his desk. The movement scared me a little. "You are *such* a hypocrite."

I was still staring at the object. If he slammed that into my pre-weakened skull, he could seriously mess me up. "What?"

"Tyson's playing like you. You don't pass. You shoot from everywhere. You complain when players don't pass to you. You don't obey your manager. He's copying *you*." He mumbled something at the end that sounded like "fuck sake."

"What are you talking about?" I said.

Bulldog was actually much better than me at controlling his temper. He gritted his teeth. "The lads send videos around. Goals from the Premier League. Mad tekkers. Funny own goals. And yeah, Max Best clips. 'Tyson,' they say, 'you play like Max!' What's he supposed to think?"

I looked to Emma for help. She shrugged. She didn't know if it was true. MD looked blank. Didn't want to get involved. "I *don't* play like that. But anyway, it makes no odds. I specifically told Tyson not to take shots. Talk about clarity! Literally one thing. Tyson, mate, it's okay that you kept shooting. That's who you are. I'm not angry about it. You do you, as a wise woman once told me."

I stopped. Nobody said anything. That seemed to be that. Quite a relief.

But then the little shit ruined it. "Can I have another chance?"

"Why?" I said, semi-exploding. "Why? You don't like it! You're supposed to get angry at me, vow to prove me wrong, go to Tranmere, get into the team, score a brace against Chester, knock us out of the cup, run around in front of the dugout flicking Vs at me." Emma cleared her throat. I eyed her. "What?"

"He wants to try it your way."

I corrected her. "He wants to try it my way *again*." Everyone was looking at me like I was being unreasonable. I knew better than all of them how much attention this kid needed. It was disproportionate. I did some quick calculations. Giving him another chance would cost very little, but it would make me look good in front of Emma, MD, and, yeah, even the dad. He was, after all, a sponsor and a member of the board. "Crazy. I can't believe this is happening. Fine. Fine, let's try it. With conditions. One, no shooting, ever. You shoot, you're out. Two, anyone leaves the club because of you, you're out. That's a universal thing, don't take that personally. But it's new so I'm mentioning it. Three, this space reserved for future conditions. Four, you're not allowed to say you play like me."

"Oh, come on," said Bulldog.

I stood and pointed to his chair. "Can I use your computer?" He gave up his spot and I went to a private YouTube channel I'd made where I'd collected clips of me from my time as a player. There were about thirty-five, mostly very short, that I'd stolen from other channels. I clicked on the first one. "Tyson, get round here. Check this out. This is my first match. Whitby Town. Not very high resolution, but that's me there with no number on my back. Get the ball, beat the man, now I'm clear." I hit pause. "What's going through my head here are the percentages. Bottom left, sixty percent. Top right, fifty percent. Square pass, ninety-nine percent. Guess what I chose?"

For the next fifteen minutes, I went through the early stages of my career explaining what was in my head just before I did what I did, including all the bullshit and politics that factored into me making seemingly bad decisions. It was a masterclass in how the shitty culture of the team made me play like a twat. I was focused on Tyson, but his dad, Emma, and MD were riveted.

While I explained why for the first time in my life I had more goals than assists, I found myself considering which snippets and angles made me look good. What if there was music playing? What if the moments I struck the ball were synced up with a drum beat? Huh. It seemed like the viral-type videos MD wanted could work with normal football skills. I wouldn't need to be a performing seal to create cool, sponsor-friendly content that would also help me attract young players. I could use real skills. Hmmm.

We drove to the place where the kids trained. We walked towards the all-weather pitch. Emma had been a bit quiet. "What's up?"

"That was so interesting," she said. "But scary."

"Scary? What?"

"You're a bit of a psycho."

I tutted. "MD, help me out."

He didn't help me out. "I'm with Emma. I had no idea so much of football is about who you hate and whose career you're trying to boost."

"We're trying to put an end to that, remember. Trying to create a culture that allows people to play without the politics and pettiness. There he is."

Spectrum was waiting on a bench. He'd met Jackie Reaper and they'd had a big ol' chat about whether I was a fantasist or not. This meeting would decide if he would work for a few more months, perhaps until the summer. If we could smooth things over, it'd give me a bit of breathing space when it came to buying the staff perks. But I wasn't sure I *wanted* to smooth things over. Spectrum was bad culture. He got up, sat down, and finally got up again.

MD did the intros, although technically Spectrum met Emma when she was my assistant manager in the Broughton match.

"Can we talk alone?" said Spectrum. "There's a coffee place just there," he added, for Emma and MD.

"I'll keep him where I can see him," said Emma. "He goes crazy if one of his players doesn't take an injury seriously, but it's fine when *he* spends a whole day working with a giant crack in his skull. What's the name for that kind of behaviour, MD?"

"Culture?" joked MD, the traitor.

I walked away and Spectrum followed. "I heard," he said, "that you got Raffi Brown to manage the teams on Sunday."

"Yep."

"I didn't mean to leave you in the shit."

"Was he that bad?"

"Who, Raffi? I don't know. I mean, you shouldn't be scrabbling around looking for people to run the touchline. I mean, I want to do my job. Until you get a proper replacement. For a month or two or whatever you need."

"Great," I said, with zero enthusiasm. I pointed to the bench where Emma was showing MD something on her phone. "We've been talking about culture the whole day. We just came from a chat with Tyson. He's getting another chance. That means I need a coach who'll coach him the way I want."

"I'll do it."

"Great. Then there's the website."

"What?"

"You do the website. Joe told me."

"Yeah. On the side. It's not much work."

"And you chose the photo of me to put there."

That hit home. He suddenly knew where this was going. He shrank. "Yeah."

"See, you've put a shit photo of me there. And that must have been a big laugh with the Maxy No-Thumbs crowd. Super funny. Thing is, I'm the guy who's out there representing the club and looking for players. How many parents will look at our website and see that and assume we're a bunch of amateurs? Altrincham have a site that makes every academy kid look like Messi. Whoever does that site really loves that club. Do you get me? Now, I wouldn't normally even mention this because the first thing you'll do is run off to your mates and laugh about how vain I am. Sometimes I'm vain, sometimes I'm not. I don't know if it's a funny trait. But if I'm representing Chester, it's better if I look good. Do you agree with that?"

"Yeah."

"It's like, you don't want to be micromanaged, but you go against my express wishes when it comes to Tyson. You make me look shit on the website, which harms the club. And Maxy No-Thumbs. I'm twenty-two and my life's going pretty great, to be honest. I didn't care about the name-calling. Until yesterday when I tried to bring a deaf player to the club. She said no and I was gutted. But then I was relieved. Because what would happen? Would you and your banter group start calling her Dani No-Ears?"

"No! No fucking way!"

"Here's what I think. I think this place," I circled my finger, "is amateur. It's all cliques and banter and tough guys and bullshit. If you want to coach the kids for another month, I'm all for that. I don't have time to find your replacement." *Or the perk I need.* "But standards around here just went up. Way up. It's not just the training. It's every-thing around it. Any questions?"

He was still reeling from Dani No-Ears. "Er, no. What do you want me to do today?"

"Whatever you want. I'll be there at the start to let the new lads know which ones will be staying. It won't be as crowded from now on."

I hung around until five and cut most of the new kids. I did it well, I think. Told them they could always tell everyone they got scouted by Chester and that they'd had real, proper training and ninety-nine percent of the country couldn't say that. They took it with good grace, and the lads who got to stay were made up. MD had had enough of me for one day and fucked off.

I noted that Vivek was still stuck on CA 1. What the hell was that all about?

Then after being in the coffee shop for a pretty boring hour in which Emma and I romantically shared earbuds while watching Harry Styles music videos, I went and repeated the trick with the eighteens. We hadn't added a lot of talent overall. It was better than nothing, but I was relying a lot on Playdar beefing up the squads in double-quick time. If it didn't work as I hoped, maybe some viral videos would be the way. Not with a Harry Styles song, I didn't think. He was fine, surprisingly good voice, but a bit bland. I definitely got why Dani would like him, and it was cute letting Emma try to explain Harry to me. She started with a familiar phrase. "What I like about Harry is . . . athleticism, expertise," she said, and I joined in for the finish, "moments of surprise."

From there we went for a bit more downtime and we checked into a hotel. While Emma was taking care of all the admin, I fired out a bunch of texts. Soon after, with me lying on the bed pretending to be asleep, Ruth arrived. She persuaded Emma to go and get dinner and have some girl talk. The door closed behind them, I quit my fake snores, caught the next lift down, and hopped into Raffi's car. He took me to one of the five-a-side places I hadn't been to yet and I did some grinding while he told me what an ordeal it had been managing the youth teams.

"I froze, Max. I didn't know what to do. All those kids looking up at me, thinking I'm some kind of expert. No, it's not funny. I was so out of place."

"Imposter syndrome," I said.

"What?"

"You did four–four–two and made the substitutions I suggested?"

"Yeah, more or less."

I laughed. "You're a first-team star helping them with their careers. They loved it. Every time you're in the first team, when you get your big move, those kids will be buzzing. *That's our manager! He managed us. No, really!*"

He *tsked*. "Serious, now. We lost."

"I don't give a shit. You helped me out. They probably feel they let you down and they'll try even harder in training. Right. Let's get onto the real reason I asked you here. What's a good song to shoot a viral video to?"

Raffi didn't have strong opinions on the subject, but I found myself wondering if the improvement in his CA was because he'd played on Saturday or because he'd managed his first game. Either would make sense. More data needed!

While I was watching a PA 23 midfielder, wondering if there was any point in training him up, a couple of lads came over. "You're that Max Best, aren't ya? Are you doing any signings? Who's coming in?"

"Oh, signings!" I said, slapping myself on the forehead. "I knew I forgot something."

They laughed, but they stuck at it. Kept hassling me. Raffi saw I was getting pissed, cooled the sitch with his ace bouncer skills, and we left.

I picked up a measly 67 XP, with 8 going towards my debt. Frustrating.

But when Emma got back to the hotel room and climbed into bed, fairly wasted, she announced that "we" had decided to create an agency. Then she tried to get frisky, aggressively cuddled me, and fell asleep, all within ten seconds.

Weird day.

Tuesday morning, 9:15.

Good sleep, head solid, neck twisty. Speed healing confirmed!

All the players, coaches, and medical staff currently employed by Chester Football Club were in the Blues Bar, at the back of the main stand in the Deva stadium. Not quite *all*. As I climbed onto a sturdy piece of exercise equipment (a sort of half-sized vaulting box), I noted that Ian Evans hadn't deigned to grace us with his presence. The first team had colonised three of the large round dining tables. Vimsy, the coaches, and the medical guys were over on another. Spectrum was there, trying not to catch my eye.

MD stood to my right. Club secretary Joe to my left. From the board, Ruth, Crackers, and Barnesy had come. They were behind me, literally and figuratively.

I introduced myself, MD, and the others, just in case no one had ever done that before. And also to hammer home the point that this wasn't just my flight of fancy. This was serious. This was happening.

"Guys, listen up. Things are changing here. This meeting is where you learn what's going on. I'll give you the quick version today and if any of you are still at the club next year, I might do it again but more detailed." The threat of them not being here next year impressed a few people but caused resentment in others. Sam Topps was giving off very smug vibes—he had a two-year contract.

"We're launching the women's team. We're bringing in talented youngsters. We want to be a selling club. We're going to train talented players and sell them for money. Money which we'll reinvest in the squad and the facilities.

"I believe the culture of the first team is incompatible with my goals. So we're changing it.

"In no particular order, unhappiness. Some of you are unhappy and you haven't told anyone why. I don't blame you; I blame the culture. But I'm telling you now if you've got a problem that's affecting your performances, you need to talk to someone. Me, MD, one of the coaches, a player you like.

"Same with injuries. You pick up a knock, you tell the manager and the medical team. If someone tells you to run it off, that someone will be working against our culture and against the best interests of the club. So do *not* run it off. Go directly to the medical team. That is an instruction I am giving you now."

Aff's hand went up. "There'll be twenty people in there every day."

"We can't afford moronic injuries. That's it. This isn't open for discussion. I know when you're not moving right, and I know when you're not self-reporting.

"Right. Onto the big stuff. There will be a lot of new faces around. It is important to the club that they feel welcome. We're investing a lot of resources in finding these players, persuading them to choose Chester, and yeah, straight up paying them. They are employees of Chester Football Club. They are not your toys. You do not get to push them around, bully them, call them names. This is me officially banning initiation ceremonies. This is me officially banning pranks." Half the team looked mutinous. "This is a place of work. This is a business. People's mortgages are on the line. You can't get through the day without pranking someone? There's the door. Clown school is to your right."

"But," said someone.

"No. No discussion on that. There is no fucking world where I bust my balls trying to bring a player here and watch you muppets drive them away. You don't get to choose who comes, stays, goes. I do.

"You might have guessed that there was an incident that provoked all this. I found an amazingly talented girl. On talent alone she walks into any team in Europe. I'm serious. I tried, but I couldn't persuade her to come."

My speech was far from over, but I stopped there. I stopped because Sam Topps and Trick Williams were suddenly whispering to each other and laughing hard. Thinking about the content of their "joke" made my blood boil. My ears were pounding. I must have been staring at Williams for ages, imagining pounding his bones into dust, one by one, because everyone in the room was craning their necks, turning, standing up, to see who I was raging at.

Ruth came over, touched my calf (because she couldn't reach my back), and whispered, "Don't bite. Ice cold."

I nodded. Ice cold. I took some breaths. "Ah, there's been some mistake. This is hugely embarrassing, Trick. Thing is, this meeting," I waved my finger in a big circle, "is for people who have a *future* at the club. So if you don't mind." I jabbed my thumb towards the nearest door.

Trick tried to stay where he was, but under the weight of everyone's gaze, he got to his feet, gathered his crutches, and slunk away, red-faced. The noise of his chair scraping along the ground was deafening; the clanks of the crutches deeply annoying.

"Well, there we go," I said, slapping my hips. "That sums it up." I stared at a spot on the wall. "That guy just committed career suicide because he couldn't resist making a crude joke about a fifteen-year-old girl." I scratched my neck. I needed to get back to Darlo to have a shave. I looked around the room. There were the obvious good guys, the ones I knew. The Henris and the Magnuses. Then a lot of dudes I suddenly didn't trust in the slightest. We'd have to keep them separate from the women's team, from the kids. "Unacceptable," I said. I scanned the room, counting players I wasn't sure of.

Ten. We potentially needed to replace ten of the first team, just on the basis of character. If we couldn't ship them out to other clubs, we'd have to pay those pricks until the summer, so their replacements would have to be guys who would work for minimum wage for a while if it meant getting their big break. CA 1 guys with high PA.

How catastrophic would that be? It'd drag our average CA down to potentially dangerous levels, but it would pay off massively after six months. We probably couldn't get away with it in the short term, but by the summer I wanted ten more Raffis, ten more Jameses. And that was just for the first team.

Include the women's team and the youth system and I needed fifty players. I needed fifty players, and I needed them to think Chester was Shangri-La *before I even met them*. The only place for them. For that, Chester needed a story.

I got down from my box and strode out of the bar, out of the stadium, and drove to a house I'd been to once before. I rang the doorbell and a woman opened it. "Oh! Welcome back! What a surprise. Come in!"

Sumo was streaming, but he didn't mind me messing up his speed run. He had the emotional intelligence to realise that I was fuming. "What's wrong, Max?"

I put the second pair of headphones on and leaned forward to see what the chat was saying. *OMG ITS THAT GUY LET ME CHANGE OUT OF MY SWEATS.* That made me laugh. "Sumo, I need your help. And your viewers', too. I need to learn how to make a Harry Styles-inspired TikTok."

18

AS IT WAS

"Sorry for barging in. What's this you're doing?"

"I'm doing a no-glitch one hundred twelve percent Hollow Knight speedrun."

"Wow. Is that what I sound like when I talk about underlapping full backs?"

"Probably." Sumo chuckled. I think he was really happy I was there, even if I was messing up his stream. "I know what an underlapping full back is, though. I did it to you when we played FIFA. You didn't notice."

"Okay, you're good at games. I get it." I watched as he mashed a keyboard to make the little on-screen character do things. "Can you do that and talk to me?"

"Oh, yeah. I talk almost all the time. *And* read the chat. There might be a few sections I go flow."

"You might go flow," I said, testing how the words felt in my mouth.

"You do it. When you play. You forget the fans, the cameras, the everything. It's just you, the team, the ball."

"Sure. Sometimes. There's normally some twat trying to ruin it." I realised what I was saying and sagged, comedically. "I'm doing it now. *I'm* the twat."

"It's okay. My *jonokuchi* liked you last time and the re-watch metrics were way above average." He glanced over. "I'm saying you bring good engagement. They want me to make a custom emote of you saying 'munkey.'" Another glance. "I'm saying it's really okay. You can barge in whenever you want."

The streaming world was mad. The economics of it baffled me. "The metrics were good? How good?"

"You're somewhere between Cat Café Manager and Hogwarts Legacy."

"Good to know. Right. Sumo. Chat guys. I need your help. You ready? How do they signal their readiness? Press F to be ready." Before I'd even finished the sentence, tons of Fs flew down the chat. "Wow. This is fun. Type *Murica* if you're from America or Canada."

"Max," complained Sumo, but the chat was going wild. Loads of *Muricas,* strings of Canada flag emojis, Statue of Liberty gifs, and one guy's "I'm Danish is that okay?" Sumo looked up at a wall clock and said, "It's mostly North America right now. Mostly. Night shift workers love me."

"With the Danish guy I could skip to the hard part," I said. "Because he knows the structures. But American sport is different; they might need a tiny crash course to understand my issue. If you're a talented player in the States, you go to high school, then college, and the recruiters are all over the schools and colleges. In football, or *soccerrrr*," I added in an impressive American accent, "it's the clubs who do it. So I'm the recruiter for a club and it's my job to find players. I'm good at that; it's not really a problem *finding* them." Especially not with me being so close to having the 8,000 XP needed to buy Playdar. "I can find the players, but not everyone wants to become a professional athlete. A lot of that's down to culture. Loads of people have had bad experiences in teams in the past. They've been bullied, excluded, misunderstood. I want to make a little viral video that people will watch and go, 'Oh that's cool. I'd like to be part of that.' Right? I want to say Chester is not like those other teams you tried. We've changed. We're different." Sumo was pulling a face. It didn't seem related to what his little game character was doing. "What?"

"We're not different, though, are we?"

I wondered what had made him say that. I decided to let him tell me in his own time, if he wanted. "We are *now*. I'm in charge of who comes in and who goes out. Can I swear?"

"Better not."

"The bad apples are getting tossed. Don't worry about that. If it's a choice between replacing the entire first team squad or signing the female version of me, I choose me." I laughed. "It's not even close. Okay so the video should be sort of generally appealing, but my main target is one girl in particular. Dani is fifteen, she loves Harry Styles, she's an attacking midfielder, and she has a really high ceiling."

"Is Dani the girl from those videos from Crewe?"

"Yeah."

Sumo paused the game so he could explain to his viewers what he knew, remembered he was trying to break a record, and instantly unpaused. He told the story of the tournament as he'd gathered it from snippets of TikToks and Tweets and whatnot. It was accurate enough.

"Right," I said. "So she's top. What I need your help with is choosing a Harry Styles song for the background, and some ideas for what could be in the video."

"That's easy," said Sumo. "You doing tekkers." He explained tekkers for his viewers.

"The future of Chester isn't me doing tekkers," I said. "It's pass and move. It's one-twos. It's isolating defenders one-on-one and smashing past them with power and purpose. It's hundreds of quick, short passes that draw defences out of position before we thrust a dagger down their gob."

"Right but tekkers is cool."

"Not to me. We don't teach that. We teach positional play, linking with your teammates, having each other's back, busting a gut to get your mate out of a jam. We teach mutual respect and understanding that everyone's got something to offer and individually we're flawed but collectively we're invincible. That's the message. That's the story. Me bouncing a ball from shoulder to shoulder doesn't tell that story. Does it?"

Sumo bit his bottom lip. I realised he was trying to stop himself from saying something he knew he shouldn't. He lost his inner battle. "Can you do that?"

"Can I bounce a ball from shoulder to shoulder? Yes. *Mate.*" I sighed.

"I'm sorry, Max, but you need to grab people's attention before you can tell the story!"

The chat was starting to understand the mission now.

HAMBO: You could do a teaser trailer. Teaser has you doing teckas. Trailer is longer, tells story, bits of buffoonery to keep Sumo engaged lol

THE_STEVE: It's tekkers. Good idea, hambo

MEGASHIRA: Didn't someone say she's deaf? It doesn't matter what song it is

I nodded. "It *does* matter. It has to be Harry. She has to know how much of an effort I'm making. So that when I say I will change the culture, get rid of all the cavemen, she knows that I mean it. That I will keep at it, relentlessly, until it's the way it needs to be. By the way, it's not just for her and the kids. I have to work there, too. I'm a player, too. I want to go to training and become better, fitter, stronger. Anything that stops me doing that, anything that distracts me, has got to go. It *will* go. Yeah, anyway. Picking the song. The problem is that I don't really listen to a lot of music."

TURCULENT_TEDDY: Neither do Harry Styles fans

THE_STEVE: lol!

"Whoa whoa whoa," I said. "Let me stop you right there, er . . . Truculent Teddy. That's a great joke. You're smart and you're quick. But I'm not here to gatekeep what people should or shouldn't like. I like football—soccer—and a lot of people think that's pretty dumb. The most common result is a draw. You call it a tie. Almost eight percent of matches don't have a single goal. Players pretend to be hurt and it's pure cringe. Sometimes when people find out I like footy, they give me this whole spiel about how rubbish and pointless the sport is. Is that fair comment? Of course it is! But I like it. Why do I have to like the same things as you? I listened to some Harry Styles songs with my girlfriend and nothing really stood out to me. She thinks they're all great—she had a big Harry phase that I'm not entirely sure she's completely out of—so I thought I'd come here and get help. Oh, Sumo, by the way, I need you to film and edit the video. I meant to say that before."

His little monster was jumping on some platforms—he missed one and fell into a chasm. "What? I can't do that."

"Mate!" I said, sweeping my hand around his room. "You've got cameras and stuff. You've got skills. I need you."

HYPECARROT: Sumo you can do it!

TURCULENT_TEDDY: Sorry Max

HAMBO: I pledge many thousands of bits to see Sumo's soccer dance video!!!

"There, that's settled," I said. "It's good Hambo is paying you because the club is skint. Right. Guys, pick a song for me."

HOOSIER_DADDY: Sorry is this a skit? It's obvs

"Hoosier, it's not a sketch. I really am this clueless. Please hit me."

HOOSIER_DADDY: As it was.

A second later the guy posted a YouTube link to a song called "As It Was." The chat went nuts—it was so clearly the right answer. I'd have liked to have watched the video there and then, but Sumo was doing his stream, which let's face it was his job. I took my headset off. "Er . . . I'll leave and listen to it in your kitchen and come back."

"No, Max, the run is dead," said Sumo. He tussled his hair and made a little *argh* noise. "I always forget the third buzzsaw. Guys, we're off *Hollow Knight* and we're temporarily becoming a Harry Styles reaction video channel." He grinned as the chat expressed massive approval. They loved Sumo's normal content and they loved when I came and disrupted it. "Wait, Max. You've *never* heard this song before?"

He'd clicked the link and brought up the video. The thumbnail was one I hadn't seen before, but that wasn't conclusive. "Er . . . I think my girlfriend was making me listen to the older stuff? The stuff she liked. This is pretty recent, is it? Yeah, I think this is one I haven't heard."

"Oh, amazing. I'll clip this. When you're massive I'll make millions. Okay, headphones on. Harry Styles, 'As It Was,' reacted to by superstar footballer Max Best, in three, two, one."

The video starts with Harry Styles walking in a crowd. He's sucked back into his memories of a failed relationship. (The chat assures me this is all about the pandemic and his break-up with Olivia Wilde.) For a massive, massive hit song, it's extremely strange. I'm not sure my reactions were very interesting—it was so far from what I was expecting. The video adds to the weirdness—Harry and a beautiful woman come close to each other but can't stay together. It finishes with him dancing happily. Suddenly it's over and I'm asked to explain my feelings.

"Shit," I said. "I don't even know. The music's so upbeat, the lyrics are almost *depressing*, then there's a kind of triumphant ending." I laughed. "I think I like it but . . . Was that a rap near the end? That was baffling. I'd need to hear it again, like, ten times."

MEGASHIRA: When Harry looked at the camera you melted

I laughed. "Did I? Yeah, sure, why not? Some stars do that, don't they? They look through the lens right at you. That's the X factor. That's why they're stars. The camera loves them." I closed my eyes. "I don't have that. I think I have it a bit when I'm running in full flow or taking a free kick or something like that. But okay, yeah. That moment did help me understand why Dani is crazy about the dude."

SHY_TORI: Would Harry be a good soccer player?

"Wow! Great question. Sumo, can you play the bit where he's walking around the circle thing?" I leaned forward and watched and asked him to rewind again. "I'm going to say probably not. He's a great dancer, you'd think he'd have a good base compared to most people. I mean, I'd need to see him live, obviously, but my guess is no. How can I explain it? To be good at most sports you need a kind of . . ." I gestured with my palm making a chopping motion. "Kind of a directionality. There's the ball, go get it. He seems maybe too fluid."

TURCULENT_TEDDY: He's only got one direction.

The chat blew up. Sumo was soon crying with laughter. My total bewilderment only added fuel to the flame.

"What?" I said.

Sumo wiped a tear away. "Max!"

"Oh. One direction. Holy shit, that's good. That's like a stealth joke." I mimed taking my hat off. "Teddy, *chapeau*. Amazing. Right, what was the name of the guy who chose this song? I still don't quite get it. Why this one, bro?"

HOOSIER_DADDY: It's about change. Things are different now. It's what you said about your team—it's not what it was. And you could understand the lyrics of the chorus to be about a team instead of a relationship. In this crazy world we can only rely on each other.

HYPECARROT: True, but there be *millions* of TikTok dance videos with this track. You've missed the party by about two years.

"That's fine," I said. "I don't need to reinvent the wheel, here. Sumo, can we hear the last thirty seconds again?" There was the rap bit, Harry went "Hey!" and then the chime of massive bells. "Epic feel to the end. Uplifting. Same chorus but opposite meaning. That's the bit I need to choreograph, right?"

"We can mix bits," said Sumo. "Bit from the start, middle, and the end. Thirty seconds total." He smiled. Maybe it was the belly laugh he'd just had and the overwhelming feeling of positivity coming from the chat. He stared at nothing. "Yeah. I think this could work. Let's spend a couple of weeks planning it out, storyboarding everything. Maybe we'll do a test run to get the equipment set up right. I might have to borrow some lights from a mate."

I slapped him on the shoulder. "Love the energy. But no. We're doing it tonight."

"Tonight?" he spluttered.

"And don't worry about lights. We'll have the floodlights on."

"You mean . . . ?"

"Yeah. We're filming on the pitch. In the stadium."

"I get to go onto the pitch?"

"Not only that," I said, grinning. Sumo being told he could go onto the pitch? That was the *real* reaction video. "You get to boss me around."

I went into the city centre and pottered, deep in thought. I was trying to get my shitty verbal brain to think in images. A thirty-second video, timed perfectly to music, telling my story through the medium of football. Good luck!

I checked my bank balance and decided it was time to finally buy myself something nice. My flea market earphones wouldn't do what

I wanted—work properly and stay in my ears—so I went into a shop and let a salesgirl convince me I needed AirPods. They were insanely expensive, but she promised me I wouldn't regret it.

"What do *you* have?" I said.

She reached into her left pocket and pulled out an AirPod case.

"You've got the Samsung ones in your other pocket, haven't you?"

"Ha, you got me," she said, and reached into her right. She came up empty. "Not really. That's a good trick, though. I might start doing that!"

Back in my office, I lay on the mattress and played the song about twenty times. I started to see the shape of what I wanted and made rather a lot of phone calls.

At five I was at the training session for the under-fourteens. The rebels were back! Future, Benny, Sevenoaks, Captain, and Bomber. Tyson was there, looking subdued.

"Spectrum, mate, I came to cut the spare players but I forgot there weren't any." I'd only offered the hundred-pound finder's fee to the two older groups. "So I'll leave you to it. One thing, though, I need half the pitch."

"Oh. Sure. I can work around that."

"Ace."

I popped my new toys into my ears—they connected instantly without me having to dick around in the settings; incredible overall feeling of luxury given what I had before—and I ambled over to the far side of the pitch. There I had a bag of footballs, some small round markers, some cones, and some poles.

I did a cursory warmup, then played "As It Was" on a loop while I experimented with skills. I did kick-ups in time to the beat. I imagined Sumo editing together multiple different types of control—parts of the foot, thigh, chest, shoulder, head—perhaps that could be the progression. From toe to head.

No, I thought. *It's not about me. It can start with me, but then we'll add more characters as we go. That's the progression. From me to us.*

Holy shit, that felt right.

So I focused on what would be the first few seconds of the video. The part where I would be alone. What mad tekkers could I do?

While the music played, I tried to combine football with dancing. A moonwalk became me dragging the ball backwards. A hip wiggle became me dropping a shoulder to trick a defender. But how to put it all together? It didn't seem possible. So I went back to the start. I did some kick-ups, then as I added something extra to the routine— swinging my foot over the ball, letting it bounce before flicking it up with my standing foot, kneeing it over my head and continuing from the other side—I added a bit more conventional dance.

Yeah, it was a bit less "pure football" than I wanted, but it would be much more entertaining. Probably. It was hard to be sure. Maybe it was total garbage.

When I paused, I noticed the under-fourteens had stopped playing. They hadn't come closer to my side of the pitch. They'd just stopped and had been watching me for God knows how long. Spectrum should have made them get on with their sesh, but he was gawping at me, too.

I popped my earphones out. "What the shit are you doing?" I said to the collective.

Benny answered. "What the shit are *you* doing?"

"None of your business, you little oik."

"Is it what we're doing tonight?"

Oh, that's right. I'd invited him. "Yes. Does it look good or cringe?"

"Good," he said, nodding slowly. The nods turned into head shakes. "But I can't do that."

"You probably can. It's a piece of piss. But you won't have to, and I'm only doing this once for a video. This is *not* how I train. This is not how *you* train. That's an order."

Future pointed to the balls I'd lined up. I'd put six there, about a metre apart, on a slight diagonal towards the goal. "What are you going to do with them?"

I followed his finger, then shrugged. "I'm thinking of ending by taking a shot, using my momentum to spin and take the next shot. You know, hitting the same corner with each go. In theory I'd time it with the sound of the bells. Not sure I have enough practice time, you know, to perfect it, but that's the general idea." Instead of returning to their drill, most of the kids came closer. "Get back to work," I said, arms wide.

"Can we see it?" said Captain.

"What?"

"Can we watch you do it?"

I rubbed my eyebrows. That was the core problem with this tekkers stuff. Kids loved it, but it was useless. On the other hand, maybe doing kick-ups and skills *was* good for their technique, and maybe this feat I was attempting would make them practise shooting.

"Fine," I said. Almost all of them went "yes" under their breath, did little punches, moved closer. "I'm gonna put my music on. When the last shot goes in, get back to work. I'm serious."

I found the place in the song where I thought something like this might work—the bit with the bells. Now that I played it again, the gaps between chimes were really short. I'd have to hustle. I tried to ignore my audience, and focused on the task. The song, the balls, the distances, the goal. Top-right corner. My favourite.

I rewound the song, flicked a ball up, and did twenty seconds of basic tekkers. Then on the first GONG I smashed the first ball. One twist later I was hitting the next. And the next. Top right, boosh! Top right, bosh! Top right, bash! Top right—well wide. Top right, swish! Top right, swish-bosh!

I reviewed what I'd done, wondering what went wrong on the fourth hit—trying to hurry because I was falling behind the beat— then turned to check how the kids liked it. They were in a state of ecstasy. I noted that some of the little cretins had been filming me on their phones. It's often hard to read faces, especially those of teenagers, but I was pretty sure they'd all progressed a level in the Cult of Max. I pointed my index fingers and twirled them. *Turn around. Get back to work.* They ran off, laughing, pointing. *Did you see that?*

Hitting free kicks to end the video was not an option. That would make it all about me.

I gathered the balls and packed away the cones.

The filming session was only a couple of hours away, but I wasn't stressed. One more little concept would do it. I had a feeling that everything would click into place.

Once we'd filmed things from different angles, we had to leave the editing in Sumo's hopefully capable hands. I pretended to leave, then snuck back into the stadium. I didn't get much sleep. I was thinking about what we could have done better. What we could have achieved if we had more time, more money. But we didn't have either. I tried to knock myself out with a camomile tea and a brown noise video. It helped.

On Wednesday we got a call from an agent who'd heard we needed a left back. He had a lad rotting in the reserves at Solihull Moors. Would we take a look at him? Inga had already got me tickets to a higher-tier match. I needed the XP, and fast. Getting whacked on the head had really slowed me down. But at the same time, the squad needed cover on the left. I checked the guy's transfermarkt page and it said he'd also played in midfield. A guy who could play left back and left mid would be incredibly helpful. He could be the difference between safety and relegation.

I drove to Birmingham and checked him out. He was CA 28, PA 39. His average rating from the previous season was 6.75. Decent.

While I collected the usual 81 XP and paid off a tiny sliver of debt, I wailed and gnashed my teeth.

We needed a guy like this. He was about as good as Prick Williams with a slightly higher ceiling. The guy would be motivated to get his career back on the rails. But he was the epitome of dead money. We only needed a left-sided player because Ian Evans refused to change formation. We were back to the ultimate culture clash—sexy tekkers *phenom* versus actual human-sized fossil.

MD had told me I could go to a hotel and put it on expenses, but I knew the club's financial situation too well. I drove back to the stadium and slept there.

Thursday was similar, but since I watched a match in York, I could at least drive back to Darlo and get a proper sleep.

On Friday, my desperate grinding continued. There was only one match being played within a million miles: Holyhead Hotspur versus Porthmadog. That involved a ninety-minute drive to Anglesey, which is in that top-most little blob of Wales close to Ireland. Probably really nice, but like most places I visited for work, I spent more time in car parks than in beauty spots.

The game was incredibly one-sided, and notable for being a rare example of a player who wasn't me getting a ten out of ten rating. Holyhead's goalkeeper must have saved thirty shots and was almost faultless in their 2–1 defeat. But neither side had any interesting players and I only got 1 XP per minute. The curse didn't think much of the Welsh League.

While I watched, I fretted about Vivek. He'd had five or six training sessions but was still stuck on CA 1. What was that about?

Adding to a vague sense of unease, a sense that things weren't quite going my way, that I was on the wrong track, came more and more headlines about a potential sale of my boyhood club, Manchester United. There were three interested parties: a hedge fund, a dubious billionaire, and the nation state of Qatar, who would use the club as a political pawn.

The billionaire was, at least, from Manchester, and he was said to be in pole position. By far the best of a grotesque bunch. Local boy gets rich, buys his favourite team? I could stomach that.

XP balance: 7,573

XP still needed for Playdar: 427

Debt repaid: 538/3,000

Saturday, January 21.

In another timeline this would have been the day I destroyed Chester while wearing the black-and-white Darlington kit. I'd told Henri the score would be 8–0, and I'd hinted that I would release a bombshell interview saying that Ian Evans had said I wasn't good enough. It would have been bye-bye dinosaur.

As it was, I was in the main stand at Blackwell Meadows alongside Emma, Henri, MD, and Ruth, and we were all backing Ian Evans. I was in disguise, with opaque sunglasses and a plain black baseball cap. I'd asked the others to call me Cliff Daps.

Emma leaned over and whispered, "Remind me why Henri isn't playing."

"He's a Darlington player," I said. "He can't play against his own team."

"That makes sense," she whispered. "I *think*."

I'd made a WhatsApp group so we could rant and rave without drawing attention to ourselves. We were surrounded by Darlo fans. I wasn't *worried* about them, it was more about paying attention to the match and not being bothered by hundreds of people with strong opinions about my life choices.

My fellow VIPs were on edge because an hour before kickoff I'd lost my mind when I saw the Chester Squad tactics screen. The formation and lineup had been untouched since the previous match, but when Evans handed in his team sheet for the match, my screen updated to show Tony Hetherington had replaced Henri.

And that was it!

The only change!

The fossil had *picked an injured player*. Aff was in the team despite his dodgy hamstring. After I'd kicked up such a fuss about how I wanted small injuries to be treated and rested so that they didn't turn into big ones. It felt like a provocation from the pensioner. He was pushing back against my authority, against my change in culture. But how we treated injuries couldn't be considered wokeism or snowflakery—it was pure common sense. A player misses one game to make sure he's available for the next eight. Why would anyone resist that?

On the pitch, the teams were ready. Lots of familiar faces and profiles. The referee blew his whistle, Blondie passed to Junior, and the home crowd roared. Game on! Darlington had been on a strangely poor run of form since I'd left, and like Chester they'd been slipping down the table. Talk of the title seemed a distant memory. Now their focus was on getting into the playoffs.

Funny how quickly sport changes. If I'd played, this game would have been the peak of Darlington's campaign. A thrilling and ruthless 8–0 win that put fear into the hearts of everyone they played thereafter. A stunning, crushing display that would have given them more than enough momentum to glide through the rest of the season without me.

But the players knew the stakes were lower, and they played like it. Darlington were sloppy. Careless. Out of position. Slow to turn, slow to support, slow to decide.

For twenty minutes, Chester were on top.

Then:

Walker collects the loose ball. He plays it neatly into midfield.

Topps gathers, lays it off to Flintoff. He sweeps it wide to the left.

Aff runs onto it, and with a burst of pace gets past Colin!

He's clear. The cross is good!

GOOOOOAAAALLLL!

Hetherington nods home.

It's no more than Chester deserve—they have started so well.

MD: You had me worried, Max! Aff's hammy seems fine. Maybe Dean cleared him this morning.

I rolled my eyes so hard I ended up looking at the stadium's roof.

Me: This is what pisses me off. It's not about what happens. It's about the percentages. If there's a 50% chance he's out for two months, you don't take it. If Evans gets away with this, great. Good for Aff, good for us. But don't pretend Evans didn't walk into the casino and bet our best player on black.

Henri: Best player?

Me: Yes, mate.

Ruth: He doesn't mean it. He raves about you.

While Henri pouted and Emma pulled a face that showed she wasn't pleased by my disloyalty, the match continued. I found myself wondering what the best outcome would be. A win for Chester, of course. But in terms of Aff, it was obviously miles better that he didn't get injured. But MD didn't seem moved by my percentages argument. If Aff really did wreck his hamstring, that would surely be the final nail in the old-school way of treating injuries.

Right?

It was the twenty-ninth minute when it happened. Aff sprinting to cover for Doug Walker. Doing his defensive duties, helping out his teammate, putting in a shift. If you put Aff on the pitch you knew you were going to get one hundred percent from him. Or, as footballers call it, one hundred and ten percent.

"*Merde*," said Henri. You didn't need a curse to tell you when a hamstring had popped. The tell-tale stumble, the hand reaching to the back of the thigh.

The injury did one positive thing: it answered the question of how it would make me feel.

I slumped forward, head in hands. The planet's gravity had been recentred to a spot somewhere in my gut. Eight weeks. If he couldn't play for eight weeks that would be . . . that would be . . . I got my phone out and checked the fixture list. All the winter's postponed matches were about to come thick and fast. Eleven matches out, and he'd be half-fit for the remaining seven.

Me: Mike, your boy just got us relegated.

I let the truth bomb explode behind me as I walked away. Michael Bay eat your heart out. I made it to the bottom of the steps, turned around, and retook my seat.

Me: I'm only back so I don't get a reputation for dramatic exits. This fucking sucks. Nobody talk to me. Bye.

Emma: Okay bye.

Ruth: Seeya.

Me: Holy fuck! He's going to put Raffi on at left mid! I can't watch this. Emma, let's go to Scarborough. They've got flamingos.

MD is typing . . .

But MD never pressed send. I knew he was writing something along the lines of "Ian would never do that." But sure enough, Raffi appeared on the touchline, went to left midfield, and MD deleted his missive.

Darlington equalised before the break and won 3–1 with a miscast Raffi putting in a four out of ten performance and contriving to make the abysmal Webby look good. The home fans were jubilant. They had three points in the bag. I got 162 XP and a splitting headache.

I'd made the mistake of inviting a bunch of people to Henri's house after the match. The ones I'd watched the atrocity with, plus Longstaff, Junior (when he had finished celebrating), Bark, Benzo, and Pascal Bochum.

I think I tried not to be a miserable bastard, and, yeah, let's say I partially succeeded. Apart from hanging out with some friends, I had an ulterior motive for the event. I wanted to introduce Ruth to Junior and Bark. They would be very good starter clients for our agency (tentatively named R.E.M. Sports—"We Never Sleep"). And I thought it would be good for Pascal to meet MD and Henri. Henri was delighted, switching instantly to German and bringing the kid over to his book-shelf to discuss goats. I *think* he said goats.

MD sidled up to me. "Did you mean that, about . . ." He couldn't say it. "About Scenario B?"

"Yes. We are fucked."

"Even if the FA hearing clears you?"

"Oh, no. Then I'd play and we'd win every match. But not under Evans. What he did today was disgraceful. Aff isn't some fucking cattle. He's the only player we've got who can run the ball from midfield to attack. Whatever point Ian was trying to prove, he's proved it. And he's fucked us. Because I won't be cleared. I won't be able to play this season. From the summer, I'm a free man. Until then, you'd best assume I can't play. Unless I can find a guy as good as Aff who'll play for free, we're toast. That's it. I'm done talking about it. Have a crisp."

"I don't want a crisp."

"An olive on a stick, then! For fuck's sake."

I strode outside and took a few deep breaths. The evening air was sharp. I went out to the crab apple and rubbed its bark. If it could talk, what would it tell me? That it had some hairy moments early on? That it nearly didn't make it through the winter of 2020? That Hurricane Whatever nearly wiped it out in '21? But it came through even stronger and now look at it.

Nope. It wouldn't tell me that because it had been grown in a massive greenhouse in Holland. The guy had been *pampered.*

I went back inside—everyone except MD was having a great time. Ruth was good at the schmoozing. Junior was eating out of her hand. Bark and Benzo were mooning over Emma.

"MD," I said, about to smooth things over. But I got a message, and the sender made me double-take. "It's from Sumo. He's finished the edit. Um . . . I think we should watch separately, to get the full effect. Do you know what I mean?"

"Sure. Send me the link."

"It's not online yet. We have to approve it, then he'll send it to Spectrum. Won't take long. Who should go first?"

"Me," said MD.

"Nah. Wasn't a serious question."

I wandered back out to the tree, put my earphones in, and pressed play.

The file was thirty seconds long and the suggested name for the video was: *Chester FC—Not the Same.*

Intro
What You Hear

We hear the first ten seconds of the track. It's poppy, fresh, upbeat, the hook is addictive.

What You See

Max Best reclining in the D of a misty, floodlit Deva stadium. He's wearing full Best 77 Chester kit, but he's pensive, lonely. We let this play out as long as modern attention spans can bear, though through-out the video the camera is always moving.

A ball rolls towards him. Max looks up. [The camera] is there. [The camera] is you, the viewer, because it could be *you* getting all this attention from Max. Max rewards you with a smile while he flicks the ball up, *doink*s it from foot to foot in tune to the music, until the ball comes to rest on his head. He stretches, gets to his feet without missing a beat, bounces it from shoulder to shoulder, lets the ball drop, kicks it up, rolls his foot all the way round the ball as it is dropping, and passes it back to you. He begins to stride forwards.

Chorus
What You Hear

Harry Styles sings, "ooh-oh-oh" and eases into the butter-soft chorus. Like most of the song's lyrics, they're melancholic, almost dys-topian, an intriguing contrast to the underlying pop sound. In this world, he sighs, it's just us.

What You See

Max walks, copying the Harry walk as far as he can manage, in a circle to the side of you. You move closer, and as your gaze sweeps longingly towards Max's upper body, he uses sign language to perform the chorus. While he has literal eye sex with you, he points down—

captions show what word he's signing—*IN*—he makes a big football shape—*WORLD*—he points one finger up—*IT*—a second finger joins the first and they "walk" upside down—*US*—both index fingers pointing up, coming together—*JUST.*

The words rearrange to follow hearing grammar: *In this world, it's just us.* The look on Max's face tells you he means it.

Coda
What You Hear

The music skips to about two minutes eighteen seconds into the official track—it's the song's triumphant, exuberant ending. You hear Harry Styles yell, "hey!" and massive bells start ringing.

What You See

Max passes to someone off screen, the video cuts to her, and now you're looking at a girl wearing a cyberpunk hearing aid, who passes to a tall, black, former bouncer, who passes to a kid with Down's Syndrome, who passes to the son of a former star player, and then a whole diverse cast of characters try to follow Max Best in scoring a free-kick, and every strike is set to the gong of the bell, *dong dong dong dong,* and all the results of all the attempts are shown in one cleverly edited moment.

Then as the bells continue, Max is holding hands with you; you're spinning round, and every rotation brings a new face into view—Vivek, Zoe, Raffi, Benny, Wilson, James, and finally, Max again. It's the happiest you've ever seen him.

Suddenly, a wide shot shows fifty players of all shapes and sizes, all in Chester kits, all taking a shot at goal. There's a guy acting as goalkeeper—he makes a valiant effort to save all fifty shots. Could it be—? It is!

The video closes with Max still in goal, daring you to take a shot. He smirks, but you wipe the smile off his face with a powerful shot that *crashes* into the right-hand post. The ball flies way over to the edge of the pitch. A Black girl is walking past in her school uniform. She sees the ball, sets herself, and smashes the ball back to Max. He winces as it stings his palms.

He looks surprised, smiles, waves her over.

She frowns and points to herself. *Who, me?*

Max is still smiling, a huge, impressed smile. *Yes, you!*

Kisi runs in and is swamped by fifty excited Chester players, parents of players, fans, and employees.

The scene fades, the Chester badge hits the screen (as though it has actual *weight* and it's bursting through a powdery film, super cool effect), and some text appears. *Not the same as it was. Chester FC. New players welcome.*

The video ends.

A little too on the nose? Yeah. On the nose like a Mike Tyson left hook. I was instantly punch drunk.

I watched, pulse racing, as MD went through all the emotions I did.

"You did *this* on Tuesday night? With no budget? I recognise almost everyone. I'm actually quite moved. Taken aback. This is community spirit, Max. Let me watch it again."

"Pass and move, mate. Don't dawdle on the ball."

We passed the phone around the room, energy flooding in from all around, my guests being converted, one by one, by the power of the story. Bark and Benzo almost refused to let go of my phone. They wanted to watch it again and again. Emma looked me up and down like she was seeing me for the first time. *She* kept replaying the bit where I did sign language. Henri watched in dreadful, impassive silence, then gave me a hug that lasted far too long and gregariously insisted I live in his house for as long as I needed. Ruth tried to play it cool, and she was the only one who didn't try to watch the video more than once. She would, though. When it was released, she'd rewatch the shit out of it.

Me: Sumo, mate. You are the greatest living Cestrian. I owe you big. I'm deliriously happy. Get it launched.

I stood there, leaning on Henri's kitchen counter, waiting for my pulse to come down. This video was going to sweep Dani off her feet, no doubt about it. When I thought of her in a Chester kit, I couldn't stop smiling.

Things couldn't possibly have gotten any better.

But they *did*. Holy shit, they *did*.

MD asked if he could have another look, and when it was finished, he smiled and handed my phone back. He wandered outside and stared at the tree. I felt something had happened, and some instinct took me into the Job Information area of the curse.

Guess what I saw? Near the bottom of the many, many managers at risk of losing their jobs was this entry from the National League North.

Ian Evans—Chester—England—NatN—Insecure

19

PLAYDAR

Another sleepless night, but this time it wasn't caused by the pain of an injury or worrying that I'd made a fool of myself. This was pure excitement. Emma sensed that I was hyper and did her best to take my mind off things. That helped. For a few hours.

While she slept, I crept down to the crab apple and made some notes. I had so many thoughts, tumbling and spinning, colliding, blocking each other. I needed to organise them. See if they meant anything.

The first note simply read: *EVANS OUT.*

MD was unhappy. For the first time, he was thinking about sacking Ian Evans. Without me, he would have thought Evans was doing a good job in hard times. My ability to "see" the future left Evans no wriggle room. I was sure that if he ever again used a player I'd flagged as fragile, he'd be toast, and if he and Vimsy didn't put some effort into training, they would be at risk. The more I pointed out Evans's mistakes, the faster MD would pull the trigger.

Any hint that Evans had tried to shaft the club with overpriced loan deals would also end his nasty, brutish, and short stint. Even if I couldn't prove financial misdeeds, if I was clever, there were many ways I could *really* land Evans in the shit.

Then again, wasn't I supposed to be using this time to learn how to deal with difficult people? It's fair to say I hadn't made much effort to get to know Evans, to find a way to work with him. And I probably never would. Sending Aff over the top didn't just maim our player's hamstring, it killed our relationship.

Long story short, he was a shit manager and he was in my way. Get rid.

The second note read: *JACKIE IN.*

With Jackie as manager, we'd get fantastic training. He'd use young players. The pathway from the youth system to the first team would open, and the entire club would be energised. And I could get on with creating the women's team and attracting young players to the club.

My last note on that topic said: *MAX IN?*

But what if, right . . . What if I put myself in a position where MD would consider me for the top job? Maybe until the end of the season. Interim until Jackie could get out of his contract at FC United. That said, let's be honest, if I got the job, I'd keep it. We'd win most of our games.

There were costs, though. For a start, we'd lose the chance to get next-level coaching. Would Jackie move from FC United to be my assistant? Doubtful!

And being the manager would massively limit how much I could scout. The women's team would get filled with randos and they would probably not win enough matches to get accepted into the women's pyramid next year.

No, the best division of labour was me continuing as DoF, with Jackie as first team manager.

I wanted to sit in the hot seat, though, I can't lie, so I decided I should at least give MD something to think about. And that meant reminding him what an amazing in-game manager I was. I would take control of the youth teams and rack up a few stupendous victories. I'd get the women's team assembled and start crushing those friendlies Inga had arranged.

Less importantly, I needed to arrange some matches to get my discount codes from the January perk. Would those glorified friendlies impress MD? I doubted it.

Getting my coaching badges would. I hadn't neglected my courses, exactly, but I was falling behind with the supervised, assessed sessions. The fastest way would be to use the kids in Darlington, since that's where my course was located. I'd have to check with Cutter if it was still okay with him.

New topic. I wrote: *TO LOAN OR NOT TO LOAN?*

If I wanted to be Machiavellian, I wouldn't bring in a left back in the January transfer window. Evans would keep having to play players out of position. Would it be worth losing the next five games to get rid of him? Absolutely. But then we wouldn't have much left-sided cover for the rest of the season. Jackie or I could deal with that, but it would limit us, and any limitation would increase the risk of relegation.

This whole line of thinking was tempting but dangerous. I couldn't rely on MD to fire Evans, and if the fossil didn't have the tools he needed, we'd get relegated. The club *needed* a left-sided body. I emailed the left back's agent and felt better about it. I'd have to get Magnus Evergreen to test my aura. Must have gained a few light side points with that decision!

Next: *PLAYDAR*.

I had 7,735 XP, and needed 265. I was absolutely determined to get them that day. The big Sunday Premier League match involved Leeds United. Leeds wasn't all that far from Darlington. About an hour in the car, which used to feel like a trek but was now a jolly little jaunt.

If I managed the twelves and the fourteens, though, I'd get 2 XP per minute while showing my suitability for the big job.

Two hundred sixty-five divided by two is 132.5. I needed to manage 133 minutes to unlock Playdar. The twelves played sixty-minute matches. The fourteens played seventy minutes. Sixty plus seventy is one hundred and thirty. Three minutes short.

I threw the pen across the garden with an annoyed laugh.

I could easily finish the day on 7,995 XP. Absurd! The only way to be sure of getting the XP was to go and watch Leeds. I noped the thought away—I'd found Dani because Henri had reminded me of the community spirit the club was founded on. The viral video resonated with MD because it was so community-minded. The community option wasn't watching a big club with millionaire players; it was managing Chester's kids. I'd do that and find some other match in the afternoon. I *would* have Playdar by the end of the day.

I went to pick up the pen and couldn't find it. Bad omen! But then it was under my foot and when I picked it up, I also found a twenty-pence piece. Yes, mate! Let the day begin!

Both the twelves and fourteens were playing Hope Farm Juniors. I'd punted our best kids from the twelves to the fourteens, so we didn't have a ton of quality at the younger age, and neither did the other team. We won 7–4 playing a simple, pass-minded 4-4-2 with no flourishes. I found it boring, Spectrum found it boring, Emma loved every second. She kept making *ooh* and *aww* sounds as though she was watching cuddly kittens and not overly competitive little brats.

When one of our kids took a whack on the shin, I delayed the match by a minute while I fussed over him and asked him to wiggle his toes one by one. But the referee didn't add the time to the end of the half, so it had been a wasted effort. I got a nice hug from Emma, though.

The fourteens had a lot more quality. They had the three best players from the twelves, Future (PA 99), and two half-decent guys with PA 25 and 22. Then there was Tyson (58), Benny (40), Sevenoaks (35), Captain (32), and Bomber (30).

I asked Spectrum to set up a 4-1-4-1, pretending it was so I could talk to Future's gran. But obviously it was because I didn't have any formations with a DM and I wanted Future to play there. I set him as playmaker, reminded Tyson he wasn't allowed to shoot, ever, and let them get on with it.

Hope Farm Juniors were pretty dreadful, but they had two guys that caught my eye. One was a left mid with PA 25. Not great, but we were short a left-sided player. I saw no reason not to bring him over. And the other guy was a PA 29 striker. Neither would ever break into the Chester first team, but they would improve the fourteens squad. And maybe bringing in another striker would be motivational. Not that Benny really needed it. I subbed him off anyway.

"Benny, mate. See their number nine? Good, isn't he? Do you think we should sign him?"

"Him?" said Benny, appalled. "He's rank."

"What does that mean? Rank one? Yeah, I think so, too. He'd give us some options up top. Yeah. Good call, Benny. Back on you go."

Talk about lighting a fire under someone's arse. Benny went on, supercharged, legs pounding, chasing lost causes, defending, getting into position for linkups.

"That was good," said Spectrum.

"You mean my man-management skills?"

"Yeah."

"That's just to keep it interesting for me. They don't really need it. They're *weirdly* fired up. Is this a local rivalry or something?"

"No, it's the last game before Das Tournament."

"What?"

"Das Tournament. It's what everyone calls it. All the best teams from the region go to Crewe, play a mini league, then a knockout cup.

Matches are pretty short but it's still a long weekend. Brutal. And the standard is high. We always get savaged."

My face lit up. "There's a tournament next weekend? Where we normally lose?" I couldn't believe my luck. The more I thought about it, the more excited I got. "And all the best young players from the region will be there? Holy shit that's perfect."

He pulled a face. "You'll be coming to Das Tournament?"

"Where else would I be? Sounds like heaven."

"It starts on Saturday. What about the first team?"

"What about them?"

He shrugged. Disappointed he wouldn't get to practise his management skills, I supposed. I didn't give a shit. If I could find, like, five talented players and persuade them to join us . . . I mean, they'd already have clubs, maybe better clubs than Chester. But if they ever got cut, they'd remember how interested I was. Yes, this might not be helpful short-term, but going to these kinds of tournaments and saying hello to some of the prospects could really pay off.

And maybe I could persuade some to pop down to Chester for a one-off match. What did the January perk say?

Disruptors Assemble!

Build a team of newly scouted talents (minimum eleven players), arrange a friendly match, and lead the prospects to victory over their age-appropriate Chester FC counterparts.

Build a team. Not "register" a team or "sign" a team. I could get the best eleven kids from the tournament to come to Chester and smash my lot. It would be painful, maybe, for the kids. But they'd get over it and I'd get a twenty percent coupon code.

God, I love a discount.

With the match still in full flow, I wandered over to the Hope Farm Juniors manager. He wasn't pleased to see me. "What?" he snapped. Most people striding towards him mid-match would be spreading aggro.

I smiled at him. "Are you going to the Crewe thing?"

"Crewe thing?"

"Der Tournament."

"Oh. No. We're much too small for that."

I pointed to his best player. "I'm going to ask your lad there if he wants to come and help us out. It'd be good experience for him."

"Oh!" The guy went through a gamut of emotions. Obviously he wasn't keen for me to steal his players, but I hadn't said I'd be offering him a permanent spot in the squad. I'd only said it was for one weekend, and it *was* a good opportunity for the kid. "Well," he said, still going through the wringer. I tried to stifle a grin when Benny noticed me talking to the rival boss. He knew what the topic was. He went mental, storming after the left back and hurling himself in front of their long clearance. He blocked the ball, and it went out for a goal kick. Delightful waste of energy. "Just for the day, is it?" said the manager.

"Obviously, if he can make that kind of step up in quality, we'd talk to his parents about what was best for him. I just wanted to let you know what we were thinking. You've done a good job with him. And the left mid. Yeah, they'll love it. Is it all right if they train with us this week?"

It wasn't lost on him that I'd added another player and two training sessions to my wish list. But what could he do? I could have taken the players without talking to him, and from a sporting perspective, he couldn't stand in their way. Hope Farm wasn't a pathway to anywhere except tractor school. He didn't have a leg to stand on. "Sure, I guess."

Spectrum had come closer to hear what I was up to. I asked him if he'd talk to the kids, since I had to rush off after the match.

I went back to my spot and rubbed my assistant manager's back. She smiled. "What was that all about?"

"Taking that guy's best players."

"That's not very nice."

I didn't tell her my impulse to recruit more aggressively had come from her father. "It's actually good for him," I said. "His team just became a place talented young players can go to get noticed by Max Best. He'll have loads of kids signing up in the next few weeks."

"Oh!" said Emma, smiling. A moment later she said, "Is that true?"

"No," I laughed. "I've absolutely dicked him."

We "only" won 4–0, which wouldn't impress MD, but we were completely dominant and had eighteen shots. Presumably, some parents would message MD letting him know how pleased they were with the change since the Broughton match. A minor step forward, I thought.

Benny had driven himself nuts trying to show we didn't need another striker. The harder he worked, the more chances he ruined. He snatched at shots, hit them too hard, tried to be too accurate, tried hitting them early, late, high, low. At one point he was so far in his head that he cocked his leg to shoot, hesitated, and stayed like that for four seconds.

While the kids drank or ate bananas or chatted with each other about highlights from the game, I took a moment to double and triple check that yes, I really had 7,978 XP in the bank. I'd lost bits of time somewhere along the way, and I'd forgotten the stupid debt! Moronic of me. Twenty-two minutes of football to find! I wanted to rush off, but I had to debrief the kids.

"Lads, good game. Totally on top from start to finish. Man of the match award goes to . . ." I looked around. Every face turned to mine. This was absolutely meaningless, but they wanted it! "Goes to *me*. I think I did a ten out of ten job managing you. Thoughts?" Lots of eye rolls. Lots of smiles. They knew I was only joshing. "Fine. It's hard to choose between Future and Seven. You guys were quality from start to finish. But I'm giving it to the goalie. You had nothing to do for so long, but when they countered you made two good saves. Great concentration. Love that. We're going to need you all to hit these levels again next week in Die Tournament. Right? From what I've heard, the other teams will get a lot more shots! I'm going to come and help out, and we're not going there to make up the numbers. I want to win. To that end, there will be a couple of new lads at training. They'll help us out in the tournament. New players. You know what I expect from you when it comes to new players. All right? Benny," I said, summoning him with a head flick.

He came over, shoulders slumped. "Yes, Max?"

"Mate," I said. And waited.

"Sorry," he said.

"What are you sorry for?"

"For playing shit."

I laughed. "You're such a nutjob. You want to see shit, try playing with Chumpy and Tim."

"Who?"

"Yeah, exactly. Look, you're an emotional player, and that can be awesome. You can get fired up and play out of your skin. We'll need that next week. But if you're seeing red, you can't see the goal."

"You want me to calm down?"

"Did you ever see Wayne Rooney?"

"Not much."

"He would get angry, storm around, do all the jobs. The crowd fucking loved it. Managers loved it. But he scored loads of goals. He wasn't angry in the penalty box. He was a killer. It was like . . . he had a radar telling him where he was. Everywhere else on the pitch he was fiery, but in front of goal he was ice cold."

Benny was absorbing all this. I expected he'd go home and watch loads of Wayne Rooney clips. There were worse ways he could spend his time. "So you're not mad at me?"

"Jesus fuck! No one's ever going to be mad at you for working too hard. What the fff . . ." I walked off, shaking my head. A bit hammy, but I'd found subtlety wasn't the best choice with footballers. I paused and looked at Tyson. He'd been watching, and now he looked away. What did he need? Time, probably. His teamwork was on the up again. I got the feeling the tournament would be as important for him as it was for me. He could either commit to the ethos or put himself on display for the other clubs.

We got into my car and I checked the map. How could I explain what I was about to do? "Babes. I'm hoping to get a tip about a player. I'm going to drive from pitch to pitch and see what's up. Will be boring. I can drop you home if you want."

"No, it's okay. If I get bored, I'll read. I just read a review of a vegan restaurant in Chester. Will you take me?"

"Absolutely." I pulled out of the car park and started my hunt.

"That's it? No hesitation?"

"You've read a review and you want to go. Must be compelling."

"You're *interesting*."

"No, I'm not."

"Most men are scared of the word *vegan*. One of my friends uses it as a sort of filter. If a guy asks her out, she says sure, I know a great vegan place. If they make stupid jokes, date's off."

"And if they're into it?"

"They go to Nando's. She's not vegan. Just doesn't want to deal with guys with no imagination."

"I wish you'd brought *her* to the double date. What are you reading?"

"There's an article about vending machines. I always wanted to own one. Or one of those little robot horses you get outside supermarkets. You're not even awake and people put money in. Yes, please! And MD sent a link. Apparently you did an interview about the Harry video. Some local journalist?"

"Yeah. MD begged me. It was pretty short. Hard to talk about the video without the video and the reporter was no Bingo."

"Well, there's an article."

"Why didn't he send it to me?"

"He did. In the Cliff Daps group."

"Oh, I muted that. You should rename it '*Succession* Spoilers,' Jesus."

The first two football pitches I drove to didn't have any matches on. It was too late for Sunday League. There was nothing on the Footy Addicts app. I drove in the general direction of a five-a-side place. They would definitely have some matches in the evening. Probably. Right? Surely.

And then the morning's excitement came rushing back—a bunch of players in bibs. I parked in front of someone's garage door—an act so obnoxious Emma berated me—and I rushed towards the pitch. Round and round I went, looking for the fence's gate. I found it, and clicking the handle open was like busting out of prison. I darted to the touchline and felt the XP stream into me.

Even better, it was a women's match and they had some okay players. A PA 17 midfielder, a PA 14 goalie, and a PA 12 centre back. Really miles away from the standard I wanted, but they were better than nothing, and nothing was all I had. I would invite them to come to training. After a season or two they would be eased out of the situation, but they would definitely leave with their potential maxed out.

But not long later, I almost forgot about them. My XP stash ticked over to 8,000. How long had it taken me to get from zero to here? Ages. It had been a slog and a half, and that was just the World Cup. I started to retrace my steps. Did I want this? Was Playdar really the best use of my resources? If I got the Contracts perks and found that Ian Evans was trying to cheat the club, that would be the end of him. And I needed to unlock attributes. Formations.

I shook my head. This decision had been made many times over. I bought Playdar.

Playdar. 8,000 XP. This perk directs you to the most talented footballer not in your database who is currently playing football within a certain radius. Can be upgraded.

One small pang of headache later, I had a new icon in my vision. As always, I checked I could hide it and bring it back, and once I was satisfied it would obey me, I took a proper look at it.

It was on the bottom-left of my awareness. A circle. Inside the circle was a piece of clipart representing a radar screen. Concentrating on it made it bigger, and when it was bigger there were three side icons— the numbers *one,* *two,* and *three.*

The whole setup seemed very familiar, and it didn't take long to work out why.

It looked like a quick-actions toolbar from video games! So that's how I'd activate the ability. Press this shortcut. And then what would happen? There was only one way to find out . . .

Although I was almost uncontrollably giddy, I forced myself to calm down. Playdar could wait sixty seconds. I interrupted the match, charmed the players, and got the phone numbers of the three women who had some PA. Emma very slightly fucked things up by getting giddy and saying they should be proud of being my first signings for the women's team. Signing them wasn't really my intention, but I went with it. They would flesh out the squad and there would be other benefits, too. Emma took some photos of me with the three ladies, but I asked them to go to the Deva tomorrow so we could give them Chester kits and retake the pics wearing the right clobber.

"I think we need to talk about you picking up girls right in front of me," joked Emma as we walked back to the car.

"Three nice-looking local girls," I said. "That's a good counterpoint to the whole diversity thing. You know what people are like. I've already seen comments calling us Snowflake FC. As Michael Jordan said, gammons buy replica kits, too. We'll plaster these pics on the website, the socials. Me and three blonde girls-next-door will reassure local bigots." Emma was giving me a strange look. "What?"

"You're being cynical. Realistic. You're normally a bit my-way-or-the-highway."

"You think I shouldn't care about the bigots?"

"Do you?"

"Not really. I don't need more enemies, though." Again I struggled to understand her expression. "You're not happy."

"I am, actually. It's nice to see you being sensible. Sometimes I worry . . . Is that the only reason you chose them? Because they'll look good in the photo?"

"No, they will do a job for us on the pitch. I'd like better players, but will I find twenty like Dani? I doubt it. Also, we've got games coming up. We need bodies."

"Bodies."

"Football term. Numbers. Substitutes. Enough guys for all the drills. Bodies. But that wasn't the main event! Let's get back to the car. My tip is about to come."

"Phrasing," she mumbled.

Back in the car—no parking ticket, no aggro, in Manchester it might have been towed already—I wondered what was going to happen. There would be some kind of radar effect leading me to a person who was currently playing football. Would it keep radarring until I found the player? Or would there be a time limit? What could I do to prepare?

First, I turned the ignition. Then I got my phone ready with the map open.

Then . . . and I couldn't believe how much time and effort had gone into this moment, I prepared to smash the Playdar button.

And as my finger figuratively hovered over the icon, I thought. "This would be a nice time for a cliffhanger."

"Do you like cliffhangers?" I asked.

Emma shrugged. "Sometimes."

"Me, too," I said.

I smashed the button and heard a distinctive *ping* noise. It sounded exactly like the reverberating submarine ping from *The Hunt for Red October*, one of my favourite movies. The hairs on my neck stood on end.

At the same time as the ping, three more things happened.

First, the Playdar icon greyed out. I didn't like *that*.

Second, a huge column of yellow light became visible in the distance.

Third, in my "screen" vision I saw a bright slice of curved yellow light that was angled towards the pillar. When I turned my head, the light moved. When I looked up or down, it disappeared. It was something like a compass pointing towards my destination. It wasn't very obtrusive, and I was able to hide it. Hiding it made no sense, of course.

I got the map, pinched the screen, and looked for football pitches in the approximate direction of the pillar.

"Got it," I said. "Buckle up, we're going in."

Emma was already in her seatbelt, still reading. "Mmm," she said.

Why wasn't she bouncing like I was? This was huge. "Can you be excited, please?"

Without looking away from her phone, she clenched her hand into a fist and made a pulling-down motion. "Whoo whoo," she said, absolutely flat.

I laughed. "I like you sometimes." I pulled away.

The column of light faded away after about a minute, as did the compass thing. A few minutes later, I pulled into the car park closest to the pitch I felt *had* to be the right one. I concentrated on the Playdar icon. It was completely greyed out, but the numbers one, two, and three looked just as shiny as before. They wanted to be pressed!

I hit the number one and with another ping, the column came back. My guess as to which pitch the column was directing me to had been spot on. I needed to get out onto the pitch right away before it faded, if only to see the graphical effect in its full glory. But pressing the button had cost me one experience point, taking me down to precisely zero XP. Did it cost one XP to retrigger the effect, or did it use whatever I had in the bank? That seemed absurd. Since I had nothing to risk, I tried pressing the number two.

You lack the resources required to process this request (100 XP).

Okay! So I could retrigger the search once for one XP—very considerate—a second time for 100, and a third for, presumably, a thousand. Or ten thousand. Would it always ping the same player? If a match kicked off between pings, would the pillar switch to a better player if one was around? And why would I ever spend a thousand XP locating a single player? Maybe when I'd bought everything there was to buy in the perk shop, when the curse was fully upgraded, I'd have loads of XP to spend on that kind of indulgence. Yes, that made a certain kind of sense. Old Nick wanted me to keep grinding. Keep watching matches, keep earning. Disposable items would lock me into the grind cycle for a good while to come.

By now I was within sight of the pitch, and sure enough, once I could see the players, the column of light disappeared and the player in question was highlighted in Playdar yellow.

A left back! The curse had blessed me with a left back!

"Hallelujah," I said, smiling.

"Who?" said Emma. "Which one?"

"That one," I said, pointing. "The short one."

"They're all short."

MARK NELSON		
		Scottish/English
Acceleration 4		
	Handling 1	Stamina 1
	Heading 6	Strength 1
		Tackling 3
	Jumping 3	Teamwork 12
Bravery 8		Technique 4
	Pace 3	Preferred foot R
	Passing 4	
Dribbling 2		
Finishing 2		
CA 1	PA 70	
D (RLC)		

Terrible attributes, for sure, but there was that sweet, sweet PA 70. Plenty of room for growth. And plenty of time, too. You might have noticed that I withheld the guy's age. Let's complete the profile.

Born 30.12.2014.

Age nine.

Nine! The curse had stitched me up, and it had gone out of its way to do so. This wasn't even a proper match. It was just some kids having a kickabout. I normally didn't see profiles unless the match was a lot more serious. This wasn't even a match!

There were eight little kids crowded around one set of goalposts. There was no net. I walked towards the players. They briefly stopped their game and looked at me. "Are you playing Wembley Doubles? Sixty Seconds?"

"Three and You're In," said one. Ah. A classic variant. You needed to score three goals to win, but if you did you had to go in goal. Kind of a perverse incentive, but I'd never met a kid who didn't try their best.

"Little kid," I said, pointing to Mark Nelson. Was he really going to become a professional athlete? I'd seen taller glasses of beer. "Do you live round here? Yeah? Let's go talk to your parents."

"Is he in trouble?" asked an older boy who also had the surname Nelson.

"You his brother? No, he's not in trouble. He just got scouted."

Once I'd dealt with the parents, I switched from full-on manic mode to chilled out, solicitous boyfriend. Emma wanted to go to a hipster café Gemma had told her about. I asked if there was a vegan menu, a request the waitress took much more seriously than I wanted. She pointed out the items that were safe for vegans.

When the waitress had gone, Emma's lip curled up. "You have to eat something vegan now, or she'll know you were wasting her time."

"I'm a professional athlete," I whinged. "I need protein."

"Vegan is all protein."

"Fine. I need protein that tastes of something."

"Can you be a vegan footballer?" she asked.

"Don't know. Probably. That tennis nutjob is vegan. I don't like him but he's absolutely incredible. Four-hour matches day after day. I don't see why it wouldn't work in football. Fuck it. Fine. I'll have the sweet potato wedges and the chickpea burger. If it's garbage we'll go to Henri's and ask if he's got any leftover pig's cheek or sheep's ears or whatever mental part of the body he ate last night."

While we ate a very late, acceptably tasty lunch, I reviewed what my massive investment had brought me.

Mark Nelson's attributes were trash, but he was nine. I'd get to watch them progress over the years. Presumably by the time he was sixteen the mental ones would be more or less set and we'd have a very clear picture of his physical ones. His father was relatively short, so if that was about the height Mark would grow to, he would likely end up being a right back who could fill in on the left. Right now he was the jewel in the crown of the under-twelves. A step in the right direction, very nice to have him on board, but I'd have liked to have found someone who could hit the first team within the next ten years.

So, then. What about this greyed-out icon issue? Would I have to spend increasing amounts of XP to activate it again?

I made the icon bigger and saw that the top sliver of the grey circle had been coloured in. Ah! It was on cooldown! I focused and a countdown timer appeared: *22:43*.

If that meant what I thought it did, I'd be able to use Playdar once per day. Which was a hassle. If I used it on Monday at 6 p.m., I'd have to wait until Tuesday at slightly after 6:00 to rescan. If I wanted it available at a certain time, like 10:00 on Sunday morning to catch a Sunday League player, then I'd have to leave it idle the day before. Just annoying!

The perk could be upgraded, though.

It came with two "slots." Playdar 2 (1,500 XP) increased the number of slots from two to three. I could slip so-called tokens into those slots. For example, one token reduced the cooldown by half, but it cost 5,000 XP. Another token doubled the Playdar range and the length of time the ping lasted. That was also 5,000 XP. There were ones I almost instantly dismissed that did things like filter for goalkeepers. It seemed an obvious way of rounding out a squad, but I knew I'd always want the top talent going, whatever position. Yeah, right now I really needed a first team left back. But if I did my job properly that would not be a problem in the future. No, my mantra was talent, talent, talent. No filters! Incidentally, the curse promised that other tokens would become available if I unlocked certain achievements.

But the token I really, really craved would let Playdar find players who *weren't currently playing*. That was exceptionally useful, and exceptionally expensive. Another 8,000 XP. Ugh! I *wanted* it, though.

"What?" said Emma.

"Huh?"

"You said something."

"No, I didn't."

She narrowed her eyes. "Are you in the room?"

"What?"

"You've been spaced out. The waitress asked if the burger was okay and you didn't blink. Are you ready to hear the article?"

"Oh, sure." I'd forgotten which article she meant but it was always nice when she read to me. I only wished I could lie down and fall asleep to her voice.

"'Chester Needs You' is the headline. They've got a little drawing of a seal in a hat pointing at us. Bit weird." She showed me. It was a reference to Lord Kitchener from the First World War. I supposed Emma's school did the Suffragettes. "'Chester's new director of football, Max Best, twenty-two'—why do they always put ages?"

I shrugged. "Old people like to know how old everyone is."

"Er . . . 'Twenty-two, has put out an unusual rallying cry alongside a viral video. In the video, Best performs "tekkers," meaning football skills, and invites talented players to join the club.'"

"Just so you know, the guy hadn't seen the video when he wrote that. You know what? Don't read it out. I think it's only going to annoy me. How can you write an article about a video you haven't seen? It's moronic. Is it broadly positive or what?"

Emma scanned it. "Yeah, I'd say so. The video's there on the page, too. You'd think he'd update the article but he's probably busy reviewing the new Taylor Swift album."

"That's not out yet."

"Exactly. You've got some good lines. 'At Chester, the only barrier is talent.' Then the article pivots from being about the video to a general update on the state of the team. It's all a bit 'by the way, the club is plummeting towards the bottom of the table.' First comment, 'Nice video,' two likes. Next one, 'Woke crap, get off your arse and sign someone.' Twenty-two likes. 'Stop dancing, start doing your job.' Thirty likes, spelled 'your' wrong. It's all *very* charming."

I tutted and shook my head. "Yeah."

"Don't worry. Kids don't read newspapers. The video will work. It's a banger."

"It's a banger? Where have you been learning footyspeak?"

"Bark and Benzo."

"Right."

"Come on. Tell me."

I blinked. "What?"

"You've got something on your mind. Something big. Fess up."

"There's a tournament next Saturday for the under-fourteens. I want to win it."

"Is that all? I thought it might be something hard."

Monday, January 23.

I asked Cutter if I could still use the scholarship kids for my coaching badges. He was extremely gracious. He even said he was curious about my style and might come to watch. Then he gave me a friendly warning about Bradley Rymarquis. Apparently Brad blew his top when he heard I was blaming him for my false registration. "I don't remember ever seeing him that angry. Tread with care, Max Best. Tread with care."

Over lunch, I went to watch a Footy Addicts match, just so I'd have some XP in the bank for when I triggered Playdar. I drove to Chester, monitored the youth team sessions, and went to the Deva stadium to take some photos of me and the three women from Sunday, plus our major new signing. Inside, the fake contracts were in place for the staged photos. Out on the pitch, our new left back was chatting to MD and Ian Evans, alongside his agent. Evans seemed chuffed and slightly surprised that I'd come through. I couldn't really take the credit. This deal had been handed to us on a plate.

"Hi, I'm Max," I said.

"Richi." This was Richard Carling, the agent who'd recommended his player to us. I knew a few things about him. He'd never played pro football and had become an agent thinking it was easy money and a way to become an insider. A lot of people thought the same, but most dropped out. It wasn't as easy as it seemed. The fact he was still going, still hustling, meant he needed to be taken seriously. He slapped his client on the shoulder. "You know Jack."

"Yep." I shook our new left back's hand. Jack Litherland was twenty-six with CA 28, decent attributes, and he was versatile enough to play midfield. I didn't like loaning players, but now that I'd made the decision I was getting more certain we'd done well. At five hundred quid a week, he was much cheaper than the guy Ian Evans had recommended. "Good speed, doesn't tire, can win a header. I'm made up."

"Me too," said Jack. "Long as I don't have to play against *you*. Was watching your highlights. You're boss, man. Boss."

I stared in horror. The guy was from Liverpool! No one had told me that. "I'm bosch?"

"Boss," he said, with just as much guttural vibration as before.

"Oh, *boss*." I smiled; he was extremely likeable. That was a relief —I'd had to take a leap of faith when it came to his character. But already I knew he'd be good around the training ground. A bit of Scouse humour and positivity would liven the place up no end. "Yeah, I'm massive. But Ian is your boss." I mentally added: *for now, lol.* "You listen to him, train hard, and we'll get your career back on track. Yeah? You're too good to be playing in the reserves. Welcome to Chester. All right?"

"Yeah, boss," he said. "You've got a lot going on round here?"

He was reacting to me being slightly distracted. "Guy from the paper is here to do some photos. Have you seen three women walking around in Chester tops? They're going to be my first signings. We'll announce *you* tomorrow. Hold off posting on your socials, please."

Jack stuck a thumb out. "Richi does that kind of thing."

Richi heard his name and turned away from his chat with MD and Ian. "Oh, the announcement? Don't worry, MD explained it. You're announcing something every day this week."

"Right. Get some positive vibes going. Bit of buzz to improve the mood. Lift the fans. Sell some tickets."

"Belter," said Jack. "It's good fans here. It's a big club for the level. I'm stoked."

"What do you think of vegan food?" I asked.

His face switched in an instant. Got serious. *Exactly* the same as Jackie Reaper. It was uncanny. "Yeah, good, good. Proteins. Anti-inflammatories. Had a mate who tried it. He swore by it, but he was in the kitchen all day. It's not for me, like, but sometimes I'll remember what he taught me, and I'll fill up on veggies and that. I could do vegetarian, I think, but not vegan. Not for long, anyway. Why? Are you vegan? Thinking about it?"

"I think it's interesting how people respond to it."

"Max," said Richi, putting a hand on my shoulder and easing me away from the others. "I heard some juicy gossip involving you. Something about you having a feud with Rymarquis." He said the name in a way that made it clear they were not on friendly terms. "Go on. I've sorted your left back crisis. Fill me in."

I shrugged. "Something weird happened. The only person who could possibly have done it is Brad. That's all there is to it, really. He's not my favourite person but all's well that ends well. If things had gone different, I wouldn't have had time to scout Jack, and he'd still be stuck."

"Max," complained Richi. "That's the *opposite* of juicy."

"When's Jack's contract up?"

Richi's eyes widened. "How about we see how he fits in and then we'll talk about that?"

"Fine, but he's going to fit in like a dream. Ah, there are the ladies. Could you excuse me? I have to reassure some gammons."

When we finalised the forms and sent them to the FA, Jack was added to the Chester Squad screen. His name was in blue, the same as Henri's, to show he was on loan. His name slipped into the left back slot on the tactics screen—clearly Evans intended to throw him straight into the first team. Fine by me.

And once we'd registered the three women (they were on minimum wage for training and matches, would barely cost anything), an entirely new screen appeared: Chester Women Squad. There were, you guessed it, three names there. But I had full control of the tactics screen! I switched the formation a few times, just for fun, then realised the women and the newspaper guy were staring at me. I knew exactly how to get out of that kind of awkwardness. "When's the last time you bought anything from a vending machine?"

Chester FC are delighted to announce the signing of Gracie Davies (19, LM), Robyn Wright (18, GK), and Erin Barnes (18, CB). The local trio were spotted by DoF Max Best and will begin training immediately.

It was way past Playdar time. As soon as the cooldown ended, I was distracted and edgy. When I was finally free to leave, I zipped down to the five-a-side place and scouted every single player there. I'd already seen most of them, but the idea was that if I triggered Playdar it would only show me players not in my database. I didn't want it showing me guys who were right under my nose.

When I was satisfied it wouldn't ping anyone on those pitches, I went out to my car and smashed the radar icon.

And yeah. *Smashed it* is a very suitable phrase.

The radar took me to a light industrial estate I'd never been to. I didn't see any pitches on the map and couldn't conceive of where a match could be happening. I hit the first re-ping and the column of light pierced a nondescript building. Bit strange, but I soon heard some distinctive thumps and shouts of "man on!" "yes!" and "get back!" I opened an unlocked door and walked into a large indoor sports hall for the employees of whatever company owned the building.

The workers were playing six-a-side and the standard was pretty high. A lot of that was down to one player.

PIPPA HOOLE		
Born 03.09.1992	(Age 31)	English
Acceleration 5		
	Handling 1	Stamina 8
	Heading 2	Strength 8
		Tackling 6
	Jumping 7	Teamwork 8
Bravery 5		Technique 5
	Pace 5	Preferred foot R
	Passing 5	
Dribbling 5		
Finishing 3		
CA 1	PA 111	
MC		

I felt like the curse was teasing me. Showing me these talented but flawed players. Too young, too old. Pippa was a good player, but she was ancient. I looked her up—as far as I could tell she'd never played football at a high level. She barely existed online, though she did have a LinkedIn profile. She had that frankly gorgeous PA, though. What would happen if we started training her? Would she learn really fast because of her vast life experience? Or would it go slowly because her neurons use walking frames?

There was only one way to find out. I had my coaching whistle in my pocket and at a break in play, gave it a quiet peep.

"Guys, sorry to interrupt. Actually, I'm not sorry. I'm hyper and I can't wait." Their faces were mostly friendly. I didn't think anyone recognised me. "I'm from Chester FC. We heard there was a talented player here. Yeah, dude, this is real; I've got a whistle and everything. Here's what I want to happen if that's all right. You," I pointed to the guy who was currently playing in goal for Pippa's team. "You switch teams. I'll go in goal. Seven on six, let's see if you can make the extra man count. All right? Spoiler alert—you can't."

The guy was more than happy to be released from goalie duty, and the match continued. At first there was a lot of intrigue about who I was interested in, but it became obvious to everyone that I only had eyes for Pippa. I didn't coach her the way I'd done with Dani, but I almost always passed to her. Once, she had a chance to play a forward pass, but she turned and gave it to me.

"You could have made that," I said, pointing.

"Too risky," she said. "Low percentage."

"Huh," I said.

Next time I got the ball I faked a pass to Pippa, then hit a low diagonal pass that split the defence. It was pretty outstanding, to be honest, and left our striker with an easy finish. I gestured. *See?* Pippa put her hands on her hips. "I can't do that."

"Yeah, you can."

"What if I mess it up? They'll get a break."

I shrugged. "That's what goalies are for."

She raised an eyebrow. Next time the opportunity arose, she tried the difficult pass. Naturally, she messed it up and the other team got a chance to shoot, and because I'd said that about goalies I was forced to go God-mode on the save. But that gave her the confidence to try again, and she very nearly made it—her pass beat the defenders but was slightly too powerful for the striker to collect. Pippa didn't look at me. Didn't want to show how pleased she was, I think. The incident unleashed a tiny but potent burst of sentimentality somewhere in my chest.

Afterwards I invited her for a drink, and a few of her colleagues came, too. This was a big story for them.

Pippa was tall and thin and like lots of tall people walked with a hunch so as not to stand out. But she was lively and funny. She confirmed she'd never played, and she fretted that there was no point in starting.

"How old are you?" I asked.

"Twenty-eight," she said. I did my best not to laugh, but she knew I knew she was lying. She blushed. "Too old for *this*."

"I'm pretty sure you're wrong," I said. "But if you commit to us we'll commit to you. We'll give you everything we've got until the summer even if it's clear I've made a mistake. We'll push you, get you fitter, work on your skills and positioning. Come train with us till the end of the season. We've got a few matches booked, too. There's going to be a massive photo in the new training centre with the first-ever women's team. You could be in that photo. Yeah, come to training. And just think," I added, eyes unfocused, "when you're, to choose a number at random, thirty-one, you'll still have five or six good years left in you. With a fair wind, you could play a hundred matches."

That clinched it. It wouldn't just be a one-year adventure. She had a future; she was in.

Tuesday, January 24.

Chester are thrilled to announce the signing of Jack Litherland on loan from Solihull Moors. DoF Max Best says, "Jack's versatility will be a valuable asset for us in the months ahead."

The two new kids settled right into the under-fourteens training. After ten minutes of drills, we got them to line up in different formations and Spectrum and I discussed which players should go where. This was all a bit of a scam to explain why the players would suddenly, instantly switch formations during the tournament. I also picked Spectrum's brains about the likely opposition and what formations to expect. Long story short, not much 4-4-2. The youth coaches tended to be much more progressive. Then I fucked off so Spectrum could do a normal session with the rest of the time. Normal, skewed towards fun. The session was an advert for recruiting the new boys. I didn't have to explain it to Spectrum twice.

Then it was Playdar time, and my first negative experience with it. I pinged, followed the light, pinged again when I was closer, and found a women's match happening on a school field. The girls were around sixteen, which was probably the optimal age for my purposes, really. There were a lot more PA 2 players than normal, which was odd. A higher base suggests a higher ceiling, but the best player was only PA 53.

She was way better than what I had or was likely to find playing five-a-side. I watched her movement, her skills. Yep. She'd do.

While I watched, a few men my age nudged each other and pointed at me. "There's the greatest living Englishman, Max Best," I imagined them saying. "Let's pluck up the courage to ask for a selfie." I ignored them for now. I had a mission.

At half-time, I went over to talk to the talent. I was annoyed as shit when the men decided *that* was the right time to make their move. The first wore a blue shirt and had a cross tattooed right in the middle of his forehead. The other's face was bent in a permanent snarl. Both looked more ready and willing to throw a punch than anyone I'd ever come across. I kept them in view while I introduced myself to the girl. She wasn't the one who replied.

"We know who you are," said blue shirt. "You're the twat turning our club into Snowflake FC."

They waited for me to reply. I didn't.

Snarl-face nodded. "Get that Marxist shit out of our city."

I blinked. Anything in the direction of "let's try to be nice to each other" was relabelled Marxism by the *Daily Heil*, Britain's best-selling newspaper, and guys like these lapped it up. They were proto-gammons. Baby gammons. Gammon-in-training.

I had a choice to make—invite them for a coffee where we would talk about the intersection of historical materialism and footballers wearing rainbow-coloured shoelaces, or pretend they weren't there.

"As I was saying," I said, to the girl and the girl alone, "I'm Max. You're really good! Would you like to—"

"Oi," said blue shirt. "That's my girlfriend. You want to talk to her, talk to me."

Bro must have been twenty-four. "Is he really your boyfriend?"

The girl nodded.

I calculated. Even if the girl was really nice, this guy was all kinds of toxic. He couldn't come anywhere near the squad. No chance. So she was out. Good player, but nah.

I decided to leave. "Just so you know, guys," I said. "I'm not just turning Chester into a Marxist stronghold. No. I'm much more radical than that. We're going to be *vegan* Marxist. All right? Seeya."

Wednesday, January 25.

BREAKING! Chester are delighted to announce the signing of James "Youngster" Yalley on scholarship terms. DoF Max Best says, "Youngster is a talented defensive midfielder who will bring energy and bad jokes to the dressing room. Chester can be proud to win the race to nab the highly-sought-after starlet."

This made me fire off a text to Spectrum.

Me: Use the word breaking again and I'll put your phone in my blender.

Spectrum: Everyone else does it.

Me: Breaking: your phone.

Spectrum: Ok.

It was after 9 p.m. by the time I could activate Playdar. Still plenty of football being played in the area near the stadium, but I had a strange certainty it wouldn't lead to anything. So I drove a bit farther, to the east of the city, and jabbed the icon.

I found the pitch easily. It was a simple playing field in a run-down housing estate. The pitch was soggy, the lines hadn't been painted in years, and the goalposts were sinking and sagging. Most of the pitch was dark, but one goalmouth was illuminated by yellow streetlights. One was flickering in a way that would have driven me mad.

But there were a bunch of teenage girls there having a kickabout. I watched for a minute. It wasn't some casual game—they were really training. Playdar had led me to one girl in particular—a PA 36 striker, but four of them were decent.

"Ladies," I said. The game barely paused, which made sense. I was some rando approaching them in the dark. "What you doing? Three and In?"

"Nah," said the striker. "Movement drills."

"It's pitch black," I said. "How can you see the ball?"

"Dun't matter. We're training."

"Do you play for a team?"

"Yeah. The Colts. But we're going for Chester Women."

"Right."

"Gonna play for Max Best."

I made a noise. "That guy? I heard he's a prick. Snowflake FC. Sleeps on a tofu bed."

"I don't care," said the girl. "He's fit. Who are you, anyway?"

"Cliff Daps," I said. "Famous scout. I heard there were some good players here. Looks like I heard right."

Thursday, January 26.

Chester are delighted to announce the signing of Pascal Bochum on a long-term contract. The talented German is highly regarded by DoF Max Best. "Pascal is fast and has outstanding technical qualities. His signing is a real coup and demonstrates the scope of our ambition."

I slept in the stadium so I could check out the first team training. When I rolled up, they were doing a drill I hadn't seen before. Progress! And Jack Litherland's CA was green. Henri's was green. There was a lot of green. I was pleased enough to initiate a conversation with Ian Evans.

"New lad training well, is he?"

"He's a trier," said the planet's youngest fossil. "Got leadership. Sets standards."

"Top," I said, trying to play it cool. Fresh face, fresh energy, new drills, change, competition, wanting to impress the new guy. I fucking loved Jack Litherland!

Vimsy jogged back. "Max," he said, slightly out of breath. "I spoke to Carl." It took me a second to remember what he was on about. Carl Carlile had been in a funk for some time, and Vimsy had finally decided to have a chat with the half-American right back. "He says he's fine. I mean, he obviously isn't, but I don't like to push. Some guys, you push too hard, you put their backs up."

I sucked some air in through compressed lips. "All right. Thanks for trying. Maybe he'll come talk to someone in his own time." I had a think about that, then realised I hadn't wandered away as soon as the conversation was over. In fact, the three of us remained there in a fairly companionable way. It was Jack! He'd lifted us. He had lifted the whole club. For the first time, I really started to understand why people were so obsessed with transfers. You weren't just registering a new player, you were ushering hope into the building. I noticed Dean and Livia had brought coffees outside to watch training.

A new first team signing was like a drug, and there wasn't long left if we wanted another hit. Seemed I was the club's dealer. "Not long left in the window, but if we could bring in another player, what would you want?"

"Another player?" said Vimsy. He exchanged a look with Evans. They communicated nonverbally before Vimsy said, "Midfield. Centre."

It was a bit of a surprise, because I thought they were happy with Raffi as the backup for that position. He was still too raw to start matches, though. Chad Flintoff had been playing MC recently, and he was CA 32. In theory, we could easily upgrade a key position. "Get another MC," I mused. "Flintoff and Anka compete for RM. D-Day drops into LM. Three strikers for two spots. That works."

"Less minutes for your player," said Vimsy.

"They're all my players," I said, meaning I didn't have favourites. "I'm happy with Raffi's minutes. You're developing him perfectly. Anything that stops him being dumped on the left is good all round. Maybe a left-footed CM so he can cover left until Aff's back. Yeah, I'll have a look."

"James Wise," said Evans.

I waited for an explanation, but none came. "What's that?"

"James Wise. Plays for Eastleigh. I've worked with him before. He's fell out with his gaffer. He'd come and help us out."

I whipped out my phone. "Eastleigh are at home on Saturday. Where is it? Shit! It's on the south coast, practically in France. No, thanks. They've got snakes and shit. Jellyfish."

"You've got something more important to do?"

"Yep."

I stared at him, but he turned away pretty quickly. Our moment of bonhomie was gone. I was certain that Evans had tried to get me to take a four-hour trip to the arse end of nowhere. But why? To get me out of his hair for Saturday's match? Or to stop me from going to Das Tournament?

I pondered the last option as I traipsed away. Was it possible, I thought, that Ian Evans knew I would crush the tournament and put myself in pole position to take over?

Vimsy came jogging and fell into step with me. "Max. What if Wise comes *here*? Will you look at him?"

"If he comes here? Of course I will. You think he'll drive four hours to come for a trial?"

Vimsy pulled a face. "Best not call it a trial. He's an experienced pro. But if you need to see him live, yes, he'll come. Ian will sort it."

There was no downside that I could find. "Sure. Let me know when so I can be here."

"I got the impression it would be tomorrow."

"Huh. Keen. What's the catch? Let me guess. He's a dick."

"According to you, everyone's a dick."

I smiled and slapped him on the arm. "Everyone apart from you, Vimsy mate. You're my favourite. Hey, have you ever been to a vegan restaurant?"

He stopped. The *V* word made him uncomfortable. "No . . . That's not really on my radar." He brightened. "If you're paying, though . . ."

I gave him a little wave as I strode away.

Threatening people with vegan food seemed to be a decent personality test, and it was funny. But why was I bothering with that? I had a psychic dog. I wondered if I could borrow Solly for a day. If I could take him on Playdar trips, that'd be amazing.

And that was the thing. Playdar was great. Top addition to my powers. And once I'd used it to scour Chester, I'd upgrade it and search even farther afield. But it only found me players with high PA. It said nothing about a player's character.

Checking people out seemed like something that could be outsourced. Who did I know who was a good judge of character? Something to think about.

Friday, January 27.

Chester are pleased to announce that veteran Pippa Hoole has joined the women's squad. Pippa is a hardworking midfielder with a great engine. Welcome, Pippa!

James Wise was at training at 9 a.m. on the dot. I talked to him, and he had indeed driven four hours to be there. Woken up at 4 a.m. for the chance to become a Chester player. I couldn't fault his determination or his ability. He was CA 40 with every reason to suggest that regular football would bring him closer to his PA of 60. He was right-footed, which was mildly annoying. Evans could have mentioned that when I said I wanted a leftie.

The guy was a hard case. Typical midfielder at this level. He wasn't charming like Jack, and he quickly struck up a friendship—kinship maybe—with Sam Topps. Not a good sign in terms of culture, but he could help us avoid the drop.

But there it was again. The buzz. The increase in standards. Raffi in particular had stepped up. Everyone was sharper. Everyone was on it.

"What do you think, Max?" MD had also come to watch.

"Good player. Experienced. You'd expect him and Sam to win the midfield battle in most games."

"He didn't like it when you offered to get him a vegan breakfast."

"No, he didn't. But if we can afford him, let's do it." I paused. If the team played as well as they were training, they'd win a few matches and there wouldn't be any reason to sack Evans. No reason not to plant some seeds of doubt, though. "Two loans plus Pascal. That's the budget gone. Most of it spent fixing Ian's mess. Giving him the tools he wants. If he fucks it up from here . . ." Had I overegged the pudding?

It seemed like it, because eggs were on MD's mind. "What's a vegan breakfast anyway? Can't have sausage. Can't have eggs. No cheese. What's left?"

I shrugged. A cheeseless brek didn't really bear thinking about. "I'm going to Crewe tomorrow. You know the way we've never won that tournament or even come close to it?"

"Yep."

When I didn't say anything else, MD turned to me. "Max! What are you up to?"

I smirked. "You'll see. By the way, I bumped into some fans who didn't like the video. I joked that I was taking the club vegan. It's probably all over their shitty fascist chat groups."

"Max! Stop calling everyone a fascist. Not everyone who buys a season ticket is someone you'll like."

"I know. Anyway, you've got the Twitter password, too, right? Maybe you can mention something about Das Tournament and make it kinda meaty? I dunno. Let's just mention meat a few times. Announce we're in sponsorship talks with a burger chain, something like that."

"I'll try to negotiate terms with James Wise's club, first, if that's okay with you. If we do it right now, he could play tomorrow."

"Go for it." I clicked my fingers. "Muesli. They eat muesli. And porridge."

"Milk, Max. Those have milk." He grimaced. "If I was vegan, I'd skip breakfast."

Chester are pleased to announce that tough-tackling midfield general James Wise has joined on loan until the end of the season. Manager Ian Evans says, "Wise is a good lad, proper old-fashioned player who knows his position inside out. I worked with him before, which is why I pushed for him to join. He'll be in the squad for tomorrow."

Chester boys under-fourteens travel to Crewe tomorrow for the annual D.A.S. Trophy. Competition is fierce but with our DoF Max Best helping out, we hope this time they can bring home the bacon!

20

DAS TOURNAMENT

The youth team training sessions were almost as good as the first team's. Vimsy had volunteered to take them, with Terry as his assistant, so that Spectrum could rest before the big weekend.

The sixteens still lacked quality, with Kian and Vivek the two best players. I was beyond relieved to see that Vivek's CA had finally hit 2. It had taken far too long, but now his own progression fantasy had really begun. While his mini team were off the pitch during one of the drills, I took him aside.

"Hey, Vivvi," I said, trying to give him a nickname. Football is almost entirely built on nicknames.

"Vivek," he said with a smile.

"V-V."

"Vivek."

I shrugged. We'd find one he liked. "You, er . . . You seem a bit different today. Bit more switched on. Bit more in it."

"I do?"

"Yeah. It's not a big deal if you don't want to tell me, but I'm wondering if there was something that . . . I don't know. Maybe you liked one of the drills from the last session. I can get them to do more." I looked at Vimsy. Spectrum had told me he thought Vivek was shit. Maybe it was no coincidence that the CA bump arrived with a new coach. "Oh! Or maybe, and it's totally okay to tell me because I need to know these things; maybe you prefer the older coaches or whatever."

While I'd been talking, Vivek had gone internal to the point of surliness. He didn't want to open up. But my last guess provoked him into talking. He fidgeted and left awkward pauses. "Spectrum's quality. I've been having fun. I like it here." Sigh. Big pause. Doe eyes. "The lads made me feel welcome. You, too. And Nisha's been pushing me to keep coming. Kept mum off my back and that." Pause, sigh, stare at shoelaces.

The kid had great eyelashes. Some girl would get lost in his eyes and the lashes would close around her like a Venus flytrap. I'd always wanted a Venus flytrap. When I got a permanent place to stay in Chester, I'd finally treat myself to one. When was that going to be? I needed to power through January—when the transfer window was closed, I'd have far, far less time pressure and it'd make sense to start house hunting. Or should I wait until after the FA hearing? That was a couple of weeks away. It was possible that MD would sack me for breach of contract if I wasn't available to play. I mean, it was vanishingly unlikely, but yeah, I had to consider the possibility. All these thoughts and more happened in the time it took Vivek to form the next words.

He swallowed so loud I heard it. "It was the video. You asked me to be in it and I thought, why? I was a bit sceptical. Token Indian? But all the kids at school kept watching it and watching it and I was in it, and it was such a big deal. Girls asked to be in selfies with me. And then we played footy in P.E. and I was one of the captains." Guy was close to tears now. "I went from being last pick to first. Pressure. Didn't like it. I'm not as good as you think. So I stayed at centre back and tried not to make mistakes, but then I saw the right mid out of position and I yelled at him and he jogged to where he was supposed to go."

"And you liked that. Being respected."

"Yes," he said, wiping his eye. "But also, I was surprised that I'd noticed it. I'd never thought that way about football. I realised . . . it was sinking in."

"I think what you're trying to tell me," I said, nodding slowly, "is that your talent has been unlocked by the power of Harry Styles's voice."

"No!" he laughed.

"You're a massive Stylist."

"Max," he complained.

"Well, mate. I'm fucking psyched about this. About you." I stretched. "But I'm pretty sure you don't do P.E. anymore. Check with the coaches later. Maybe there's some form we send your school."

"I don't do P.E.?"

"Vivvo, you're one of the best footballers in Chester! You don't fucking do random shit while your teacher reads fascist newspapers. You're a full-time football kid slash part-time TikTokker. All right?"

He didn't quite know what to do with his face, but a little twitch of the lips suggested he didn't mind the idea of having some special treatment at school.

So that was top, and it was also top watching the eighteens, newly reinforced by James and Pascal. Suddenly, we had the basis of a very decent team, and we had assets. Assets we'd be able to sell for money I'd use to utterly transform the club.

"What's tickling you?" said Vimsy, as the lads put the equipment away.

"What do you mean?"

"You've been grinning for over half an hour. Terry's been timing it."

"Yeah?" I said. "So have you. You can feel it, can't you?"

Terry was shaking his head, face blank, but I knew he was grinning on the inside. He had to be. "Feel what?"

"We've got stars at every level now. A conveyor belt of talent. It's not just a dream; it's happening. We're on the up." I think I briefly lost my mind, because I suddenly found myself with one arm on Vimsy's shoulder, leaning in, sort of jabbing his chest. "Vimsy, great job today. Love it. Loved every second. That's the standard. *That's* the standard, yeah?" I eased away, holding my palm out for him to clasp; he did. I pulled him towards me and slapped him on the back, three times, the most slaps permitted by England's unwritten rules of male bonding.

I hugged Terry, strode away, gave a Maxy Two-Thumbs to several players, and left a trail of motivated happiness in my wake.

But no one was as motivated and happy as me. It had been a hell of a week.

Now to cap it off by winning Das Tournament.

The competition was hosted by Crewe Alexandra's famous academy in association with a college that looked like Downton Abbey. They had all-weather pitches, plus immaculate grass ones. The drainage alone probably cost more than Chester's annual budget. I felt my old friend poverty come back to say hello.

While I walked around the pitches, getting a feel for the event, I thought about my short- and medium-term goals. Short: win the tournament, blow MD's mind, put myself into contention for the manager's job when Evans sabotaged himself. Medium: catch up to Crewe. If I had a kid and lived in Cheshire, "Alex" would be my first-choice destination. Overtaking Crewe in terms of squad quality and reputation would be huge. Megahuge. The first hill we'd have to climb.

I found our kids sick with nerves, huddled together like disaster survivors. Jackie Reaper once told me I'd infected the Beth Heads with my absolute certainty of winning. Well, that seemed an appropriate tool to take out of the box.

When the lads saw me, they were all, "It's Max, Max is here," which did give me a brief 2d6 boost to smugness, though I had just enough awareness to feel sorry for Spectrum. He was the one who had herded these cats onto the team bus and done all the organising and all the preparations. Well, if he wanted adulation, he should have tried harder to get chosen by the curse demon, shouldn't he?

"Guys, shut the fuck up; you're giving me a headache," I said, and they stopped whispering. A couple grinned nervously. I jabbed my thumb behind me. "We're supposed to play these pricks? They're shit. Winning this isn't even a challenge. I say we hop on the bus and go to Alton Towers. Who's with me?" Alton Towers is a well-known theme park, not all that far from Crewe.

Spectrum had a tiny curl on the edge of his mouth. He had started to understand my sense of humour, even if he rarely laughed. "The boys are very motivated to play *football*, Max. Even if it's sooo easy."

That got a laugh. The ice was broken. I could almost *see* the group's nervous energy evaporate off them. "Fine," I said. "We'll whump some chumps. But just so you know, they've got a roller coaster that they set on fire . . . *while you're riding it*. And loads of bees come out and attack you. I can't believe you'd rather play . . ." I pointed at Spectrum.

"Oh, er . . . Crewe B."

"You've chosen to play Crewe B instead. What the fuck." I put my hands on my hips, sighed, then clapped once. To business! "Spectrum, what's the deal?"

"So, there's two mini leagues of five teams. We play the other four teams in our group. Three matches today, one in the morning. The top two go into the playoffs. Top from Group A plays second from Group B, vice versa, winners into the final. Third-, fourth-, fifth-placed teams play each other to decide the final ranking. So we'll get at least two matches tomorrow."

"Bonanza," I said. "Who's in our group?"

"Crewe B, Wolves, Wrexham, Nottingham Forest."

"Piece of piss," I said. "It's not even Crewe A. Jesus Christ, don't they know who they're dealing with?" I gave stern looks to all the kids. "Listen up, everyone. This is the most important thing I'm going to say to you today. Do I have your complete attention?" You'd better believe I did. They were *agog*. "Top. Nobody, and I mean nobody, is going to use the word *Nottingham* today. We are all, and this includes you, coach, going to say *Notts Forest*. Repeat after me: Notts Forest."

"Notts Forest," chanted my players, while Spectrum rubbed his nose.

"Excellent. They hate that. It will wind them *all* the way up." I laughed.

"Forest is tomorrow," said Spectrum.

"Who?"

"Forest."

"Who?"

The kids were staring from me to him like they had centre court seats at Wimbledon. Spectrum cracked. "Notts Forest," he said. He shuddered. "Ugh! I don't even support them and I hate saying it wrong."

Benny put his hand up. His arm quivered with the effort of being noticed. I nodded. "Does that mean we're doing mental disintegration?"

"A bit," I said.

Benny went "woah!" and then started explaining it to his teammates. I tried to avoid spoiling the effect by laughing. I'd only been around for a couple of minutes and I'd turned them from being nervous wrecks into thinking they would be given cheat codes.

I turned away from the kids for a private chat with Spectrum. "Who's up first?"

"Crewe. They've done the fixtures based on their needs. Start with us, the weakest, and get progressively harder fixtures. By the time they play Wolves, they might already be through to the playoffs and can rest players."

"Rest is important, I guess?"

"Yeah. It's vital. It's the difference. Our best players aren't a whole lot worse than the average, but the bigger teams just have way more resources. Wolves could play a different team in their second match if they wanted to rotate, and they wouldn't be any weaker."

"But they can only make three subs in one game, yeah?"

"Yeah. Matches are forty-five minutes on a full-sized pitch. It's tiring. It's good we have more subs this year."

I gave him a long, hard look, wondering if I should say what I wanted to say. Since he'd had his talk with Jackie and come back to work, he'd done what I told him with no friction. There wasn't any point in trying to persuade him to stay—that ship had sailed—but maybe he could learn a lesson that would help him in the future. "Everyone comes to every training sesh because it's fun. Everyone's here today because it's not Toxic FC." There wasn't any point in continuing the lecture. The serious moment was over. I smiled. "Haven't you heard? It's Snowflake FC now."

Spectrum gave me a strange look as he said, "Teamwork FC."

I couldn't work out what emotion he was transmitting, whether it was a joke. I didn't want to get bogged down in personal drama. "So Crewe think we're the weakest team? That pisses me off. Let's go bulldoze their little tournament, yeah?"

Ten minutes before kickoff, my screens kicked in. I was offered Bench Boost and Triple Captain. More old friends! Based on what Spectrum had said, I'd need those for the next match, against Premier League Wolves. I thought of saving them for the final, but we had to *get* to the final first.

So, Crewe B. They had a squad whose PA varied much more than ours. They had a surprising number of what I'd started to call "Fool's Gold" players. They were tall, fast, or great athletes who didn't have high PA. To normal people, even to experienced scouts, they looked like great prospects. I knew better, but that didn't stop them being good performers at this level.

The tactics screens told me that Crewe would line up in a 4-2-4. Very ambitious, very attacking. Good tactic against a team of no-hopers who would spend the whole forty-five minutes defending.

"Spectrum," I said, as the kids waited to be told our formation and starting lineup. "Do you normally park the bus in these games?"

He looked away. "We try to play. But . . . yeah. We get pressed back."

I raised a palm. "No shade, man. I beat Man City with a bus the size of Pep's bald spot. So guys, Crewe are going to do four-two-four. Lots of fast attacks down the wings. Captain, Bomber, they'll try to get crosses in. Deal with them, thank you very much. Right," I said, rubbing my chin. We had a medium-sized whiteboard. In a small section of the top, I moved the red magnets into a 4-2-4 formation. Then I started putting out blue ones. I talked out loud as I went. "How mental do I want to go? Pretty mental, I think. Two centre backs, obvs. Future as DM. Yes, please! How about . . . five across midfield. Yeah. Our five against their two. Lol! Enjoy building attacks with a fucking zombie horde attacking you! Guys, you're the zombie horde. In case that wasn't clear. Two strikers? Nah. Tyson, you'll play CAM. Benny. You're up top. Wow. I love this."

I stepped back, luxuriating in the magnificence of my creation.

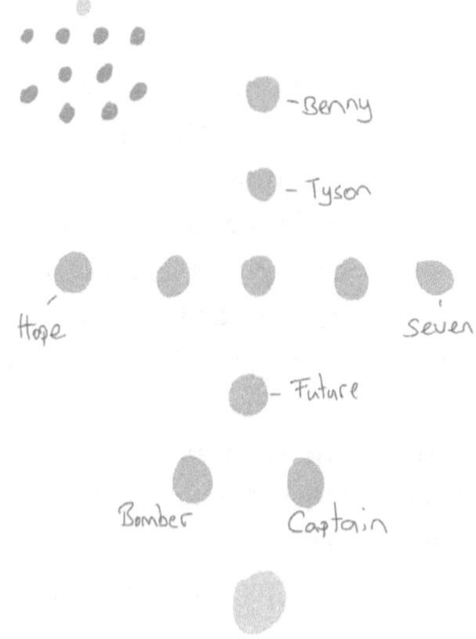

Spectrum's mouth had dropped open. He closed it in time to say, "You want us to play . . . two . . . *one*-five-one-*one*?"

"Yes, please."

"You do realise," he said, coming close to me and hissing so that the kids wouldn't hear his disloyalty, "that when they attack it'll be four on two?"

My tongue swept across my bottom lip as I tried not to grin too hard. "Better not let them have any attacks then, right? Set that up while I go pee. Thanks."

He couldn't help it—the next statement burst out of him, completely audible to all the kids. "But we haven't practised this!"

"Yes, we have," I said, stroking an imaginary kung-fu grandmaster beard. "Yes, we have."

I wandered off and found myself at the Wolves match. Based on league position—they were about 120 places above us in the pyramid—they should have been our hardest opponents, but they had their fair share of Fool's Gold and players out of position. They did have a handful of guys with very high PA—in a couple of years this group would be far, far better than ours. But for a one-off match taking place today, I rated our chances. Our average CA was about 4, with Tyson leading the way on CA 7. Wolves had an average CA of 6 with their best player having CA 11.

The manager spotted me and nudged his assistant. I knew exactly what he was saying. "Look! There's the greatest living Englishman, Max Best! Let's pluck up the courage to ask for a selfie." They were fucking drowning in equipment. Laptops, tablets, bags, cases, match balls, enough water bottles to put out a house fire. A kid pulled on a yellow shirt; he wore a GPS performance tracker. Three hundred pounds, per player. These little yobs were better equipped than Chester's first team.

I gave the men a little wave, then went back to the pitch where my kids were playing Crewe. Their CA was much closer to ours, but they had confidence. They had experience. They got to play in Fuckingham Palace twice a month. Their best players were their forwards, and their entire system was based around bringing that firepower to bear. My plan was the equivalent of piling a few sandbags in front of a thundering tank.

Spectrum's back was stiff. He had obeyed me, but he didn't like the tactics. He thought I was deliberately setting the team up to lose. Maybe he thought I wanted to make him look bad. When I retook my position on the touchline, he bent to pick up a water bottle, took a swig, and put it down again. This process left him very slightly angled away from me.

I checked out my subs. There were the two guys with PA in the twenties I'd promoted from the younger group, but they were CA 2, and they were eleven years old. I also had Nine as a half-decent backup for Benny. But basically, all my good players were on the pitch. Changing the team would mean diluting our ability to win, but I wanted to stick to my principles as much as possible. "Coach," I said. "Help me make sure everyone plays at least a few minutes in at least two games."

"Everyone plays every game," he mumbled, repeating a phrase I'd learned when I managed the Beth Heads.

"Yeah. We can't do that in this tournament, but we can always use the three subs and we can rotate the starters."

"Right," he said, somehow with minus a hundred percent enthusiasm. Such an annoying man!

The match kicked off and Spectrum sucked in some air. I realised he was holding his breath, waiting for the onslaught to arrive.

One minute later, his anxiety had turned to confusion. Crewe hadn't been in our half. Where was the invasion?

Two minutes in, his frown was so deep not even Botox would have smoothed it. The match was chaotic, but those plucky underdogs, those cannon fodder, those no-hopers from Chester were in the ascendency.

By five minutes in, the match had fallen into a predictable pattern. Predictable to me, anyway. Spectrum sometimes pointed and said, "But."

Crewe would have a goal kick or a throw-in, and they would move the ball around their defensive third, as they'd been trained. My guys would react by doing absolutely nothing. A couple of times, Benny tried to press, but I yelled at him not to. So Crewe would pass the ball from side to side. At first, they were quite happy to do that, and indeed their manager was pleased with their approach.

But every time they played the ball *forwards*, our five midfielders would swarm. They surrounded the ball carrier, they put pressure on him, they made interceptions, they forced mistakes. Crewe's talented attackers barely got a kick. They were beautiful, gleaming tanks—and I'd stolen their petrol.

When we turned over the ball, we'd push it to Tyson, who'd dribble and try to find a pass to Benny. Benny was on his own against, in theory, four defenders, so he was going to find it tough to get shots away. That was fine. He'd probably be a lone striker for most of his career. It didn't hurt him to do it in tournament conditions.

Spectrum's back was much less turned away now. Crewe's possessions still stressed him out, but in his mind the worst-case scenario had come down from 10–0 to something much more acceptable. The 4–0 and 5–0 defeats Chester were used to in these games.

At the fourth time of asking, Crewe finally got through our midfield and Spectrum's anxiety showed with his hands partially covering his eyes. He couldn't watch! I was annoyed by our bad luck—it was really way too much of a random ricochet in Crewe's favour that led to a striker dropping to get the ball, bursting past Future, and playing it wide to the right. The right mid, unopposed, moved forwards and crossed. Captain headed it behind for a corner.

Spectrum said, "Okay, we got away with that. How about we go more defensive for a few minutes?"

I pulled a face—*er . . . no*—and instructed four players to attack from this defensive corner. "Spread out," I said, gesturing manically. "All across the halfway line!"

Spectrum was right back to hating me, but my move caused pandemonium on the Crewe bench as they struggled to get players to drop back. By the time the corner was taken, Crewe only had four players in the box! I'd frazzled their tiny minds. Bomber won the header, we cleared, and things went back to normal.

"Captain and Bomber are unusually good in the air, it seems," I mused.

"They're proper defenders," said Spectrum, talking on autopilot. "They actually love it. Oh."

"What?"

"Future's gone."

I snapped my head around to check out the pint-sized prospect. He was holding a finger, forming a kind of protective barrier over his head. He was taking tell-tale gasps of air.

"Captain," I called. Our main centre back heard me. I pointed to Future. "Send him over here."

Captain put his hands on Future's shoulders, pointed him at me, and cajoled him into jogging to the touchline. I gave Captain a thumbs-up and he jogged back into position, fists clenched, ready for the next battle.

"Hey, Future," I said to the tiny, teary mess, noting his performance was currently rated four out of ten. "Whatchya doing?"

"They're too fast!" he blubbed. "Too big and too fast. I can't . . . I can't . . ."

"Ah, I see." Our subs inched closer. Both to find out what was happening and to offer support. But also to see if Future would be subbed off and one of *them* would get to play most of this match. None of them could fill in at DM, so nah. "I don't want to alarm you, mate," I said, which normally got people's attention. "But what you're doing is called catastrophising. What happens is your negative thoughts create a little vortex in the brain. It looks sort of like a tornado. Have you ever seen a tornado?"

Through his tears, he nodded.

"Yeah, you probably watch *Twister* every Christmas morning. I know I do, before I open my presents. So what it is, is, imagine a tornado but it's round. It's small and it's round. And your negative thoughts are actually making a tiny spherical tornado in your brain. And the dangerous thing is, if you do it long enough, it makes a hole." He blinked. "Yeah. An actual hole. And when there's a hole in your brain, you know what it fills with?"

He thought he knew where this was going, and it didn't help with his tears. "Bad feelings."

"No," I said. "It fills with orange juice."

The crying stopped. "What?"

"When you drink orange juice, it goes round your body, yeah, on the way to the stomach. And if there's a hole in your brain it goes there. It loves it. It happened to me. Every time I moved my head I could hear like one cubic centimetre of orange juice sloshing around. It was really fucking weird."

He kind of did one more cry while rolling his eyes at me. "I should stop having bad thoughts."

"No, do what you want. It was cool hearing stuff in my head. I got used to it. And I found a cure."

"Cure?"

"Plasticine. You put a tiny bit of plasticine in your orange juice and it starts to fill the hole. Ten glasses and you're good."

"My gran told me not to eat Play-Doh."

"Does she let you drink orange juice?"

"Yes."

"That's weird. Something doesn't add up there." I'd been squatting, leaning my head towards him. I stood and rolled my head around. "Thing is, bro, we've been chatting here for about an hour, right? And look." I pointed at the match going on behind him. He turned. "We're doing fine. We don't need you." Spectrum gave me a sharp glance that triggered a burst of anger. I glared at him until Future looked back at me. He saw the calm, relaxed, almost angelic face of Max Actual Best.

"The other kids are tall. Pffft. No one asked you to win any headers. We've got Captain and Bomber for that. The other kids are fast. You're fast, too. It's okay if a guy dribbles you today. That's why we've got goalies. Don't stress about it. Now, it'd be super helpful if you did an interception or two and it's important that you get into the positions your coaches taught you so *that* lot can't do easy passes. Yeah? But your main job is getting the ball from Captain and Bomber and passing it to midfield. We can do it without you but it's slow. When *you* do it, we move up the pitch really fast and we put pressure on these chumps. What happens then is they *buckle*. And I go mwahahaHAhaaa and all the orange juice in my head sloshes around and it feels good."

"You're crazy!"

"Yeah. Just go be a connector, please. And later I'll tell you about my trial at Chester and how I had a big freakout for twenty minutes and then when I calmed down I took the piss so much Ian Evans ended the game early."

"What!"

"Actually, now that I think about it, that's the *whole* story. Never mind. Okay, off you pop."

Future trotted back into his position.

Spectrum stared straight ahead as he said, "We don't conventionally encourage twelve-year-olds to eat plasticine."

I shrugged. "There's a cure for plasticine."

"Apple juice?"

"Close. Cider."

That got a tiny, reluctant grin. "That was one of the most mental interactions I've ever seen." His attention was focused on the rear of midfield, where Future and Captain were discussing something. "But it worked."

Another thing that worked was my tactic. We stifled Crewe, strangled them, and their rare breaks were ruthlessly ended by Captain—an eight out of ten performance that would have been higher if he'd been any busier. With Future back in the game, doing his linking work, Crewe didn't get any breathers. We attacked, we attacked, and we turned *their* attacks into more attacks. Spectrum went from a state of constant anxiety to being almost zen. If we lost this, it would be because of random chance. I could almost *see* the moment he realised my strategy was right. He sort of popped out of himself, and instead of becoming an insect crawling into its shell for protection, he became the team's coach, running up and down the touchline, clapping, cajoling, yelling out praise and encouraging players to adhere to their tasks. The switch from pessimist to optimist cost him—he started to sweat, his hair got frazzled, and he got his glasses dirty and felt he couldn't spare the few seconds needed to clean them.

For now at least, Spectrum was *in*.

The bottleneck for us was Benny. He'd had a couple of half-chances and one that was a quarter-chance at best. None had turned into anything close to a goal, and he'd started to wind himself up. I wanted to call out to him, but I made myself wait.

Two guys from Wolves appeared in their pristine tracksuits and big coats. They stared in astonishment at the patterns of play, bickering with each other about what the formation was, then began furiously scribbling on notepads. One of them ran back to base while the other stayed to watch the end.

After twenty minutes of seeing their tactics backfire, Crewe buckled.

The move started on the left, where one of the players I'd stolen from Hope Farm was stationed. I'd nicknamed him Hope, proof that the orange juice in my head was ruining my imagination.

Hope collects a loose ball. He turns inside and passes to Boyce.

Boyce plays it back to Future, who hits a first-time pass to Nugent.

Nugent lays it back to Future, who hits a first-time pass to Sevenoaks.

He feints to dribble on the outside but cuts a perfectly-weighted diagonal pass into the stride of Tyson.

Tyson chips a ball over the defenders.

Benny latches onto it. He shrugs off a challenge, approaches the keeper.

It looks like he has taken it too wide . . .

GOOOOAAAALLLL!!!!

He slots it home!

The goalie got a touch but couldn't keep it out.

The goal had been coming. It's a fitting reward for Chester's performance so far.

While the kids celebrated wildly—a bit too close to Crewe's goalie, I'd have to talk to them about that—Spectrum ran up and down the touchline, not knowing what to do. I waited, amused, until he calmed down. He seemed surprised that I wasn't bouncing. I wondered if his teams had ever taken the lead in one of these tournaments. It seemed not! I waited a bit more, and when I felt he was ready to listen, I said, "I can't coach much, but I can show Benny a better way to finish those chances."

"What do you mean? It was perfect."

"Nah. Those two touches made the angle worse. I'll show him a better way. Can you make a note of the time? Is all this being recorded?"

He gestured to a camera on a tall pole and some sort of robotic one on the other side of the pitch. "Yeah. No close-ups or anything, and sometimes robocam loses the ball."

"If you don't mind, clip out that move. Any different angles and that. I'll demo, like, three better options."

"Three?"

I misread what he meant. "Yeah, two's better. I'll show him a Hugo Sanchez first-timer and a Max Best fake-out."

"You know Hugo Sanchez?" said Spectrum, eyes wide.

I was too pensive to engage. "There's the chip option, but he might snatch at it. Or . . . or practising that might help with his new Iceman persona. Let's think about it. So there's footage from this. Have we got a club tablet we can bring to sessions? Show the videos then work on it, that kinda thing?"

"No."

I scratched my chin. "I'll see if I can get us a few. Beg Wolves for their hand-me-downs. This haves and have-nots shit is winding me up big time."

The match continued. We were straight back onto the front foot. So much so that the Crewe manager was almost literally tearing his hair out. There were no breaks where he could make tactical changes, so all he could do was beg his players to move into new slots, one by one. It looked like he was trying to get his team into a formation the players were comfortable with.

"Max!" said Spectrum, practically yipping himself into a one-eighty like those tiny dogs. "They're going four-four-two!"

"I *know*," I said, unable to stop my annoyance reaching my voice. A tiny sliver of professionalism kicked in. "Thanks, though."

"So what are we going to do?"

"Do? Nothing. Four-four-two doesn't help him." I scoffed at the very idea.

Spectrum put his hand in his mouth and when he took it out, all his fingernails were gone. If I'd liked him, I would have done a Darth Vader voice. "I find your lack of faith . . . unimaginative." But I didn't, so I didn't.

Then came a moment that really got my juices flowing, almost for the first time in the match.

One of our midfield swarm, Clive, PA 1, played a nice, simple pass to Tyson. He looked up, saw the keeper off his line, and shaped to shoot. My anger rose to preposterous levels, but while the keeper scrambled backwards, Tyson did a little foot shuffle, a hip wiggle, and played a dreamy pass out to the right for Seven to run onto. It was really gorgeous, Teddy Sheringham-esque, and the final flourish was Tyson wagging his finger at the goalie. *That was a warning.*

"Yes, Tyson!" I yelled, and both Spectrum and I clapped enthusiastically. No filters, no agendas. Just appreciation for a move of rare quality. He seemed stunned by the attention and retreated into his shell for a minute.

But then he came back with a vengeance.

It's Tyson again. Crewe must be sick of his dribbling.

He shapes to shoot and a defender slides in to block it.

Tyson cuts back onto his left, pushes the ball forwards.

Benny holds it up. Plays a neat reverse flick.

Tyson is through on goal! He rounds the keeper. He has an open net!

He pauses. What is he doing?

He passes backwards—Benny applies the finish.

GOOOOAAAALLLL!!!!

A wonderful move!

A strange thing happened then. The players celebrated in a big huddle, as was becoming their thing, and when it broke apart and they started the long journey back to our half, someone on the touchline shouted something to Tyson. He looked surprised, replied, and then looked over to me. He looked away. Guilty as fuck!

"Spectrum, would you please find out who those men are?"

"Are you serious?" He was eyeing the pitch like if he left, everything would fall apart. The prick!

"Yeah," I said. My voice must have conveyed my worry, because he walked away without another word. He came back a few minutes later.

"They're scouts. They wouldn't say who for. They only asked what his name was, they said. I think I believe them."

"It's a bit shit, messing with his head mid-game."

"Yeah." After he'd agreed with me, he thought it through and realised he really agreed with me. He began yelling at the players in a much deeper voice. Super committed now. Come on, lads! Head up, Tyson! Roar!

But the next five minutes proved I was right to worry. Tyson's rating dropped from nine to seven. I subbed him off, replacing him with Nine, the other guy we'd poached from Hope Farm. I switched to 4-4-2. Matched the other team, who would spend the next five minutes bewildered at our sudden change. Five minutes closer to an impressive win.

While Spectrum returned to pointing at the pitch going "Wut?" I turned to focus on my newest problem.

"Tyson. Nicely played. What was that little weirdness at the end?"

He swallowed and looked at Spectrum. I jerked my head away and he followed me to a more private location. I had a strange feeling in the pit of my stomach. I checked it out and was surprised to find it was labelled *fear*. I'd invested so much time and energy into this little brat and now that my work was paying off, the idea of some bigger club swooping in to take him from me the way I'd taken the kids from Hope Farm was . . . was painful. It would be a setback. A step backwards. Number goes down.

"What's up?" I said.

He looked a bit shifty for a while, typical teenager, but then his time at his posh school showed its worth. He had the confidence to put his feelings into words. "There's scouts here."

"Yep."

"They're interested in me."

"Yep."

"I could move to a different club, like you said. A *Premier League* club."

I blinked. "Wolves?"

"Forest."

"Excuse me?"

"Forest."

"Excuse me?"

He made an exasperated little movement. "Notts Forest," he said, but saying it made him grin.

"Okay. And do you *want* to go to Nottsssss Foresssst?"

"I don't know. Maybe?"

I inhaled. "Thing is, if you want to go, fine. I'll wish you the best of luck and everything. Like I said. But let me know, because if you're off to Notts or wherever, it's not fair that I give you minutes instead of people who want to play for Chester. Do you know what I mean? I'm doing a project here. Pathway to the first team."

"Well, yeah, but . . ."

"Spit it out. Jesus."

"You don't like me."

That was surprising. "What's that got to do with anything?"

"You coach Benny. And Future. And Captain. But you never tell me anything. You never coach me. You only tell me what not to do."

"That's not true. I also told you to get a proper haircut."

He frowned, and his hand instinctively went to his hair. "No, you didn't."

"I wanted to. Not with this one. The last one. This one's good. Suits you. Well, you want coaching, you've got coaches. You want something from me, I can't promise that. But I can promise you won't get private chats with the manager of Notts. Or their DoF if they have one. Or their star player. Or anyone except one little Spectrum-type guy. Not a single one of those other guys will know your name. And right now, you don't need coaching. You need to be told what not to do. And that's what you're getting."

"I don't like it."

"I wouldn't, either. I'd think, *I'm better than you, you old hack. You don't know what I need.*" I smiled. "But you don't get that choice. Be-cause I'm me. And I know best."

"Other teams would let me shoot."

I was ninety-nine percent certain that the scouts had shown interest in Tyson because he'd created two goals. Because under my cruel thumb he was the ultimate team player, to a fault. Because the fake long shot showed he had imagination *and* restraint. Because it hinted at superior decision-making that Tyson didn't actually possess. Yet.

But the thought of explaining all that repulsed me. Saying it would feel like begging. The guy had talent. The guy could make it. But only with my help. If he wanted to fuck off, he could fuck off.

"If selected in the next match," I said, becoming distant. Patrician, "I expect you to give a hundred percent and ignore outside distractions."

"Yeah, course."

"I have you in mind for an important tactical role," I said. "You'll think it's a punishment. It's not. It's for the team. If you don't want to do it, you can go off to pitch five to meet your new mates."

"What is it?"

I ignored the question and strode back towards our technical area. "Mitchell, get warmed up. You're on for Benny soon. Adam, you, too. You'll go for Boyce." Adam was one of the under-twelves I'd promoted. He was eleven, and only slightly bigger than Future.

"Max," said Spectrum. "That'll be a very small team out there. They'll get overrun."

I nodded. "Adam, you'll replace Future. All good? Great."

"Replace Benny? Are you sure? They could get two quick goals."

I was sick of his doubts. "We're here to win," I said. I left all the rest unspoken. That we were rotating our squad assuming we'd reach the final. That Benny was our most important player and we couldn't grind him into dust. That I didn't want to hear any more negative shit. He didn't *believe* the way I did, but Spectrum got the message. He shut his fucking gob, and I was thankful for it.

That was all I had to do. The rest of the match was quite dull, for me at least. Spectrum reacted to every incident like Gemma had at the World Cup final—reactions turned up to eleven. But if I wasn't getting 2 XP per minute, I might have gone round and scouted all the other players. I needed to scan everyone so that I could trigger Playdar. I'd decided not to use it on Friday in case Crewe was bursting with players like Dani. But I could still grind like in the old days. I saw the match out. Easy 2–0 win. Yawn.

Spectrum and I crossed the pitch and shook hands with the guys from Crewe. They looked shellshocked. I had a sudden idea. It was absolute genius. "Guys, you've got loads of subs. After the matches today, can I borrow a few? I want to do a tiny, tiny demo match. It'll be fun. Chill. Short. Nice end to the day."

They mumbled some confused maybes, and we walked back. Spectrum didn't comment on the demo match thing. He was still fixated on a match I'd mentally consigned to the dustbin of history. "I don't get it," he said. "That was . . . that was comfortable." I let him keep talking. "I mean, we rested our best players! We won and Benny only played half the match. Tyson got a break. Even Future. It's . . . What the fuck was that formation?"

"Language," I said.

"How did you know what formation *they'd* play?"

"They did it in the warm-up," I said. "How long till the next game? About an hour? While you were setting the lads up, I had a look at Wolves. Looks like they've focused on technical players. Could be hard. We might have to get weird. Just saying."

I gathered the kids around for a quick debrief. "Good job, lads. You've beat the hosts in their weird Harry Potter Forbidden Forest. Yeah? Didn't expect that, did they? Guess what? Chester's in town. Deal with it. Man of the Match goes to . . . me. Second place, Benny. Great composure on your goals. *Ice Cold in Alex*, yeah? Shit, that's a *great* line. Wasted on you lot. Also second place, Captain and Bomber. Also second place, everyone else. Third place, goalie. Did you even have a save to make? No? You took a great goal kick, though." Lots of laughs. "Seriously, though. Everyone chipped in. That's it. It's that simple. All right? Try to stay calm. What we did isn't unusual. That's what we *do* now. We give teams *headaches*. Save your energy. Do some sunbathing or whatever." We all looked up at the sky. "Or cloudbathing."

My phone rang. It was MD, saying that a reporter was at the tournament and wanted to talk to me. I said I was busy. He begged. I said no. While I was talking, I saw something. Something miraculous and unexpected.

A man, a woman, and their child. Dani!

I punched the air and in a foolish rush of blood to the head, told MD I'd spare a few minutes for the reporter. "Send him over," I said.

I jogged to Dani and stood in front of her, smiling just as goofily as James Yalley often did. She smiled back. I opened my mouth to speak, but remembered I couldn't. And she'd deleted herself from the chat. How did I do this? I ended up looking at the clouds for help. They were useless.

Dani pointed to her phone.

"You left the chat," I said.

"Invite her back," said the dad. So I did, and then the four of us stood close by, texting each other.

Me: Emma. Guess who's got two thumbs and is back?

Emma: What! Wow! Daniiiiiii

Me: Dani, point two thumbs at yourself so I can take a photo of you and surprise Emma.

Dani: She knows.

Me: Yeah but if we don't close that conversational loop it'll bother me. What has two thumbs and is back . . . this girl. Come on. Thumbs.

Mr. Smith: Dani liked your video.

Me: Is it top-ten viral in Crewe now? My IT dude said the numbers didn't really count as viral. Said it needed more cats.

Mrs. Smithe: Our coach got it from your coach.

Me: Oh.

Dani: You're a good dancer.

Me: Emma said I'm better than Harry.

Emma: Don't listen to him, Dani, I would never.

Dani: I know! I liked when you signed, Max.

Emma: That was my fave too.

Dani: You did ASL though.

Me: What does that mean?

Dani: You did American sign language.

Me: Wait. Do I have an American accent?

This delighted me no end, for some reason.

But then it was time to take the next step. I hadn't prepared for this moment. I kind of thought I'd get some warning. There was an awkward silence. Different from the previous silence. I wanted to ask Dani what her intentions were, but there was no way without involving everyone, which was quite inhibiting. Maybe when her parents started to trust me I'd be allowed to chat one-on-one.

Me: Sooooooo

Still no one so much as twitched their thumbs.

Me: SO WHAT BRINGS YOU TO CREWE

Dani: Duh. We live here.

Me: Are you going to make me say it?

Dani: Say what? Also: yes.

Me: Would you please pretty please with a cherry on top sign for my football team please thanks

The family turned away and started signing to each other. I was worried at first, but the mum was a terrible actor. They were teasing me. Finally:

Dani: I want to try.

I nodded, calmly, and calmly gave the three of them firm but polite handshakes. "Yes, that will do tremendously well," I believe I said.

Emma: What's happening?

Dani: Max ran away. I think he was shouting.

Mr. Smith: He was screaming "f*ing come on yes mate" and similar things**

Mrs. Smithe: He's very fast. He went quite a long way. Is he coming back do you think?

I ran back and waved at Dani. *Come on. Follow me.*

I introduced her to the boys. They knew she was my white whale, the star I'd discovered from the previous Crewe tournament, the one who'd made me embrace social media and do tekkers. And here she was! They treated her like a celebrity. Tyson, the little shit, annoyed me by being super extra nice. *Ooh teach me to sign my name.* Ugh. He didn't fool *me*. A bunch of the bolder boys coaxed Dani into a skills circle, doing kick-ups and *boing*ing the ball around to the next person.

The dad gave me a quick lesson in deaf culture and pointed out a big mistake I'd made in the video. I thanked him, and he said they knew it'd be hard for everyone but we'd get through it. He and his wife went for a coffee.

Future looked from them to Dani. "How do we talk to her?" he said, amazed at the existence of deaf people.

"You learn sign language, but not the American one, because that's totally different and apparently Dani only understood what I was doing from context. Ugh. I spent ages learning that, and it was like learning Portuguese to talk to a Brazilian."

"You're joking, aren't you?"

"Yes, actually."

"But really, how do you talk to her?"

"Chat group."

"Can we do one? Just for us?" He meant the boys and her.

"I don't know. Ask the dad." Future raced away in the direction of the café. Super speed! His tears were long forgotten.

So soon the boys who had phones were doing chats with Dani, supervised (remotely) by her parents. I wasn't invited in and while I was burning with curiosity, I had to let them get on with it.

And that was the scene when the reporter arrived: me off my head on good vibes; Spectrum watching Dani, wondering what I saw in her while being happy for me and for the club; some kids doing skills; Dani joining in when she wasn't texting; the kids laughing, joking, every now and then turning to look at me and then laughing even harder and returning to their phones; kids without mobiles leaning over to see what the latest jape was.

We were an island of unity in a sea of rivals, reefs, and sharks. Dani looked at me. I smiled and gestured in a biiig circle. *Look at this mess.* Then I signed: *in this world, it's just us.* But the us wasn't the "me and you" gesture I'd used in the video. It was us, Chester FC. This little circle. She smiled and looked down at the grass.

Spectrum said he wanted a coffee, too, and fucked off in the same direction Dani's parents had gone. I felt a presence behind me. The reporter. "Bizarre tactics. Improbable wins. Disruptive newcomers. Looks like I stumbled into another Max Best masterclass."

I didn't turn around. I didn't need to; I knew the voice. "If you're looking for a great story, you've found one. But why should I give *you* the inside scoop?"

"Because you owe me fifty quid."

My snort turned into a cheeky grin. "Fine. Get your notepad out, Beth. Things are about to get intense."

WE'RE OFF TO SEE

30-minute read

The Wizard of Us
by B. Alban

Max Best likes movies.

"*The Wizard of Oz* had eleven writers," he tells me, bouncing on his heels like one of the youths in his charge. "Imagine the chaos! A little idea from here, one from there. You can see in the final edit there are lines that make no sense. They're remnants from one of the scripts that got competed out. It's not perfect, then, but it's still taught in film school. There are books about how well it follows mythic structure and all that. Eleven writers. That's a football team. These kids today, this weekend, they're writing their own script. You've heard of Das Boot. This is Das Tournament."

When I catch up with the normally media-shy Best, 22, widely thought to be Europe's youngest director of football, Chester Boys Under-14s have recorded a shock win over D.A.S. Tournament hosts Crewe. Now, he's preparing for a clash against Premier League Wolverhampton Wanderers. There are well over a hundred places between them in the English league pyramid. Wolves regularly play Manchester City, Liverpool, and Tottenham. Chester's upcoming fixtures include matches against Banbury and Leamington. The financial disparity between the club he runs and his rivals could not be more stark. It riles Best, and he brings up a mutual acquaintance from our time in Manchester. "Do you remember that Turkish guy who sold kebabs at Platt Lane? Emre? He loves this chef called Salt Bae. The guy who puts a bit of gold on steaks and charges a thousand pounds. That's Wolves. Gold burgers morning, noon, and night."

"Then it doesn't matter if you lose," I suggest.

"Oh, we're going to win," insists Best, and for a naive moment I'm willing to believe that this story might have a happy ending.

The Munchkins

"Guys," announces Best, as he begins his preparations for the Wolves match. There are twenty minutes to go, and Best still has not named the team nor decided on a formation. The boys are unfazed—they have a saying, "Max Knows Best." They are a ragtag bunch—a few starlets who catch the eye of rival teams, some functional players who stick to their tasks, and a clutch of two-foot-high cutie pies who look like the mascots for a team of mascots. Other teams have brought eleven- and twelve-year-olds for the experience, but only Best dares use them in the white heat of tournament play. "Guys, this is Beth." I have asked him to call me Bethany. "She was my first-ever captain and she taught me about women's football when I was a bit ignorant. She wants to know about our project at Chester. Project? I don't think I like that word. How about story? Yeah. Oh."

Best side-eyes me and demands one of the players hands over his phone. The player is Benny, 14, son of Chester legend Nice One, who scored a famous goal against Leeds in the FA Cup. Benny is in the team on merit, scoring both goals in the 2–0 win over Crewe. He is reluctant to let go of his phone, but Best makes noises like a chimpanzee until he gets the device. Best types, then points to his face. Every child in the area stares at him. He types some more, and everyone looks at *me*. It is disconcerting. Best hands the phone back.

At that moment, a small child dressed in the yellow of Wolves enters the inner sanctum of Chester's technical area. The Chester boys bristle, but the child has one simple question. "Are you Max Best?"

It is clear that Best is cycling through many jokey responses, but he settles on "Yes."

The intruder flees.

Max points to Adam, one of the youngest players. "Follow the yellow prick chode! Tell me where he goes!" Adam gets to his feet and sprints away. Best tugs at an imaginary beard. "So . . . it has begun." The boys laugh. Best's humour is exactly their level. "Is anyone telling Dani what's going on?"

"Me," says Tyson, 14. He's the star of Chester's unheralded academy, and is already drawing admiring glances from teams such as Nottingham Forest and Stoke City.

"Thanks, bro," says Best. I ask who Dani is, and his mood turns. "Do not ask about Dani. Do not write about Dani. Do not bother Dani. Do not print this bit. Do not even use the letter D in your article."

Best glares at me until Adam returns. "He went to the Wolves coaches! He said, 'Yeah, he said he was' and one guy said, 'Okay let's do plan A,' and then they noticed me so I looked at the main one and I said, 'Are you Max Best?' And he said 'No' and I ran back."

Adam is swarmed by his mates, who praise his daring and his quick thinking.

"What does it mean, Max?" This is Spectrum, 25, the youth team coach and Best's reluctant assistant for the tournament. If he's annoyed that Best is in Crewe instead of watching the first team, he doesn't say it with anything except his entire being.

Max is smug. "It means I have finally found an opponent worthy of my attention." He pulls his beard, and the kids cheer.

If I Only Had a Brain

About ten minutes before kickoff, Best gets serious. He invites the children to shut the fuck up and goes to a whiteboard. The kids gather round and sit cross-legged. Spectrum licks his lips, apprehension etched into worry lines a man his age shouldn't have. Now that the match against their storied opponents is near, the Chester squad looks young. Callow. A lot of scared little boys.

Best faces the semicircle. "Boys, put your phones down. I need your undivided attention for this. Not you, Tyson. You see, there are two types of motivation: intrinsic and extrinsic. Write this down, Beth; this is good stuff. Way better than what the Wolves guy is saying, and you can quote me on that. Intrinsic is you want to win because you want to win. Extrinsic is because if you win, I give you something.

You've already won one game, so now it's time for your reward. I need a volunteer." Almost every hand goes up. Best points to Benny. He goes to stand next to Best, whom he clearly idolises. When Best's hand alights on the young man's shoulder and gives him an amiable shake, his smile widens. "Great. Now, some of you are still in what I call the *ew, girls* phase of life. But many are starting to get just as interested in girls as football. So I'm going to teach you how to flirt. Let's start by seeing how you normally do it. Beth, come over here for a second."

"No way!" says Benny, wriggling out from under Best's grip.

There is uproar. Benny tries to flee to the safety of the middle of the pack. The other boys—the ones who aren't rolling around laughing—try to push him back. After a slight delay, the girl called Dani laughs, too, and Tyson rushes next to Best, who is wiping a tear from his eye. The hubbub subsides so everyone can watch Tyson's contribution.

The young striker straightens, points at me, and shouts, "I volunteer!"

The laughs come twice as hard, twice as loud. Benny clambers back to the front and pretends to try to wrestle Tyson out of the way. "She's mine! I'll batter you!" The fight is strangely fascinating.

Best claps a few times, and the boys settle down. It takes a while. "Right. Tyson, ladykiller confirmed. Let's not flirt by shouting at women, though, yeah? Keep it classy. So. There's like a match or whatever." He goes to the whiteboard, swipes the blue magnets away and rearranges the red ones. "Wolves are going to play three-four-one-two." He pauses. "Where have I seen that before?" He slaps his forehead. "Holy fuck! This guy's going to do the Max Best Challenge on us! What the actual!"

"They wouldn't. That's crazy," says Spectrum, who seems to accept as Gospel that their opponents will use an obscure formation.

"I swear to fuck," says Best, pointing to the red magnets, as though *they* have told him Wolves's plan.

"What's the Max Best Challenge?" says Adam, one of the newer players in the Chester system. So new that he hasn't been fully indoctrinated into the Cult of Max.

His teammates strive to be the first to explain it to him, while Best glares at the whiteboard. The Max Best Challenge, Adam learns, is a coaching method developed by Jackie Reaper at FC United, in which a team with superior technique attempts to drag their opposition horizontally across the pitch and back again, disrupting enemy defences. The superior team then attacks the large gaps that have opened up.

"How do we stop it?" says Captain. He's one of Chester's two centre backs, taller and stronger than almost everyone in the tournament.

"The Dutch used this in the World Cup," says Best. "Against the U.S.A., who did four-three-three. The Dutch won easily. So it would be really stupid of us to do four-three-three."

Spectrum groans. All the kids groan. After a slight pause, Dani looks away from her phone and puts her hand over her eyes. I realise, stupidly late, that Tyson is texting her what's happening.

Max begins laying out the blue magnets in a narrow 4-3-3 shape. He follows a narrative order instead of a footballing one. "Goalie. Hope at left back. Seven at right back. I know it's not your fave, but just do your best. Put a shift in—for the team, yeah? Strikers, we'll start with Adam, John, and Future."

"What?" snaps Spectrum and regrets it instantly.

Best narrows his eyes but decides to leave it. "Yeah. Tinytown FC. Guys, you'll be my flying monkeys. Absolute silence. Tumbleweed. Haven't you seen *The Wizard of Oz*? How can I set up a *team* when no one's seen any *movies*? Guys, you have to watch all the same movies that I ever watched so I can reference them. Ugh. How to explain flying monkeys? Just imagine some well-dressed monkeys and they've got wings. They might be blue, which sounds really weird now that I say it out loud. They're only in the movie for about a minute, if I remember. We'll come back to that.

"Where was I? Three tiny attackers. Lol. Wait till Wolves see *you lot* coming. Oh, man. This is exciting. My heart is *pumping* right now. Look, I can't hold my hand still. Beth, is my hand still?" I step closer. "Oh," says Best, reaching for his pocket. "Reminds me. I've got a new phone. Let's exchange deets." He pulls out his phone and I pull out mine, and we're standing next to each other, arms touching. Before I can open the contacts app, Best gives me a little push away. "And that, boys, is how you get a phone number. Boom! See how smooth that was? Jesus Christ I should be a dating coach."

I wander back to where I started, slightly stunned, and when I come to my senses, Best has named a centre back and the three players he wants to go into midfield. There is one spot left to announce—the second centre back. His four best players have not been named: Tyson, Benny, Captain, and Bomber.

Best makes everybody wait. He takes a red marker pen and draws two striped zones either side of midfield. "Do not go here. Do not go here. Here, do go not. Not do go do you. This is the trap, right? So don't go there. Simples." He draws a solid red line around the defence and the midfield. "We've got seven guys here. Seven plus the goalie. All you do is defend. Do not attack. Do not go forwards. Do not go into the trap zones. When Wolves come, wait, be patient, then get the ball. Okay? What they won't be expecting is for us to play long ball."

"Long ball?" says Spectrum, surprised.

"Yeah. Welcome to 1985, guys! Ugh. I really want to talk about *Back to the Future* right now. This player," Best picks up the final blue magnet and places it into the second CB slot, "needs to be a guy who can kick the ball really far. Who's our player who can boot the ball the longest?"

The kids look round at each other, but Tyson has stopped tapping on his phone. He can somehow predict where this is going. "You want me to play centre back?"

"Yep."

"There are scouts here to watch me play striker and you want me in defence? So I'll play shit, or what?"

Best doesn't reply. He waits.

Dani touches Tyson on the arm and gestures a question. *What's going on?* Tyson taps into his phone, the sound of thumbs on glass growing louder by the second. Dani's phone vibrates. She devours the text, laughs, and writes back.

Tyson slumps.

"So?" says Best.

"She says you made *her* play as a goalie." He looks up to the sky. There's no help for him there.

Future says, "He wants me to play striker!"

"Maybe they could swap, Max," says Spectrum. "Play in their natural positions."

"I'd rather win," says Max. And then we're all back to watching Tyson. He glances at the girl. She nods. Tyson copies the gesture. Best claps his hands together. "Fucking yes. Guys. This eleven will go and warm up. No offence, Future, John, and Adam, but you are about as scary as a bowl of ice cream and an afternoon nap. When Wolves see you, they'll relax. They'll switch off. After a minute, all their motivation will be gone. They'll be complacent. And then we're going to sub you off and bring on the hulks."

"Who's coming off?" said Spectrum.

"The three of them."

"And Tyson will go up front?"

Best betrays a moment of exasperation. Why can't everyone understand his plan instantly, without him having to explain it? "Tyson's our playmaker, mate. I need him pumping accurate long balls forward. The whole plan relies on him being there."

"Then who's coming on to be striker?"

"Benny, Captain, and Bomber!"

"Two of them are centre backs!"

"They just need to win headers! They're the best at heading in this whole tournament." Best starts slapping the whiteboard—the magnets shake. "We defend. We turn over the ball. We give it to Tyson. He leathers it. Captain wins it. Benny gets the flick-on. Goal. What the fuck is the problem? It's self-explanatory."

We stare at the whiteboard. I look across the width of the pitch to see the Wolves coaches. They do, indeed, look complacent. I realise I am feeling sorry for them.

"But Max," I say, even though I'm trying to fade into the background. "Why not start with those three up top? Why the theatrics?"

His spat with his coach has made him tense; he loosens his neck. He inhales, then breathes out. His answer finally arrives. "Because it's *funny*."

The Wicked Witch of the West (Midlands)

The Chester team walk onto the pitch, and they are incredibly tiny. Best has asked them to warm up in their formation, so the three youngest players are the ones nearest to the Wolves boys. The latter are too polite to laugh, but Best is right—they relax. This match will be the equivalent of a small boy throwing punches at a bigger one who simply holds the pipsqueak's head a safe distance away.

"Why aren't they worried?" I say.

"Who?" says Best. He's still surly from having his insane strategy questioned.

"The Wolves bench. They must know you're up to something."

"Why would they think that? We played good, modern, attacking football against Crewe. Now we're going to try the same with younger players. They think I'm happy to lose this one and rest my best lads for Wrexham. They think six points out of nine is beyond our wildest dreams."

"Isn't it?"

"My dreams aren't for publication, Beth." He turns to his substitutes. "You guys know what to do, right?"

Captain shrugs. "Win headers. But then what?"

"Whatever you want, mate. Talk to each other. Maybe you'll come up with some little plan. Think what you'd hate to happen if you were defending . . ."

"And do that," says Bomber, 14.

"Exactly," says Best. "Just let me be really clear here. I'm not looking for dribbles and backheels and skills. You are battering rams. You're going to trample those defenders, terrify them, drag them out of position."

"Get aggro on us," says Captain.

"It's all about Benny. Get him some space. Try not to head the ball straight at goal or the keeper will come. Do angles, let his speed do the rest. Know what I mean?"

"Yes, Max."

Best grins, tries to hide his grin, grins wider. The kids reply in kind. Whatever else happens, they've been told they are Best's secret weapon. They've been told they matter. And mattering to Max *matters*.

The game kicks off. Wolves pass the ball around for a full minute, letting all their players have a touch. Chester's three forward players run around like whirling dervishes, knowing they might only get a few seconds of game time. Wolves move the ball to the left-hand side of the pitch, waiting for a Chester boy to press them. Nothing happens. The Wolves player looks confused and passes the ball backwards. Spectrum mumbles, "Holy God." He has just realised that Best's prediction was entirely accurate. The sides of the pitch are traps. They try the right-hand side, and again, no Chester player moves to stop them, not even the flying monkeys. The Wolves player stands there, turns to his manager, and flaps his arms. *What am I supposed to do now?*

I have my first belly laugh of the day.

My second comes shortly after—the ball goes out of play, and Best replaces the flying monkeys with Benny and the Hulks. There's just over a minute on the clock. The referee comes over to check if Best knows the rules. "It's not rolling subs. You can't make any more changes if you do this," he says.

"I know," says Best, gathering the three kids round him like a mother duck. "But it's time for their ice cream and afternoon nap."

If I Only Had Courage

The Wolves team become cautious. They know something is up, and they don't like it. They keep the ball for a while, but seeing that Chester have almost no intention of pressing them, they work it forwards through to their central attacking midfielder (CAM). He puts his foot on the ball and finds there are seven Chester players between him and the keeper. He tries an ambitious through-ball, which is easily cut out. A couple of passes later, the ball is at Tyson's feet. He looks up and pings the ball downfield.

Bomber rises, easily winning the header, and flicks the ball on. It's much straighter than Best would have liked, but the defenders are not alert to the danger. Benny is. He latches onto the ball, takes a touch, and smashes it low into the bottom-left of the net.

Best doesn't react. He's lost in thought. "So who do you work for?"

I'm still buzzing from the goal. "What?"

"You did journalism. Then you got a job."

He's asking about my career. "My course finishes in the summer," I say, trying to bring his attention back to the match. It's like he's forgotten it's happening and somehow it's my job to remind him. "I'll write this, try to get it published somewhere. *Manchester Evening News* maybe. Hope it helps when I start applying for real jobs."

"When's that?"

"Yeah, soon."

"What's your dream job? *The Athletic*, something like that?"

"Oh. Maybe the *Daily Mail*."

Best reacts like he's been slapped. "How to kill a conversation in two words. Fuck me. You can go now."

"Are you serious?"

"Yeah. Interview's over. Spectrum, make sure no one talks to her."

"Max," complains the coach.

I have no choice but to pick up my bag and start to wander off. I pause as a long pass from Tyson reaches Benny. He lays it off for Captain, who flicks the ball up to knee height and then over his head towards the goal. The defenders are more switched on this time, but Benny is more determined. He gets to the ball, takes a touch, and fires a shot. The goalie gets a hand on it and pushes it wide. It's a corner.

"Everyone," yells Best. "Everyone up."

Once again, Spectrum complains. Chester will be open to counter-attacks, a fact Best should be all too aware of, having made his name as a player with a fast break from a corner. This decision is an emotional outburst, a petulant response to me, nothing more. But Wolves respond by pulling everyone back into their penalty box. Only as Tyson and Sevenoaks, 14, discuss what to do with the corner does the Wolves manager finally decide to leave one striker on the halfway line. If Chester don't score, Wolves probably will. The odds are massively in favour of the latter.

I notice Best touch the air. He's having some mental argument that's expressing itself through body language. He sees that I'm still around and shoos me away.

I walk along the line, towards the corner where Tyson has both hands raised over his head. But instead of firing it into the box himself, he plays a 15-yarder to Sevenoaks, who hits the cross with spin and quality. The penalty box is crowded, but somehow it feels inevitable that Bomber should get to the ball first, and for his flick to go directly into Captain's path. He throws his whole body at the ball, almost a diving header, and as it crosses the line he is already clambering to his feet, running away, yelling, demanding his team follow.

They run en masse to their base, their home for the tournament, and bounce around.

Dani and the rest of the squad bounce with them. They are learning that it takes more than eleven to write a script.

If I Only Had a Heart

Chester's crushing 5–2 win over the tournament favourites is the talk of the town. The underdogs are top of Group B. Casual observers are delighted; experts are not.

I speak to an employee from Wolves. They are dismissive. "Anyone can lump the ball up to a big man. If that's the only way you can win, I suppose that's fine. But you ask me, that kind of football has no place here. We're trying to develop young players. He won't win any friends with that kind of win-at-all-costs mentality."

Another observer, a very experienced administrator, agrees. "I've heard about this Max Best. Heard he's got a few tricks up his sleeve. That's all well and good but I've seen all that before. People like that get found out. Fool me once, shame on you. Fool me twice, shame on me. These professional coaches aren't fools. Chester won't win another match, mark my words."

The Chester boys, though, are in dreamland. As they wander around the complex, their kit marks them out as the team to fear. "See them? They're *Chester.*" The boys hear, and their cheeks flush. This is new, and they like it.

I fall into step beside Tyson and Benny. They don't seem aware that they're not allowed to talk to me. "Hi, boys."

Tyson rolls his eyes. "I *have* a girlfriend," he says, and he and Benny fall into each other.

"Can I walk with you anyway?"

"Course," says Tyson. He checks with Benny. Benny agrees.

"Where are you going?"

"Oh." Tyson's feet stop moving. Benny takes a couple of strides before he realises. He waits. Tyson scratches the back of his neck, then starts forward again. "I got scouted but I told Max I wanted to stay at Chester."

"That's good. But?"

"Er . . . he said he was pleased but I shouldn't decide just coz we won. He said I was hyper because he'd Wizard of Ozzed me."

"Whatever that means," says Benny.

"He'd Wizard of Ozzed me into being the best centre back in the universe, but the spell would wear off."

"He's so weird!" says Benny.

"I know, it's top," agrees Tyson. "Yeah and he told me I should go and check out Notts Forest."

"Oh, wait," I say. "There's a team called Notts County. That's short for Nottinghamshire. Nottingham isn't shortened to Notts."

"It is if you want to mess with their heads," says Benny, and the boys fall into each other again. "Yeah. Max said I should go to Notts, too. He reckons they've got top packed lunches with all, like, nutrition inside. He says we're allowed to eat one but we have to bring the other one back."

"He's doing, like, research, for when the club's got more money."

"Oh," I say, "so he doesn't really want you to talk to Notts. He's using you as spies."

Tyson's face opens. "That's what I said! Didn't I, Benny? That's what I said! And he said, well yeah but no. He said it's going to take years to upgrade the facilities and all that, and if I want to go to Notts for a bit, why not? They'll let me shoot."

"You're not allowed to shoot?"

"Yeah. Max subs me off if I shoot."

"What if he's used all his subs?"

"I go off anyway and we play with ten." Tyson shrugs. He's so used to this extraordinary restriction that he doesn't know how shocking it is. "But if I go to Notts and do well, great. That's the best thing. But if I go and I get released, I can go back to Chester and I'll have had all that top training and I'll be miles ahead of Benny."

"Fuck you, no you won't. Max Knows Best. I'm staying. I'll learn way faster than you. He fucking scores from corners, you bell end."

"What does Dani think you should do, Tyson?"

I've asked the question with maximum innocence, but the boys both stop dead. Tyson holds up a finger and pulls Benny away. They have a hushed conversation and return. "Why do you want to know about Dani?"

I'm on thin ice, for some reason. One wrong move from losing a source! I try to look unbothered. "Just curious."

The boys look at each other. Tyson comes to a decision. "I think we can walk on our own from here." He waits for me to move away, then taps on his phone. I'm eerily certain he's sending a message in all caps.

The Ruby Slippers

As I circle the tournament, looking for stories and subplots, gathering background information and colour, I spot Best again and again. He's at pitch 1 watching Derby vs Shrewsbury, then he's by pitch 2 watching Crewe A vs Stoke. Then he's over at Derby's base camp, chatting to their coaches, giving feedback to their players. At one point, he seems to be giving tips to their goalkeeper, and if there's one thing Max Best is not, it's a goalkeeper.

"He's ridiculous," says a Chester FC fan who has come to watch the next generation play and is mortified by Best's antics. "Either he's delusional or he hasn't recovered from that smack on the head. Either way, he shouldn't be here, and he shouldn't be coaching other teams' kids. I suppose it's better than having him coach ours. It's a while since we won a game here, so I'll give him that. Credit where credit's due, I never thought I'd see us beat a team like Wolves. Now if he'll leave the rest of the job to the professionals, we'll have had a good day."

Best has no intention, however, of letting the highly qualified Spectrum take control of Chester vs Wrexham. I watch from the other side of the pitch as Best sends his players out in a banal, conventional 4-4-2. This turns out to be yet another masterstroke, as Wrexham's coaching staff dash around trying to reorganise their team. When they've done that, they are sent into a panic once more. I stifle a laugh as one coach shouts, "Diamond! He's gone diamond!" And while they are responding to that, one coach throws down his water bottle in disgust. "Now it's four-three-three! He's taking the piss!"

While Best seems to be winning the war of the sidelines, on the pitch the sides are more closely matched. Chester have their strengths, but so do Wrexham. The team from Wales have learned a lesson from the Wolves debacle: Chester are not to be underestimated. There is no complacency from their side. It's a tough battle. Too tough—a savage, two-footed lunge from a Wrexham midfielder on poor Benny sees Best sprint onto the pitch, carrying a medical bag, before the referee has even blown his whistle.

As Best leans over his player, gently tucking his hoodie under the boy's head, I move closer. Best asks a question and discovers that the referee has no intention of sending off the Wrexham player. It's not even a booking. Best is incandescent, briefly loses his mind. The Wrexham gang shout in defence of their player. Best turns away from them, summons Spectrum, summons Captain, then sits on a ball next to Benny. From his new throne, he issues commands. Spectrum covers Benny's leg with several layers of magic spray. He gets on the phone and either speed dials or inputs a very short number. I'm on the pitch now, edging closer to the drama, and I notice that as Spectrum dials,

Best reaches into his pocket and does something to his phone. The incident means nothing to me until much later.

"Ambulance!" yells Spectrum into his device. "We need an ambulance!" Shock spreads around the onlookers.

Meanwhile, Captain has gathered the rest of the team and formed them into a protective circle around their fallen comrade. From the sidelines, the subs run on to bolster the wall. Dani rushes on, too. Her parents remain, guardians of Chester's meagre equipment.

The building of the wall is too much for Wrexham's manager. He strides onto the pitch and launches a foul-mouthed attack on Best and the referee. He insists that the match continue. Best stands, checking that his players are in no danger from this man, and notices me. "Beth. I'm DoF. I'm not allowed to say what I think. You be my avatar. *Benny's* avatar. Ask that twat why he told his players to go in hard. Go on. Hard tackling. Why? Ask him why. Ask if this is going to be in the documentary. Ask if that little hooligan gets a special episode every time he breaks someone's legs. Go on. Ask if that's how you get ahead in life, ordering your kids to go in hard. Ask him why he's such a fucking coward."

Bombs dropped, Best sits back down on the ball. I'm left facing the target of his wrath—a man so angry he's turning purple. There's the slightest delay before he can reconnect his brain and his mouth, and in that time I realise: Best is telling the truth. He knows what formations the other teams will use. And he knows this man has ordered his players to launch into reckless tackles, dangerous tackles. I approach him and give him a piece of my mind. For some reason, his defence is to yell, "You can't prove anything. You can't prove anything." Which, some might say, proves *something*.

I realise Best has tricked me into fighting his battle for him, into becoming part of his latest dramatic scene. The realisation exasperates me, but it's nothing compared to the injustice Benny has suffered. Seeing him there on the grass, protected by his all-sorts mates, hands over his eyes so we can't see his tears, triggers a part of me I haven't tapped into for some time. I storm over to the yob who made the foul and demand he take off his ruby red football boots.

"What? No. Why?"

"We need them for evidence. For the police. To check if Benny's blood is on them. If there's blood, you're getting done."

I've gone too far. The Wrexham coaches push me away, crowd around their player. As I start to cross the pitch, I'm thrilled to see that he has burst into tears. I'll feel ashamed of myself later, but I'm still exulting at being the vehicle of Benny's revenge when I hear my name.

"Beth." It's Best. He bites his bottom lip. He's trying not to smile. "Interview's back on. We're playing Notts in the morning. See you there."

"What about this?"

"Game's over. Can't move Benny," he says. "Got to wait for the—" He bites his lip again, sticks out his tongue. Soon after, he's back in command of his face. Deadly serious, he says, "Got to wait for the ambulance."

There's a tiny court case involving the tournament administrators. Best wins. The match is called a draw. At the end of the first day, Chester have 7 points and are top of Group B. Their best players have played much less than the best players from other teams. The only cloud on the horizon is poor Benny. The last I see of him, he's being carried away by Best. Not quite as injured as it seemed, but still apparently distraught. Best takes small steps forward, letting the left foot catch up to the right. I realise he's carrying Benny like a soldier might carry a coffin. And when I see Tyson on the touchline, laughing and joking with Captain and some others, I'm sure of one thing: Benny is just fine.

As It Stood

PLACE	TEAM	PLAYED	GOAL DIF-FERENCE	POINTS
1	Chester	3	5	7
2	Wolves	2	0	3
3	Notts	2	-1	3
4	Crewe	3	-3	3
5	Wrexham	2	-1	1

Escape in a Hot Air Balloon

I go to the canteen to get a coffee and a quick sandwich. I make some calls to get out of my plans for the following day. I eat half the sandwich and take the rest with me. I'm heading towards my car when

I stop, mouth open, cheese dangling from my lips, and watch a scene unfold on the closest pitch to the café.

Chester, *sans* their four best players, are playing an impromptu friendly match. Spectrum is in charge of Chester, it seems, while Best is managing a team built from underused players from other squads, plus one boy who is wearing a puffer jacket and trainers. Best is running around, animated, yelling instructions and cackling to himself.

The Chester boys are happy that their Max is happy. The misfit team play with immense concentration and desire. They zip around scoring goals and using this unexpected opportunity to impress their coaches. Best blows his whistle and the match is over. He pauses, then suddenly punches the air. He runs around high-fiving the children, then ushers them off the pitch and welcomes a new group. He rapidly organises them into a 4-3-3 formation—presumably it isn't worth the time it would take to ask each stranger what their favoured position is—and once again they score freely while Chester's boys make half-hearted attempts to stop them. Best ends the match, pauses, and punches the air again. He finishes the day with more high-fives, profusely thanking the managers who had lent him players, and by gathering his flock and leading them back towards their team bus for the journey home.

I ask people with hundreds of years of combined footballing experience. No purpose for these micro-matches can be divined.

Return to Oz

Owing to a plumbing emergency and traffic, I arrive late, twenty minutes into Chester's crucial match against Forest.

Spectrum fills me in. "So this morning, Notts smashed Wrexham and Wolves whupped Crewe. Wolves are third, but they're in pole position, really. They're playing Wrexham now and Wrexham are toast. Their morale is shot and they're a shambles. Forest need to beat us. If we get a point, we'll finish second. If we win, we win the group."

"What about Benny?"

"He's okay. He's bruised. Max says we can use him for the last fifteen or twenty. Nine is playing instead. He's doing okay."

He shows me the league table as it stood before kickoff.

PLACE	TEAM	PLAYED	GOAL DIF-FERENCE	POINTS
1	Chester	3	5	7
2	Notts	3	4	6
3	Wolves	3	3	6
4	Crewe	4	-6	3
5	Wrexham	3	-6	1

"Okay," I say. "And what's the score?"

"It's two–one. We were two–nil up but Notts have this midfielder who's a little genius. He's running the game."

"Didn't Max have some insane plan?"

"No, it was pretty conventional. We're just slugging it out. Taking turns to throw big punches."

"You don't like it."

"It's stressful. But the real drama is Tyson." He looks worried and turns to Best. "Can I tell her?"

"Sure, whatever," comes the reply. Best looks subdued. His attention seems to be fixed on a short player in Forest red. He's two-footed with a low centre of gravity and Chester don't have a midfielder who can compete with him.

Spectrum is in a gossipy mood. "So you know Notts are interested in Tyson, and last night they called his dad and made some extravagant offer."

"The moon on a stick," says Best, who refuses to clarify the comment.

"So Tyson showed up all tormented at the meeting point and he said that his dad said that Max had to cut the shit or they were leaving."

"Cut the shit?"

"Oh, right, you don't know. Tyson isn't allowed to shoot." He frowns again. "Max, are you sure about this?"

"Yeah, let it all out. Whatever. Who cares?"

"And Max gets all pissy like he does and says the rules have changed and now Tyson can only play if Tyson gets a tattoo saying 'I won't shoot' and I complain and Max backs down and says, 'Fine, no tattoo, and Nottsss can poach my players all they want but if you're one of us, you're one of us and if you're one of us, you get on the bus.' So Tyson snaps back and they have a fight, but then he hops on and sits at the back, hiding under a hoodie all the way here. He's out there now playing CAM, but he's playing shit. His head's a mess. Max reckons near the end of the match he'll shoot and then run over to the Forest bench and ask for amnesty."

"What do *you* think?" I ask.

Spectrum shakes his head. "For once I think Max is right. It'll go something like that, anyway. We're all just kind of waiting for it to happen."

They lapse into silence to the extent that I consider working my way round to the Forest side of the pitch to be there when Tyson defects. I'm struck by the atmosphere—it feels like being in a Cold War spy thriller, not a sports tournament for boys.

Every now and then, Best spits out instructions and the boys on the pitch reposition themselves. It's far smoother than what other teams can manage. The Best-Spectrum axis, for all its obvious disunity, has produced a team that acts as one. I point this out to Spectrum. His eyes drop. He whispers, "That's Max. That's his mania. Teamwork FC. That's why Tyson can't shoot. It's about making him a team player." He shakes his head. Still inaudible to his boss, he continues, "Tyson should stay. His improvement recently has been . . . startling. But he won't. He'll see the Premier League badge. He'll think he might get turned into a FIFA character. He won't get that at Chester. Max is acting like we're a big club, which is inspirational when it isn't annoying, but we're not. We've got nothing to make him want to stay. Not really."

"What if you win the tournament?"

My question is badly timed. Forest's midfield maestro gets the ball, skips past a weak challenge, body swerves around little Future, and threads a pass between Captain and Bomber. A rapid striker is first to the ball and applies a cool finish. Two–two, and Chester are starting to look like the small team they are.

Best swivels his finger, and his players revert to 4-4-2. He's barely present. It's hard to believe this is the cocksure wizard the boys have come to love. The curtain has parted, and Best is just another hollow man in a cheap hoodie. A man with a talent for kicking a ball who believes this makes him talented in all areas of life.

His shoulders slump even further as Forest score again. Chester are going to finish third in their group. It's actually a remarkable achievement, but after the glory of yesterday, it feels like winning the wooden spoon.

The match starts to peter out. Best summons Benny. At the next break, he'll replace Nine. Benny only has a few minutes to impact the game, and he's moving gingerly. As Nine comes off the pitch, Best reaches out an arm and turns Benny towards him. He brings his face close to the young man's. "Look at that," he says, pointing. "See that? They're fucking terrified of you. Top scorer. They can't live with you and they know it." He releases the striker, who, instead of sprinting to position, walks. Every Forest player turns to track him. As Benny passes the midfield schemer, Benny stops, stares him out, then continues up the pitch.

Suddenly, I'm reinvested. Best is striding up and down like a panther. His jaw is set, his stance is wide. He radiates confidence.

"Attack!" he yells, startling me. "Attack! Attack attack attack!" He repeats the chant, and it seems to me that most Chester players move forward ten yards. Spectrum quivers with horror—there are massive gaps in the defensive lines. But *this* Chester won't lie down and die—they'll fight to the end.

The next passage of play is a high-wire act, with Chester controlling the ball, using Future as a conduit from left to right, from north to south. Sevenoaks is suddenly the dominant player on the pitch—everything goes through him. He dribbles and dribbles, and his opponent starts to make mistakes. The ball comes to Forest's star man, and Benny appears out of nowhere, barging him off the ball. The referee gives a free kick—ludicrous, grossly unfair—and Forest's captain claps his hands furiously, trying to revivify his team.

"United!" yells Captain, bizarrely, but the effect is incredible. I swear the Chester players grow an inch. The next few minutes are mayhem. It's carnage. It's all-out attack from Chester. They're potent down the right. They conjure a few nice moments down the left. But the middle is a wasteland. The chances there should come from Tyson, but he's still not in the game. He's still torn between two possible versions of the future.

It seems that will be the difference between the teams. That Max Best's philosophy breaks down if one player isn't fully invested.

But then comes the highest moment in the entire tournament. Impossible drama. Sevenoaks skins his man, surges towards the byline, then Ronaldo-chops the ball into the penalty area. He drags the ball back and his standing foot is swept away.

Even before the referee has decided, Best is screaming for Tyson to come. Chester's director of football rushes down the touchline, and Spectrum and I follow. The ref awards the penalty. Tyson jogs across towards the side of the pitch. Forest complain. If Chester score this penalty, Forest are out of the running. By complaining, they are only giving Max Best time for one last madcap intervention.

"Tyson!" he yells.

"What? What?"

"Take the pen."

"Oh! Sure. *Wait. What?*"

There's an awful moment as we all realise what Best is planning. "No!" says Spectrum. He is furious.

Tyson will have to take the penalty. But as per Best's rules, he won't be able to shoot.

Everything that has gone before is vaguely understandable. The rules, while bizarre, have a noble goal—to improve Tyson as a player.

This, though. This is pure cruelty. This is sadistic. A grown man hurting a young player before he can hurt him back.

"Max," I say. "Do not fucking do this. I swear to God."

"Seriously," says Spectrum. He bursts out into a fierce laugh. "I will fight you. I will actually fight you."

Best isn't listening. Tyson is his whole world. "Take the penalty. Don't shoot."

"Fuck me," says the boy. He grinds his fists into his temples. The referee is blowing his whistle. *Hurry up!* "You don't want people to see how good I am."

As he does in situations where someone doesn't believe in him, Best stands to his full height, becomes distant. "You're so good, you don't need to shoot."

Tyson trudges off. He looks more like a boy who has been sent off in an important match than one who has been trusted to take a decisive penalty. There are between fifty and a hundred spectators—Chester are box office now—and they believe they are about to witness a fateful moment in the tournament. They believe this is a fair contest between penalty taker and goalkeeper, albeit one tilted 75:25 in favour of the striker.

I am mildly in shock. I've seen horrible things on a football pitch, not least the tackle on Benny. But I've never seen a manager go in two-footed on his own player like this. Later, I wonder why I didn't charge onto the pitch and stop it.

Benny rushes up to Tyson and asks what is going on. Tyson whispers into his mate's ear, and Benny gives him a big hug. It's a sweet moment.

But then Tyson is putting the ball on the spot. It will be almost the last kick of the match. Almost. The weight of the world is on his shoulders. He wipes something away from his cheeks. My heart breaks. I steal a glance at Best. He is as impassive as the bust of a Roman Emperor who butchered his own population. I have never hated anyone more.

The referee blows his whistle. Tyson is too busy wiping tears from his eyes to strike the ball. I wonder if his plan is to delay taking the penalty so long that the ref will simply end the match. But no—the young striker steps forward.

Time slows.

The tournament flashes before my eyes.

The Wizard of Us. It's just a man behind a curtain. Smoke and mirrors. Max Best is weak and scared and no more talented than the rest of us, but he tricks us into believing that maybe . . . maybe. Yes, there have been accomplishments. He swats the hosts aside. He masterminds a one-in-a-billion thrashing of a team that eats golden burgers. For one glorious evening, his team prance around like cocks of the walk. It's a memory this defeat can't take away.

Tyson's right foot arrives at the ball. It seems like he has decided to smash it into the net, leave his boyhood club, and decamp to a bigger, better team where he will be treated like the young star he so clearly is.

Max Best has courage. Max Best has a brain. But Max Best has no heart.

Tyson, face contorted, strikes the ball. The goalkeeper dives to his left, Tyson's right.

The ball . . .

I can't believe my eyes.

The ball trickles a few inches forward and left. Tyson steps back and to his right.

What the fffff . . .

And then I understand!

The hug wasn't a hug—it was a planning session! Benny has timed his entry into the penalty box perfectly. He's far ahead of all the other players. Tyson has *taken* the penalty. The ball is live. The ball is live!

From his position a yard away from Tyson, Benny passes the ball into the left-hand side of the net.

It's there! Chester have done it!

The players lose their minds. The crowd erupts. I'm hugging Spectrum. It's unbelievable. It's the greatest moment of my life. Best has turned football into a thrill ride. A roller coaster built on the hopes and dreams of young men. He wrapped Tyson so tightly in a cocoon of restriction that the only way to escape was to grow wings. Eleven boys plus subs are streaming around, flapping their arms, trying to take flight, believing they might.

I pull away from Spectrum and click my pen. I *have* to write this down.

When you first see him, Max Best is a powerful mage, warping the very fabric of reality around him.

But pull back the curtain and you'll find Max Best is a small, weak nobody.

But pull back *another* curtain and you'll see: Max Best is *actually* a wizard.

Back in Kansas

I need to apologise to Best for doubting him, but when I finally look up from my notebook, he is nowhere to be seen.

The kids have a break before their semifinal against the winners of Group A. They eat, drink, and, little by little, calm down.

Best reappears as if by magic. "Guys," he says. "Shut the fuck up, you're giving me a headache." The players smile and edge closer. "Listen. I'm really proud of you. You've got everything. Brains, courage, heart. You're such a good *team*, holy shit. Now, this is really important. Not like calling Nottingham Notts important. This one's real."

I swear I see him swallow.

"I've had a ton of fun bossing you around this weekend. Giving you weird missions, putting you in the wrong positions, messing with the millionaires. It's great fun. I'm going to do it again. But we've got a bit of a saying, me and the coaches: *everyone plays every game*. It's from when I managed an obscure team called the Beth Heads. They had brains, courage, and heart, just like you. And some of you haven't played much, so we haven't done the best we could in that respect. We'll make it up to you in the next league game, yeah?" He looks at Spectrum, who nods. "When we first came to Chester, we were all shit. I mean, not me, I was mint. I was the white Ronaldo." The kids laugh. Ronaldo is white. "But *you* were all fucking garbage and Spectrum turned you into this."

Best points at the last pitch they played on.

"You're an absolute nuisance now. You're a menace. Every team who ever plays you is going to have a sleepless night. *Chester are coming.* Are you with me? This is almost all because of Spectrum. So he's going to manage you for the rest of the day. Because that's his job that I'm paying him for," Best says with a sly smile. "But also because he fucking deserves it. He turned you into one of the four best teams in Das Tournament and he stood up to me when he thought I was doing something wrong. All right?"

The kids agree. They love Best, but they've lived with Spectrum for years. He's as popular as any coach I've ever met.

"There's just one last thing." Best's face hardens. "Tyson. Have you made a decision?"

The young man returns his gaze in a way few can. "I want to stay. I want to play for Chester."

"Give me your phone."

Tyson thinks about refusing. God knows what's in his chat history, and I hope I never find out. But Best merely sets up a FaceTime with Tyson's dad.

A large head sees Tyson and breaks into a warm smile. "Hi, son! How did you get on?"

Best swings the phone around onto his own face. "They drew. Tyson missed a penalty." The joke provokes uproar. Best silences the gang with a gesture. "Listen. I just wanted to tell you that you won't be able to not watch Tyson in the under-fourteens anymore."

"Oh," says the dad. "Is that right?" He is pissed, in a restrained way, but I'm still trying to parse all the negatives. *Not . . . watch?* Has Best banned Tyson's father from attending matches?

"That's right. From now on, you'll have to not watch Tyson play for the under-*sixteens*."

The roar is deafening. Tyson is swarmed by his mates. Best holds the camera up for the dad to see the melee, waits ten seconds, then swings it back round. I want to slap the smirk off Best's face, and so does the dad. But we're happy, too. Tyson's been promoted!

"Bye," says Best, and hangs up. He stretches, massively. "Tyson," he calls out, throwing the boy's phone back. The tumult dies down. "One more thing. You can shoot."

"Yesss," hisses Benny, shaking his mate by the shoulders.

"Of course," says Best, his voice rising above the new clamour. "If there's ever a match where you shoot more than you pass, I'll fucking knock you all the way down to the twelves. Are we fucking clear?"

"Yes, Max!"

"Right. Spectrum. You've got Stoke. Expect four-four-two, but I'll text you if I see them change it. All right? Seeyas."

Best strides away. I look from him to Spectrum and the kids. Should I follow the Wizard, or stay with the Us? But I soon realise that it doesn't matter what happens next. The story is complete. Max Best has a heart. Spectrum has courage. Tyson has a brain. And more boys have realised something that Benny already knew: there's no place like home.

ABOUT THE AUTHOR

Ted Steel is the author of the Player Manager series, which features a charming but secretive main character. He also wrote *Nerves of Steel*, a LitRPG featuring a charming but secretive main character. When asked to provide a bit of color for his biography, Steel was charming but . . . secretive. Learn more at www.ted-steel.com.

DISCOVER
STORIES UNBOUND

PodiumAudio.com